WORLD OF SHE

A POST-APOCALYPTIC FRESH START

INVERSION
BOOK 1

G.W. DARCIE

Wavecrest
Books

Wavecrest Books are published by

G.W. Darcie, 600 Ontario Street, P.O. Box 27015, St. Catharines, ON L2N 7P8

This book is a work of fiction. All names, characters, places, and events are products of the author's imagination, and any resemblance to actual persons, living or dead, is entirely coincidental.

WORLD OF SHE

Cover Design by G.W. Darcie

ISBN: 978-1-7781811-3-9 (Paperback)

Visit worldofshe.com

To Ann, my heart's fulfillment, who keeps me grounded by making our world together better than any fantasy world.

Humanity's Epitaph:

They squabbled as extinction approached.

— Anonymous - circa 2040 (old calendar)

1

DISCOVERY

Every She tells me I'm the worst kind of trouble: a curious man. Here I go again, but how do I back out now?

These straight steel edges are jarringly out of place in the pristine wilderness that surrounds us, yet I feel a strange connection to this mysterious thing. It looks like the top of a large air vent, emerging from this small bluff in front of me. I shiver in certainty that this is from the Before, a piece of history, forbidden fruit. And it's calling me.

All I'm allowed to know of the past is that there was once a vast global civilization, and humanity came close to extinction when it all collapsed. But our She have carried us through seven generations since then, and we men need to be looking forward, not back. Still, I've always wondered what that Before world was like. Could whatever's under here shed some light?

I tighten the thigh straps of my safety harness, avoiding Dray's eyes, though I'm sure my trembling hands reveal me. Am I really doing this? Breaking into an undiscovered historical site? This is crazy.

A She like my mother would be thrilled to claim finder's rights to whatever this is, but men have no such rights. Strictly prohibited. No She can ever know about this.

I try to focus on breathing. A light March breeze whispers a secret I can't quite hear as it flows across the rolling hills, carrying the fresh, earthy scent of the wilds. No one ever comes out here, but to be sure, I climb to the top of the twelve-foot mound and scan the surrounding wilderness one last time.

In the far distance, the skyline of the 'Shell'—the crumbling remains of a once-great city—is a faint cluster of spikes on the horizon. Much closer, a few miles to the south, jagged lines of collapsed walls mark what's left of a vast industrial park, dead now for well over a century. We're standing in an area thought to be free of dangerous ruins, so no one cares that we're out here. But if they knew about this vent ...

Our storm-battered world is littered with crumbling remains, but whatever's under here looks like it was deliberately buried. How can I not be curious?

I fill my lungs with cool air and snug up the zipper of my jacket as I descend the mound to focus again on the vent opening. We still use gooseneck vents today, with their shafts curled over at the top so that the opening faces down to keep the rain out. From the erosion pattern on the bluff, I'd say the side of the mound collapsed to reveal this vent within the past year. Curious. What could need an air vent this big?

Dray grips the harness around my waist. "Tye, look at me. You can do this. You're a natural explorer." At thirty-two, he's only six months older than me, yet he still treats me like a child who needs his encouragement. My eyes cling to the deep brown reassurance in his. My best friend knows me too well.

I pull away and nod, checking my short ponytail to make sure the elastic is secure. "This might be what we've been looking for," I say. What *I've* been looking for. I'm the one who likes to play historian in my spare time, a role forbidden to men. Dray just likes scavenging. If it weren't for my mother's ancient, discarded map, we'd be off every weekend, blindly scavenging elsewhere. But the map shows something out here—something she could never find—and now I've discovered ... something.

I should've reported it to the authorities. It's stupid of me not to. The law is clear about historical sites. They are off-limits to men, and violators are dealt with harshly, often taken away and never seen again. But Dray loves to break rules, and besides, they'd send historians out here and I'd never hear another word about it. I want to know what this is.

We tried dropping stones to sound the depth. It only confirmed that this is a really bad idea. But something this deep must be important.

But ruins are deadly dangerous places. Is this worth dying for?

I grit my teeth. Is it worth clinging to a small, irrelevant life as an inconsequential man? Anything would be better.

Dray puts a calloused hand on my shoulder. "I'll be right here on the pulley. I've got your back."

"I know you do." If anything goes wrong, there's no way he can get in to help me. "Look, Dray, this far out in the wilds, we're on our own. If something goes wrong—"

"Nothing's gonna go wrong." He brushes his wavy black hair back from his eyes, and it flutters around his shoulders.

"But *if* ... don't get yourself in trouble by telling anyone we did this, okay? Just say I disappeared."

"You're gonna be fine, Tye. This will be a big payday. I can feel it."

There's a rich timbre to his voice that inspires confidence, whether he knows what he's talking about or not. It's easy to be optimistic when you're oblivious to the risks. "Dray, it's not that simple."

"You're sure, right? You're sure there are artifacts down there?"

No, I'm not sure. "That's what I'm hoping, but—"

"Because everything is riding on this."

I nod and take a deep breath. Two weeks. We've got two weeks to pay the fine on my overdue taxes or my place gets repossessed. "Don't worry. You're not gonna end up back in the homeless shelter."

He shrugs. "I don't know. It would be nice to eat three meals a day again."

"Can we go five minutes without talking about food?"

Dray examines the opening. "Actually, it's a good thing you're so small. Who else could fit through that?"

"I'm not small. Five-nine is average for a man." Average. I've spent my whole life looking up at people. "You've only got two inches on me, you know."

"Can we go five minutes without talking about dicks?"

I give him a shove that doesn't budge him, and we return our attention to the opening. For a moment I wish our positions were reversed. But I couldn't bear to be waiting out here, worried about him. He can do the worrying. He's the strong one.

He dusts off his cargo pants. "The sun sets in just over five hours. We've got a three-hour bike ride back home, so if we're gonna do this—"

"We've got two hours. I'm ready," I lie.

"It'll be like I'm lowering you into a well."

Yeah. If the well were barely wide enough to fit my shoulders. I'm not scrawny, but I don't have Dray's brawn.

"Okay," he says, "the pulley's ready." He's got it secured to a nearby tree trunk, with over a hundred feet of rope ready to go. How could that not be enough?

He grabs the pulley rope he'll use to lower me. I need to go feet-first up into the down-facing opening, so that once I'm over the gooseneck bend, I'll be right-side up in the vertical shaft. Dray gets under my shoulders and lifts until I get my hips on the bend, and I wriggle in from there. Hanging in the harness at the top of the shaft, both hands gripping the rope, I take a moment to catch my breath. *What am I doing?*

The shaft is almost two feet square here. My climbing skills do me no good in a space this cramped, so I'm just along for the ride.

Below me, black depths. A knot of dread in my core makes it hard to breathe.

"How are you doing in there?" Dray's voice booms and echoes in the shaft.

"You don't need to yell. Sound carries like crazy in here."

"Are you ready? Go find us some treasure."

Treasure. Okay. I ease down into the safety harness, try three times to get my reluctant hand to let go of the rope, and switch on my headlamp. With the shaft wall only inches from my face, the reflected glare blinds me until I crane my neck to look down. Beneath my feet, there is nothing. Just like going down into a well. A bottomless well.

The line jerks as Dray lets off the pulley and I start descending. He checks with me. "Everything okay?"

My tongue is almost too dry to form words. "Yeah, keep it coming." I strain to see into the black void below me, but it's like looking into the future.

This is by far the craziest thing I've ever done. By far. I tighten my jaw.

I'm about fifteen feet down now, and grateful for my headlamp. I see the dim reflected glow of daylight above me, too far away to ever reach on my own. My life is now in Dray's hands. I clutch the rope. If it breaks—No, it's a good rope. I inspected the whole thing myself, triple-checked the knots. *Stop worrying and focus.*

I wish my mother could see me now, doing historian work, following in her footsteps, even succeeding where she failed. No, I should be glad she *can't* see me now. She'd be furious. History is not for men to know.

That was drilled into my head my entire childhood, as I watched my mother become prestigious as a historian. She did well for herself, and I always benefited—when she was there. But she was away a lot, more so as I got older. And then she was gone. Gone where I could never follow, swallowed up by the dreaded Shell. I'll never see her again, never see where she works. The Shell is out of bounds to men. Too much Before history there. Too much death.

And though we're in an unrestricted area, this must be an unknown historical site, which makes us criminal trespassers. It's the last thing I want. I'm not cut out for the criminal life. But if we can pawn enough valuable artifacts to pay the bills and get us afloat—

A gleam underfoot catches my eye. An edge. I'm, what—thirty feet down? It's an opening into a horizontal duct. "Stop. I'm at a branch. I'm gonna see where it goes." I hoist myself into the new shaft and wriggle my way forward. It's hard to breathe in here. About twelve feet in, I come to a grate-covered opening in the duct floor, and through it, my light reveals a hallway. I knew it. This *is* something. I grab the grate and rattle it, bang on it until it falls open in a cloud of dust.

"I found an open space," I call up. "Take up slack." I feel a reassuring tug on the rope, let my legs swing down into the hole and sit back into the harness. "Okay, down again."

I pant in the foul air. Forget about two hours. I light the hallway floor as Dray lowers me toward it, land on both feet, and I'm in. Shadows from open doorways leap at me and vanish as I sweep my light around. *In where I should not be. This is crazy.*

I fight down panic as I struggle for air. Focus. Treasure.

Choking in the old dust, I pull my undershirt collar up over my nose. I've got to move fast. With the dust I've stirred up, the hallway in front of me extends beyond the range of my light. It's like looking into the depths of the lake, wondering what might be down there waiting to rush up at you, mouth wide. A shiver runs down my spine.

I had planned to disconnect the rope from my harness and go exploring. Forget that. Dragging the rope behind me, I approach the closest open door and shine my light inside. Looks like some sort of office. And ...

Great Mother. I've hit the jackpot.

Artifacts. Lots of them. The large office desk and credenza both hold numerous items that look to be in pristine condition. I pick one up, dust it off, and examine it with wonder. I have no idea what it is, but it has an elegant beauty that takes my breath away.

I gasp and cough. No time for this. I quickly scoop up what I can and fill my sack, then stand sucking air through my shirt. It doesn't help. I can't stay down here. One more glance around the room, then I rush to the ceiling hatch and holler up. "You there? ... Dray?" If he's not, I'm dead.

"Ready and waiting."

"Okay, go! Haul me up!"

I recheck the strap that ties the sack to my harness as Dray's pulley lifts me off the floor. The sack dangles about three feet below my feet as I reach the hatch and climb in. "I'm in the shaft. Go!"

Sliding on my belly toward the vertical shaft, I yank to a stop. Alarmed, I call up, "Keep going."

I feel the line vibrate under tension, and my whole body matches it. *No no no. Don't get stuck here.*

Dray's voice jars me. "We're stuck. Check your lines."

My mind wildly flails in the fog until I figure out what he means. We're snagged on something. Nothing in front. I crane to look behind me and see the problem. "The sack is snagged on the ceiling hatch. Gimme some slack."

"You okay?"

He can hear in my voice that I'm not. "No air," I manage.

"Hurry up, then."

I slither backward in the tight ceiling shaft until I reach the opening, the sack dropping out of reach as I do. For a frantic minute, I try to haul it up, but there is no room to get it in with me, and if I back out of the way, I have no leverage. The sack needs to go in first, in front of me. "I've got to ... go back down ... Let me down." I hope he heard me.

"Cut the sack loose. I'm hauling you out."

"No! Ease me down."

"You sure?"

"... Do it. Hurry!"

Clear of the hatch, I haul the sack up and have it in my arms by the time I reach the floor. "Okay ... back up! Go!"

I strain to hold the sack over my head as I'm hoisted up, then push it through the hatch above me and wriggle in behind it. I push it ahead of me as I'm pulled along, then I flip to my back to enter the vertical shaft. But the sack gets there first and falls in, its strap trying to strangle me. I fight the urge to cut the sack loose, imagining it plummeting into the endless depths. *No. I'm taking this with me.*

I'm dizzy, panting and helpless, as I hang there in the slowly ascending harness. I feel the hunger pull of the void beneath me and focus on the faint light far above. There is no way in the world I could climb this shaft on my own. Impossible.

Dray will get me out. I know he will. Lightheaded. Need air. A wave of fatigue drags me down, and I strain to look to the light above, getting closer with each yank. Relief washes over me as I reach the gooseneck and greedily suck in air. And then Dray's hands are hauling me out into the open. I flop onto my back, and my heart swells as I gaze up at my rescuer.

"Are you okay?"

Not wasting breath with words, I nod.

"You did it, Tye! Good job. So, what did you see down there?"

Panting, I shake my head. "Later."

"Okay," he says. "Let's have a look at the loot."

The loot. Yes. I watch as he opens the sack, pulls out an item and examines it.

"Whatever this is, it's in perfect condition. It must be worth a fortune. Look at all this stuff. And it's all ours."

And it's illegal for us to have it. I sit up as we both eagerly explore a world of trouble in a sack.

For the past week, I've been weighing the pros and cons. We're desperate, and this is the big score we need. But if we're caught, we'll be separated and shipped off to different penal colonies for 're-education,' and I'll lose him forever. I can't let that happen. Score in hand, the risks loom much larger.

We're criminals now.

2

SHELTER

I LIE AWAKE, walking through my forbidden adventure in my mind's eye, trying to picture the treasure room as it was when I entered. I curse my cowardice, as I often do. I was too scared to pay close attention to what was there, too focused on trying to breathe, and I panicked. There's no other way to describe it. Threw stuff in my sack and ran. So like me.

What would it be like to be strong, just once?

Now I've seen my first glimpse of the Before world, and even brought back artifacts. But they have revealed nothing, and for the last week I've been too scared to try to cash in. The one She I thought would act as a fence for us, a local roughneck who owed me a favor, took one look at an artifact and backed out. It would draw too much attention, she said. Any unknown She unsavory enough to deal with high-end contraband is someone I wouldn't trust. Not with our lives on the line. I wish I'd thought this through.

My ears perk up at the sound of the door to the attached bunker dome opening. The high-pitched hum from the triangular windows eighteen feet above me has been unrelenting. I was able to tune it out until now. The wind would be a deafening roar outside the protection of this sunken geodesic dome. Like all the other homes in town, only the top eye of the dome lies above ground, where the wind harmlessly skims over it.

"Tye. Tye. Wake up. It's the year 140. You've been asleep for two years."

A moment of alarm eases. It's just Dray being Dray. And it's still 138 N.E.—one hundred and thirty-eight years since the dawn of the new era, since the end of the Before world.

I prop up on an elbow and peer into the gloom, where I can barely make him out. "You're a riot, Dray. How old are you again?" Thirty-two, going on seven.

"Oh, so you *are* awake. Just dozy, like usual."

"What? What do you want?" I know damn well what he wants. My annoyance fades.

"It's the storm," he says.

"I know. But it's okay. We're safe." Like they say, you get to shelter, you get to live another day. Still, it's always nerve-racking, being pinned down and helpless. It wears on you.

"I can't get warm," he says, voice forlorn.

We lie trembling in the roaring dark, two six-year-olds clinging to each other. The wind monster howls right up there, hungry to get at us. Each scrape jangles our nerves; each bang jolts us until it's too much. Life and death. I bolt for the door, Dray on my heels. My father sits up in bed as we burst in. He lifts his blanket, and we both dive for safety. We snuggle in, one on each side of him, and in the glow of the night-light, Dray brushes back his wavy black hair, and the tears in his eyes tell me what it's like to have no father. To have a mother who doesn't care about you. And me, an only child, happy for a part-time brother, happy he's safe here with me. And my father coos to us and I'm grateful to not be alone, as I so often am. But my mother's work doesn't allow for children, and everyone knows I was a mistake. None of that matters because I know she loves me. And as our matria—the head of our family—if she were here, she'd protect us all, as a matria does. But right now, Daddy's love is enough. I cling to him in the semi-dark until my eyes won't stay open.

. . .

DRAY WAS A PRETTY BOY. The girls always went for him. The grownup She still do, unfortunately for him. Once they start fighting over him, the winner figures he owes her. That never goes well.

And right now, he needs me. I lift back my blanket, and he climbs in beside me and rolls into my open arms. He does feel cold. I quiver as his icy hands grip my back. I snug the blanket in around us and revel in the embrace, the closeness of another living being, the indulgence, the nurturing, the sense of safeness. If I could feel this safe with a She, I'd be a happy man, and he would too. But at least we have each other.

We lie listening to the uncanny silence induced by the whistling white noise of the wind. I try to imagine what it must be like outside. The image intrudes, as it has countless times over the past twenty years. I'm nine years old, clinging to my father's leg. He's trying to hold the storm door open for a man who's struggling to reach it, unable to get his footing in the buffeting wind. The man tries to crab his way forward and is suddenly gone, lifted and thrown from sight. The breath being sucked from my lungs. The storm door slamming down. My father sobbing.

I clutch Dray, and his solidity grounds me.

"How long do you think the storm will last?" he says.

He's hurting. I can tell. This must be one of those nights when continuing seems pointless. I wish I knew how to ease his pain.

"All I know is, it's gonna end way too soon," I say, tickling his ribs.

He squirms. "Don't."

Okay, so that's not gonna work tonight. Just cuddling, then.

At five-eleven, he's two inches taller than me, but he likes to bury his head in my shoulder for some reason, in sharp contrast with his daytime bravado. It's fine with me. It gives me a chance to feel paternal.

The thought triggers the memory, and my body goes rigid under the crushing weight of powerlessness. Then the floodgates open and the grief pours in. I catch my breath as my eyes stream.

Dray pulls back in the dark. "You okay?"

His presence draws me back to now. "Uh, sorry. Yeah." I wipe my eyes and pull him back to me. "It's just, you know, old stuff."

He sighs. "Yup, I know."

What a pair we are. In many ways, an unlikely pair. He's bigger, more rugged, more daring. I'm the thinker, with my father's finer features and cautious nature. He has lighter skin but darker hair and eyes, while I have browner skin, some of my mother's pigment, but less body hair. He's got the guts and good looks, and I've got ... what? I'm average in every way. I don't know why he sticks with me, but I'm grateful.

He feels warmer already. There is comfort in human contact. Sometimes it's enough to get you through.

"You stink," he says. "When was the last time you had a shower?"

"Last time I needed one. You can always go out for some fresh air, you know."

He swats me as the storm howls above. "I'll just hold my breath."

"Wow," I say. "I'm not used to good ideas coming from you." Another swat, right on cue.

He'd much rather be with a She. We both would. But it's so risky. We're freemen for a reason, and since most of my scars are on my foolish heart, I've been lucky compared to Dray. Punishment starts to feel deserved after a while. No, Dray, you didn't deserve it. You didn't deserve it from your matria or your sisters, and especially not from any of the She you served. You didn't deserve the beatings, and you didn't deserve to get thrown to the wind.

"You're safe here," I say.

"Unless your crazy is contagious."

"Must be," I say. "I caught it from you." I'm reassured by his banter. I need him to be okay. Being a freeman in a world of She is not something you can do alone.

"We'll get through this, buddy," I say.

"I know we will." He inhales and seems to settle.

I lie listening to the occasional clunk of flying debris hitting an overhead window, confident in the heavy armor-glass above us.

Maybe not confident. More like resigned to the possibility of disaster. Nothing you can do about it. Another clunk.

He rolls over, and we fight for control of the blanket until I realize I'm not sleepy anymore. His light snore is my signal, and I slip out of bed and pull on my socks.

On tiptoes, I sneak through into the adjoining dome, close the door, and turn on the lights. The bunker dome, my mother's former workshop and storage room, doesn't have the same quality of insulation, and the wind noise is much louder in here. I can see why Dray couldn't sleep. Still, I marvel at how well our geodesic dwellings protect us from the extremes of this hostile environment using such a simple design—a design brought forward to us from the Before by heroic historians like my mother. We owe so much to those ancient designers I know nothing about.

I look around at the disassembled parts and feel my mother's presence. It evokes a familiar ambivalence, the deep longing crushed by the heavy confusion of abandonment. She used to love tinkering with this stuff, wouldn't throw anything out. Could turn it into cash. She supported us by selling artifacts. If only I could do the same.

But I'm a man.

3

SECRETS

Standing alone, I let my eyes wander around the familiar mess of the bunker dome. I've got a week to come up with the money to pay my fine or I'm gonna lose everything. The storm rages overhead, demanding caution. Providing cover.

With renewed determination, I head straight for a bin against the wall. I pull off a tarp and stand gazing in at my loot as the frustration churns within me. All this treasure I'm too scared to sell.

Part of me doesn't want to sell it. I select an object and examine it. Curious. The gleaming artifact in my hand, the size of a deck of cards, is what my mother used to call a "device," and it's supposed to do something. If only I could figure out what. I have another like it and one twice the size, a strange keyboard with no typewriter under it, a hard blob that molds to your hand, a metallic mesh cylinder the diameter of a mug but twice as high, and several other artifacts I have a tough time even describing.

If my mother were still here, she'd take them away to keep me safe. If any She even knew I had these, I'd be shipped off to some re-education colony and never seen again. So I can't ask. It's up to me to figure these out on my own. I sit down at my workbench and again pull up the magnifying glass.

The device is smooth except for one small hole and a couple of raised bumps on the side. My mother knew how to open these, but she never showed me, and I don't want to damage it by trying to force it. Sometimes she'd remove parts and put new ones in, and they'd light up and she'd be so excited, but then she'd hide them from me. It was to protect me, she said. I accepted that. I was ten. When I asked if they were weapons, she said no, it had something to do with the rules against men learning about the Before.

And really, what's the point in looking back? The future lies ahead of us, and that's where we need to focus. History is irrelevant. We're busy serving our families and our communities, and we have a growing population to support. We know what we need to know. How many times have I heard that?

The problem is, I grew up exposed to too many mysteries and too few answers. And now, I've only made it worse.

As a last resort, I figured I could count on the freeman community to help me fence these artifacts. But now I can't bring myself to put anyone else at such risk. No, to have any hope of selling them, I'm gonna need the help of a She. And you can't trust She. Ask the wrong one, and losing this place will be the least of my problems.

My unfocused gaze falls upon the well-worn letter sitting in its place on the corner of my mother's old desk. It's her last message to me, written shortly before she left. I push through the familiar, bitter ache and reach for it. In her handwriting, I hear her voice, see her face. Her scent has long since vanished from the envelope, but I inhale her essence as I remove and caress the folded sheet within.

My darling Tye.

I always linger on these words, reluctant to move on. If only the world had stopped right there. I look away and wipe my eyes, already disappointed in myself. She so wanted me to be strong.

Life has a way of taking us to unexpected places, no matter which course we set for ourselves. All we can do is try to make the best of wherever we end up. I know this must be hard for you, but I need you to be brave and strong.

I'm glad she'll never know how badly I've failed her. But she must have expected I would, leaving me behind like that.

Remember, strength comes in many forms. Find yours. Respect the strengths of others, but find your own. Find it, develop it, and use it to contribute as no one else can.

When did I stop trying? Was it when I learned that obedience is safer than strength? Or was it when my spirit was drained fighting unfair rules? Find your strength. Easy for She. Shaking my head, I go back to the page.

I hope one day I will be able to share the details of my work with you. But until that day comes, I want you to know that the purpose of my life's work is to give you a better future.

If only.

Please know I will love you forever.

Liar. You abandoned us. I toss the letter down. Just when we needed you most. No, maybe not. That would be now. You could sell our loot for us. You could tell me all about our artifacts.

But of course, you wouldn't. You never taught me anything about the past, just let me hang there in ignorance, choking on my questions ...

The book.

No. Don't even think about it.

But the book contains my mother's own words, always denied me. When she wasn't fiddling, she was always writing. I see her arriving home that day, all excited, with a box full of copies of her first published work. I'm sure it's one of those. She never shared any of her work with me. Of course, she couldn't, under penalty of law, but I always felt shut out.

Maybe there is something in the book that would explain the artifacts. My eyes go back to the bin. If I ever needed answers, it's now.

But the book contains restricted material. Six months ago, when I found it, when I realized what I had in my hands, I panicked and dropped it right back in its hiding place. I had to. And I've left it there ever since, not knowing what else to do. To be caught with it would …

But I'm already a criminal, already in possession of illegal contraband. What difference does one more transgression make?

My curiosity spikes. They always said I was dangerously curious, as they waved their secrets in my face.

For six months I've deprived myself of the illicit chance to learn about history. Six months of pretending the book doesn't exist, of fearing the consequences of giving in to my yearnings. Six months of being a proper, law-abiding citizen. And for what?

The roar of the storm overhead echoes the battle raging inside me. I push myself to my feet and struggle into a fierce headwind of inner resistance. Bringing illegal artifacts here was bad enough, but I can justify that; I need the money. What excuse do I have for reading restricted material?

The fact that my mother wrote it and accidentally left it behind makes her culpable, too. Is that what I want? Do I want her punished?

I don't know. Maybe.

I strain to pull the old desk out from the wall, just far enough. Last time, I was retrieving a bill that slid down here. The desk looms more menacingly this time as I reach in behind. Am I really doing this? I pluck it up like it's some dead thing and scrape my knuckles pulling it out. Guess I am.

It's just a book. Brushing off the cover, I read, *The She Manifesto: Notes from a Cultural Historian.* Then the author's name, *Celia.*

A chill runs up my spine. So this is it. Okay, what do we have here?

The cover page leaps at me, as it did before.

Warning. This book contains restricted material. For the eyes of She only.

I fight the impulse to push it away. I know what comes next. And I'm entirely in the wrong.

If you are male, close this book immediately and hand it to the nearest She. Any male caught in possession of this book or having been informed of its contents shall be removed from society by order of the High Council. Any She found to have revealed any of the contents of this book to a male shall be subject to a period of imprisonment to be determined by tribunal.

I glance around again, wary. I have seen this mandatory warning many times, been trained to respect it. But handing this over to the authorities would have been foolish. They'd assume I'd already read it, and no freeman is gonna be given the benefit of the doubt.

What's the point in denying myself? I am bursting to know what I have in my hands, what knowledge lies within. On these pages, my mother's secrets are exposed.

I glance around one more time, certain now that even Dray must know nothing about this. I skip past the preface, and with hungry eyes read the introduction.

The She Manifesto, our guiding charter, documents the rules of the ForeMothers of the first High Council, rules that have safely guided us back from the brink of extinction. In what follows, I offer a discussion of these rules from the perspective of cultural history. This work is supported by the generous support of The Historian Guild: Mining the past to enrich the future.

From the work of historians, we have regained knowledge about how to grow crops indoors, how to extract hydrogen from aluminum waste, how to make solar panels and armor glass, and a thousand other things to help us survive and thrive. But we have also learned about ourselves and our culture.

A culture is a set of rules and values that guide the attitudes and behaviors of a particular group of people in adapting to a specific ecological niche. Most are entirely unaware of the culture they grew up immersed in until they are confronted with something different. In our sparsely populated world, until long-distance travel becomes practical, we will rarely encounter such differences. However, the study of history exposes us to the cultures of the Before, and from them we can learn a great deal about ourselves.

So this is what a cultural historian studies. I always wondered.

We learn that each culture evolves in a specific ecosystem, passing down rules to aid survival in that context. The rules of desert cultures, built around surviving in an environment of scarcity, are not useful in the forests where resources are more plentiful, and vice versa. It is not that one culture is better than another, it's that they're each tailored to different needs.

For example, the dominant cultures of the Before had many prohibitions regarding sex. Few recognized that their negative moral values existed to support the patriarchal family structure.

Patriarchal? What's that?

Men wanted to pass their wealth along to their 'blood' heirs and didn't want to pay to support the children of other men. Since they had no other way to control fertility, and no defense against sexually transmitted diseases, sex outside of marriage was prohibited.

'Blood' heirs? Marriage? Okay, you've lost me. What the hell is this about?

But it's hard to discourage sex without the weight of moral authority, and so most aspects of human sexuality became culturally defined as 'immoral.' We find these attitudes absurd today, with our enhanced immune systems and control over our own fertility. But those strange values were perhaps appropriate in the context of those times.

They saw sex as immoral? Weird. Harming others is immoral, but sex?

Our context is very different. Those who survived the collapse were different in some unpredictable way from all those who perished. When it comes to the survival of a species, diversity is strength. Understanding this, the ForeMothers taught us to prize genetic diversity above all else in our procreation choices.

I droop. Which is why Rose always chose the seed of other men after Matty was born. I can't blame her. I just wish she'd given me another chance after we ... after we lost him. The vision hits like a kick to the groin—the crib, bright and airy, his skin blue, cold. Still fresh after all these years. I wipe my eyes, waiting for the sting to subside. Maybe she was right. Maybe I do have bad seed.

I stand and wander across the room, rolling my shoulders, then realize I've left the book open on the desk and hurry back. Careless. I check the doors, then sit and return to the page.

The fall of civilization required a fresh start. As people banded together to persevere in a dead world, the old rules were not only irrelevant, they were dysfunctional in the new context. The Fore-Mothers, struggling to ride the wave of change, saw the need for a new social structure and wrote the Manifesto to pass along their hard-learned lessons. Its publication unified the young world of She. The resulting cooperative social system helped the population flourish and spread, and the Manifesto found loyal adherents wherever it went. It forms the framework of our culture, and so deserves our careful attention.

But cultures must evolve with their populations, and change is always difficult. If we are to avoid repeating the mistakes of the past, we must learn from them. The very survival of our species is at stake—

I hear a noise and close the book, looking up in alarm. Nothing. A piece of debris hitting the armor glass. Looking back at the book, I hesitate. I hold the answer to all my questions in my hand, but it will take me many hours to read through this. How am I gonna do that without Dray noticing? Maybe I should show him. How can I keep such a huge secret from him? No, I must. I've already put him in enough jeopardy. He's a terrible liar, and as long as he knows nothing about this book, he can't be caught in a lie. It could save him.

But why is this book so dangerous in my hands? The standard answer seems hollow, a false façade—it contains history, and history is not for men to know. Okay, but why? Any She can know it, so why not men?

As I fume, a small voice rings through the turmoil like a bell. *What if there's a good reason?* I go still. Then I am making a terrible mistake.

But what possible reason could there be? No, if there were a good reason, they would tell us what that is, instead of keeping us in the dark.

I riffle through the pages, looking ahead with frustration. It's all right here, but when am I gonna get a chance to study this? I'll need to read it in snippets whenever I get a few moments of privacy. It could take months.

I sigh. If Dray wakes up, he'll wonder where I am. Just a bit more, then I'll hide it. I flip ahead to a section titled "The Rules."

Rule One: A law is meaningless unless enforced. The laws of She shall be enforced by the strongest among us. Semiannual competitions shall be held to establish a ranking, and the top-ranking combatants shall earn the title of Enforcer ...

4

SCARS

Rule One (A): Contestants shall be ranked in semiannual tournaments, Spring and Fall. There shall be two divisions of competition: Hand and Sword. In hand-to-hand, contestants will fight empty-handed in unarmed combat. In sword-to-sword, contestants will fight in armor, armed with bokken. Contestants shall be rated in each division, and rank determined by combined standings. All who achieve the status of enforcer shall be awarded the rank of Charlie and employed to enforce the peace and the rule of law.

Commentary: As social primates, we instinctively form a dominance hierarchy, and conflict is minimized when each member knows her place in it. Physical force is the primal form of dominance. Here, the ForeMothers have established rules to constrain and direct the fighting instinct into a nonlethal, cooperative channel. Note: Other forms of social power emerge as a society becomes more diverse and complex, and physical dominance becomes less influential ...

THE DAY IS crisp and dry. Beyond us, outside of town, the crater fields of the northern farms shelter their crops and livestock. I spent summers in those craters as a teen, helping to maintain the solar screens and irrigation systems. My only fond memories are of flying my kite after work, but at least I learned excavation.

"It's all about power," says Dray, pedaling beside me down the hard-packed roadway, finally dry after the storm. "If you had all the power, would you treat people this way? I'm telling you, Tye, it's not right. If She had hearts, they'd see that."

There's a whole chapter on power in the book, but I haven't been able to get to it yet, or any other topic, for that matter. The frustration simmers, but I have other priorities right now.

We're in an affluent neighborhood. Down in our older area, the underground geodesic homes are evenly spaced, with only their tops visible above ground. Here, pods of dome tops mark multi-dome dwellings that sit on large lots. We pass a playground where fathers chat while their children frolic on shiny new equipment. Girls wrestle to claim the top of the slide. A boy gets pushed aside by a bigger girl as he tries for a turn on a swing. I sigh. Playgrounds were where I learned my place in the world.

Dray continues. "They think they can treat us any way they want."

"Because they can," I point out.

"Yeah, but that don't make it right."

It's not much further to our client's place. I've been dreading this confrontation. I'd rather do this by telephone, if only I could afford one, but we can't wait any longer. We're days away from eviction. We need the money now.

"What's 'right' got to do with it?" I say. "She who can enforce the rules dictates the rules. You know that. There's no point in arguing. We need to focus on getting paid."

We spent a week excavating a foundation space for Lacy, our client, so she can add a new addition—a larger sunken dome. That was well over a month ago. The foundation is already in, and we still haven't been paid for the dig.

On the ramp down into Lacy's home, I stop and steady myself.

One of her daughters, maybe eighteen, greets us with an infant on her hip and calls for her matria, then invites us in. Lacy sits at her desk going over papers, while her consort, Cam, refills her glass. I wonder if he's the daughter's father. A She controls her own fertility and strives for genetic diversity in her offspring, so you never know. Lacy looks away in disdain when she recognizes us.

"What do you want?" she says.

People say my voice has a childlike quality to it when I'm anxious. I straighten and do my best to sound grownup. "We're here about our outstanding invoice, hoping you can see fit to pay us. The job's been done for a while now."

Her expression sours and she turns away. Then she seems to reconsider. "Give me a minute," she says, then disappears into a back room. I grin at Dray. Over his shoulder, I see a plaque on the wall. It reads, 'Guard the rightful place of She. Preserve the status quo.'

Crap. Lacy is with 'the Quo,' that anti-progress extremist movement that thinks all men should be slaves. Wish I'd known that before we took this job.

She returns and hands me an envelope. "Here. Now you can't say I never paid you."

"Thank you," I say, then glance at the check. "Uh, this is only half."

"You only did a half-assed job. You think I'm going to pay full rate for that?"

"We did exactly what you asked, and we did an excellent job. Come on. We have bills to pay. Don't—"

She sneers down at me. "Two men with a piece-of-crap machine can't charge the same as a professional company. If I wanted to pay full price, I'd have called the professionals."

"We are professionals," protests Dray.

She laughs. "You guys are hilarious. Now get out of my house."

He bristles. "You can't just—"

When she hardens to confront us, Cam cringes back, signaling danger. I grab Dray and yank him toward the door. "Thanks for your business," I say, pushing Dray up the steps to the exit ramp.

He is still fuming as we pull away on our bikes. "Guns, Tye—"

"Watch your language." I glance around to check that no one is within earshot of such vulgarity.

He ignores me. "You're such a limp little dick. Why did you let her—"

"She's with the Quo. Don't need any more scars. And neither do you. Half is better than nothing."

"It barely covers our expenses. If we're not gonna get paid, we might as well not bother. Maybe we should focus on selling the loot."

"Keep your voice down." But he's got a point. I can't lose my mother's place. I can't. If we were just unclaimed, we'd get to live in a men's residence. As freemen, we're on our own.

We've always done our share of community service, daycare, and infrastructure maintenance. But I'm done with trying to attract the attention of a She willing to take me in only to put me to work serving her. We're on our own, but at least we're free.

As we ride along, Dray pulls in beside me. "Why are She so aggressive all the time?"

"It's in their nature, I guess." I hope to learn more about that from the book.

"What about the loot?" he says. "When is that gonna pay off?"

Ah, the loot. I grind my teeth. "I'm still working on that."

"How are we gonna sell stuff we're not supposed to have?"

"That's the part I'm still working on." If I could present my artifacts to the world, it would prove I have what it takes to be a successful historian in my own right. I'd prove men can earn wealth and respect the same as any She.

In the meantime, I've got a dozen devices I can't even name. They must do something, or else why would She pay so much for them?

"You know," he says, "the longer we hold on to them, the more likely we are to get caught."

"I know that. Don't worry. I'll think of something." I'm running out of time.

"Oh, I'm not worried. They try to haul me off to re-education, they're in for a nasty surprise. They're not taking me without a fight. I'll crack heads."

"Dray, stop it. You can't fight them. Remember Mouse, back in school?"

He grimaces. "Yeah. She was tiny. Your size."

"There are small She and there are big men, both rare. But I remember her rubbing your face in the dirt. You really think you're going to take on enforcers?"

He pouts.

"Besides," I say, "we're not gonna get caught."

I don't even want to think about—

"I wonder where they'd send us," says Dray. "Where is re-education, anyway?"

"It's nowhere in the Eastern Territories, I know that. My mom said that each of the six regions shares the same culture and laws as us. None of them want seditious men in their midst. So it must be somewhere far away."

"Huh," says Dray. "Provender seems far away to me, and it's only a two-day trip. I've heard the next closest city is two weeks away. Two weeks of dangerous travel."

"Two weeks is nothing. My mother's been to two other central cities, each crowded with a hundred thousand people or more. She was gone months."

"Yup, I remember she was gone a lot."

"So who knows where we'd end up? I don't want to find out, so let's just play it safe, okay?"

The aggravating part is that there are plenty more artifacts where these came from. Treasure beyond measure. Our secret could make us rich. Dray could afford to build his freemen apartments and develop his dream of a self-sufficient local brotherhood.

Now I'm the one fuming. She like Lacy can lie and cheat and steal from men with impunity, while men are browbeaten into obeying every stupid law.

And every unreasonable demand. I should have said *no* when Marsa made me go out in that storm to rescue her mucking cat. She obviously valued it more than me. And I knew what would happen when Barb made me take those eight brats to the market by myself, and then blamed me when they caused a ruckus. A hundred times, I should have stood up for myself.

Dray's right. I am a limp little dick.

That stops now. Why have I worked so hard at being a 'good little boy' when it's always at my own expense? If She are so determined to drive me into a life of crime, why am I resisting? All I need to do is play it safe.

How hard can that be?

5

SHEENA'S BAR

Rule One(B): Each of the six local regions shall establish a company of champions from the pool of Charlies to serve in protection of the local Councils. The champions from each region shall be awarded the rank of Bravo.

Rule One(C): A company of top champions among the Bravos shall be established to serve in the protection of the High Council and its rulings. Henceforth known as the Elite Guard, this company shall consist of the top fighters from the whole of the Eastern Territories, each of whom shall be awarded the rank of Alpha, with the duties and privileges afforded such station ...

THE A-B-C RANKING SYSTEM, Alpha-Bravo-Charlie, is imitated in every schoolyard competition. So that's where it came from.

THE DEEPENING DUSK is heavy with the hum of pumps as rain runoff fills the reservoirs of the surrounding geodesic homes. Ahead of us, the wet dome tops glisten as though holding back tears.

Another early April day lost to rain. It's been a wet spring.

Terrible conditions for digging. Our flatbed truck sits out of commission, the power shovel needs repairs we can't afford, and we have no new jobs on the horizon. And I chose this life?

One day. I have one day to come up with the money to pay the fine, or they're gonna take my mother's home from me. Homeless freemen. So cliché.

I'm just a man in a She's world. What was I expecting? It's all predictable, in a random kind of way. I finally take charge of my life, and nothing changes; I'm still at the mercy of She, still controlled by the weather.

Snap out of it, Tye. It won't help to get depressed about it. Tomorrow I'll go in and argue my case for another extension. One month. That's all I need.

Who am I kidding? They won't give me another extension. Lots of She have been after my place, expecting me to fail, ever since Elona and her daughters moved out. Some of them probably already have their bids in.

Down the street, a group of children laugh and squeal as they play in the puddles, splashing each other. Dray walks beside me on the gravel laneway, swinging his arms around to shake out the kinks of being indoors all day. Out of nowhere, he gives me a nudge, and I have to grab his arm to avoid splooshing into a puddle. A million times he's done that, and I still never expect it. I give him a swat, and he plays innocent. But his eyes are full of fun, and that mood is broken, and I can't help but smile. *I love you, man.* "Watch it, you moron."

I'm so glad he's in better spirits. His carefree playfulness and oblivious optimism always seem to come out when I need them most. He even shaved and prettied himself up for tonight. I always hated getting dolled up, but it's expected of men. You don't want to embarrass your matria. Now, I don't need to care how I look.

And he's right. There's no point in sitting at home moping about the situation. Tonight, I get one last chance. No more playing it safe. I've got to reach out.

There are She in the criminal underground who sometimes come to the bar trolling for freemen. Maybe I could lure one in with the sample device in my pocket and the promise of a big score. It's a bad idea, getting mixed up with those She, but what choice do I have?

Around us, patches of light appear from below as the Hillhaven villagers open their sunken doors to the fresh night air. I know the comforting illusion of freedom those open doors provide to the men inside, the ones who wish they had permission to be out. A year ago, that was me. Now, if I want to go out, I go out. Freedom is wonderful. I never expected it to be so expensive.

Dray's gone quiet. What's going on?

"It's a topsy-turvy world," he says, as we make our way down a dark laneway between the dome tops.

"Oh?"

"The earth, the very cradle of life, tries its best to scour us from its surface with deadly winds and temperatures, and we surface creatures are driven to shelter underground."

Okay, that's uncharacteristically deep. Where did he pick that up? "Yeah. Topsy-turvy." There's history to explain that, but I'm not supposed to know it, let alone talk about it. I'm not supposed to know that a once-benign climate was somehow changed by the vast civilization that died. Seven generations into the new world, I can't talk about the Great Pandemic that ended the old one. Because I'm a man and it's history, which makes no sense to me, but I'm not gonna dwell on it. Not when there's a nice cold beer and a chance at solvency waiting for us.

At Main Street, the view opens toward the river. Down there, the new topsider district stands defiant amid the huddling town, its industrial and apartment buildings hardened against sun and storms with thick walls of reinforced concrete. The newest boxy, two-story monstrosity covers an entire block, yet in my old neighborhood, we still think of ourselves as villagers. Things are changing too fast.

Dray brightens. "Hey, maybe we'll get to see Sheena tonight."

"Maybe. Be careful what you wish for."

"Yeah, yeah, I'm always careful." He steps into the street without looking. I grab his shoulder and pull him back as Norma's delivery van blows past with complete disregard.

The bar's large, open storm shutters welcome us onto the entrance ramp. Descending, we push open the door under the Sheena's Bar sign and embrace the sweet, yeasty smell of the brew. The place is half-empty, the clientele familiar, though I only recognize a couple of freemen among them. It's mostly local unclaimed men, here hoping for a tryout if some She come in later. A tryout might lead to being claimed and "living the good life" under the care of a She, exactly what freemen want to avoid. Despite all the hopeful makeup and coiffed hair, some of them have been unclaimed for years and will end up with each other again tonight.

I look around and see no shady She. One of these men may have a connection. We make our way to the bar and pull up stools. I'll need a couple of drinks to screw up the courage to ask around.

"Evening, Danner," says Dray. "Glad you didn't close early because of the rain."

"An essential service," says the burly bartender with a smile and a wink. He's keeping his eye on three loud drunks to our right as he pours our drinks. Our toast is practiced and efficient so we can get right to that first swig.

By our second drink, the trio of drunks has become quite raucous. We send them annoyed looks, but somehow that doesn't settle them down. At least we tried. They're a little close for comfort as they horse around, so I nudge Dray, and we push our stools further away.

A slurred voice yells, "Bartender. Another one here." A good six feet tall with a solid build, the ringleader sways on his feet as he pounds the bar. Danner, an inch shorter but heftier, is serving another patron. The guy lays into him with a verbal barrage that somehow turns into a drunken three-way shoving match with his buddies.

Dray says, "Oh, oh. Here's to blowing off steam." He drains his glass.

"Yeah, we'll be seeing Sheena, all right."

Danner straightens and puts his hands on the bar. "Okay, pack it up, boys. That's all for tonight."

One of the drunks says, "Come on, guys. Let's get out of this dump." He grabs the big guy by the arm and pulls him away from the bar. The big guy wheels around and swings, knocking him back into a table. Everyone in the bar stops and looks. The second drunk tries to restrain the big guy and ends up on the floor. Before I can grab him, Dray steps over to intervene and gets punched in the face. Now it's a brawl, as several nearby locals try and fail to quell the trouble-makers. The people at the far tables are on their feet, the men cowering behind the larger She, who shake their heads in disgust.

The six-foot-four Sheena appears behind the bar, her lush red hair tied back, her freckled, fine features compressed into a stern scowl. Ravishing, regardless. She drops a hand on Danner's shoulder to prevent him from jumping into the fray, then points her thumb toward her office. Danner defers.

Sheena draws herself up to her full glorious height, and her big roaring voice hammers the room. "*That's enough.*"

All the men freeze. It's an involuntary response, ancient, primal. It's what happens when a She uses her real voice, not her social voice. Human ears hear the deep, angry roar of a large predator, a sound that activates an instinctive warning that one's only hope for survival is to avoid being noticed.

Even when you're used to it, the effect lingers. All the men straighten up and back right off. The large drunk, still spoiling for a fight, goes back to grappling with someone.

I look for Dray and see him holding his face, backing away from the action. Before I can call out, an alarmed male voice cries, "Heads up!"

All eyes turn toward the entrance, and the men shrink back as two towering figures stand blocking the doorway. Their short-cropped hair, form-fitting leather regalia, and angled thigh-high boots announce them. *Enforcers.*

But not just any enforcers. In a world where female beauty is universal, it is dominance that catches the eye. Dominance is power.

Every man desires selection by a dominant She for the status and privileges that accompany her, and men learn to recognize dominance at a glance.

It shines from these two. The tops of their tight leather boots parallel the upward slope of their hard thongs, which connect to armored hip guards. Elbow-length forearm guards cover their hands down to the top knuckles. The molded breastplate features low-cut cups sitting astride a diamond-shaped shield, center chest, above an open midriff. Shoulder guards connect through a neckband collar of gleaming gold. Their dominance on full display, they stand half-naked, brazenly exposed, like they're daring some fool to try an attack.

They say attentive men are easier to control, so enforcer regalia has two functions. The first is to convey authority, and the second is to catch and hold the attention of men ...

Where was I? Yeah. We have a kleek of enforcers in town, but all six are only ranked Charlie. The golden neckbands on these two signify the rank of Alpha, the toughest of the tough, the hardest of the hard. Alphas are renowned for their exceptional allure. Their posters adorn men's walls.

I've seen a couple of Bravos in the village before, but never an Alpha. What are they doing here?

I go cold. *Oh, crap. Are they here for us?* I slide my hand over to cover the device in my pocket. *How do they know?*

6

———————

PINNED

I SIT FROZEN to my stool, scared to breathe. I need to run. I need to hide. I need to—*Stop. Be invisible.*

Dray's eyes check with me about bolting. That would draw attention to us. We'd never make it out. I gesture to stay put.

I glance around and see a room full of men with guilty faces, all watching in alert fascination as the two appraise the situation. Their curvaceous beauty inspires awe and dread in equal measure.

The average height for a She is six-two. These two are both big, maybe six-five. But it's not their size that makes them imposing. Their very bearing shouts, *You mess with me, you die.* Each has a bokken—a blunt-edged hardwood sword—strapped at the waist.

I've heard an Alpha can take your eye out before you can blink, her sword work is so quick and precise. She can crush a windpipe on a whim, or burst a heart, mid-beat. I've heard an Alpha wouldn't bother to draw her bokken against a man; she could just kill him with a punch.

I wish I didn't know any of that. I'd be enjoying this view a lot more.

The one in front looks to be in her thirties—it's hard to tell with She—with rich-brown skin, a brush-cut crown of dense white hair, broad shoulders, a tight waist, and long, powerful legs. The one following seems a bit older, with a tan complexion, brush-cut blond hair, and the shapely, feminine musculature of a champion. But as the image of that second face sinks in, it holds me spellbound, like the dance of approaching flames.

A taunt of recognition, untethered, lustful, impossible. She commands the room with her eyes as the Alpha in front heads straight for the grappling men and stops, towering over them.

"She said that's enough." Social voice. Most She use a social voice to show a lack of hostile intent. A She's social voice is usually music to men's ears, but this one carries an imperative.

The man trying to subdue the drunk immediately lets go and backs away, hands showing submission. The drunk troublemaker turns away and staggers toward the bar. "Piss off. I need a drink," he says.

I hear a collective gasp from the room. The Alpha grabs his shoulder and pulls him around to face her. As he turns, he swings out to strike her. Her head snaps back out of the way and he misses. The room goes silent. The drunk sways back with a grimace as the Alpha wags her finger in his face, the message clear. *Shouldn't have done that.* Then, lightning quick, she grabs him by the collar, yanks him clear off the ground, presses him above her head, turns and tosses him backward onto an empty table, then drags him to the floor where she drops astride him and raises her fist. My stomach contracts as I see his coming death.

But she holds back, fist high, poised to strike.

His eyes are blood moons focused on her fist as he gapes, unable to take breath. Then she eases and examines his face, stretches her long, lovely neck, and leans in. Her voice steams like dry ice. "I don't hit men, or your suicide attempt would have been successful."

She pops to her feet above the stunned drunk, then looks down at him and hesitates before stepping away. He gasps, then struggles to roll over and push himself onto his hands and knees, retching.

The blond Alpha takes command, addressing the room, voice only edging toward real. "Who wants to defy *me*?" Everyone shrinks back as she surveys us. "Good. Then there will be no more nonsense." She turns to the felled drunk's companions, voice back to social. "Get your boyfriend cleaned up and take him home. You know he'd be easy prey in this condition."

The men sheepishly comply as the two enforcers check the room, then saunter straight toward me at the bar. My heart drops. I knew it. I knew they were here for me.

The blond reaches the bar and stands right beside me. She's got me. I sit pinned to my stool, stomach clenched. She looks down at me, and I hold my breath. Body rigid, I check her face for my cue to flee for my life. But I'm seized by large eyes shining luminous aquamarine in the bar light, and that face—that exquisite face—takes the fight out of me. Our eyes meet, and my reaction is involuntary. I surrender.

Then she turns to Sheena behind the bar, and Sheena's face opens in awe.

"You're her! You're Kay—"

"And this is Onyx. Are you Sheena?"

Kay ...? I gasp in recognition. Kāya. The Alpha Kāya. It floods back: boarding school, her fight posters on the wall, my teenage crush. And I'm impossibly face to face with—oh no.

The slightly shorter Sheena straightens. "At your service."

All that time I spent as a teen gazing at her face. She's older now, even more magnificent.

Sheena throws out both hands in greeting. "It's such an honor to meet you. I was a big fan." Then she looks around and shakes her head. "Unclaimed men. Most of my business, unfortunately. I could've handled that, by the way."

"Thought I'd save a sister the trouble," says Onyx.

"Appreciate that," says Sheena. "So, how can I help you?"

"We need information," says Kāya. "We're looking for—"

She notices me right beside her and turns to look down at me. *Me. It's me you're looking for.* And now she has me. I gaze up into a face that astonishes me and fall into her eyes, lost.

"Is there a problem?" she says.

I blink. "Problem?" I gulp air. "No. No, I won't cause any—"

"Do you mind?"

I'm flummoxed until she nods toward where she wants me to go, and the light dawns. She's not arresting me. She's not? Not yet. I quickly stand—I barely come up to her shoulders—and withdraw to find Dray sitting at a table nursing his jaw.

"She let you go?"

"I don't think they know it's us yet." I nervously finger the device in my pocket. Why the hell did I bring this? "We need to get out of here."

Dray grabs my thigh. "Not now. They're watching the door."

"Yeah. Yeah," I fluster. "Let's just sit tight."

This is wrong. I should run. *No.* That would catch their attention, which would lead to detainment, which could go very badly, with my big mouth. This could be the day it gets me killed. I'm an expert at keeping a low profile and avoiding attention, but then, always at the worst times, I lose it and mouth off. I need to keep it together and stay small and hope they don't notice me.

Dray keeps his voice low. "You got a close-up look. What's she like?"

I sigh. "Perfection." I lean toward him. "That's Kāya. Remember her? Fight posters? Boarding school?"

"All the Alphas had posters. Don't remember her, but I think I remember the other one. The hot white hair on hot brown skin. Wow."

"Yeah, that's Onyx."

"Onyx. Right. I sure remember her."

"Okay, cool it." We can best avoid their attention by ignoring them, but my disobedient eyes betray me and reward me, and I curse my weakness. Then I remember Dray's jaw and shake my eyes free. "You okay?"

"What gets into these idiots? Why would he swing at her?"

"Unless it was an attempted suicide, I guarantee no thought went into it."

Dray's eyes are all over Onyx at the bar. "How stupid would you have to be? I mean, look at all that pent-up power just itching to come out."

"Most She underestimate how stupid men can be. She obviously doesn't."

A tall, buxom matria herds her two men toward the door. Sheena calls out to them as they leave. "Sorry about the disturbance, folks."

The matria calls back as she shakes her head. "Men. Thick heads and thin skulls. A bad combination."

"You got that right," says Sheena. The She at the bar resume their conversation under our appreciative gaze.

Kāya glances our way, and I take a mental snapshot of her face before averting my eyes. I luxuriate in the glow of the afterimage, then catch hold of myself. There's danger in being drawn in. I don't know that I've ever seen a more dangerous face.

Dray is still nursing his cheek. "I have to get some fight training."

"Why bother? You seem to love getting beat up. Why the hell did you do that?"

"Somebody had to do something."

"Sheena would have handled it. And we'd have had a front-row seat, you dummy."

"Not all bullies are She. Men bully other men, too. If I knew how to fight, I could handle men like that."

"Maybe, but any She would still crush you."

"Maybe, maybe not. But it would be nice to be able to fight them off if I had to."

I sometimes wonder how many concussions he's had. Female physiology makes their muscle and bone density much greater, and their skin tougher and more durable. Every schoolboy knows you can't fight someone who's bigger and stronger and tougher. It's no contest.

The two Alphas conclude their conversation with Sheena and turn to inspect the men in the room. They're on to us, all right. But they haven't identified us yet. They're putting on the pressure, waiting to see who tries to bolt.

I put my hand on Dray's bouncing knee to still it. *Don't even think about it.*

Now, they're making their way around the room, checking everyone out. All eyes watch furtively, with a few notable exceptions where men offer smiles and nods. Kāya stops and exchanges words with a big guy, six-three and beautiful, who works at the sawmill. She gives him a smile that could melt rock. What would it be like to be strong enough to interest an Alpha?

"Hi, cutie."

The voice startles me. It's Onyx, standing right in front of Dray. His eyes dart around, looking for an escape route. I knock my knee against his, and he looks up at her with a fake grin. "Hi."

"Relax," she says. "I'm just checking to see that you're okay. How's your jaw?"

Dray touches his face and shrugs.

"You should have stayed out of it," she says. "Men aren't built for fighting."

He nods, then leans forward. "You're okay?"

I cringe. Why is he talking to her?

She tilts her head. "Of course."

Concern clouds his face. "For a second there I thought ..." He touches his lip.

"What?" she purrs. "You thought he was going to touch me? In one of my tender areas?" With an alluring smile, she rubs a tantalizing finger across her lips. "Not without permission, sweetie."

My heart stops. She's got him.

Now Kāya is coming this way, with sawmill guy in tow. Did she ask him to point me out? She's closing in. Onyx is saying something. "Time to go, Dray," I blurt, interrupting. "It's getting late."

Rising abruptly, I knock over my chair, and it bangs to the floor. Now the two enforcers are right on top of me, and I scramble, trying to back away, but trip over the chair and go down hard on my ass. Kāya is frowning at me. She knows.

I roll to get back to my feet, hear a clack beside me, and look down. The device has slipped from my pocket and lies gleaming on the floor. *Oh no no no.* On hands and knees, I grab for it, and in my panic, it fumbles out of my fingers and hits the floor with another clatter. I feel her presence right above me as I lunge to cover it with both hands and try again.

My heart jumps as a heavy hand drops on my shoulder, fingers lining my neck, thumb soft on my throat. I can't bring myself to look up. An open hand appears in front of my face.

I should break free and run. But I learned the futility of that at an early age. The hard way. Repeatedly. I'm simply too slow. And back then, it wasn't life and death. *What do I do, what do I do?* My grip loosens.

Obedience inspires mercy. It's my only hope.

I gingerly place the device in her hand.

7

INTERROGATION

KĀYA EXAMINES the artifact with interest. "What have we got here?"
Then she covers it with her hands and looks over her shoulder to
sawmill guy. "Another time. Leave us." He cautiously backs away,
then turns and hurries back to his table. She looks around, and all
faces in the bar turn away. "Let's go somewhere quiet."

Still sitting on my ass in shock, I stare at the floor. I feel a hand
under my armpit, and I'm weightless as she hoists me. I stretch my
legs down to reach the ground.

Sheena points toward the back. "Use my office."

Dray grabs my arm and says, "Yup, it's getting late. We should—"

Onyx holds up a hand, freezing us, and Dray puffs up. I clutch his
arm. "Dray!" *Don't. Please don't do anything stupid.*

They herd us toward the office, where we see Danner, the
bartender, pacing with an infant in his arms. To my surprise, Onyx
rushes over and tenderly brushes the baby's hair with her fingers.
"Oh, isn't he sweet," she says. The She join in, cooing together over
the baby.

I breathe again.

"Danner," says Sheena, "look who's here. It's Kāya. *The* Kāya. Can
you believe it?"

Danner's face betrays alarm, in sharp contrast to Sheena's delight. "Yes, I ... It's an honor." He clutches the baby to his chest and gives a shallow bow.

"Please take Bo home now. I'll finish up here."

My hope sinks.

Danner nods, wraps the baby, and eyes us with suspicion as he goes by. Sheena closes the door behind him, and we are trapped, held captive by enforcers who caught us red-handed, guilty of a crime I don't understand. I hastily wipe tears from my cheeks to avoid revealing my despair.

Kāya examines the room. "Thank you, Sheena. Please keep this incident to yourself. You are dismissed."

Objection flashes across Sheena's face but is quickly masked. She bows her head in deference and withdraws. Even Sheena fears this one. This one carries an aura of command that sets my nerves tingling. My survival depends on my ability to give her no reason to kill me, which she could do with one hand, in twenty different ways.

Kāya holds out the device. "Where did you get this?"

I try to shrink into the floor and fail.

"Answer me."

I squeeze my eyes and mouth shut. *Wake up, wake up.* This has to be a dream.

Dray steps forward, hands raised. "It's not what you think."

They both turn to him, and Onyx speaks. "Explain."

"We're collectors. We find things."

"You mean you're scavengers."

"No, no. We—"

The pair of them box us together. "Names," demands Kāya.

"I'm Dray, and this is Tye. We just—"

"Were you scavenging in the west end of the Shell?" It's an accusation.

Dray answers for me. "Of course not. We're not suicidal. We only search locally. Tye, here, is famous for his searching skills. We find a lot of stuff. Uh, amazing stuff."

Kāya's face broadens as she suppresses a smile, and I notice several faint scars. "You're a terrible liar, Dray." She continues with an old, familiar trope. "It was lying men who caused the collapse of civilization."

I clench. Now who's the one lying? I know that to be false. I'm not supposed to, but I do. I bite my tongue.

"Now, you're both going to start telling us the truth." The sharp edge in her voice slices away all hope of evasion.

"You don't hit men, right?"

Dray's question makes me cringe. Even I can see the difference between drunken fools and criminals. I hold my breath as Kāya steps closer to tower over him, examining his face through narrowed eyes.

"We don't hit *helpless* men. I'm getting a dangerous vibe from you."

Onyx suppresses a chuckle, and Kāya gives her a look of exasperation. Onyx responses with, "I'll bet Sheena hears things. Before we get carried away, let's see what she knows." She's still trying to keep a straight face. Curious.

Kāya scowls again at Dray before turning away.

"You boys stay where you are," says Onyx, back under control. "We'll be conferring right outside this door."

We submit, of course—what else are we gonna do—and they close the door behind them. A reprieve. I catch my breath as I look around. The office, a medium dome adjoining the bar, is well lit, though its ceiling windows are dark in the night. Its east wall exposes the geodesic structure of the subterranean exterior. Sheena's desk sits beside the door, across from a couch, several chairs, a safe, and a crib. Dray and I look at each other. I expect to see blame on his face but don't.

"I really mucked up, Dray. I'm sorry. I—I guess I panicked."

"We should have ducked out as soon as they walked in. I was happy to stay and watch. Stupid."

"Why did I do that? I knew better than to try to run. It's like I have no self-restraint."

"Self-restraint? We've lived our whole lives on a leash. Who needs self-restraint when you're always being restrained?"

"And now that we're freemen?"

"Okay, point taken." He looks around. "Yup, we mucked up this time, we did."

We listen for a moment and can't hear any voices through the door. We lower our voices anyway.

"I don't think they were looking for us," says Dray.

"Yes, they were. I heard them at the bar."

"They came in looking for something, but after, I think they were just trolling for men."

"What? No. Why would you think that?"

"Uh, well, Onyx offered to gimme a treat tonight."

"What? When did that happen?"

"Right before you—you know."

I grab my head and moan.

"I was ready to say yes. I'm sorry, Tye. What gets into me?"

"No, I get it. She's gorgeous." They both are. I shake my pitiful head. "Doesn't matter anymore."

He looks around, woeful. "She have a strong survival instinct. Men, on the other hand, we're dimwits born with—"

"We're not dimwits."

"—born with a self-destruct instinct. We grow up learning to avoid danger, but then we reach puberty, and everything flips, and we're involuntarily drawn to the world's most dangerous predator."

"Keep your voice down. They hate being called that."

"So what? It's true, isn't it?"

"Yeah, but—" I deflate. We wander over to the desk and pull out two chairs, their metal frames like prison bars, and sit.

You need to be strong to take risks and survive. I can't afford to take risks. I knew that. Did I really think I could get away with this? And if they find out about the book...

"Whatever happens, Tye, don't say anything about the site. If we need to, we can give them the rest of the stuff. We can always go back for more later."

If we have a 'later.'

He continues. "But if we tell them about the site, we'll lose it."

"Yes, but they'll want to know where we got that thing." Better to show them the site than have them searching through our twin-domes.

"Let's say we found it on the street."

"What if they don't believe us?"

"They'll try to beat it out of us, but as long as we stick to our story, they'll give up and move on." He touches his sore cheek.

Beat it out of us? I squeeze myself to hold back a moan. I've avoided beatings for a long time with a clever combination of avoidance, submission, and fake obedience, but I still remember. Beatings have a way of staying with you.

And now my luck has run out. I can't do this. I won't survive a beating, not from an Alpha. Not from Kāya. To see cold cruelty on a face I've adored would kill me. "I can't, Dray. I'm sorry. I just can't."

"Then let me do the talking. You just—I don't know, whimper or something."

I can do that. I'm good at being nonthreatening—a necessity when you're small and fragile. I used to hate it when people said my long, dark lashes gave me doe eyes, but for defusing female hostility, helpless tears can work miracles. Maybe they'll keep me alive now.

Unable to sit still, I stand and walk over to the exterior wall, where I examine the geodesic beams. Polished wood. Good workmanship. Impenetrable as a dungeon. I rock, tapping my forehead against a beam. The baby smell still hangs in the air, but it only brings up memories I can't deal with right now.

I've just returned to my seat when I hear a noise at the door and alert to my predicament. I'll bet all men are disposable to a She like Kāya, yet my life is in her hands. I anticipate her return with eager—dread.

I jolt upright as the door bursts open and the two enforcers flood in. My eyes find her before I can brace myself, and I'm enthralled. She moves with the agile grace of a wildcat, her posture impeccable, her towering form enticing. Her face hard. Our peril reasserts itself.

They drag our chairs out from the desk with us in them, then Onyx takes up station near the door. Kāya sits on the edge of the desk, feet flat on the floor, and leans toward us. The strength of her presence radiates heat.

"Here's the way it is. We have no interest in wasting time here," she says, and holds up my device. "You will tell us where you got this. Now."

Dray and I exchange glances, and he says, "We found it on the street. On our way here tonight."

Kāya stares at him, calling his bluff. I watch with growing concern.

Dray sees it's not working. "Uh, we did. Just tonight."

Onyx speaks from the doorway. "We've already established that you're a terrible liar, Dray. We're giving you an opportunity to cooperate."

"I am cooperating," he protests.

Kāya chuckles, shaking her head. She turns to me, and I shrivel.

"It's Tye, right?"

I nod, tentative.

"Do you have a voice, Tye, or does Dray do all your lying for you?"

"No, I have—" No voice. I clear my throat and try again. "I have a voice."

"Tell me, Tye, where did you get this?"

"I found—"

"Don't try to tell me you found it on the street. This is not from around here."

I deflate.

"I'll ask you one more time. Where did you get this?"

Dray leans in. "Look, I told you—"

Kāya blurs, and her large hand is around his throat, his head stretched high. His mouth gapes like a fish out of water as he grips her forearm guard with both hands. "I've heard enough from you," she says, examining his bulging eyes. "I'm asking him."

Onyx intervenes. "Kāya."

Kāya glances over, releases her grip, and turns back to me. Dray guards his neck with both hands, gasping.

"What's it going to be, Tye? The truth? Or—"

"The truth," I blurt, tearing up. "Just ... don't hurt him. Please. Please. It's my fault."

Dray grits his teeth. "Tye!"

"Well, it is. I'm the one who knows history, not him. He's just trying to protect me."

"Tye, what are you doing?"

Kāya shoots up a finger, silencing him. She looks back at me, and I see interest in her eyes. The entirely wrong kind of interest.

"How is it that you know history, Tye?" she says. "It is not for men to know."

I wince, cursing my big mouth. "I hear things, is all. When people talk about the past, I listen."

"Who talks about the past? I want names."

I do my best not to squirm. "Nobody. I mean, people talk about how things were in the early days. New World history ... mostly."

She's not buying it. Her eyes are right there, and I wither under her glare. The truth, then. It comes out as little more than a mumble. "I want to be a historian."

The enforcers exchange amused looks, and I notice the scar on her cheek. Kāya says, "Do you know why it's forbidden for men to be historians?"

"No. Why?" *I can only guess there's something you don't want us to know.*

"It's because it's highly dangerous work. Men are not made for that kind of work. Don't you agree?"

I give a meek nod. Men do dangerous work, too. You think excavation is safe? On the verge of speaking out, I pull back.

Kāya studies me with a scowl. "A man could never be authorized to do historian work. Are you in violation, Tye?"

She knows. I hug myself, rocking. It's pointless to try to hide it; she sees right through me. Years of grievance well up within me. "Why can't a man be authorized? I know men are slow learners, but we can still learn." There. I said it. I brace for a blow.

She straightens, frowns and squints at me, highlighting a pale scar on her forehead. "And how exactly have you come to learn history?"

No blow. Another reprieve. How, exactly? I can't implicate my mother. "Like I said, I just picked it up here and there."

Kāya turns to Dray. "What about you, Dray? You know history too?"

"Nope, not a bit," says Dray. "I only help him sort and carry the—"

I cut him off. "He doesn't know anything. He's totally clueless, as should be evident."

"Hey," protests Dray.

Kāya's eyes don't leave me. "So, you have more of these."

I squeeze my eyes shut as Dray curses himself.

Onyx steps closer to Kāya, and I overhear, "Check the spread of the damage."

Damage?

Kāya turns back to me. "Tye, do you tell other men about history?"

I emphatically shake my head. "Never. I only listen."

"If only I could believe you. Get up. You're coming with us."

"Where?" says Dray.

Onyx takes Dray by the elbow. "Let's go."

"Don't hurt him!" I call out. "Let him go. He doesn't know anything." They all ignore me.

There are people in the bar. We can call out for help. They'll rescue us.

The Alphas flank us as we file through into the bar. I look out and see frightened men looking away, trying not to draw attention, as two apex predators prowl through their midst.

There will be no rescue.

8

ALPHA

Our shuffling feet echo as we are ushered out of the bar and up the ramp. We emerge into the open night, and the sudden silence rouses me. I breathe in through my mouth, hoping the still-damp breeze will dilute the acrid taste of fear, and look up to examine the sky. My future is written in the stars up there, somewhere, but all I see are clouds being herded off to some unknown fate.

Out in the open air, escape seems possible, but that's an illusion. We wouldn't get ten feet before being taken down. No, we're bound tight, even at a loose distance.

I get a shove and don't resist. Defiance would be stupid. All I can do is submit and plead for mercy. Wherever they want us to go, we go. To a formerly claimed man, a consort, the sense of resignation is familiar. I had hoped to never feel it again.

As if reading my thoughts, Onyx says, "You two are unclaimed?" She looks us over, dubious. "Only two kinds of men are unclaimed: the undesirable and the unmanageable. In your case, it's obvious."

"Thanks," says Dray. "We freemen are unclaimed by choice."

The Alphas exchange glances. Enforcers hate freemen, and now he's given us away. I flare my eyes at him in protest, and he shrugs.

There are men who commit suicide by attacking enforcers. There is a lunatic fringe of men who are dangerous, so part of me can understand why enforcers must be alert to threats. But that's not who freemen are. Freemen want to live free. Emphasis on live. We don't commit suicide, let alone attack enforcers. Yet because we resist being under She control, we're always the first they suspect, always guilty in their eyes. And now that they know, we can't expect fair treatment.

A large fuel-cell safari truck, certainly not local, looms ahead of us, parked on a laneway. We're making our way down the road toward it when a deep growl prickles the back of my neck. I freeze and search the dark shadows behind the dome to our right. If that's Sally, we should be quietly backing away. Onyx squares to the sound and steps toward it.

Dray gives a warning under his breath. "You shouldn't have done that."

Another growl, more menacing. Both backing up, Dray and I bump into each other as Kāya corrals us. "We should be running now," I implore. Onyx ignores me and takes another bold step, and another. What is she doing? Something shifts in the darkness, and I strain to see. Something large. A rumbling shape emerges into the dim light, all sleek muscle and white fangs, ears folded back, angry. My muscles seize as the large Doberman starts barking fury. Yet Onyx presses forward past the property line. *Don't. Don't do that.*

Suddenly, it's charging, leading with its fangs. I gape in horror as she strides toward it. The Doberman leaps at her, jaws wide.

With a quick motion, she catches it by the neck in midair and, to my astonishment, holds it hanging with both hands around its throat. Its legs flail at the air, forepaws clawing at her arm guards. She draws its face close, glares into its eyes and snarls. Then she drops it down on its back and pins it with one hand. With the other, she grabs its windpipe and squeezes, while she again leans in and growls through bared teeth. The dog goes limp under her.

From the alley comes a frail voice. "Sally! Sally, get back here."

"Don't!" I cry. "Don't kill it. Please! That's old Hanna's dog. Her only protection."

Onyx huffs. "Don't be ridiculous. I'm not going to kill it. I'm just establishing who's alpha here." She releases pressure on its windpipe. "It won't attack us again. Will you, girl?" She strokes it lovingly, coos to it until it calms, then lets go. The dog flips to its feet, gives one quick lick of her hand and hurries off, tail between its legs.

As Dray wipes his brow, I find myself clinging to him and let go. His eyes are wide, voice barely audible. "Did you see that?"

I steady myself, still trying to process it. "Alpha, as in top dog, I think."

"Obviously," says Dray, composing himself. He turns to Onyx. "You're both Alphas, so who's on top?"

She ushers us into the back of the truck. "Kāya, here, holds the rank of Alpha Lead."

"You have a team? Here in Hillhaven?"

Kāya ignores him. "Onyx, that's enough talk. Let's focus on the task at hand." She climbs in.

In the back of the safari truck, we sit on the lone bench under a collapsible roof. Around us, piled and stowed, lie crates, canisters, and a variety of other supplies. My voice leaks fear. "Where are you taking us?"

Kāya turns to face us. "Here's the way it is. You have more of these. You are going to show us. Directions. Now."

"I never said I have—"

"Now."

I clutch myself, mind racing. We can't take them to our place. What if ... "What are you gonna do to us?"

The enforcers look at each other. Kāya is slow to respond. "That's going to depend on you."

"What do we need to do?"

"I'm still waiting for directions. You're stalling."

I sink. If I show them our collection, it will prove our guilt. If I don't, well, they already know we're guilty. They'll search through my whole place and find the book and then I'm really screwed. Maybe it would be better ... No, we'll be banished either way. I grab Dray's hand and gaze at him with welling eyes. *We're gonna be separated, and I may never see you again.*

My heart slams as Kāya swings in and lands at my feet. I squeeze my eyes shut, then when nothing happens, peek out. One foot forward, she squats casually in front of me, forearms resting on her knees, and we're face to face. I try to look away, but her face is right there, and I can't. Though I'm braced for pain, I find no cruelty in her eyes. Curious. She tilts her head, examining me.

She squints as she sees my tears flowing. She detects my tremble. She looks away and sighs.

I alert to a movement to my right and see Dray launching himself from his seat, and I know he's gonna try a surprise attack. "No!" I cry. Kāya spins and blurs, and Dray slams to the floor face-first, her foot on his back. "No! *Please!*"

She glances at me, then eases. She lifts her foot, and he rolls to face her, eyes wide, hands raised. "You should stay seated, Dray." She nods consent, and he drags himself back to the bench as I suck air.

She squats in front of me again, and her questioning eyes melt the ice in my veins. She reacted to his attack and defused it before he even got close. She would have been within her rights to claim self-defense. She could have killed him.

But she didn't. My gratitude bursts out through a broken voice. "Thank you."

She nods. Her eyes caress mine with a soothing silkiness that licks my wounds. "How about returning the favor?"

I will give you anything. "What?"

"I think you know."

I know. My home. Now Dray has given her cause to take it out on him if we don't cooperate. Resisting was foolish from the start. "Go straight ahead four blocks, then turn right for two, then left, and it's the large double, three domes up."

"Thank you, Tye." She smiles at me, and my heart melts. And I know all is lost. But all was already lost. What difference does this make?

Dray turns away and glares into the distance, like I let him down by being unwilling to watch him die. *Well tough shit, Dray. I'm not gonna let you throw your life away like that.* The truck lurches and we're underway.

I can't hold it in. "What's *wrong* with you? You thought that drunk at the bar was stupid, and then you go and try the same thing."

"I thought she was gonna ..." He looks away.

He doesn't need to say it. He was trying to protect me. What a hopeless pair we are.

Riding in the back of the truck, queasy and breathless, I see the familiar surroundings as if for the last time. Everything looks different. Nothing stands very high around here. From the dome tops to the squat trees to the collapsible windmills, everything cowers, hunched in deference to the punishing storms. Riding up here affords a good view as we pass through the old neighborhood. It's reassuring to see the ground blistered with the familiar, glowing dome tops all the way down to the topsider district.

Dray's looking too. We're both wishing we were over there right now, on the other side of the river. The blister clusters of those newer neighborhoods look bigger, and now, in the darkness, brighter. It's visible evidence that our small farming community, after seven generations, is starting to grow, prosper and diversify. We now have over eight thousand residents, including men. And a promising future ... that I've squandered all hope of seeing. I curse my stupidity.

The problem with a small town is that it takes no time at all to get where you're going. The enforcers do a quick survey of the area as we arrive, then hop out and stand waiting.

Bypassing my living quarters, I lead them to the bunker entrance. I open the latch on the sunken door, and Onyx pushes by me down into the dark interior.

"Lights," she demands.

Even from the doorway, I can smell the musty tang of rust and dust I only notice when someone new comes in. I point to the switch, and she flicks it, exposing the whole mess. The workbench in the middle is cleaner than usual, and the shelves lining the walls don't look too bad. But it's the piles of junk on the floor that first grab the eye. Old parts, plastic and aluminum cases with tubes and wires sticking out, small, rusty appliances with parts missing, all lie waiting to be sorted and stripped for parts.

Kāya strides in. "Who owns this double?"

"I do." I swallow.

Skepticism hardens her face.

Onyx cuts in. "Few men even own domes. What is an unclaimed man doing with a large double?"

"Not an unclaimed man," says Dray. "A freeman."

Kāya squints at me. "Again, whose bunker is this?"

"It's mine," I say. "I have full rights to it and everything in it."

"You own this bunker? How?"

"It belonged to my mother. She left it to me."

"She let you collect all this stuff?"

"Most of it was hers." I shouldn't have said that.

Onyx scowls. "Was she a mechanic?"

I puff up in my mother's defense. "No. A historian."

Not the answer she was expecting. "Your mother. Name."

"Celia."

Kāya shakes her head. "You're off to a bad start—"

"No, it's true. Look." I point to an old photo on the wall.

Kāya's eyebrows shoot up. "You're Celia's son?"

Onyx says, "Celia has a son?"

"Wait. You know of my mother?"

"How could we not?" says Kāya. There's more, but she holds back.

"Then you know more than me," I say. "She abandoned us when I was young."

The two Alphas exchange puzzled looks. Then Onyx says, "Ah, the book fallout."

Oh crap. The book?

"Makes sense," says Kāya. "Smart, actually."

"What book fallout?" I'm holding my breath, but they ignore me.

Kāya frowns. "This complicates things."

I can't drag my mother into this. "No, she didn't teach me any history, if that's what you're thinking." At least, not on purpose.

"But you saw enough to make you want to be a historian."

I shrug and nod.

"When was the last time you saw her?"

"When I was ten."

To my relief, this seems to satisfy her, and I look to change the subject.

Onyx, doing a quick sweep of the room, beats me to it. "Does anything here actually work, or is this all junk?"

"There are some good parts in here, but I haven't found any buyers yet."

"I can see why," says Onyx, wrinkling her nose as she pokes around.

The more promising-looking items, intact devices and clean components, sit on shelves. The enforcers do a slow scan as they explore, avoiding the rusty piles on the floor.

The Alphas look even bigger here in familiar surroundings, and half-naked, the stuff of fantasies. My eyes slide up Kāya's shapely thigh-high boots and snag on her half-exposed glutes as she pivots. How can something so perfect be so—

"What's in here?"

"Dray's room."

Onyx glances in. "You live here?"

"I like to surround myself with the finer things," says Dray.

Both She look around through the door.

Onyx confronts him. "Where do you really live?"

"Here. What are you—"

"No freeman would keep his place this tidy. Don't lie to me, Dray."

Worried, I speak out. "He's not lying. He's a bit of a neat freak."

Dray lifts his shirt to show the scars on his back. "I was very well trained." Her face twitches.

Kāya steps into his room and sniffs, then nods. "It's his scent."

She smells us? Curious. I remember hearing that some Alphas have enhanced senses, but it seemed far-fetched. So far, they've lived up to all the stories.

The Alphas turn away from his door and return to examining the room. They soon make their way over to the shelves holding the better stuff.

"Look," I say, "you can take whatever you want. We just—"

"Everything here is for sale," says Dray. "You can't just come in here and steal it. There are rules, you know."

For a moment, it's like they're trying to figure out what to make of a man who's telling enforcers about the rules. I'm tempted to help them out, but he wouldn't appreciate being called 'a bit of a clown.' Luckily, they figure it out on their own and return to exploring.

A minute later, Kāya holds up the device she took from me. "You have more like this. Show them to me."

"We're cooperating, right? You won't hurt us?"

"I'm still waiting."

Dray cuts in. "Don't do it, Tye. It's all we've got."

Onyx investigates a box. "We will find them anyway."

She's right. And that's not all they could find. I nod and start toward the far wall, where the bin sits hidden beneath an old tarp.

"Tye, don't."

I stop. "Dray, it doesn't matter. We lose anyway. We always lose. When we're claimed, we lose. When we're free, we lose."

"So, what? We just give up?"

"Maybe if you're strong, you fight to the end, I don't know. It's pointless for me."

Onyx cuts in. "I see you're quite the fighter, Dray. How's that bruise coming?" A hint of a smirk softens her face.

Dray rubs his cheek. "Just a return visit from an old friend. I've had worse."

Her eyes again wince. "Then why do you—"

Dray rails. "You come in here and you take everything from us, and you expect us to just roll over and take it? Because we're only men? Well, we—"

"Dray! Don't. It's over." I'm not gonna let him dig himself deeper trying to stand up for me. I fill my lungs and cross the room, looking over the crates and shelves lining the wall. When I first learned all this was mine, I felt rich. I was so hopeful back then, when selling old artifacts seemed like a lucrative possibility. Then thinking new arti-facts would be more valuable and easier to sell, and being hopeful again.

I was so naïve. I gaze down at the old tarp in front of me, revealing the location of my treasure. My treasure. Lost now, like my home. Like my life.

I stand for a long moment, like preparing to jump into chilly water, unable to commit to taking that leap. But I've already given it away. Stalling is pointless. I plunge in, grab the tarp, and pull it off. I reach in to touch my treasure one last time, flanked by two giants, as the enforcers stand witness to the contents of the bin.

Contents that convict me.

9

———

EXPOSED

Rule Two: The lessons of history shall be taught to all young She, such that they may learn the horrors of subjugation and the immeasurable blessings of the Inversion. In conjunction with such education, all young She shall swear an oath to forever stand on guard against a return to that subjugation. Insofar as the High Council of She is the governing body overseeing the protection of all She, the oath of allegiance shall be to the rule of the High Council. All transgressions shall be punished according to the rulings of the Tribunal ...

The room is suddenly airless, the exit stairs impossibly far away. The triangular panels on the wall curve up to the strip lights overhead and bathe me in the glow of their harsh judgment. The illicit contents of my secret bin, now well lit, lie naked and exposed.

In the suffocating silence, I lean back and await sentencing. The two enforcers exchange looks, then, with wide eyes, they both reach in and pick out devices. They seem surprised. What were they expecting?

"You might as well take them," I say. "I was about to lose them tomorrow anyway."

Kāya looks up. "What do you mean?"

"I'm being evicted tomorrow. The town will own my home and sell it off to the highest bidder."

"Then we certainly can't leave these here."

Onyx examines another device. "Why are you being evicted?"

Aren't you shaming me enough already? "Too many business debts."

"You have a business?"

Dray's back goes up. "We're not the only men to run a business."

Onyx shrugs. "No, but you have to admit, it is a bit of a novelty. What business?"

"We do excavations," says Dray.

"Oh, so you're diggers."

"We have our own power shovel, and we do excellent work. When we can get it. And then there's the problem of getting paid. A contract with a She isn't worth the paper—"

"Dray." I give him a quick head shake. Then I gaze longingly at the artifacts. "I hoped these might help me pay the fine and keep my home."

"You've been fined?" Onyx asks.

Dray cuts in. "Yeah. For being broke. How does that even make sense? Men make such good scapegoats, don't we?"

"Dray, please. You're not helping." I look up at Kāya. "He's just upset, is all. Please don't take it out on him. I'm the one who ..."

Kāya ignores me, fixated on the device in her hand. She takes something out of her satchel and plugs a cable into the device. It lights up. We all gasp in unison, and she quickly unplugs it.

"How did you do that?" The question barges out before I can censor it. I wince. That was inappropriate. Her eyes narrow like she's making a note of it.

"Where did you get these?" she demands.

"We just wanted to pay the fine and back taxes," I plead.

"How? There's no way you could sell these. Unless you had

someone helping you." She abruptly turns and looks down at me. "Who is it? Give me the name."

My resentment leaks out. "There's no one helping me. Do you think I'd be losing my home if I had help?"

She leans in close, and I cringe, but she only sniffs the air, then straightens back up. "I doubt you would." She brushes me back and leans over the bin. "Again, where did you get these, and what do you know about them?"

"All I know is, She think they're valuable. I don't know why."

She shows the device she took from me. "What is this?"

I spread my hands. "I wish I knew. What is it?"

She scowls. "I think you know. Why did you have it with you?"

"In case I came across a potential buyer."

"Yeah? What would you charge for it?"

I throw up my hands. "I don't know. What's it worth?"

"Am I supposed to believe you're trying to sell something you know nothing about?"

I slump. Yeah. That sounds bad.

Dray steps in. "We weren't worried about being cheated. We're men. We get cheated all the time. We just needed to get some money to pay down some debt. Why does it matter what we know?"

I clutch myself. Why does he have to be so confrontational? He's gonna get himself pulverized. But I'm eager to hear her answer.

Kāya peers at him. "Rule Six: Any man in possession of such knowledge shall be removed from society. We need to know how dangerous you are."

What does knowledge have to do with being dangerous? Maybe it's explained in the book, but I have to violate the rule to understand it? That's crazy.

Dray is defiant. "There are no weapons here, if that's what you're worried about. We're not stupid. Do you know the penalty for a man found in possession of a weapon? Oh, yeah. I guess you do. You probably do the executions."

Onyx shakes her head in amusement. "That's a lot of hostility, Dray. You've had it rough; I can tell."

He warily nods to her, and their eyes hold. Curious.

Kāya dismisses them both. "Artifacts cannot be allowed to fall into the wrong hands."

Dray sneers. "You mean men's hands."

Onyx, standing a full head taller, slides behind him and drops both hands on his shoulders. I cringe, seeing him stiffen and gasp as if getting in one last breath. But she grins at Kāya, shaking her head. "Unmanageable."

It must be an inside joke, because Kāya eases. "As enforcers, we swear an oath to the Sisterhood to protect our We first; the community takes priority over all private contracts. Where need be, we keep the peace. If we see an act of sedition being committed—"

"Sedition? We're not—" I start.

"Teaching history to men? But you *are* in possession of historical information you could pass to other men. Digital records from the Before, such as those contained in found devices, are fuel for insurrection. If we determine that your sedition threatens the We—"

"We are duty-bound to eliminate that threat," says Onyx, speaking softly into Dray's ear. "This is your chance to show that you pose no threat."

I fight down panic. "What threat? What are you talking about, threat? How is my knowing history a threat to the We? Please. I've never understood."

Kāya squeezes her eyes closed and runs a hand through her hair. The hairs on the back of my neck warn of a lightning strike. But when her eyes return to me, they show—bemusement.

"So, you have trouble comprehending the words 'not for men to know.'"

I bow my head. "No, I understand the words." Just not the reason. But there's no point in asking this sexist. "What are you gonna do with us?"

They glance at each other. "We haven't decided yet," Kāya says.

"Then let Dray go. Honestly. He doesn't know anything."

"No," says Dray. "Let Tye go, and I'll tell you everything."

I moan in exasperation. "Dray, stop. Don't do this. You're only making things worse."

Onyx confronts him. "You should listen to your friend, Dray. I seriously doubt you're all that useful to us. You lie too easily."

"Here's the way it is. Neither of you is going anywhere," says Kāya. "Your time is up. Sit."

Dray and I look to each other with alarm. They wouldn't kill us, would they? All at once, I'm not so sure.

There are two old armless mid-back chairs at the workbench, each with at least one missing slat in the straight wooden backrest. We sit facing out.

Kāya says, "You'll start by telling us where you got these artifacts. The truth this time."

They're running out of patience, and they seem to see right through us. Resisting any longer is too dangerous. The truth, then. I take a deep breath. "We found them out—"

"Tye." Dray clenches his teeth as both enforcers turn angry faces toward him.

I bark at him, "Shut up, Dray." The enforcers look to me expectantly. "Out in the wilds. Not in the Shell. You wouldn't get me near that place. No, over near the old industrial park. But not in it."

"Where, then?" Kāya asks.

"Near there. I can't be more specific. There are no landmarks."

Kāya frowns. "Not very helpful, Tye."

"I'm sorry, I am, but how do I describe one spot in the middle of the wilds?"

She scowls and folds her arms. "How are they in such good condition?"

"They were underground."

"They're too clean to have been buried."

"Yes, they were in some kind of underground structure."

"An underground structure from the Before? All underground?"

"Yeah."

Onyx says, "Not likely to be from the Before, then. They didn't build to accommodate storms in those days. If they had, we'd have all the artifacts we could ever use."

"No," I say, "it's from the Before for sure. It's not like anything."

That seems to have piqued their interest.

"And how did you find it?" Kāya asks.

"I ... uh ..." I better not mention the map, and I can't bring my mother into this. "People used to search that area all the time. I think they were searching for this place but never found it." And then it hits me. Kāya will never find it either, not without our help. She *needs* us. Maybe I can use this. "It's very well hidden. That's why no one ever found it. I'm really good at finding things."

The two Alphas exchange looks. I bite my lip.

"So," says Kāya. "It sounds like you are going to need to show us this place."

"Yes, that's the only way you'll find it." I wring my hands.

"I wish I could trust you, Tye. I really do."

I feel it slipping away. "You can. You can."

"I don't think I need to tell you what will happen if you are lying to us."

"I'm not. I swear."

The enforcers withdraw and confer. I use the time to check on Dray, who's turned away from me, glowering. Then I make the mistake of looking over. Side by side, they are breathtaking. Identical in height and regalia, each has a distinctive beauty. Onyx's stance is unpretentiously boastful. Kāya's stance carries the authority of She perfection. They both have wonderfully long, powerful legs, with Onyx an inch higher at the hip. Their molded breastplates suggest average chests, though Onyx pops more. Both have taut abs on full display. Yet my eyes always seek Kāya's face, and when she looks our way ... that face ...

"You just gave it all away," says Dray, shaking his head, refusing to look at me.

I whisper, "We need to be useful to them."

"Of course we do. They're She. It won't last, Tye."

"But it gives us time."

"To do what?"

"To figure something out. Dray, we need to work together here. Please don't aggravate them anymore. I don't want to see you get hurt."

"Tye, you know it don't matter what I do. She just hate me anyway."

"When was the last time you tried to be nice to one?" I sigh. "I know. I know. What difference would it make? I'm just saying, it's been a while. Maybe it's worth another try."

"What, with these two?" He looks at me aghast. "If you think I'm gonna be nice to my executioners, you're crazier than I thought."

"You want to make it easy for them? Is that what you're saying?"

He slumps.

I put my hand on his arm. "Dray, we're gonna get through this."

He meets my eyes, and we tremble together in the raging storm.

I sniff and straighten as the enforcers return. I wish I knew what they had in store for us. Why did I ever think I could decide my own fate?

Kāya nods at Onyx, who says, "Dray. Come with me."

"Where? Where are we going?"

"Out to the truck. Don't worry, I'm only going to ask you a few questions."

Why are they separating us? I don't like this.

"Dray. Now." Onyx beckons.

Our eyes connect and linger, each of us looking to the other for reassurance neither can give. Dray puffs out his cheeks and lurches to his feet, then follows her up the stairs to the door. I need his strength here with me. I want to call out, *Don't leave me here alone,* but don't dare.

As they leave, Kāya pulls out Dray's chair and sits in it backward, arms crossed across the chair back, examining me. I can't stop trembling. What happens now? I'm within easy striking distance with no way out. Staring at the floor, I steal glances at her face that confirm

I'm still in the glare of her spotlight. Then she leans in, and the scent of leather binds me.

"I think it's time we shared some secrets, Tye. Let me go first."

A trick? My gaze flits around as I try to check her sincerity without getting lost in her eyes.

"I have no desire to hurt you. You seem like a nice man. Sensible."

Her eyes snag me, and I'm caught, until she looks away.

"But it's clear you have visited a historical site—"

"I didn't know until I was in it," I plead.

"—and removed valuable artifacts. You must know I have a duty to turn you in—"

"You can have them. Please don't—I won't tell anyone. I swear. I'll never say a word."

She examines me. "Tye, come on. You're a man. How can I believe anything you say?"

"But ..." I sag. Why would I expect anything different? My eyes well.

Her voice softens and takes on gentle, intimate tones as she leans in closer. "Actions are more telling than words, don't you agree?"

I nod, trying to swallow. "What can I do to prove ..." Prove what? I can't think straight.

"You can show us where you found these. Would you do that for me, Tye?" The heat of her breath turns my resistance to ash.

"Yes. Of course. I—"

"But you need to understand, I'm taking a big risk, trusting you. I need to know if it's a risk worth taking."

"How? What can I do?"

Her voice, all satin and suede, caresses me like a hand down my pants. "Now it's your turn. I need you to share some secrets with me."

I close my gaping mouth. What secrets? Is this about the book? She couldn't possibly know about that. Could she?

"Will you do that, Tye?"

I nod, uncertain.

"Good. Now, tell me about history. I need to know what you know."

I see what she's doing. She's forcing a full confession. I wipe my eyes. Wow. She's really good at this. And I'm a starving mouse, trying to resist the cheese in this trap.

Just one bite before I die. That's all I ask.

10

A LOT TO LEARN

Rule Three: A She may lay claim to one or more men, and in so doing, gain exclusive rights to his/their services, including domestic and child-rearing. In laying claim, a She takes on the responsibilities of the role of Matria, head of a family, assuming care and control of all men and offspring therein. It is the sole right of the She to determine the status of the claim. A She may dissolve a claim at any time, dismissing the man from his station. A man so dismissed will return to the pool of unclaimed men, providing general services to the We until such time as he is claimed by another ...

KĀYA SITS FACING ME, awaiting my confession, alone together in the bunker. Mine is the voice of a frightened child. "Uh, I'm not sure what you want." The voice feels genuine, but she doesn't buy it.

"I want to know what you know of the Before." Her gaze becomes hot. Now I know what a bug feels like, pinned under a magnifying glass. It doesn't even feel like my own bunker, as her overwhelming presence makes it seem small and cramped. What do I know about the world of the Before? More than most men, I know that. How much is too much?

I can't focus when I look at her, but where do I look when she seems to fill the whole room? I fill with the perfume of her scent. Where to start?

"I know the Shells were once enormous, shining cities full of people, with towers that scraped the sky. I know the surrounding burbs were once an endless sea of dwellings that housed an unimaginable number of people." This is all common knowledge. "So many people that they were consuming the entire earth out from under them, dirtying the water, spoiling the atmosphere, heating it up until it raged against them. That's why we have the storms, right?"

"Where did you hear that?"

Careful. "I don't remember. I've always known."

Kāya stands and looks around. I steal a look and marvel at her tight waist. She steps toward a shelf and examines an ancient toaster. "Go on. What do you know of those people?"

I'm helped by the fact that so far, all I've learned from the book is that the past was bad, and they don't want to repeat it. I stick to what I learned in school. "There were so many people packed close together that when one got sick, many got sick. Then the Great Pandemic killed most of the human population."

Amusement softens her eyes. Something about that public version of events is obviously off. I move on to the safer territory of New World history.

"Then the survivors had to organize to survive in a hostile world." And I know damn well it wasn't the fault of lying men that civilization fell. That's just a story She tell to keep men honest. But I must be cautious here.

"Tell me more about the Great Pandemic. And Tye, I want to hear all of it."

I shrug. "What's to tell? Most everybody got sick and died. Something like eight billion people. To be honest, parts of the story seem far-fetched. I mean, there were eight *billion* people?"

"Go on."

She's a cool one. "There weren't enough survivors to maintain the machinery of civilization, so everything ground to a halt and then started falling apart. They managed to gather into small communities and keep going, and gradually built things back up, and here we are."

Kāya sits back and studies me, waiting.

I wish I knew what she was digging for. I need to give her something. "Apparently men fought a lot, violence, wars. It makes no sense to me. Maybe you can explain it."

She looks at me, expressionless.

I continue. "I mean, men aren't built for fighting. We're small and weak and slow to heal. And where did they get the weapons? Maybe overcrowding drove men mad. Maybe there were too many men for the She to properly supervise, I don't know."

Kāya sits back and seems to ease. "Yes," she says, "we have rules now that they didn't." She looks away, thoughtful. "Do you know the difference between electric and electronic?"

"Uh, not really. Electric means it runs on electricity. I'm not sure about ... Oh. You mean *pre*-electronic? That's a description of our culture, I think. I heard my mom ..."

She studies me for a moment. "Not important. The artifacts you found were obviously stored under special conditions. We need to investigate those conditions. Do you understand?"

At that moment, Onyx enters. "How's it going in here? That one poses no danger."

"Same," says Kāya, to my surprise. "I think we're okay here. Celia was careful."

"That's a relief." Onyx motions behind her, and Dray walks in.

"She threatened to chase me down if I ran," says Dray, looking her up and down. "I was quite tempted."

My alarm abates when Onyx shakes her head and chuckles. A lucky break. She gets his humor, and he knows it. I wipe sweat from my brow.

Kāya joins in. "Onyx is a sprint champion. She'd hit you like a diving eagle hits its prey. It would be quite entertaining."

Yikes. I'm not sure she read their signals.

But hold on. What was that they said? We pose no danger? When did we ever pose a danger? Oh, right. Sedition. I guess that means I don't know enough to be dangerous. Which means—I have a lot to learn.

As the two She confer by the stairs, I take Dray by the arm and lead him to the other side of the room. "Are you okay?"

"Yup, it's all good."

"What did she ask you about?"

"You know, history and crap. Easy stuff."

"What do you think they—"

I turn, wary, and see Onyx head back up the stairs to outside. Kāya approaches, and I again feel small. I can see by her bearing they've come to a decision.

She addresses us in her commanding style. "Here's the way it is. You have tonight to prepare yourselves." I prepare for the worst. "Tomorrow, we have business to attend to here in town. When we are done, you will guide us to the location where you found these arti-facts. You will remain in our custody until we make a determination about your futures. Is this clear?"

"Uh ... but tomorrow we have to move out. All our stuff—"

"You can each bring a bag."

A bag? What about all—

"So, we get to live through the night," says Dray. He always sees the bright side.

"Better than that," says Onyx, as she comes back in with a duffel bag over each shoulder. "We will be staying the night."

No, no, no. We have to get them outta here. If they find the book—

Onyx continues. "You, Dray, will get to work off some of that hostility, if you're up to it." There's that alluring smile again.

Dray gulps. Then he glances at me. I grimace at him with a subtle head shake. "You are more than welcome to stay the night," he says, his eyes openly wandering over her. "Do you really think you can take that much hostility?"

What are you doing?

Onyx matches his grin. "Oh, I'm pretty sure I can."

Kāya turns to me. "That's Dray's room. I assume you have your own accommodations."

My heart pounds. I've hidden the book under some clothes in my dresser. If she goes searching—"Uh, nothing interesting over there."

"A bed, though, I hope," says Kāya.

I wipe my face. Maybe she won't search. We watch the two warriors embrace, then gaze into each other's eyes before kissing. I stand transfixed.

"Have fun," says Kāya as they separate. "And Onny, if the bed's comfortable, sleep in."

"Best boss ever," says Onyx with a sly grin. She addresses Dray, ushering him toward his room. "I'm going to look around first before we settle in. You just sit tight."

I clench. That's not what I wanted to hear. I know there's nothing in Dray's room that could get us in more trouble. Still, when the door closes, I'm worried for him. For both of us. How am I gonna manage this?

Mind flipping around like a trout out of water, I look to Kāya. The turmoil disappears. Those aquamarine eyes flare in my vision, and I surrender to my fate. With a sweep of her hand, she directs me to lead the way. "Show me where you live."

Knees weak, I take her through into my dome, relieved to see the dresser closed and unobtrusive, reassured by the cozy comfort of the living space. Here I am, at home alone with the most beautiful She I have ever seen. My face flushes. She closes the door behind her, and my heart does a flip inversion—the most *dangerous* She I have ever seen.

And I haven't yet seen her angry, not like she'll be when she finds I've been hiding something. She's gonna rip me from my home, force me to reveal the source of my treasure, then discard me to some distant penal colony. My tense apprehension is buried under an avalanche of loss, and I sag under the weight. But my eyes come back into focus, and there she is, the real, live Kāya, right here with me in my room. My head swims and I clutch the promise of the present moment. Maybe if I can please her ...

Kāya looks around my quarters with disapproval. "You've been a freeman how long?"

"Over a year."

She shakes her head with pity, and a profound emptiness deflates me. I thought being free and alone would be better. But free and alone is still alone.

I hold my breath, watching her explore, then seize up as she pulls out a drawer and glances in. But she doesn't poke around. Just closes it again and moves on. I lean against the table, feeling faint.

"Tell me, Tye. What does being a freeman mean to you?"

The question surprises me. "Uh, it means being able to live my own life, make my own decisions, come and go as I please. It means I get to choose who I want to be, not have some role forced upon me."

"No, I mean, what does it mean about how you relate to She?"

I hesitate. "I'm not sure what you're asking."

"Most freemen have no interest in becoming attached to a She. You?"

"No. Absolutely not. I don't want to ever be claimed again."

"Good."

Good? She removes her sheathed bokken and sets it on the floor beside the bed.

"You know never touch this, right?"

I nod.

She slides off her arm guards and sets them beside her bokken as my heart pounds. Taste is a personal thing, and everyone has unique preferences, but I can't imagine any man not being stunned by her beauty.

"Since I'm staying the night," she says, "there's something you can do for me."

Please, please, please. "What's that?"

"I've been out in the field for weeks. You know, in the Shell. No men. And right now, I'm in need of a good rocking. Are you willing?"

Am I willing? "Yes," I say. "Definitely."

She nods, then sits on my bed and starts pulling off a boot. I watch with rapt fascination.

"When was the last time you pleasured a She?"

I'm taken aback. "It's been a while."

"I asked, when?"

"Yes. Uh, maybe three weeks ago?"

"Tell me about it." She starts on the other boot.

Curious. What's she after? I don't trust her. "A group of She were passing through on their way somewhere, and one of them decided to try me out, you know, to see if I was worth claiming. I told her I was a freeman, but she seemed to think she could change me."

"And?"

"I did not live up to her standards."

"How hard did you try, once you got off?"

Not a question I expected. I shrug.

She stands and looks down at me, unclasps the back of her gold collar and pulls her shoulder guards over her head. "Is that how you play it? Passive-aggressive? It's easy to fail, right?"

How could she know that? I hesitate. "When necessary."

"And when is it necessary?"

I feel like she's stripping me naked, and I can't refuse her. "When I ... feel trapped, I guess. To be claimed again would kill me. Please. I'm not worth it."

Her smirk is dismissive. "Men and their melodrama. Your worries are misplaced, so don't bother with your failing act." She turns away and sets her shoulder guards on a chair.

I hope she didn't misunderstand. "But it's okay if you want to try me out."

She chuckles. "I don't try out men. If I want a man and he's willing, I take him. I have no interest in claiming one."

I blink. "But you could have any man you want."

"Any time I want."

All at once, I see. She has no need to take on the burden of claim.

My back stiffens. I mean nothing to her. But—that's what I want, isn't it?

My unexpected uncertainty vanishes as she unfastens her breast-plate. I lick my lips, and the taste of hope loosens the bonds of my better judgement.

11

EVICTION

Rule Four (Amended): All unclaimed men shall be housed and fed in exchange for their community service. All She shall contribute to the care and wellbeing of unclaimed men. To the extent possible, all men, claimed and unclaimed, are to be kept sexually active to maximize both their willingness to cooperate and their ability to provide healthy seed if called upon to do so. It is mandatory that explicit consent be obtained for all sexual activity, and She are expressly prohibited from forcing sexual submission.

Commentary: As the first generation matured, they came to understand that 'happy men cooperate.' Hence, this amendment. To avoid male rebellion, all She are encouraged to do their part in meeting the needs of men and rewarding desired behavior ...

ALL SHE ARE BEAUTIFUL, but Alphas are in a league of their own. I watch Kāya remove her regalia, piece by piece, and can't help but wonder how other She feel around her. I hope it gives them a hint of the inadequacy I feel every minute of every day.

What am I doing here, in the presence of this goddess? I stand in awe, trying to be invisible, as she wipes down the inside of her breast-plate. I look away when she glances over.

She chuckles. "You might as well get comfortable."

I allow myself the thrill of watching. Her modest breasts embellish her athletic build. I hardly have time to adore them before she pushes down on the hip pads of her hard thong. She steps out of it, puts it with the rest of her regalia, then stands unabashed, facing me.

I assure her that the tiny shower has hot water, then stand uncertain, mouth dry, waiting for her to step back out. When she reappears, it is not as a fearsome Alpha. Oh, she's still magnificent, still imposing, but in a softer way. Her skin glistens as she towels down.

"Come take a shower. Wash some of that fear off you. I'm not going to hurt you."

Yes, I need one too. I'm sure she can smell me from across the room. I tear off my clothes and rush in to wash. Not gonna hurt me, she said. I hope she means that.

Like everyone else, I've grown up with nudity as a natural part of life. There is nothing sexual about being nude. It's our natural state. A She's sexiness is determined entirely by her intention. What men watch for is the sexual invitation, usually nonverbal in the form of explicit display, always confirmed by explicit eye contact. A She uses the 'invitation' to signal accessibility and arouse a man to readiness.

I step out of the shower and almost drop my towel. I should have known Kāya's invitation would not be subtle. Still, I'm astonished to see it directed toward me.

"There," she says. "Doesn't that feel better?"

It takes a moment to realize she's talking about my shower. "Yes. Much better."

"Why don't you come over here and help me feel better?"

I fluster, trying to come up with a clever response. I have no words.

I would be insane to not take advantage of this. This could be the most amazing night of my life. It could also be my last amazing night, if I end up in some penal colony. Maybe if I please her enough, that won't happen. I desperately need to please her.

"You're still okay with this?"

I force my mouth closed. "Yeah. Uh, yes."

She shakes her head with a chuckle and takes charge. She rolls to her feet and pulls me onto the bed, then pushes me to my back, and just like that I'm under her, looking up in awe. And we both know it's just sex, but her mouth is right there, and even knowing a kiss is out of bounds, my lips long for hers. And in the heat of connection, I'm lost in a dream, mindlessly soaring through the heavens until, spent, I slide back to earth.

Then panic sets in. I'm finished, and she's clearly not.

Uh-oh. What do I do now? All She have different preferences, and I have no idea what would please her. The only way to know is to ask. "Kāya, please guide me. I'm so grateful to you right now, and I want nothing more than to give you pleasure. Help me. Tell me what you want, what you like. Guide me. Please."

She stills, and I alarm, sensing something is wrong. She sits up, then climbs out of bed without looking back. What? What just happened? Did I say something wrong? Maybe I sounded like I don't know what I'm doing. I'm sure she's used to men who know exactly how to please her. Why did I say that? I chase after her, desperate to make amends, and find her stepping into the shower.

She rebuffs my approach. "I'll be out in a minute."

I raise my hands and back away, then sit on the edge of the bed, rocking. I have failed her. My chest closes in.

She comes out wrapped in a towel, and I know we're finished. And I left her unsatisfied. "Kāya, please. Did I say something to offend you?"

She looks away. "Let's just leave it."

"Are you angry?" She doesn't seem angry.

"Look, Tye, I need to get some sleep. I think it would be better if you slept on the floor."

The floor collapses under my heart.

————

WARY EXHAUSTION TOSSES and turns me through the night, like I'm trying to sleep in a cage with an unpredictable predator. Unable to get comfortable on the floor despite the extra blankets under me, I give up at daybreak and sit quietly at my table. I consider trying to sneak out and make a run for it, but where would I go? And what would happen to Dray if I did that? No. I couldn't do that to him.

I replay last night in my mind for the hundredth time. What did I do wrong? I was in paradise and then ... what? She won't sleep forever. What happens when ... I don't want to think about it. What's the point? I close my eyes and rest my head on the table.

A sound wakes me. I lurch upright and grab my aching neck. Kāya is up, and already dressed. I groan, dreading what's to come.

"Tye, the bed's free. Go lie down."

I wipe my mouth, uncomprehending, until she gestures to the bed and nods. My words are slurred but desperate. "Kāya, I'm sorry if I—"

"Leave it be." Her tone and manner are neutral, and my mind is in a fog. All I can think to do is comply. The bed is soft and warm, and I give in to it.

————

SOMETHING ... What's going on? I fight to come awake and hear it again. A heavy knock on the door. A jumble coalesces in my mind. Kāya. Where is she? Did she lock herself out? I must have fallen asleep. *The book.* I left it unguarded. Did she find it? I quickly check the drawer and there it is, untouched. The knock again, more insistent this time, along with a call. "Open up." Not Kāya's voice. I moan. This is eviction day.

My home. The place I've called home my whole life. Even when I was away at boarding school, or living under the claim of a She, this was always 'home.' Without it, I am lost. A chill quiets me. I fight to push through my rigidity and stand, then look around. I should get the door.

This is when my last link to my mother gets ripped away from me. Why should I care about that? She obviously doesn't, or she would have come back and helped me. Anger swells in my chest then boils into shame. She entrusted all this to me, and I've lost it.

The futility of it all drains me. Losing my home doesn't even matter anymore. My life in Hillhaven is over. I have no idea where I'll be by the end of the day.

"We know you're in there. Open up."

"Coming," I snap.

Wondering where Kāya is, I drag myself up the stairs, still in my nightclothes, and unlatch the door. Standing there in the light wind is a town official I recognize from the lawsuit. I clench against the suicidal urge to lunge and punch her in the face. Behind her stands the six-foot-seven Rimora, one of the local enforcers who's had it out for me ever since I became a freeman.

The official steps forward. "Tye Celiaso, I have here your final eviction papers. You have until noon today to vacate these premises or be subject to arrest."

I glare at her, my stomach shriveling. I want to tell her what she can do with her eviction papers. I want to rail against the injustice of their oppression. I bite my tongue, not trusting myself to speak without jeopardizing my life.

I jump, startled by a demand from right behind me. "Show me the papers." Kāya, in her regalia, stands behind my shoulder. I slink out of her way.

The taller Rimora draws back, and I tighten, uncertain. The official shifts uncomfortably on her feet. "I heard there were Alphas in town. May I ask your business here?"

"You may not. Papers." Kāya holds out her hand.

The official glances back at her enforcer, who is clearly deferring to Kāya's rank. For the first time, I notice the neckband on Rimora's regalia. Black. She's a Charlie. Bottom of the A-B-C enforcer hierarchy. Kāya's gold collar gleams in the morning sunlight. The official places the eviction papers in Kāya's hand, and we fidget as she takes her time reading through them.

The official breaks the awkward silence. "I'm sure you'll find everything is in order."

"I'm not finding that at all," says Kāya. "According to this, the amount owing is a tiny fraction of the true value of this property."

The official blushes. "It's a matter of insolvency—"

Kāya speaks over her. "Wait here." She disappears inside, and I am left standing in the shadows of two large and now angry She.

"What is she doing here?" demands Rimora. I have a flashback to the time she dragged me out of Sheena's Bar and threw me in jail overnight for refusing her advances. I guess she didn't like being told I wasn't her plaything. My big mouth again.

"I'm afraid you'll have to ask her," I say, trying to hide my glee at her discomfort.

Kāya steps out to confront the pair, and their eyes widen as Onyx fills the doorway behind her. Kāya addresses the official. "You have placed a value on this property." She hands the astonished official a slip of paper. "This covers the amount owing. With full payment of the debt, I hereby take ownership of this property."

The official stammers. "You ... you can't—"

Kāya holds up the eviction papers and tears them in half. "I can't what? Are you saying your valuation was fraudulent?"

The official examines the check in her hand. "No, no. This is just ... irregular."

"Here's the way it is. You will have a deed prepared in the name of Kāya Larada by noon today. Your business here is concluded. You may go."

Even I can see the enforcer is fuming. Kāya confronts her. "Is there to be a challenge here, Charlie?"

The enforcer's eyes flare, then look down as her face flattens. "No, Kāya. No challenge. But ... may I respectfully ask what Alphas are doing in Hillhaven?"

Kāya surveys the surroundings. "What is your name?"

"Rimora."

"Well, Rimora, it would seem we have just established a satellite office here." She leans forward, eyes narrowed. "You may want to stay on my good side."

As they defer and withdraw, I try to hide my exhilaration. To see my tormentors intimidated into submission was utterly delicious, and I savor the taste of vicarious power. My captor has overturned my eviction ...

But then she took my home. My head swims in confusion. I clutch the edge of the doorway and take in the familiar scent of the neighborhood to steady myself.

Kāya and Onyx have gone back inside. I stand in the open doorway, looking around at the bubble tops of my neighbor's domes, remembering when neighbors used to help each other. The Alphas have left me alone out here, and I again suppress the temptation to run.

I've lost my mother's legacy, my last ties to her, but I knew this was coming. I expected I'd be scrambling to try to figure out what to do next. I don't need to worry about that anymore. My fate is no longer in my hands.

Was it ever?

My mother's words come back to me: "Life has a way of taking us to unexpected places, no matter which course we set for ourselves." It's not enough, telling me to make the best of things. I needed more. *If you'd been here to guide me, maybe—*

"Tye. Inside."

I wipe my eyes. I'm familiar with feeling like a prisoner, but this time, I literally am one. Until I outlive my usefulness.

12

APPRAISAL

Rule Five: In the We, every child is the responsibility of every man. All unclaimed men shall participate in community childcare in addition to their other duties, and in exchange shall receive room and board and good standing. A man found to be in dereliction of these duties shall be ostracized for a period of six months, during which time no She shall have sexual contact with him ...

I DESCEND INTO MY ... former home and find the others sitting at the table for a quick breakfast of dry granola, berries, and instant coffee. "I'll pick up some milk next time I'm out," Dray says to Onyx with a sneer. "Oh, that's right. There isn't gonna *be* a next time."

So, he knows we're homeless now. "Morning, Dray," I call out, hoping to defuse a tense situation.

"I'm still not sure there's going to be a *this* time," says Onyx, rising to confront him.

In a panic, I blurt, "If you hurt him, you might as well kill me, because I'll never, ever show you—"

"Tye! Tye, calm down," says Dray, holding out a mug. "It's okay. No threat here, freeman. We're just goofing around."

I look from face to face and see surprise, then amusement. Onyx reaches across the table, and he hands her the mug. My face flushes. Kāya leans back in her chair and looks at me askance.

I fluster. "I'm sorry ... I thought ..."

"Come and sit down before you pee yourself. Have some breakfast with us." Dray retrieves the boiling kettle.

What is he so cheery about? ... Oh, right. Looks like he had a better night than I did. Good. I'm glad. He needed that.

Lips squeezed tight, I sit and stare at my empty bowl as the others eat. Onyx passes me the granola, and as I spoon some into my bowl, I feel her eyes on me. Reluctantly, I look up.

She locks eyes with me, but I sense no hostility. The gentleness in her voice surprises me. "You're a good friend, Tye. Dray's lucky to have you."

Before I can refute the lucky part, she turns away. "We're got a busy day ahead."

"Yes, we do," says Kāya between mouthfuls. "You two must have a vehicle. Where is it?"

Dray says, "We have a flatbed truck. We use it to get our power shovel to work sites."

I correct him. "Used to use it. It broke down a couple of weeks ago. Couldn't afford to get it fixed. We were hoping ..." I trail off. What's the point? We'll never see it again. "It's yours too, if you want it."

Dray directs a disgusted look my way. I ignore him. *Get a grip, Dray. In case you haven't noticed, it's over.*

"One more part, and I would have had it on the road again."

"I know you would." Then I remember our best hope is for them to see us as useful. I turn to them. "Dray can fix anything."

Ignoring me as usual, Kāya helps herself to more granola. "Any other vehicles?"

"Just our bikes," says Dray. "Why? Do you need one?"

Onyx says, "We need to know how much of a flight risk you are.

We have errands to run, and we can't afford to lose track of you while we're out, so we'll take those bikes. To be on the safe side."

Dray shrugs. "We were planning to run away at the first opportunity."

I slap my hand to my head.

Onyx chuckles. "Maybe I should cuff the two of you together."

"Yup, that's probably a good idea," says Dray. "It'll give us a challenge, so we won't get bored."

I implore him, "Dray, stop it. Please."

Onyx cuts in. "He's being bad, isn't he, Tye? Would you like me to punish him?" This time I see the mischievous twinkle in her eye before I panic.

Kāya drains her mug and stands. Onyx straightens her face. "Onyx, since you're having so much fun here, you can stay and babysit. The men need to pack and be ready to travel, and I can take care of this morning's business on my own. I will need you this afternoon, though."

Onyx is all business. "Understood. Nance should be here by then. I'll start sorting."

Kāya nods, grabs her duffel bag and leaves without looking back. The sun seems to set as the door closes behind her, and I'm left without a single clue about what went wrong last night.

"You heard the boss," says Onyx, rising from the table. "Tye, take your time eating, but when you're done, this is your chance to pack. Dray, when you're done, come over and help me do some sorting."

"Sorting what?"

"Artifacts, of course. Some of them might be worth keeping."

Dray says, "We'll give you our best sale price for whatever you buy."

"Oh, we're not buying anything, cutie," says Onyx.

Dray protests. "You can't just—"

"You obviously can't sell any of it, so it's no use to you."

"She's right." I put my hand on Dray's arm. "Let it go."

Onyx rubs an eyebrow. "Dray, you're in enough trouble as it is. I'd like to be able to help you, but I can't unless you help us."

Dray sobers. "I know."

"I'll be next door. Don't you boys go anywhere." She winks at Dray and goes through to the bunker, leaving the door open.

I look at him with suspicion and keep my voice low. "She trusts you?"

He shrugs.

"How did that happen? What went on last night?"

He avoids my eyes but can't keep the grin off his face. "She's … different." He glances at the open door. "I'll tell you about it later. How about you? You okay?"

"Not so much."

His face straightens. "What happened?"

"Wish I knew."

"Don't muck things up, man. They're not gonna hurt us unless they have to."

"Why would they have to?"

"They've been enforcers, but now they're historians. This stuff is really important to them, and they don't want us telling anyone else where we found it."

"So, we need to keep our mouths shut and show them the goods, or …"

"That about covers it. Look, I better get over there."

"Dray? Do you think Onyx might be willing to talk to you about Kāya? You know, why she's mad at me?"

He shrugs. "I can try. You look bagged, man. We've got a couple of hours. Why don't you try to get some shuteye?"

I yawn. "How could I sleep at a time like this?" But the fatigue presses down on me, and I have no will to fight it.

I sit in a swirling cloud of conflicting emotions, unable to bring anything into focus but the freeman's need to wall off his heart or be consumed. But her scent in my bed brings her flooding back to me in all her glory. I collapse onto the mattress, overwhelmed with an empty longing that terrifies me.

———

I WAKE FROM A DEAD SLEEP, disoriented, and find it's already past noon. Another loud knock on the door. Kāya must be back. I pull myself together.

Bracing myself, I answer the door and am taken aback. The She standing there is older, fair-skinned, about six-three, and looking down at me with penetrating hazel eyes. There is a no-nonsense look about her, a strong chin framed by shoulder-length sandy hair. She wears the casual working clothes of a field historian: khaki cargo pants and a matching loose shirt. With practiced restraint, I resist her allure. "Can I help you?"

"Tye Celiaso?"

"Yes?"

Her face clouds as she looks past me on both sides. I glance back. There's no one there.

"Where are they? Okay, uh, let's just go inside." I become alarmed as she crowds me through the door and down the stairs, scanning the interior as she presses. "Kāya," she calls.

"She's not here, but—"

The bunker door bursts open and Onyx rushes in. "Nance. Welcome. You made good time."

"Got away early." The newcomer leans into Onyx. "I found him outside on his own. Is that a good idea?"

"He's harmless. And extremely valuable." My ears perk up as Onyx continues. "I'm keeping an eye on him. Kāya should be back any time now."

"I see." Nance turns to me. "So you're Celia's son. Yes, I see the resemblance."

"You knew my mother?"

"Yes. I'm Nance Emmada. Kāya sent for me."

"How did you know her?"

"Who, your mother? We were once colleagues. I have great respect for her." She turns to Onyx. "Now. Where are these—special items you've come across?"

"About my mother, I'd love to hear—"

"Not a social call, Tye. The artifacts?"

Oh. One of those. "Why are you here?"

Onyx is waiting in the doorway. "She's a field historian, specializing in technology. She's going to help us appraise your collection."

"You work in the Shell, too?"

"Just came from there," Nance replies.

Field historians are a tough breed. These She work out there in the "Big Death." Everyone knows what happens in the Shell. Walls crumble, roads cave in, buildings collapse. There are toxic fumes, enforcer-guarded kill zones, roving gangs of She bandits, countless ways for the Shell to end your life. A man would face certain death going in there.

Onyx shows her around and points out some items of interest. After a quick survey, Nance says, "Where's the good stuff?"

Onyx reveals the bin, and I hear a gasp. Nance gapes at the devices, then reaches in and tenderly picks one up. She examines and caresses it like a baby. Then picks up another. "Where did these come from?"

Onyx gestures toward me.

"We found them."

"Where?"

"We're gonna show Kāya," I say. *Not you.*

She checks with Onyx, who shrugs. Then she says, "I'm afraid you must have misunderstood. A historical site is no place for a man."

"You won't find it on your own."

Nance flashes a skeptical look and goes back to examining another device. "You say there are more?"

"She wanted you to look at the rest of this stuff?"

She looks around with scorn. "Yes, she did."

———

IT IS late afternoon when the Alphas return from their errands. Nance has combed through the bunker, examining and sorting. She has kept Dray and me busy, moving trash and cleaning casings.

"How did it go?" asks Nance.

"Good. We got what we came for," Kāya says.

"And more," adds Onyx with a smirk as she holds up what I assume is the deed. She glances at me, then quickly changes the subject. "Anything here we can sell?"

"Apart from the obvious?" Nance says. "The rest is standard miscellany. This kind of stuff is everywhere, and not much of a market for it. There might be some good components, but it would be a lot of work to extract them. I'm not sure it's worth it. Not when there are devices like this around." She holds one up. "Where do we get more of these?"

Kāya juts out her chin, looking at me. "Yet to be determined."

I studiously polish away and pretend not to be listening.

"They won't tell you?"

"They claim it's out in the wilds, with no landmarks."

"Then how did they—"

"They're going to show us." She raises her eyebrows. "And they've already been in and seen it."

Nance's lips form an O. "How much did they see?"

"Nothing dangerous."

"So, what are we going to do?"

Onyx cuts in. "They're going to show us the site they found, and we're going to consider lesser charges against them. Maybe supervise them for a time before ..."

I see the surprise on Kāya's face. She says nothing.

Onyx continues. "Well, I'm not going to leave them in the hands of these local thugs. Who knows what they'd do?"

"Let's just see what we've got here before we make any hard decisions," says Kāya.

I've got to stall that. I jump in. "It will be worth keeping us around, I promise. There's a lot more where this came from. A lot more." I hope.

That catches Nance's interest. "Tell me."

"This is all from one room. The place is huge. You need us."

Nance says, "This site you found. It's intact?"

"Far as I could see."

"How did you select which artifacts to take?"

"I just grabbed what I saw."

Nance looks at Kāya, then shrugs. "You may be a historian now, but you're still in charge here. It's your call."

"First, what can we sell right away?" Kāya asks.

"This crate has materials we can recycle, and this one, well, you should be able to get something for the parts. As for the good stuff, I've separated out the well-known devices from artifacts that need further study. You can sell what's in this bin. This stuff will draw attention, and the criminals will come after you, so I'd suggest using a private sales agent to keep the source anonymous. I'd like to be able to appraise the historical value of this new site before it gets plundered."

"Good idea. Great work, Nance," says Kāya. "No need for you to hang around."

"Yes, I'd like to get back during daylight. I don't want Aida worrying."

"You can take a load of supplies with you. There's whey protein and fresh fish on ice in the truck. Let's go transfer it over."

Kāya beckons, and I leap to my feet.

"Help Nance with these things," she says.

"Sure. I can do th—"

"When will you be back?" says Nance.

"We'll get this stuff to the local outpost, then we've got a few more things to pick up, so we'll head out in the morning. We'll go take a look at this find of theirs and we'll radio from there, I would hope by early afternoon."

So ... we'll be staying another night? My relief vanishes as quickly as it came. Another chance for them to discover the book. Another night on the floor.

Nance drives off in a covered jeep, and the Alphas head back inside. I stop at the doorway and run my hand along the wooden frame. Firm and solid, stable. Safe. The home I grew up in. The home I finally found my way back to. And then lost. I get a few more hours here before they haul me out into the wilds. I have no choice but to show them. And then?

If we cooperate, if we're lucky, the best we can hope for is to get shipped off to "re-education." I don't even know what that means. It could be a life of hard labor, or it could be a euphemism for "buried in the woods," for all I know. You can't trust She.

It was always held over our heads as a threat. But then I went through my teen years in boarding school and came out thinking, *How much worse could it be?* Then, a few years back, Brody—he's the one who told us about guns—got dragged away, and we never saw him again. Then, just last year, Arny was taken away in custody and never came back.

I massage my temples. Men come back from boarding schools.

13

THE KINDEST THING

Rule Seven: Possession of firearms, projectile weapons and explosive devices is strictly prohibited. Found weapons are to immediately be turned in to the nearest Weapons Enforcement Office. The penalty for the use of such weapons is exile.

Commentary: Despite the physical dominance of She, the first generation often found themselves at the mercy of armed men. The terrible weapons of the Before could kill from a distance, negating all physical advantage and giving the weak the power to slaughter the strong. The only way for She to establish and hold their newfound power was to eradicate the weapons that made their strength irrelevant. They decided that the safest course of action was to rely on their inborn physical advantage, which could never be turned against them. They melted down mountains of firearms, and it still took generations to get rid of them all. Making it a capital crime to retain a found firearm from a historical site and mandating that they all be turned in to the authorities for recycling, has been an effective strategy. The "hundred-year purge" makes finding an old firearm a rare event today ...

DRAY and I spend the evening as we often do, in his room, sitting together on his bed, with him strumming on his uke and me reading. The normalcy is almost comforting, except it's false. Even Dray's *Technology for Men* magazine can't hold my attention. Innovation, to us, simply means tinkering with ancient designs restored and provided by historians. And two real historians sit at the table over in my living quarters, playing with actual working "electronic" devices that are beyond us.

I throw the magazine down in frustration. Dray stops and looks up. "What?"

"I don't know, Dray. Why? Why can't we see what they're doing over there? Why can't we know of the Before?"

He puts his uke down and rests his hand on my arm. "You ask too many questions. We're only men, Tye. We can't know everything."

I want to smack him. No, I don't. I'm sure he's looking forward to being with Onyx again tonight, whereas ... "We're not 'only men,' Dray. We're freemen. If we simply accept our assigned ignorance, how can we possibly make it on our own?"

"By not letting them push us around. By not ..." He sags back. "I don't know."

Yeah. Hard to win that argument when we are literally prisoners being pushed around. His sudden sadness breaks my heart, and I reach out to caress his hair, resting my hand on his shoulder. "We'll get through this, buddy. Hey, how about playing something lively, like 'Free o' You'?"

Before he can start, we hear raised voices coming from the other side. Angry voices. We look at each other. "That's not good," I say.

"No shit. What do you think's going on?"

The bathrooms in both domes share the same air vent outlet, known to carry sound from one side to the other. I hurry to the bathroom to listen, and Dray crowds in behind me.

Onyx is yelling. "Kāya, you're such a coward when it comes to men."

Huh?

"Is that what you think this is?"

Then something I can't make out. I strain to hear Onyx, her voice now quieter.

"Look, I know you're scared of emotional attachment, and you've got good reason. But if you ask me, you go way overboard. I was looking forward to being with Dray tonight."

"It's just for one night, Onny. Don't be so selfish."

"Okay, sure, too many men try to attach themselves to you. I know you hate that. But he's a freeman, right? He's no threat. What's your problem? I mean, I can see why you want to do Dray, but I think it's more than that. I think Tye scares you."

What?

"Onyx, you need to shut up right now, before I ..."

"What? You would fight me over a man? Fine. Take him. But you owe me."

The voices stop, leaving me mystified. Scared of emotional attachment? She asked me about attachment. She avoids it, she said. That's got to be why she's so cold all the time. I bump into Dray trying to back out of the bathroom. "We weren't supposed to hear that. Quick, let's get back."

He settles on the bed with his uke, brow furrowed.

"Onyx wants to be with me?"

"So does Kāya, sounds like."

"She's scared of you, freeman? What did you do?"

"Nothing." What did I do? "Hey, if they ask, we didn't hear anything."

"Not a thing. We were in here singing." He strums the intro, and we both sing.

The first chorus is interrupted by Kāya's appearance in Dray's doorway. "Tye. Bedtime." She tips her head toward the adjoining door, and I do my best to conceal my surprise. I've been praying for this and dreading it. Maybe she's giving me another chance. Dray grins, looking for Onyx.

But as I move toward the adjoining dome, she doesn't follow. Instead, she steps into Dray's room and closes the door. A wave hits me, almost buckling my knees. Relief, despair, I'm not sure. I knew she'd want Dray tonight. I knew it. But I hoped … I don't know what I hoped. I go through into the living quarters and see Onyx still sitting at the table, the dejection on her face unmistakable. Great.

I stand hunched. "Uh, where do you want me to sleep?"

She seems to notice me for the first time. "What?"

"Where do you want me to—"

"Why are you … Oh. Tye, it's not you, okay? I've got nothing against you."

"I wish … I wish I could satisfy you, Onyx, I really do. But I'm not very …"

She squints at me. "I'm not that hard to satisfy, Tye. What are you talking about?"

"Kāya must have told you about …"

She abruptly stands and looks toward the adjoining door with a pout.

I try to console her. "He's always been popular with the ladies."

"No, Tye. She's avoiding you." She folds her arms. "What did you do? Did you pledge your undying devotion, or some shit?"

"No! No. I didn't say anything like that."

"Because if you're lying about being a freeman, things are going to go very badly for you."

"I'm not, Onyx. You've got to believe me."

Her face is a brick wall of skepticism, and I feel an urgent need to convince her.

"Okay, do you want to know why I'm a freeman? Why I avoid She? Because I saw what happened to my father." I drop my head. "Mom's work took her away from home all the time. When Elona challenged her for my dad, my mother didn't even fight for him. Just gave him up. Not that she didn't love him, so she said. She was too busy with her work—work we couldn't be a part of." I glare at her. "Yeah. I know what you historians are like. Do you think I'd be foolish enough to give my heart to a historian?"

She squints at me but says nothing, so I continue. "That Elona and her spoiled daughters were merciless in their demands. She had my father running all day and night, busting his butt to please her, even when he was trying to care for me. Even after he got sick. She used him up, like he was disposable. My father died young, body and soul worn out at an early age. Drained by demanding She. As a consort, I was on the same track. But I'll be damned if I'm gonna let that happen to me."

I sit down, face flushed. All at once I worry that I've gone too far, that my big mouth has gotten me in trouble again. We both sit in silence, until she says, "You two are quite a pair, you and Dray."

"Oh, he's had it worse than me."

She hangs her head. "That's rather obvious. And I'm sure it's not helping that Kāya gets carried away sometimes with her *'fear me'* act. Let's change the subject. It's getting late."

Her what? ... Curious. I rub my head, trying to compose myself. "What do you want to talk about?"

"Anything else. How about that weather?"

The superficial silliness of the question tickles me, and I laugh. We talk about close calls we've had with storms. After a few minutes I catch myself sprawled comfortably in my chair like I'm talking to an old friend, and abruptly sit up. She takes notice.

"Is everything okay?"

"Sure. I'm not accustomed to having She in here, is all."

She looks to the bed. "Do I appeal to you, Tye?"

The question catches me off guard. "Uh, do you want to?"

"Answer the question."

My face goes hot. "You're gorgeous, Onyx. How could you not appeal to me?"

"Personal preferences are unpredictable."

"Well, sure, but—"

"We only know them ourselves when we experience them, don't you think?"

"I guess so."

"How would you like to help me out with an experiment?"

"Uh, like what?"

"I try you out and see if you're a pleasant surprise."

My jaw drops.

"No point in wasting an opportunity," she says. "It's just sex. Don't feel like you have to live up to your friend. I'm confident you won't, so no pressure."

I pause, uncertain. "Yeah, I'm not that competitive."

Her eyebrows go up as she grins. "Oh, so you *do* have a sense of humor." She removes her forearm guards.

Sense of humor? Does she think I was joking? I watch as she continues to undress and decide not to set her straight.

She reclines on the bed, leans back and raises a foot toward me. "Why don't you help me out of my boots?"

"Uh, sure. Okay." I grab on with both hands and savor the curves of her long leg as the boot slides off. I slow down with the second, trying not to seem overeager. Legs bare, she stands to tower over me again.

"Oh, and Tye? You need to tell Kāya what you told me about your father. It's convincing, and I have a personal stake in her picking you next time. Now, are you sure you're okay with this?"

In a state of disbelief, I nod my consent.

She pulls my shirt over my head and tosses it aside. "No matter what happens here, tell her you enjoyed me."

It takes me a moment to understand, and by that time my pants are around my ankles. Kāya is determined to avoid any risk of emotional attachment. Onyx is doing this to reassure her that I'm independent and opportunistic, not clingy. I see Onyx in a whole new light, and my heart warms. It's maybe the kindest thing a She has ever done for me.

———

DAYLIGHT STREAMS in through the bunker's ceiling windows as I awaken to find a She asleep beside me. I am alarmed until the previous night comes flooding back. Onyx could have taken me by force, but she didn't. Oh, she took me, all right, but it was playful, not like with Kāya. For a moment, I watch her with deep gratitude. I won't forget her kindness. And her face is certainly pleasing. But it's not Kāya's face.

Here in bed, I feel inexplicably safe, but now I'm cursing the daylight. I'm not sure why. Even if this is my last day, I have no right to complain.

But daylight favors prying eyes. I don't want Onyx looking around in here. I can't let her find the book. I putter in front of my dresser until she is up and ready.

Kāya and Dray are already preparing bowls of granola and tofu when we emerge from my tiny bedchamber. Kāya is still wearing her nightclothes, a tee shirt, and loose panties. I try to emotionally distance myself, but her still-sleepy face is the morning sun. I work at keeping my eyes averted as we all sit down to eat.

I'm trying to figure out how to raise the topic when Kāya throws Onyx a casual question. "How was your night?"

I jump at the opportunity. "Fantastic. Hottest night I've ever had with a She. She's a goddess." I gaze admiringly at Onyx, stealing glances to catch Kāya's reaction.

"Yes, she is," says Kāya.

"Yes, she is," echoes Dray, who straightens when Kāya looks over.

"Yeah, that was great fun," says Onyx, beaming. "Left me sleeping like a baby. How about you, Dray?"

"Yup, very good. I slept on a log."

Kāya stops and looks at him. Onyx raises an eyebrow.

Alerted to a problem, Dray looks from face to face. "What? It's an old expression. From the Before. You're historians; you should know it."

Kāya looks away, lips pursed. Onyx's dimples reveal her efforts to keep a straight face.

Dray is worried now. "Celia taught it to us as kids. Am I not supposed to know it?"

Unable to hold back, both She burst into laughter. "I've never been called a log before," manages Kāya. "Talk about shameless flattery." They both convulse.

Onyx wipes away tears. "I told you he was a silver-tongued devil." Still chortling, the two swat at each other as Dray looks on, baffled.

I jump to his rescue. "It's 'slept *like* a log,'" I say. "But we like your version better."

To my relief, the mood is light as we finish breakfast and start to clean up. Then Kāya demands our attention. "Here's the way it is. We're going outside for a quick workout and to do some final errands, so we'll be in and out. And to be clear: if you try, you won't escape, but you *will* piss me off, and you really don't want to do that." She examines each of us until we nod understanding. "The two of you will go now and pack for a long journey. You have two hours."

"It's not that far, where we're going," I say. "About an hour, by vehicle. We should easily be back before sundown."

She confronts me. "Pack for a long journey."

My chest tightens as the bottom falls out of my world. *We're not coming back.* I knew it. I *knew* it. I look to Onyx for rescue, but the fun is all gone. She avoids my eyes. I grasp at straws. "What about all my belongings?"

"They will remain where they are, in my possession."

The air goes out of me. So it's final. It's really happening. I thought things were going okay, that maybe they would go easy on us. But they've just been using us. It's what She do. Why don't I ever learn?

And what do I do about the book? I can't leave it here. When they clean the place out, someone is bound to find it. But if I bring it along, getting caught with it would be disastrous. What do I do?

———

It's late morning when we head out in a stiff breeze under overcast skies. We cross the river I used to swim in as a kid and take the main road south. I expect to feel sad, watching my hometown slide by for the last time. Instead, emptiness. Our friends in the freeman community will wonder what happened to us, as we have wondered about others who disappeared. They'll hear stories of us being taken off by enforcers and feel renewed helplessness. But as for the She of Hill-haven, good riddance.

Ten minutes out, where the road bends east toward Cedarton, we turn south again on the Indy Park side road. Dray and I ride in the high-roofed back of the safari truck with the supplies, each lost in our own solitude. I've given Onyx general directions, but I'll still need to warn her when we're approaching the next turnoff. Our secret trail is not marked, and easy to miss.

I notice Onyx check the mirror.

"We're being followed," she says.

"You sure?" Kāya turns to look back and curses.

I look back but see nothing. Oh, there. A glint on the road behind us. Weird. Nobody comes out here anymore.

Onyx shakes her head. "Looks like we stirred up some interest in town. Got people curious about us."

"We can't even go into town for supplies anymore without—"

"Oh, come on, Kay. You've never gone anywhere without creating a splash."

"Me? You're the one who—"

"I'm not the one who made a rather large impulse purchase in a small town. Okay. Let's turn back and stop them. Disable their vehicle."

"No. It's most likely Luce's trackers."

I interrupt. "Trackers?"

Onyx says, "They're an enforcer subclass that specializes in tracking people down. They're not much good in a fight, but you can't hide from them for long."

"Stopping them would make Luce think we're trying to hide something and increase her curiosity," Kāya says. "And I'm not going to lead them right to it. I want to keep this new find to ourselves. We need to throw them off."

"How do we do that?"

Kāya bites her lip and squints into the distance, then swivels to scrutinize me. "You're being straight with me about this underground site, aren't you, Tye?" Her intensity makes me wary.

"I am, yes."

She turns back to Onyx. "New course. Don't turn off where we were going to. Stay on this road until we get to the next junction, and head east over to the Shell road. We'll check in at our site, and whoever's following us will report that we've gone back to where we came from."

My skin prickles. What?

Onyx raises an eyebrow. "We can't do that. We've got men with us."

You can't do that.

Kāya wrinkles her nose in consternation and rubs her scalp. "They're in our custody. I can claim an exemption for one night. We can manage them and make sure they don't see anything they shouldn't." She looks over her shoulder. "You can be good for one night, can't you?"

My body goes rigid. Overnight in the *Shell*? I look to Dray and see my own panic reflected in his face.

14

THE BIG DEATH

There is no way of predicting where the next explosion will occur, let alone its cause. Explosive device or gas deposit? Accidental or intentional? Did something trigger a bomb, or did an old mechanism simply fail? The Shell is a deathtrap. But as historians like to say, no risk, no reward …

"DON'T TAKE us in there, please!" We're men, and we *can't go there*. We'll never survive in the Shell. How many stories have I heard? How many years did we get this prohibition drilled into our heads?

Dray has gone pale. "Onyx? You still need us, don't you?"

They exchange looks, then Kāya turns to address us. "We're not taking you near any dangers. You are in our protective custody. Do you understand? We'll keep you safe."

Protective custody? That should be reassuring. But I soaked up too many stories about death in the Shell, spent years imagining what it would be like to watch a mountain fall on you. Like what happened to my mother's friend. She was in the vicinity of a high-rise collapse, her body never recovered. Somewhere under a mountain of debris.

How can they protect us from that?

And then there's all the humrem. Human remains everywhere. Skeletons in every building, bones and skulls littering the streets. I remember being sick to my stomach when they showed us pictures. I don't want to see it.

I catch Dray watching the road go by beside us, like he's estimating his chances if he were to jump out. I grab his knee. We can't outrun them, can't hide from them. I lean over and put my arm around his shoulder. "Looks like we're going into the Shell."

His face is tight. "Looks like it."

————

TWENTY TENSE MINUTES after leaving the highway, we're driving along a gravel road through the ruins of what was once a place called Suburbia. It stretches to the horizon in every direction. All that remains of the ancient dwellings are fragments of box-shaped walls that emerge from the prevalent shrubs and grasses. The surrounding woodlands are all the common stunted varieties, capable of surviving the winds.

Onyx is driving, with Kāya beside her. Dray and I sit in the back with the large hydrogen canisters, water bottles and boxes of food and equipment. I count canisters and marvel at how they can afford all this stuff. And how Kāya could afford to buy my home like that.

The truck we're riding in, with its high-capacity fuel cells, is further evidence of their success as historians. A success withheld from men. The bitter taste of injustice curls my lip.

Kāya holds something up to her mouth, then I see the curly cord and realize the truck is equipped with a portable radio. I should have known that. How else could they have asked Nance to come? I try to listen over the road noise.

"... change of plans. We're inbound, ETA less than two hours, but we have two men in custody."

The speaker crackles. "You're bringing men here?"

"No choice. I'll explain when we get there. Secure the site."

She glances back at us as she stows the microphone. "Looks like you're going to get to meet the rest of the team."

A historian team? A sprout of interest pokes up through my shivering dread. Onyx did say something about Kāya leading a strong team. I thought she was talking about enforcers, but Nance isn't an enforcer.

I find my voice. "How many on your team?"

"There are six of us. Four historians and four enforcers."

Uh ... Oh, right. Kāya and Onyx are both. An efficient combination. And they must know what they're doing, right? They wouldn't all be jeopardizing their own lives, would they? "Where are they?"

"We're doing an excavation in the North Cambria Junction, not that that's going to mean anything to you. We've set up a temporary claim-site shelter a couple of blocks away. That's where we'll be spending the night."

An actual historical dig site. In the Shell. And we're going there. It's a dream come true, only to reveal itself as a nightmare. I remind myself I've already visited a historical site and survived, even without protection. Of course, that one wasn't in the Shell. Still, I'll never have a chance like this again to see for myself what it's like.

A stronger man would be thrilled to be in my shoes. My last couple of nights would be the highlight of any man's life. Sex with two Alphas, and now this. And all it took was to throw my life away.

I glance over at Dray. I'll find a way to get him out of this. Somehow.

He must see my distress, because he reaches over to take my hand. "It's gonna be okay." He holds my eyes until I nod and ease back.

I hadn't noticed the sky darkening until the rain surprises us, and we scramble to let down the canvas sides. It's a common spring downpour. Nothing to worry about. Dray and I huddle together, and I close my eyes, listening to the hypnotic drone of the rain on the roof and the fizz of the tires on the wet ground. The irregular jiggling of the vehicle is somehow soothing.

I must have dozed off. When I open my eyes again, my neck is stiff, and I see the rain has stopped. Through the windshield, I see where we are and gasp, waking Dray.

The familiar, jagged profile of the Shell has expanded to fill my view. The central peak of large towers now stabs into the sky, with the surrounding smaller clusters spread far and wide. Everywhere, the skeletal remains of a vast civilization stand teetering on the verge of collapse. A chill runs through me.

For my entire life, the Shell has been known as the Big Death: the death place of millions. And more die here each year. I've heard countless stories of catastrophe, of fatal accidents and unforeseen dangers taking the lives of She.

Yet here I am, speeding helplessly toward the Big Death, knowing full well I should not be here. I clutch Dray again for reassurance, but he's doing the same with me. My eyes go to Kāya, sitting up front, and find her casually watching the scenery go by. It hits me that she lives and works out here among the humrem, facing death every day. I shudder.

"You said your site is outside the burb ring," says Kāya. "I trust you were being honest about that."

"Yes," I say. "It's back there in the outskirts."

"There's not supposed to be anything left in the outskirts. How did you find it?"

How much should I reveal? "I remembered seeing an ancient map. It showed the location of some kind of facility, not far from Hill-haven, but my—no one could ever find it. I did." With a little help from erosion. But I need to look useful. "Guess I have an instinct for finding things."

"One of your mother's maps," says Kāya, seeing through me again. "Do you have it with you?"

I knew she'd ask. She doesn't want to have to depend on us. I'll make it clear she does. "No. When we got home with the loot, I got scared and destroyed it. It wouldn't help you anyway. It didn't help my mother, and she was exceptionally good at finding things. The place is well hidden."

"Uh huh, and you're sure you can find it again?"

Dray and I exchange glances.

"I'm sure," I lie. "We've been back a couple of times."

"We'll stay at my claim-site shelter overnight and get underway in the morning. I'm gambling on you, Tye. You're not going to let me down, are you?"

"Of course not." I try to swallow but can't.

The Shell has always been some fearsome thing way off on the horizon, jagged and menacing, the resting place of millions of lost souls. As we get closer, it looks like another world, grotesque. The remnants of enormous buildings poke out from mountains of rubble to jut into the sky. From here, in its outer fringes, I can see the individual buildings of the closer clusters. Some look almost intact, others like sharp-angled spines and ribs sticking out of half-missing corpses. The tallest of the buildings are further away, in the densest cluster that marks what was once the city core. And surrounding that, to the horizon in every direction, are smaller clusters, growing more sporadic as they recede from the core.

From the edge of the Shell, looking in at the ruins, I try to imagine what the city must have been like when it was all shiny and alive. I can't do it. It doesn't at all match my dreams. The scale of things is mind-boggling.

A small cluster of buildings grows as we approach, and my sense of alarm grows with it. I've never seen anything stand so defiantly high. They tower before us now. *Close enough. This is close enough.* I clutch the seat and stomp on a nonexistent brake pedal. I breathe again as Onyx slows the truck to a crawl and turns off to the right to skirt a large debris field, overgrown with vegetation. From the looks of it, a building toppled sideways here, years ago. We curl around the far end to an opening in the ground, and my stomach lurches as we drop down a large ramp into the darkness.

Except it's not completely dark. There are lights over there, and a truck and a jeep and two people. And hulking old wrecks of vehicles scattered about. It's a space unlike anything I've ever seen, at once both enormous and crushingly cramped. Heavy cement pillars in neat rows hold up a ceiling so low the truck's roof barely fits. On the side away from the lights, the space is completely closed off by mounds of debris that seem to be reaching out to consume us. It's clear the ceiling has collapsed over there. Why would they think we're safe over here?

I don't want to point out the obvious, but I feel like ants are crawling all over me. "Are you sure we're safe in here?" The musty odor itself is enough to make me want to be anywhere else.

"It's okay," Kāya says. "The building above here came down long ago. This section is stable."

It sure doesn't look stable. I bite my tongue as we pull up into an area bright with makeshift lighting and park beside another truck. This one carries a pair of enormous cylindrical water tanks, fitted lengthwise, side by side. I recognize the jeep as the one Nance drove. Two new enforcers, eye-catching in their shaped regalia, stand glaring at us, guarding a doorway. Do they think they need a show of strength here?

Not knowing what to expect, Dray and I wait for Kāya to make the first move. We ease when she greets both enforcers with warm hugs, as does Onyx.

Kāya introduces us. Bree, about six-four, has warm black skin with a clean-shaven head and luscious full lips. Her deep brown eyes, with their prominent lashes, have instant appeal. In her regalia, she seems streamlined from head to toe, all lean muscle with no body fat. Her hips taper to long, powerful-looking legs, while her biceps bulge above her arm guards. She wears the silver collar of a Bravo.

Val, also a Bravo, is easily six-eight, with little headroom above her. Fair, with a ruddy complexion, she has a prominent chest and an hourglass figure. Her reddish-brown hair is trimmed in the traditional enforcer buzz-cut—nothing for an opponent to grab on to—and freckles dance across her nose. Her face seems friendly, and I'm drawn in until I remember she's an armed enforcer. And she's scrutinizing me. I avert my eyes.

Bree's voice is terse as she reports, "Everything's locked out of sight. This is still crazy."

"It's only for one night, Bree. They'll be good boys, won't you."

It's not a question. We nod.

Kāya calls through the doorway. "Nance? Aida? Come on out and meet our guests."

They emerge together as a couple, and Kāya introduces them. "You've met Nance, our archivist." In the stark lighting, her sandy hair looks darker, her chin more prominent. "And this is Aida. Best technologist in the business. You want to know what something is and how to fix it, these are your experts."

The two academics wear matching khaki coveralls. Shorter at six-one, with exquisite, soft features, Aida has center-parted, chin-length, straight black hair that shines like her distinctive black eyes. With slim hips and strong shoulders, she seems to flow like water as she approaches, examining me.

"Yes, I see it," she says.

I wipe my face, wondering what's on it.

"Not that it matters," she says. "His heritage won't protect him here. Or us."

We cower beside the vehicle as the four new She stand glaring at us. I have the oddest thought: I've never felt so special. All this attention, simply for being a man where men shouldn't be. There's a delicious freeman flavor to it.

Kāya addresses the group. "We'll be away again tomorrow, so you can carry on with your work until you hear from us."

"You're going to check out that new site?" asks Bree.

"If the weather looks promising, we'll head out in the morning. Okay, enough standing around. Let's get the supplies inside."

As the She get to work, Kāya approaches us. "This is what they used to call an underground parking garage. It provides decent shelter for the vehicles, and you will stay out here. Through that door is a basement wing we're using as a home base while we work in the area. You will *not* go in there. Is that clear?"

"Perfectly." I watch as the shapely Val transfers canisters, two at a time, from our truck to a compartment in the other. I would have trouble carrying one. Not to mention she's bigger than me by almost a foot.

Bree stops to confer with Val. Their regalia matches that of Kāya and Onyx, marking them as a team.

When Onyx returns from inside, she's carrying sleeping rolls under each arm. "You'll want to sleep in the back of the truck." She tosses the rolls in among the supplies. "It might be a bit crowded, but you can move stuff around if you need to. Oh, and Dray." She leans in, glancing around. "Don't do anything suicidal tonight, like leaving, okay? I want you to still be here in the morning."

As if on cue, a rumble in the distance makes my skin crawl. A storm coming?

Nance and Aida both hurry out to join the group. "Was that thunder?"

"No," says Onyx. "Another collapsing building. I hope no one got caught."

Aida shakes her head. "It's getting worse. This is starting to get too dangerous. Maybe we should cut and run."

"Tech is gold," says Bree. "No risk, no reward."

"You got that right," says Dray, drawing all eyes. He shrinks, bites his lip, and studies the floor.

Val says, "You're taking a big risk bringing men here, Kāya. I hope this is more than just stud service."

"I assure you it is."

Bree turns away, shaking her head.

Kāya steps toward her. "Is there going to be a challenge here?"

Bree straightens and glares back. Her voice is firm. "It's my duty to question your judgment. Step back and take a look at what you're doing."

Big Val cuts in, coming between them. "No challenge, Kāya. It's a big risk, is all. I mean, what if they learn something they shouldn't?"

Kāya looks away and eases.

Bree adds, "How can we trust men not to shoot off their mouths?"

"They're here for a reason, Bree."

Now Nance intervenes. "It's your call, Kāya. Don't say we didn't warn you."

"Noted. Okay, I'm starving. What do we have to eat around here?"

As if being in the Shell weren't bad enough, the team clearly doesn't want us here. Watching Kāya head toward the door, a sense of peril overwhelms me, and I call out. "Protective custody, right?"

Without looking back, she brushes us off with a flick of her hand and is gone. I wish I could trust her.

15

NIGHT IN THE SHELL

AFTER A DINNER of cold cuts and bread, Dray and I are left alone for the evening, though Onyx comes to check on us from time to time. Exploring the garage, we even screw up the courage to peek into the dark corners to reassure ourselves we're alone in here. There is an unfamiliar dank, musty smell that pervades the whole place, but to my great relief, we find no humrem. I trace the odor to the interiors of the old vehicles, their tires flat, their windows smashed, the victims of a century of scavenging. Over by the collapsed area, some of the debris is slick with mold. They said the place is stable, but the cement is crumbling off several of the support pillars. We can only hope they hold through the night.

"We're turning in early," says Onyx, on her last check of the night. "Big day tomorrow. You two get some sleep."

We say goodnight, and the disappointment shows on Dray's face as she closes the door behind her. The lights go off and we settle into our borrowed sleeping bags. To my surprise, the evening sky is still light enough to illuminate the entrance ramp.

Dray sits up and looks at the opening. "What do you think it's like out there? We should have a quick look."

"No way."

"Come on. We're here already, so let's at least take a look."

"I don't think that's a good idea."

"A quick peek. They'll never know."

The idea seems ridiculously reckless. But this is a once-in-a-life-time opportunity. Why do I always back down? "You're right. Let's do it." I think of Rose demanding I be in before dark, Marsy denying me that river raft ride. Why did I never push back?

We creep in silence to the ramp and up into the dusk. Then, entranced in morbid fascination, we stray further out to get a better look around. The evening is mild, but I'm trembling like a leaf in the wind. The air smells of old concrete and rust as I scan the nearby ground, desperate to avoid humrem. Millions died here, and I don't want to be haunted by their remains. The area looks clear.

I always knew the Shell was a huge and dangerous place. But to see it from this close, even in the fading light, I can't fathom its breathtaking enormity. Right in front of us, several high-rise build-ings stand clustered in various states of collapse. One round building, now just a mesh frame, stands above the rest. I imagine it was once covered with glass, one of the wonders that made the city shine, and I'm saddened by what it's become.

And there, those must once have been twin buildings, their rectangular bases identical, standing proud, side by side. But only one remains standing, the other sheared off near the bottom. My heart aches for the lone survivor, and I have to look away.

But it doesn't help. I stand engulfed in the ruins that stretch out before me, a vast wasteland, the very embodiment of despair. A glimpse of transcendent loss guts me. What is the loss of one infant against that of an entire world? In sudden revulsion, I turn and hurry back into the garage.

Dray follows, and we zip ourselves into our bags. Still unsettled, I look to him for rescue. This is where he's supposed to say something distracting, something funny.

"This is too weird," he says, still trembling.

I wait for more, but it doesn't come. Okay, so it's my turn to distract him.

"What's with you and Onyx?" I ask.

"What do you mean?"

"Look, I know you, Dray. You're not exactly friendly toward She. And then it's like you two are old pals. How did that happen?"

"I told you before. She's different."

"Yeah, no question about that. She's amazing. But I mean, can we trust her?"

I hear him sigh. "She's gonna do what she needs to do, and that's whatever Kāya says. But I trust her to be straight with us. Tye, I'm telling you, it was like nothing I ever experienced. There I am with a She and we're being honest with each other, and ... it was good."

"Okay, you gotta tell me, freeman. What happened?"

He leans up on an elbow, and even in the gloom, seems to brighten.

"Remember when she took me outside that first night?"

Good. Let's forget about where we are for a while.

"She said she was gonna ask me some questions, and I needed to tell the truth. Then she asked me what I knew about history. I said I didn't give a shit about history. She asked me about a couple of things I never heard of, then she asked me about you. I said you're a good man. She asked me if I would lie to protect you, and I said damn right I would."

And I'd do anything for you, freeman.

He continues. "I said, if you're gonna beat me, just do it. She said, does that mean you're lying to me? I said, what difference does it make? You're gonna beat me anyway, and she said, I'm not gonna beat you for telling the truth, and I said, that would be new, and she said, what do you mean? And I said, if a She doesn't like the truth, she'll beat you for telling it. She started getting pissed and I said, see? And she ... I don't know, it's like she heard me."

"You mean she stopped being pissed? Just like that?"

"Just like that. She asked me about the scars on my back, and I said, none of your damn business, and she said, a She? I just shrugged. And she said, don't judge all She by the behavior of those 'brutish, small-town roughnecks,' she called them. I'm sorry you had to grow up in that backward hick-town, she said, but we're not all like that. That's what she called Hillhaven: 'a backward hick-town out in the sticks.'"

"That seems a little harsh," I say.

"Does it, though?"

I concede with a shrug.

"Then she said the weirdest thing. She said, can we please start again? I'm not gonna beat you. Lie if you want, she said. Or tell the truth. Don't matter. I won't beat you. I said, I'll believe that when I see it. You She lie all the time. She said, men lie all the time, too, but I'm gonna believe what you tell me. I said, why would you do that? And she said, it's a risk, and I may come to regret it, but I want to help you."

I remember his boldness when they came back inside. Envy flares within me.

A fluttering sound startles us and is gone. Birds? Bats? It's completely dark in here, and I can't see his face, but I know he's listening, too. There is nothing now but a faint dripping sound in the distance, and I notice a clamminess in the air. Maybe it was always there. I snug up my sleeping bag and shift over closer to him.

"I can see why you're so taken by this one, but we need to be cautious here. They seem to have a thing against emotional attachment. I'm just warning you. Don't get yourself in over your head."

"Are you jealous, Tye?"

"No, no ... Okay, a little. But not because I want Onyx. I'm jealous because I wish Kāya were more like her."

"Yeah, that Kāya's a cold one. You should keep your distance."

"She thinks so, too."

"Sorry, man. I know she's your type."

More than 'my type.' Perfection isn't a type. Arrrgh. I don't want to think about it. "Anyway, the other night. What happened next?"

"Oh yeah. Onyx said some She can be brutes, and she was sorry about how bad it must have looked in the bar with that drunk, and I said, yeah, bad as in damn hot, and she said, what? And I said, he deserved it. She seemed relieved about that. Then I said, well, I don't deserve it. Sure, I might have deserved it a couple of times, but not those others."

My heart glows. I'm finally getting through to him.

"Then I told her, if you need to hit me, you know, draw blood or something, to show your boss you did a good job, I'm okay with that. She looked at me like I was crazy."

"So she sized you up pretty good, then."

He gives me a cuff. I'm about to cuff him back when he turns serious.

"I asked her if they were gonna kill us, and she turned all sad and said it was awful that we would think that, but she could understand why we might. But no, she said. No, they would never. They weren't even after us, only interested in the artifacts."

I clutch his arm. "You believed her?"

"I really did. I think she meant it. Then I said, what is it with She and their trinkets and baubles? Which is all those things are, far as I can tell. She asked me why I thought She wanted them, and I said I didn't care, as long as they were willing to pay good credits for them. Oh, yeah. She asked me if there was anything in our collection I would like to keep for myself. I said I'd trade it all for a good pump."

"A good pump."

"I might have said, for a good hump, then corrected myself."

"That's more believable. But you know she was testing you with that question, right? If you picked out something valuable, she'd know you were lying."

"Huh. I don't know, but she seemed—friendly after that. Then later, after she looked around my room for a bit, I told her I preferred men, so there was no point in her trying to claim me. She laughed. I said, I'll prove it to you. Show me your breasts and I won't even be interested. She laughed again, then she called my bluff. She won that one. I told her that trying to claim me would be a waste of time and effort, but she could try me out if she wanted."

"Let me guess. She said, I don't try out men."

"What? No. She said, hell yeah, I'll try you out, but I have no interest in claiming a man. I didn't know what she meant, so she told me that as an enforcer she didn't need the complications, and being a historian meant living where men aren't allowed. Can you believe it? No interest in claiming a man. You know what that means? Safe sex."

"Yeah, I know." Sex when you are safe from being claimed is a dream come true for a freeman.

"What can I say? We had a good time together. She was even careful with me. She didn't seem so scary after that. Except when she's with her boss. Then all bets are off, because she's totally loyal, and who knows where that might lead? Anyway, I thought that amazing night would be the end of it, but you know what? I'm kind of hoping it's not."

"Don't get your hopes up."

"Oh, come on. Don't tell me you don't want another night with Kāya."

"I ..." I sigh. "We really are dimwits, aren't we."

"Only according to all the evidence. But we're here now. Let's see where things go. As my granddaddy used to say, when you're sittin' under the cow, you might as well milk'er."

"If you're waiting for me to say, 'Let's milk this cow for all she's worth,' I'm not gonna say it. I'm just not."

"No, but you're thinking it, right?"

"Yeah, I kind'a am."

As we say our goodnights, I'm left with a vague determination I can't pin down, something vital I can't quite see. The Alphas still need us, but tomorrow that will end. We don't have much time left. To do what? There's nothing we *can* do but go along.

Except now, I *want* to go along. Let me see what I can learn before I'm shipped away.

———

I LIE AWAKE, still restless. Something intrudes in the gap between Dray's snores. Is that ... voices? The faint sound calls to me, and I quietly climb down from the truck in search of it. Yes, it's definitely voices. I'm at the wall now, moving away from the door, following the sound toward the crumble, when my hand hits the jagged edge of a broken-off pipe. I kneel down in the mustiness and put my ear to the opening. It's Onyx, and she's arguing with someone.

"This isn't like her." It's the other voice. "Why is she being so reckless?"

"Cut her some slack, Bree. She's going through some changes, and I think it's for the better."

"Well, it's putting us all at risk. This is a clear Rule Six violation. All men are prohibited from learning the ways of the Before world, up to and including the Inversion. Any man—"

"Don't quote Rule Six at me, Bree."

"You two need a reminder. Any man in possession of such knowledge shall be removed from society to avoid the inciting of insurrection. Any She—"

"Bree, that's enough."

"I don't think it is. Any She caught passing such knowledge to a male shall be subject to a period of imprisonment to be determined by tribunal. Is that what you want for us? Has Kāya forgotten about us?"

"Bree." Kāya's voice rings with authority.

Fear edges Bree's voice. "Kāya. I didn't know you were—"

"You know I hear everything. If you want to question me, question *me*. And no, I haven't forgotten about you. I wouldn't be doing this if I didn't think it was to your great benefit. Yes, there is risk involved, but this could be big, Bree. You saw the artifacts."

"Yes, but—"

"Your concern is valid, and if you want to leave, you are free to do so."

"But what about you, Kāya? The rules ..."

In the dark stillness, I strain to hear.

"I have devoted my life to enforcing those rules, Bree. And now I have to live with some of the things I've done, things that felt wrong, but I did anyway, in the name of duty. For all those years, I enforced the letter of the law as if it were written in stone, but you know what? It's not. All those years on the Elite Guard, standing watch over the

High Council as they deliberated over how to interpret the She Manifesto, as they argued over which of the rules of the ForeMothers to emphasize and which to downplay. Laws change, and with good reason. Some laws need to change. Some, like Rule Six, are outdated."

"But until they are changed, they are still the law, and we will still face judgment."

"In order for a law to be changed, someone has to stand up and challenge it. Many now accept the Celia Hypothesis. There is wide support for a change."

"But why now? Why this law?"

"Tye Celiaso. We will never have more leverage on the High Council. And if he is being truthful, and I think he is, this find could make our careers. So, now you know my mind. I'm not going to drag you into this, Bree, either of you. But I truly hope you'll stay with us. Talk it over and decide."

Onyx speaks, her voice receding. "Now you know why we left the Guard. But this ... chance of a lifetime, Bree ..."

I wait in the darkness for more, head spinning. Kāya spoke my name. What did she mean about leverage on the High Council? And what is the Celia Hypothesis? She would challenge the law? Kāya is a rebel? The voices were muffled. I may have misheard some things. Maybe I misinterpreted.

Fearful that someone will come out to check on us, I creep back to the truck and climb in. Should I tell Dray about this? What would I tell him? What did I overhear, exactly? Mind swimming in uncertainty, I pull the cover over my head and close out the world. But my heart is grasping at a new straw. She would stand up for me?

A surge of certainty ambushes me. *I will stand up for her.*

The thought hangs in the dark silence until it collapses under the weight of my own scorn. In what world does a simple man stand up for an Alpha? Certainly not in a world of She.

<h1 style="text-align:center">16</h1>

<hr>

MANKILLER

The wisdom of the ForeMothers is evident throughout the Manifesto in rules clearly aimed at avoiding the mistakes of the past. Rules Three and Four, with their guidance on managing men, are prime examples. But the mistakes of the past are the mistakes of men. The Manifesto marks them for avoidance.

Rule Eight: She shall never war against She. The amassing of an army of more than twelve fighters is strictly prohibited. The penalty for participating in such an army is a minimum of two years in prison. The penalty for leading such an army into a battle that results in fatalities is exile.

Commentary: To know history is to know of war. No one should doubt that She are capable of the crime against humanity that is war, and no one should doubt that war could end us. To remove any temptation, all She must be on guard against the buildup of military force ...

I startle awake in the sudden glare of floodlights and hear the door open. It's Bree, come to check on us. The exit ramp is bright with daylight.

We're both still sitting in the truck when she returns with a tray holding boiled eggs, strips of dried beef, berries and a jug of coffee. As soon as she's out of sight, we dive in. It's been a while since we ate this well.

It's almost an hour before she comes back out, along with Val and Aida, all carrying bags and cases out to the trucks. I'm starting to get desperate. "Uh, Bree? Is there a toilet we can use?"

"Okay, you two. You've got five minutes outside. Do what you need to do and come back in. I'm assuming you both want to stay alive."

We nod.

"Then don't go far."

The glare of the morning sun has me squinting as I look for a good spot to relieve myself. I reject a nearby patch of tall grasses and go for the grove of dwarf ash trees around the corner. When I'm done, I steel myself and look around. The scene looks different in the daylight, mottled in various shades of green by a fringe of covering vegetation. A more recent debris field stands out in the distance, not yet overgrown. The jagged skyline remains forbidding, though the impression of destruction and decay is tempered by the abundant new life.

On my way back to the entrance, a glint in the distance catches my eye. I'm looking down a long, straight stretch—an ancient roadway—and yes, there is definitely something moving this way.

Dray sees it too. We dash back to the entrance. "Bree! Come see. There's somebody coming."

A few quick strides and she's beside us. I jump as her voice cuts the air. "Val! Vehicles!"

Val dashes out, and the two Bravos climb a nearby mound to get a better look.

"They're inside the claim markers. Coming this way. Kāya! We have company!"

Moments later, Kāya appears beside us, eyes intense, then moves ahead, peering out. "There's trouble coming. Make ready."

"I'm seeing two trucks," says Val. "It's got to be Luce's team. Hide the men."

"No," says Kāya. "She knows they're here." She turns to us. "You two stay where you are. Onyx?"

Onyx runs to her side, and the two exchange a long look. She grips Kāya's forearm. "You sure?"

"Watch them for me."

"Got it," says Onyx.

What are we doing? Shouldn't we be hiding? We're not supposed to be here.

Bree approaches Kāya. "You called it right."

Kāya juts out her chin. "Our followers yesterday saw us take men into the Shell. I figured they'd send word to Luce."

"How did you know she'd come?"

Kāya studies the approaching vehicles. "It's me she's after. And this claim, of course." She shakes her head. "She's Quo. I figured the men would give her the excuse she's been waiting for."

She's Quo? *Crap.* The Quo hate men. Especially freemen. *We can't be seen here.*

I look to Kāya in dismay as she explains to Bree, "She's been pillaging other historians in the Shell for years. She's as much bandit as historian. Done quite well at it, they say. She's got the power to get away with murder out here in the frontier. She who can enforce the rules dictates the rules."

"She's that good?" asks Bree.

Good at what?

"Once an Alpha, always an Alpha. She was selected to the Elite Guard a couple years ahead of me, but then dismissed for unethical conduct shortly before Onyx came in, back when I was still going through my ... dark period. Last she knew, I'd been removed from active duty, a washed-up drunk, someone she could push around."

What?

"And then five years later, she's the washed-up drunk, scratching out a living in the Shell, and I'm a squad leader. It was my testimony that closed the door on reinstating her, so she hates me. Now she's discovered I'm out of the Guard and on my own. It's payback time."

What does she mean, 'on my own'? The whole conversation makes no sense to me.

"And she's still with the Quo?" asks Bree.

"Of course she's Quo. So are her goons. They'll use the men to justify this."

"Doesn't she control most of the central northeast?" asks Val.

"Took most of it from others who had prior claim, from what I've heard. Always finds a legal justification. Out here in the badlands, if you're strong and immoral, it's a good way to make easy money." Kāya glances back at us, then stands tall. "It's time somebody put a stop to it."

Onyx says, "The central northeast has been thoroughly picked over. Not much left to find there."

"I expect she's desperate."

"Not much left here anymore, either," says Bree.

"But she doesn't know that," Kāya says. "Let's see what she's got, after all these years."

What she's got? Are they gonna be trading?

We watch in silence as the vehicles draw up. One pulls in front, and a large beauty in enforcer regalia jumps out. With a solid build and pale skin, her dark brush-cut hair frames a stern, angular face. Her stance is confrontational as she surveys us. Her eyes rest on me, and my chest tightens.

Kāya steps forward. "What can we do for you, Luce?"

"We came to see if the rumors were true," Luce says. "I see they are. You are in violation, Kāya. I'm disappointed in you. You know we can't stand for it."

"Is it true you killed two men recently?" demands Kāya.

Oh shit. I shift closer to Onyx.

"They were trespassing. We don't abide scavengers."

"That's no justification for murdering them. I will see you brought to justice."

"Says the She violating the law. You soft on men now, Kāya? I never would have expected that from you, of all people." She looks to her team with a smirk. "Killer Kāya—"

"Shut up, Luce."

"—has gone soft." There are chuckles around the group. "What is it, Kāya? Guilty conscience? Or are you—"

"Shut your mouth, Luce. These men are not trespassing."

"They're where they shouldn't be. What would you call it?"

"They're here in my custody."

There is no surprise on Luce's face. "Then it's your transgression, and it can't go unpunished. But I'm a reasonable She, so here are your options. Either I take these violators, or I take this claim. You choose."

We're dead.

Kāya stands tall. "I claim single-case exemption."

Luce looks back to the others, who are all shaking their heads. "Denied by consensus."

"This is not consensus. These are all your people."

Luce spreads her hands and looks around. "I don't see many contrary votes, do you?"

Kāya glowers at her. "You wouldn't get away with this anywhere else, and you know it. You are not taking these men."

Protective custody. *She's honoring her word to us.*

Luce gives a crooked smile. "Then you are hereby stripped of this claim."

What?

"I challenge," says Kāya.

"Accepted," says Luce.

I clasp my head in my hands and watch as the two She remove their weapons and hand them aside, then strip down to their hard thongs. Dray tugs on my arm and leans in. "Are they gonna fight?"

I nod without averting my eyes. The two She don padded chest protectors, insert mouth guards, then walk out to face each other, and the spell breaks. *This is bad.*

Bree and Val join the other She circling the two fighters. I survey the ring of enforcers, each one displaying powerful Shehood in its most beautiful and lethal form. There are seven of theirs, but Bree and Val are Bravos, and I see only one silver collar among the others. The rest are wearing black: all Charlies.

"Aren't they gonna talk about this?" I ask.

"No point," says Onyx. "Brute force trumps discourse. It's a law of human nature."

"Yeah, a law dictated by the strong."

"All laws are dictated by the strong. Now shut up."

Kāya's voice is deeper than I've ever heard it as she sneers, "I'm going to enjoy this."

"You and me both," growls Luce. "We fight to domination!"

The witnesses echo in unison, "*To domination!*"

The two fighters tighten into mountains of rock, exchange nods, and leap at each other. They trade quick kicks and punches that don't get through, then settle in, strategically looking for openings. Yells and grunts accompany each attack as they clash and withdraw, circle and clash again. The speed and ferocity of their attacks is shocking. It seems impossible that anyone could defend against such onslaughts. Yet they keep going.

The She encircle them, intent, breaking discipline only to yell encouragement, heckle, or groan in sympathy. There are hoots each time Luce lands a blow.

What if Kāya gets hurt? What if she loses?

Grappling now, Kāya manages to throw her opponent onto her back but is unable to take advantage before Luce bounces back up. Luce sweeps Kāya's feet from under her, and they go down, but Kāya kicks her away and they're both back on their feet.

I can't bear to watch, but I need to see what's happening. Vibrating with fear, I huddle close behind Onyx.

Onyx curses as Luce connects another solid blow. Kāya struggles to stay on her feet.

I gasp. "Is she gonna be okay?"

Onyx doesn't take her eyes off the fight. "Kāya can take care of herself."

"Do something," I implore.

Onyx ignores me. Both fighters are wet with sweat, breathing hard. Kāya is wincing, with blood on her face.

I can't bear it. I cry out, "Stop! Please, stop this! We'll go with them."

Many heads turn my way. The fighters collide in a flurry of arms and legs, and Kāya staggers back, hunched, one hand raised in surrender. Luce steps back and straightens as Kāya buckles to her knees.

"*No!*" I try to go to her, but Onyx holds me in place.

Luce backs away, blood in her mouth, touching a cut over her swollen eye. She turns and limps back to her vehicle as Kāya collapses into a fetal position on the ground. Bree and Val kneel over her as the others withdraw.

I'm rocking in Onyx's grip. She shakes my shoulder. "Stop it! You've embarrassed her enough."

"But she's—"

Another shake and a stern glare freezes me. *How can she be so cold?* With help, Kāya sits upright, still hunched.

"She's breathing, no thanks to you. Now shut up."

"But ... what now?"

"She lost the challenge."

"What does that mean? Is Luce gonna kill us?"

Onyx scowls down at me. "Weren't you listening? You stay with us."

"But—"

"Enough." Onyx waves me off.

With painful knots in my stomach, I watch as Kāya's enforcers help her to her feet. They support her arms as she gingerly makes her way toward us. Her cheek is bright red as she tries to wipe blood from her mouth. I feel sick to my stomach. Luce's Bravo says, "Good fight," as she directs the rest of her team back to their trucks.

Onyx says to her, "Tell Luce we'll be out of here by morning."

"The rest of your team is welcome to stay and join ours," says the Bravo. Then she nods and follows the others.

Val and Bree sit Kāya down on the ground and lovingly attend to her, as Aida assesses her injuries. When she's done, Aida nods and steps back, then looks to Nance and shakes her head in disapproval. "This is what I hate about the fucking wild frontier."

Watching the trucks pull away, Nance says, "Yeah. Not the outcome I expected."

Onyx kneels beside Kāya and whispers something I can't hear. Then she wipes off blood with a towel and examines her face. "You okay, otherwise?"

Kāya stretches her neck, and I can't hold back any longer. "Please tell me you're okay."

Kāya chuckles dismissively, not even glancing at me. She blames me. She thinks I'm an idiot, not even worth yelling at. My entire world, what's left of it, is crumbling. I try to wipe frantic tears away.

Onyx notices me and shakes her head. "She'll be fine. It's nothing she hasn't done to me a dozen times."

Kāya reaches over and ruffles her hair. "You keep coming back for more, and I love you for it." She wheezes as she sits back. "How about that? She still packs a punch."

Dray leans into Onyx. "You two fight all the time?"

Onyx huffs. "When we train together, we go hard. Got to keep our edge."

I need Kāya to understand. "Why did you do that? You didn't need to ... We would have ..."

She doesn't look at me. "You would have what? Gone off to be killed? It's a good thing it's not up to you." She finally looks up at me, but her eyes are cold. "Stay out of it next time."

I stiffen. Next time?

She sits watching as the visiting vehicles pull away, then struggles to her feet and looks around at her team. "Okay, we've got packing to do. Let's get at it."

"They'll be back in the morning," says Onyx. "Armed."

Aida doesn't hide her resentment. "What about our site?"

Kāya straightens and winces. "Sorry Aida. It's theirs now. But I think we're onto something much better. Aren't we, Tye."

It's not a question. The whole team turns and looks at me, and I wither. Then, without waiting for a reply, they all head toward the shelter, leaving us standing alone.

I look to Dray for—something. He looks as lost as I feel.

"She fought for us," I say, grimacing. "Traded her site claim here for our lives." I throw my head back and squeeze it between my hands. "I should have kept my big mouth shut."

And now the whole team has lost their claim and their livelihood because of me. And Kāya thinks I can save them. What have I gotten myself into?

Dray scratches his cheek. "I guess we're here until tomorrow."

"Guess so." I stand dreading the day ahead. They'll be busy packing up their whole operation. How can I ever face them again? And I'm dreading the coming night. No way I'll be able to sleep. What if I can't find the place again? What if it's not as important a find as I think? I thought all the junk in my bunker had value. What do I know?

Only that everything is on me now.

Dray must see my distress, because he takes me in his arms and rocks me. "We'll figure this out."

There's that oblivious optimism coming through again. *What would I do without you?*

But the situation is dire. We have learned Kāya is not the big threat I feared she was, that she is, in fact, protecting us like she said. But we've also learned there are far worse threats around. Powerful enemies who would quite happily kill us. And for what? What is our crime? Being somewhere dangerous? That makes no sense.

The more I think about it, the crazier the whole thing seems. I look around. Here we stand, in the Shell, and the closest we've come to being killed is by some crazy Alpha. The fact that we're still alive puts the lie to the dogma. Sure, there are plenty of dangers out here, but where is life safe?

As we drag ourselves back toward the entrance ramp, I stop. "I just can't believe it. Why should Kāya have to pay such a steep price just for bringing us here? How could it possibly be such a big deal to have a couple of men out here in the ruins? Shouldn't that be our risk to take?"

Eyes wide, Dray spreads his hands, mystified like me. All at once, after a lifetime of certainty about the Shell, those unquestioned beliefs seem as fragile as any of these ancient structures.

So, what is the real crime? Being where we might learn history? The law is clear, but the crime? Seeking knowledge? Why should there be a law against that?

What are they afraid of? What are they trying to keep from us?

I know where I can find the answers. If only I had some privacy.

17

TAKING LEAD

I PACE the parking garage at dawn, partly to chase off the chill, and partly because I can't sit still. We've got to get out of here before Luce returns with her goons. We can't be here when they arrive. We've got to get going. Where is everyone? I hold back from pounding on the door to get them moving, knowing they're already pissed at me enough as it is.

I dash outside to check again, hoping not to see approaching vehicles. The door finally opens, and the team emerges. Kāya isn't with them as they bring out boxes and crates to load into the vehicles. I fish for information about how she's doing but get nothing.

At last, Onyx stops and confronts me. "Haven't you humiliated her enough?"

I grab my head, wincing. "Onyx, I ... How can I ..."

She sees my torment and sighs. "Okay, maybe that's not fair. The truth is, she did this to herself. It's not like her to show off. She's far more disciplined than that. It's almost like she wanted to impress you with a demonstration of her strength, and it backfired on her. She's pissed, all right, but mostly at herself. Anyway, she'll get over it, but you should probably, you know, back off for a while."

At herself? I'm dubious. I've never met a She who would blame herself when she could blame a man. The rest is good advice. Unfortunately, under the circumstances, backing off is not an option. This is bad on top of bad.

Dray and I try to help with the loading but quickly learn to stay out of their way. It's clear they're shunning me, but I get it.

Kāya finally comes out moments before we all board. She's not in her regalia, but a casual khaki shirt, shorts and trail boots. I wince when I see her swollen face and again curse my stupidity. She avoids looking at me. We don't speak.

When we finally head off, Dray and I are wedged between the packs and boxes jammed into the back of the lead truck. Onyx drives and Kāya rests beside her. Nance and Aida are in the overloaded tank truck behind us, followed by Bree and Val in the covered jeep, also crammed full. We head back out of the Shell the way we came in.

I need to act now, and yet the situation with Kāya couldn't be more volatile. But I have no choice; this is my last chance to negotiate. If I can appeal to Onyx, there's some hope. I suck in a lungful of air. "Onyx, you don't know where we're going."

She hesitates. "And you're going to give me directions."

I clench my teeth, then leap. "I'll take you to the new site on one condition."

I see Kāya's shoulders slump, and squeeze my eyes shut against the pain in my chest. Onyx's voice is cold. "No conditions, Tye. We're not playing games here."

This has to work. It has to. "No games. You need to let Dray go. I'm the guilty one. He was just tagging along, and he doesn't know anything. Ship me off to wherever, but let him go back to town."

I hold my breath ... Nothing. No reaction. The silence is crushing. Finally, she says, "I can't do that, Tye."

I fold inward. Then what's the point? I curl up with my head between my knees as I'm jostled along the heartless road.

"Tye, a whole bar full of witnesses saw the two of you with an artifact, being arrested by us. We can't just let you go."

Dray lurches forward. "Onyx, don't worry about it. I'll show you where it is. Tye gets like this sometimes."

I show him the shock of betrayal.

"Well, you do."

"I was trying ..." My voice trails off.

Kāya's voice surprises me. She doesn't look back as she speaks. "Here's the way it is. Tye will lead us. I trust him."

My mind stumbles. What was that? My eyes keep blinking until I wipe them, and Dray looks at me expectantly. I turn and glare at him, and he narrows his eyes in defiance. I give up and focus instead on Kāya's startling words. Trusts me? I brace. No. It's another manipulation. Cheeks burning, I hang my head.

She knew I was bluffing. She sees right through me.

I lean forward. "Onyx ... I shouldn't have ... I'm really sorry."

She gives a subtle nod without taking her eyes off the road. "Me too."

I'm not sure what she means by that. Sorry as in disappointed in me? Or sorry she can't protect Dray? I settle back to stew in my uncertainty.

I trust him, Kāya said. I can't shake the words.

Our three-vehicle convoy makes its way back out through the burbs the way we came in, and into the outskirts. All we have to do is cut across to Indy Park Road and head north toward Hillhaven. Then it's up to me to point out the turnoff to our secret trail.

I can't stop wondering about Kāya, sitting so close, yet a world away. She keeps surprising me, showing lenience, even protecting me. But it's stupid to get my hopes up. To her, I'm a means to an end. Once she has her new site, she'll have no further use for me, and then ... then I'll see the real Kāya. I know that. I'm not so naïve. But let me pretend, for these last few hours, that we're friends. No, colleagues. Give an exiled man a final fantasy and let me live in my dreams till then. I will lead this expedition.

When I figure we're getting close, I start watching for the turnoff. This is where my usefulness gets put to the test, and I start tensing up. The whole team, this entire convoy, is following me, depending on me.

I'm looking for a section of roadside that rises up level with the road. It's beside a grove of trees on the side of a small hill, but as we drive along, the whole area is full of groves of trees on small hills.

Dray grimaces. "What do you think?" he says. "We should be close. See anything yet?"

"Not yet. It's still up ahead."

After a few more minutes, we're both worried. Dray says, "Do you think we've gone past it?"

I sure hope not. I'm supposed to be leading this expedition. I can't already be lost. But we've always come from the other direction, by bike. "Onyx, slow down."

We crawl along, studying the roadside, until I see it. "There. On the right. Go over that flat area, and on the other side you'll see a trail."

Onyx perks up at the wheel. "It's about time."

We call it a trail because it's easy to travel, but it's not an actual trail. Rather, it's a wide swath of grasses bordered by bushland on both sides.

"This is an ancient roadbed," says Onyx. "How did you know it was here?"

Dray answers. "We've been exploring out here for years. Found some interesting stuff, too. No, nothing like what you're looking for. There are ruins up ahead at an old crossroads. All cleaned out generations ago, so everybody knows it's safe. But you never know what you might find out here."

I add, "You know what we search for? Flat squares of ground surrounded by debris. I heard my mom talking about it. It could be a sign that there's a basement under there. Might be one that's watertight and hasn't been found yet." I suddenly realize what I'm doing.

Onyx chuckles. "A real amateur historian."

I take that as permission. "For my whole life, I've dreamed of being a historian." I can tell by the crook of her head that Kāya is listening. "A chance to rediscover lost knowledge and know-how. Like special building and farming techniques, manufacturing processes, antiviral vaccines, recipes for amazing materials, insights into the sciences. It's because of the work of historians that we have most of what we have today."

"That's our role, sweetie," says Onyx. "Mining the past to enrich the future. It's too bad it's—"

"Don't say it. I know."

"That's the way it is, Tye. I'm not sure I agree with it, but—"

"Tye." It's Kāya again. "Please don't forget we are also enforcers. Don't let careless talk become a habit when there are others around."

"No, I ... Of course." Others. But she's okay with it? Curious. I wish I could talk to her. But I'd only get shut down again, like that first night. Or I'd get angry about the injustice of our laws, and that would only make things worse.

There's got to be something safe we could talk about. I come up blank. I don't know anything about her, other than she's the subject of a stupid war raging within me. I'm dangerously drawn to her, but the reality is, she opposes everything I believe in. She enforces the subjugation of men. And I mean nothing to her; I'm a mere annoyance she's putting up with to get what she wants. And what kind of idiot would fall for someone like that?

I come alert as we pass the crossroads ruins—several collapsed structures overlaid with sprawling steel beams. From there we head into an area of low hills, lush with new-growth forest. A flock of birds bursts into the air as we approach, twittering their annoyance.

"Up ahead, we need to head off the trail and into the bush on the left. I'll let you know where."

We crest a small hill, and there in the distance are the ruins of the old industrial park. And there is the series of hills and bluffs I've been searching for. "Not far now. Okay, up ahead, go left."

We turn off into the bush and onto an animal trail, probably deer, that we had no trouble following on our bikes. "How far?" asks Onyx, as she swerves back and forth, looking for a route through the growth.

"Not far. Over through there."

We pull to a stop. "This is about as far as we can go with the trucks," says Onyx. "I still don't see anything."

"It's just up ahead."

Soon we're walking through familiar patches of spindly, squat evergreens covering the hilly ground. But this is the part that gets tricky. We're surrounded by clusters of trees, large mounds overgrown with grasses and, here and there, a concrete fragment or scrap of rusted steel. It all looks familiar. It all looks the same. Without our trail markers, scraped into flat surfaces, we'd be lost. I look back and see Dray and all the others in single file, following me. Me. Leading a team of historians to a historical site *I* discovered. I get a tingle in my chest.

An unfamiliar stump tells me I'm not where I thought I was. *No.* I can't get lost now.

I hear Nance's voice from behind. "Well, this is off the beaten trail."

"There's asphalt crumble here," says Onyx, "but no sign of a former roadway.

Nance adds, "That building debris back there didn't come from natural decay. An old demolition site, maybe? How far are we going?"

"It should be right around here somewhere." Great Mother, where is it? Uncertain, I circle back.

Onyx looks irked. "We're lost, aren't we."

"Uh, no, no, it's around here somewhere."

"What exactly are we looking for?" says Kāya.

"It's a small entrance. On the side of a small bluff. On the side of a hill. Hard to spot."

Where is it? My alarm is reaching a fever pitch when I finally see what I'm looking for. A rock leans against a tree trunk. Right where we left it. And across from it is the small bluff. And there it is. My heart leaps.

And then plummets. My job is done.

But seeing the vent again makes clear what I should have known all along. They still need me. At least for a while longer. I've still got time to prove to them how useful we are.

With renewed determination, I call out, "Here! Found it."

18

CRAZY TIME

THE SUN PEEKS through the partially overcast skies as I pat the head of the incongruous gooseneck vent emerging from the side of the small bluff, half hidden in new growth. The others draw around and gawk.

"What's this?" Kāya's disappointment shows.

My triumph dissolves. "The entrance."

Aida scowls. "That's no entrance. At best, it's an air vent."

Kāya gives me a dubious look. "You climbed in there?"

"The old map said there was something here. I was curious."

They take turns examining the opening.

"That's not going to do us any good," says Onyx. "There's got to be another entrance."

"That's what we thought, too," says Dray. "Searched the whole area. Couldn't find one. And Tye's the best searcher in the region."

"If there is something down there, there has to be an entrance," says Aida. "Unless whatever was here was demolished and buried."

"The part I saw was intact."

"If the entrances were deliberately hidden, they may be easier to find from the inside."

"Didn't see one. Don't worry, we have a system. You lower me in, and I'll tie stuff on, and you can haul it up."

Nance objects. "Absolutely not. If this is a Before facility of some sort, in good condition, we need to get in there."

"Agreed," says Kāya. "Val, Bree, see if you can get the vehicles closer, then we'll do a thorough search of the area."

"You won't find anything," I say. A twinge of uncertainty has me looking to Dray, who gives me a confident nod. But they might. I should enjoy this while I can. I step back and look skyward. I did it. I got us here. And unless they find something we missed, I get to go back in, but with historian supervision, from real historians.

"If anyone was still in there when the place was buried, we can expect to find humrem."

Human remains. Thanks, Nance. Why did you have to bring that up? The place is haunted, is all I know.

Aida asks, "Tye, how long ago did you first go in there?"

"Uh, two weeks ago, maybe a bit more."

"At least we know it's not an active biohazard."

They all look at me, and my skin crawls. How many hazards don't I know about?

Dray says, "Unless that's what caused his insanity."

"Shut up, Dray."

"Just kidding. He's always been insane."

"Dray, I swear—"

Aida interrupts. "This is where you got those artifacts?"

"Yes. Down there."

"If it was deliberately hidden, then the big question is, why would they go through the trouble of burying this place without cleaning it out first? Unless there was some urgency ..."

Nance looks at her. "You mean, like the world ending?"

"So ... why would they bother burying it?"

———

I told them there was no other entrance. How long are they gonna keep looking? I stand waiting near the trucks, now camouflaged in a meadow some thirty yards from the vent.

All eight of us have been scouring the area for almost two hours and come up with nothing. Nance, Aida and Dray are already back, the historians digging around in the vehicles. I watch for Kāya's return, but all I see is the surrounding wilderness. Even the old roadbed is far out of sight. This far out in the wilds, we are safe from prying eyes.

The spring air is more humid than usual, and breathing it in calms me. The scents of pine, cedar and wood rot compete with the fragrance of wildflowers and crabapple blossoms. What must this be like for someone with enhanced senses?

Finally, she emerges from the bush. She shakes her head, and I release caught breath. They still need me. I join the others, then wince as Kāya approaches, her swollen cheek livid.

I want to shake her and demand, *Don't fight, ever again.*

Aida catches my attention. "How did you find this vent out here in the first place?"

"This is a hilly area, right around here. If you look closely, there are subtle differences between natural mounds and mounds of rubble. The vegetation growth, for one thing. Rubble snags wind-blown seeds, so you get different patterns of growth. See up here? And over here? And if you dig down a bit, the earth is lighter than natural soil. That's crushed concrete."

Aida interrupts. "Did your mother teach you these things?"

"Not on purpose, but I might have picked up a few things spying on her. She had an apprentice one summer. And I learned a lot from exploring the old safe sites around Hillhaven as a kid. It was my dream to be—" Should I be talking about this?

"Tye can find anything," says Dray. "Best searcher in the business. One time, we were doing an excavation down by—"

"Let's not get into old—"

"My friend here knows what he's doing, is all I'm saying."

"To get back to your question, bluffs are always good places to see below ground level without having to dig. Whenever I come across one, I check it out, and I got lucky here. You see where the soil has fallen away? This vent was completely buried until recently."

Onyx and Bree appear, pushing through the squat vegetation. Onyx shakes her head.

"I told you," I say. "This is the only entrance."

Kāya seems perplexed. "If people worked here, there must be entrances and exits. Did you search the whole inside?"

"It's pretty dark in there." And I was trying not to piss myself. "I didn't see much of it."

The She exchange glances. "Tye. Dray. Give us a minute. Go take a leak or something. We'll call you back."

As we reluctantly wander off, Dray mutters, "So much for trusting us."

"They were hoping they could be done with us by now, but they've got to send me back in. There's no other way."

"You hope."

"I hope."

The overcast sky doesn't threaten more rain, but it's already midafternoon. Where will they be staying tonight? Hillhaven is only an hour away, but we wouldn't all fit in my—

It's not mine anymore.

The call interrupts my mood slide, and we hurry back. I'm not sure what to expect.

Kāya addresses us. "Tye, we're going to need you to get inside and try to find an entrance. Would you be willing to do that?"

"Yes, I—"

Dray takes over. "You need something found, Tye's your guy. He'll get you in."

"Good. Now if there's no easy way in, we may have to dig one. But we need to know where to dig."

"Got it. Uh, how do we do that?" I ask.

Aida steps forward. "We're going to give you something called a transponder. It works with a radio signal that will point us to you. All you need to do is place it at the best entrance you can find. Now, how did you manage to breathe down there?"

"Uh, it was hard."

Aida digs into a pack and pulls out something that looks like an oblong glass bowl. She holds it up to her face, pulls its straps over her head and looks out at me. Some sort of mask. Then she takes out a small cylinder and attaches it to the chin of the mask, turns a knob and takes a deep breath. She turns the knob again and removes the mask. "Supplemental oxygen. This should be good for about half an hour. You can stretch that out by using it sparingly, as needed." She helps me put it on and try it. The taste of the air is cool and fresh, though somewhat metallic. Then she stows it back in the pack. "We'll lower this down after you."

She hands me the pack, and with trembling hands I check inside. Extra lights, the small box they called the transponder and several tools. Wow. They come prepared. It hits me that I'm standing here with a team of serious professionals. And I'm the one leading the way.

"Right," says Kāya. "Tye, let's get you inside. Go find us a way in."

The horrid black void awaiting me comes vividly to mind. My heart thumps as a sudden panic seizes me. I'm gonna screw this up. I know I am.

I can't think like that. I did it before, in the stupidest way possible. Now, I'm equipped and backed up by a team of historians. It'll be different.

I find Kāya watching me with concern and straighten. It's not about treasure this time. I'm gonna prove my value and show her what a man can do. I set my jaw.

I climb into the harness Onyx gives me and stand passive as she tightens it. We surround the vent opening in silence while Nance works at securing the hoist around a nearby tree trunk.

"How many times have you done this?" asks Kāya.

No point in keeping up the bravado. "Once."

"That's it? Never mind. Tell me again what's down there."

"About thirty feet down, there's a side duct that opens into the ceiling of a hallway. It's about ten feet down to the floor. The place is huge."

She scowls at me. "That's a hell of a risk you took, going in there."

"Believe it or not," I say, avoiding her eyes, "freemen enjoy a little adventure once in a while."

"I hope you're ready for another one," says Kāya, "because once you're down there, you're on your own."

"I can handle it," I say, trying to convince myself.

Kāya looks around, then calls out, "Okay. Let's go." I startle when she touches my hand. "Be careful down there." She drops her eyes and turns away.

But that unusual image of her eyes burns itself into my soul. Was that concern in them? She must expect me to screw up. Well, I'm not gonna.

Dray gives the harness a final check.

"Am I doing the right thing?" I whisper.

"Tye," he whispers back, "we're freemen without assets. We have nothing to lose. And who knows where this will lead? I'd go in your place if I could."

"That's crazy."

"Yeah, it's crazy time. Go show them what a freeman can do."

Crazy time. I used to always try to play it safe, but look how that worked out. If there was ever a good time for crazy, this is it. I've got a chance to live my dream. If I let my fear stop me, what's the point in dreaming? And if I die, well, at least it will be as a freeman, on my own terms, not as a victim.

Dray is still waiting. I hold his eyes. "This is my chance—our chance."

He nods.

My chance to prove to Kāya I'm worthy of her trust. To prove that Dray and I are worth having around. To prove I'm capable of being a useful member of a historian team, that I could have followed in my mother's footsteps as well as any daughter.

Part of me knows I can do this; part of me doubts. I need to prove myself to me.

I stand tall and face the She. "I'm ready." Then I falter as the tongue of fate draws me toward the mouth of the beast about to swallow me whole.

19

THE BIG DARK

DROPPING down a dark shaft my shoulders can barely squeeze through has got to be the stupidest thing I ever did. So, of course, I'm back doing it again.

Except this time, it's different. I'm doing it right. I'm proving my worth to a team of historians. I can do this.

I reach the side duct and call up for the pack. Pushing it ahead of me, I crawl to the grate opening and look through. Within the small pool of my light, the empty hallway looks the way I remember it. Beyond my light, nothing. Complete darkness. I lower the pack to the floor, then follow, checking all around me. Nothing has changed. No cause for panic. My arrival has stirred up the dust again, and I try to slow my breathing but can't.

I take out one of the spare flashlights, a fuel-cell cube with a big lens and carrying handle. Then I sling the backpack over my shoulders. This light is more powerful than my headlamp. Good. Down here, the more light, the better. It still doesn't seem enough. Next, I remove a small waypoint marker light, turn it on and sit it below the access vent. This will mark the way out, and should glow for a few hours, Aida said.

I stand in place and examine my surroundings, trying to acclimatize to the alien environment, not ready to plunge in. Straight walls and square corners everywhere. The walls are smooth and white, with some kind of matte finish that diffuses the reflected light. I see no sign of water damage and smell no mustiness or mold. Unlike the clean walls, the floor and ceiling up ahead are a mess. I'll need to watch my step as I make my way around the flat, broken debris of fallen ceiling tiles. The dark gaps above leave the impression that the whole ceiling could come down on me at any moment. I peer up and see a solid ceiling two feet above this one. It's likely not as precarious as it looks.

I ease when I notice that with this new, stronger light I can see the far end of the hall. It's not endless after all. There are doors at irregular intervals, except for a large black gap toward the middle on the right side. An open space. I shiver and check my closer surroundings.

The dust is as bad as I remember, and the stale air threatens to choke me. How did I survive this before? I was planning to save the mask for emergencies, but I'm already coughing. I need that mask. I struggle to get it on, and as the oxygen flows, I savor the clean air. I peer around as I get my breath, then continue exploring.

I see footprints in the dust and, with relief, recognize them as mine. Why do I keep thinking there might be something down here other than me? That's not possible. Is it?

The first open doorway I come to is the room I was in before. The one I've been trying to visualize. It all comes back: the big desk, the large cabinet, the suffocation. But I'm not here for loot this time. And I'm not suffocating. A sense of illicit freedom fills me as I step back into the hall. I've got this whole place to myself.

I check through a few more doors and see a variety of rooms. Several are interconnecting, but with no other way out. I'm hopeful when I find a pair of doors side by side, but they're for large washrooms, each with many sinks and enclosed toilets, their bowls all dry. I try a tap. No water.

Right next to these is the gap, a large, open area I recognize as a cafeteria, judging by the tables and chairs. Entering, I sense the volume of the surrounding space even before swinging my lights around. At the back of the room is a wide set of stairs going down. That's the wrong direction. I need to be going up. But Great Mother, this place is huge.

In the eating section of the room, I count four pairs of rectangular white tables, with six chairs at each table. The chairs have clean, efficient lines with no visible joins, as if molded from a single piece. I confirm all the tables and chairs are empty. Like I expect to find someone sitting there, waiting for me. I don't even believe in ghosts. But what do I know? This is not a good time to find out I'm wrong about that. This place gives me the creeps, and I haven't even come across humrem yet.

As I approach the far side of the cafeteria, it opens up into a long hallway identical to the first one. I retreat the way I came, determined not to get lost down here. I need to keep my bearings. One hallway at a time.

The last time I was down here, it was a quick grab and dash, and even that came too close to disaster. If Dray hadn't hauled me out when he did ...

But this is not like last time. This time, I'm well equipped and playing a crucial role, part of a professional team. Of course, none of that matters if something happens down here. They can't help me. I'm on my own. I shake myself. I've got to stop thinking and keep moving.

Behind a row of counters, I see the entrance to what must be a kitchen, lined with gleaming metal. There's a sink, and what looks like a huge stovetop, and walls of shiny cupboards I'm half tempted to look in. They'll have to wait.

I'm breathing too fast. *Slow down.* Each room I go into is a dead end, and in each room, I marvel at the wealth of devices lying around. We've hit the jackpot for sure. But I can't get distracted. I've got a job to do.

Back in the hall, I continue checking doors until I come to a shorter hallway heading off at right angles. I check around me for landmarks, then head in. About halfway down, I examine what look like three large double doors, but none have knobs or handles.

Unable to find a way of opening any of them, I take out my hammer and strike a door with a good, hard blow. The bang echoes through the enclosed space. That *was* an echo, right? I turn and swing my light around to check the darkness engulfing me, shadows shifting as I do. Creepy.

I return to hammering on the door. Each blow sends echoes reverberating through the void, trying to wake the dead. *Wrong thought.* I'm compelled now to check around me every few blows. Stupid. There's nothing here. Right?

If these doors lead to the surface, they should hear this hammering. I stop to listen for a response from outside. Nothing. Time to move on. It's slow going, with my light flitting around in the blackness, but things are trying to sneak up on me from behind. I just know it.

I'm panting again. How long has it been? I haven't been keeping track, but not that long. I've got to keep going. I've got to find a door to the outside. Not far from whatever I was hammering on, I come to a smaller door with a bar across it. Above it, I find the word 'Exit.' *This is it. The way out.* I test the bar with a push, and it collapses against the door, making the door bounce. I push again and the door opens. Behind it is a landing for a stairway. To the right, it goes down, but in front of me it goes up. This must be the way out. I go through and start climbing, and a few steps up I hear a clunk behind me as the door closes again. I keep climbing. This is good. This must be going toward the surface.

The stairs rise and turn, rise and turn, with landings at regular intervals. I'm relieved when I come to another door, like the one at the bottom. I push on the bar and shove. Nothing happens. I lean into it and give it a good shove. Nothing. I throw my whole weight against it, and again. Not budging. This door is not gonna open. Okay, no problem. I must be near the surface. I'll make some noise for a while, then keep looking. There might be another exit.

I bang away for a while, then make my way back down the stairs and find only a handle on this side of the closed door. I grip it and pull. *Uh-oh.* I think back. Yes, it opened out this way before. I try pushing anyway. Nothing. I try pulling again. My heart pounds. I'm locked out.

There is nowhere else to go but down, but I balk at doing that. No choice. I climb down, circling from landing to landing until I come to another door, identical to the first. Also locked. And the stairs keep descending. *No.* I'm not going any deeper. I yank and swear and rattle the handle and yank again until my fingers ache.

Panting heavily, I drag myself up the long climb back past the first door and on to the top, where I try again. I kick at it, throw myself against it, hammer away at it with fury, my ears ringing. I cry out, "In here! I'm in here!"

In my panic, the flashlight slips from my grasp and bounces down the stairs, its last moments a flashing frenzy of desperation. Then it hits the landing hard and explodes in a lingering flare of blue flame. The flash of heat shocks me, though the mask has protected my eyes and face. What in blazes was that? The still-flaming cube must be ten feet below me, but within seconds the black smoke pouring off it dims the throw of my headlamp.

The light's hydrogen fuel cell must have cracked open on the granite steps. I don't know what's smoldering, but I have no doubt the smoke is toxic. I scramble down to it and kick it off the landing, down the steps. It's lucky I'm wearing an oxygen mask. *Oxygen.* I go rigid. There can't be much time left.

And I'm trapped.

20

———

EXPENDABLE

A HAZE of smoke hangs in the air as I try to guess how much oxygen I have left. I need to get out of here. I climb back up to the door and resume hammering until I remember the transponder. I pull off my backpack and dig through it, fingers trembling, and place the transponder by the door. I hope it's working, but have no way of knowing.

My energy is fading as I make my way back down, past the blackened husk of the light, to the first door. There's got to be some way of opening this. Working to gain control of my breathing, I try to approach the problem methodically. But I find no point of attack. It's a metal door, sealed all around the frame, no access to hinges, no play in the latch. I become frantic, muscles spasming as I scream. I throw my weight at it until I hurt my shoulder.

I've got to get out, and outside is up there. I start the long trudge back to the top, and even through the mask I can smell the soot in the air. This is bad. I've gotten myself into a trap and I can't see a way out. My first taste of historian work, and I get in over my head. I guess I wasn't as ready for this as I thought. Reckless.

I get it now, Mom. I know why you tried to keep me away from this. It was an act of love, and I just couldn't see it. I thought I could prove to you—

I remember the book. Crap. They'll find it when they go through my things, after I'm ... Kāya will regret ever trusting me. If only I'd gotten rid of it. I hardly saw any of it anyway. I've got to get rid ... I need to get out of here.

I finally reach the top, without even the strength to try throwing my weight again. I can't catch my breath. The oxygen is running out. Do I take my chances with the toxic smoke, or suffocate in the mask? I lift the edge of the mask to test the air and immediately choke, coughing until I get the mask secured again. That was stupid. I go back to hammering until, arms and lungs exhausted, I sink to my knees and drop the hammer. If they were on the other side of the door, they'd be signaling back. I hear nothing but my own panting, the loud ringing in my ears and the hammering of my pulse.

I can't think straight. I try to start back down the stairs, head swimming. Feeling my legs start to buckle, I grab the handrail and sit on a step, gasping.

My senses swirl with the sound of my wheezing, my rapid pulse, the hot pressure in my face. I'm still coughing, even in the mask. The headlamp seems to weigh a ton, so I pull it off. It falls and lights up the painted cement block wall across from me. Even without it, my head grows heavier until I can't hold it up.

So close. I was so close.

Poor Dray. What's he gonna do without me? He can't make it on his own. Onyx will look out for him. Won't she? And what about Kāya?

Despair fills me as I see it all clearly. Dray is on his own. They'll ship him off somewhere and be done with both of us. It's been obvious all along, and Dray tried to warn me. We are nothing but useful pawns to them. Expendable, like my dad. Why has that reality been so hard for me to accept?

Kāya's face comes to me, shining in the darkness, and I calm. That face. Those eyes.

Ah, yes. This is why.

It is said that for each man, there is a face he will die for. I've seen a thousand beautiful faces, loved a couple of them, but always thought it was just a cute saying. Now I know it's true. And now, for the first time, I understand the last line. *Pity the man who sees that face.*

Yes, pity all men, for we are the weak, the powerless, the losers in life's lottery. But one day, a man will rise up, with the strength to stand tall, and he will lift up his brother men to freedom. And all men will be freemen, free to choose whom to serve, whom to love.

Dray sits beside me on the step and puts his arm around my shoulder. "You made it, Tye. You're free now, never to be claimed again."

Free now. Yes, free. A cold emptiness swirls around me. Free and alone is still alone. I try to warn him, but he dissolves into shadows, and Kāya stands before me in her regalia. Odd; I have no fear of her.

"You missed your chance to love me," she says.

"No," I protest. "You wouldn't let me, coward."

I see that familiar look of skepticism in her eyes as she fades to darkness. Why doesn't she believe me? *She's* the coward. It's not me. It's her ...

Doesn't matter anymore. I can't feel my body. I grasp for her face but can't quite form it.

To see her one last time ...

Too late ...

... missed ...

From impossibly far away, I hear my mother calling me home, debris hitting the dome's armor glass, the storm door rattling in the wind. I look down at the book of knowledge in my hands and watch its blank pages flutter off in the wind like autumn leaves.

As I sink into the blackness, I'm holding Matty tight to my chest, nuzzling into the smell of his baby hair, feeling his tiny heartbeat as mine overflows with joy. The beat gradually slows, and I'm lying against my father's chest, immersed in his scent as his chair gently rocks. He's speaking of love, but I lose the thread ...

21

HELLHOLE

I GASP, and light stabs my eyes until I squeeze them shut. Air. I gasp again, head and heart pounding. I'm on my back, taking in full breaths, my chest aching with each one. Where am I?

I pry my eyes wide enough to see I'm in the open air. Someone is leaning over me. Two people. "Okay ..." The voice is breathless. "... Okay, he's back." Aida? She moves away.

"Tye. Tye, you with us?" It's Dray, distress carved into his face.

"Breathe easy. Relax." It's Kāya, voice also breathless, an oxygen mask pushed up on her head. Her face seems distorted. Oh yeah, swollen cheek.

It all comes back. How did I get out here? As my eyes adjust, I see I'm surrounded. There is Onyx holding a sledgehammer, shining with perspiration. Big Val holds a spade. Their chests are all heaving as they wipe sweat from their brows.

"What's going on?" I try to say. It comes out as a mumble no one hears. Kāya holds up my head and puts a bottle to my mouth. The first sip is hard to get down. The second feels like a wet kiss. I try again. "What's going on?"

"Thought we'd lost you there, buddy," says Dray, eyes full of concern.

"You're going to be okay," says Kāya, cheeks puffing as her head falls forward, eyes closed. She brings her face back up. "Sorry it took us a while to get through. Glad you're still with us." She squeezes my hand.

The black nightmare is gone in a blaze of joy that leaves me bewildered.

Onyx comes over. "Well done, Tye. You led us right to it. Whoever buried this place did a good job. We'd never have found it."

I sit up, and dizziness spins me. I groan and slump forward.

Kāya puts a hand on my shoulder. "Just sit. No rush."

Large piles of chunked concrete and fresh dirt lie heaped around a hole in the side of a small hill. "The entrance?"

"Aida says it's an emergency exit. But it's still a way in."

An emergency exit. Not so much.

On the other side of us is a large clearing, beyond which the ground flattens into fields. We're sitting at the front edge of the raised, uneven terrain, with all its brush-covered mounds. Out in front, Bree is removing a punctured door from a large T-hook attached by a chain to the back of the truck. They must have yanked it right off its hinges. After they punched a hole through it. After they dug out the steps leading down to it. Saving my life took some serious determination. And I don't know what to make of that. Men like me, we're disposable. She use us up and throw us away. And yet ...

Nance and Aida emerge from the hole and lift their masks. Aida says, "It's a one-way door. You can come out, but you can't get back in." She looks at me. "The top door would have worked the same way if it weren't buried under a ton of dirt."

A one-way door. I've never heard of such a stupid thing.

Nance wipes her face. "Bit of a trap you got yourself into. Good thing we picked up the transponder again, and then heard you."

"We lost the signal when you went inside," says Aida. "The structure must have blocked it somehow, until you got up close to the surface. This is a long way from where you went in."

"Yeah, the place is big," I say.

Dray leans over and throws his arms around me. "You scared me half to death. I was waiting with the pulley and you didn't come and you didn't come and time was running out and ... Guns, Tye, you scared me."

I rest my cheek against his. "Yeah. Me too. But you found me. Thanks. Thanks, everyone."

"No, thank *you*," says Aida. "Now we've got a way in."

I cough. *Ow*, that hurts. "I guarantee you're gonna be happy."

"I can already tell this is major," says Aida. "I haven't been this excited since—"

"Last night?" says Nance with a sly grin.

Aida's eyes sparkle. "You're so bad."

I've never seen this group in such good spirits. The relief shows on their faces. They must've worked hard to rescue me. *Me.* I'm still bewildered. Were they seeing me, just for a moment, as a fellow historian, someone of value? My heart flutters, not daring to hope.

"We've got another locked door," says Kāya. "How do we get through it?"

Onyx shrugs, hefting her sledgehammer.

"Hold on," says Aida. "Why is the first answer always brute force? There are other options, you know."

Onyx says, "What's wrong with—"

"Let's try not to destroy any more of this place than we have to," says Kāya. "Aida, what have you got?"

"I've got tools and I've got know-how. I'll pick the lock."

Nance grins. "Now there's some sexy brainpower."

"This is why academics have such power on the High Council," says Val, as she and Bree collect the other tools. "They always come up with lazy ways to do things."

"Power comes in many forms," says Nance. "It seems like you enforcers sometimes forget that."

Did she get that from my mother?

"Aida, go see what you can do," says Kāya.

As Aida and Nance disappear back into the hole, she turns back to me. "So, Tye. What did you see down there?"

Another interrogation. "A long hallway, lots of rooms, a big cafeteria—"

"What's in the rooms?"

"Desks and chairs and cabinets and shelves, yeah, lots of stuff."

"What else?"

"I don't know, uh, oh yeah, three big doors, side by side, but I don't know what's behind them. No handles. And—that's about it."

She looks puzzled but says nothing, then rises with a nod and gathers the enforcers. "We don't know how long it's going to take to get in, but let's plan on staying here for the night. Onyx, call in for an updated forecast, and you two bring the other vehicles around."

"On it," says Bree, as they head off.

"Dray, sit on him for a few minutes. Make sure he rests."

As she goes over to join Onyx at the truck, Dray ruffles my hair and gazes into my eyes. He breaks into a big grin. "You did it, you lunatic. So tell me. What did you really see down there?"

I cough, then check that we're alone. "Treasure beyond measure, freeman. I was right." My grin collapses. "Not that we'll see any of it."

"They'll go easy on us, though. That's something, right?"

"You still trust them?"

"You're still alive, aren't you? And just so you know, I wasn't the only one scared when you didn't come back."

"Who else?"

"You know."

"What are you saying?"

"Look how hard they worked to save you. Why would they do that if they were gonna get rid of us anyway? No, I think we're safe here as long as Kāya's in charge." He sits back with an easy grin as he watches Onyx and Kāya at the truck.

There's that oblivious optimism again, and I smile, though I'm sure he's misreading the situation. I'm nothing to her. An image from the recent nightmare flashes to mind. "Missed your chance." Well, I have another chance, and I'm not gonna make the same mistake ...

Except, in the cold light of day, there's nothing I can do that won't ruin everything. My heart sinks. No, the only way I can survive this is to fully commit to the freeman way: to steel my heart and stand apart.

Where am I gonna get the strength to do that? I cough and cautiously fill my aching lungs.

Dray's right. She hasn't hurt me yet, and she's had plenty of opportunity. And oddly, I'm not scared of her anymore. They will soon be sending us away, so time is running out, but ... this is ridiculous. I have no right to expect anything between us. And how can I earn her respect if I keep groveling in front of her? Like Onyx said, I've got to show her the freeman spirit and stand up for myself.

The other truck pulls into the large clearing out front and parks. The jeep follows, then the She start unloading packs. Onyx beckons us over and tosses a large pack to us.

"This will be your tent. We've got lots of space, so there's no need to crowd. Find a good spot for it in the trees over there."

They're letting us stay. I allow myself a glimmer of hope. How long? "We've got safe weather ahead?"

"Don't worry, we've got storm tents too, if we need them. But since we could be here for a while, let's be comfortable while we can."

Here for a while. Hope bubbles up in my chest, and I caution myself, focusing instead on my task.

It's a three-She dome tent, simple to erect, spacious and freestanding, and we have it up in no time. It's a good five feet high, with a sturdy frame. We take a few minutes to figure out how to do a quick takedown in case we should need to. I'm feeling lighter now, almost floating.

Three other tents have sprung up around the tree line of the clearing. "Looks like we'll be sleeping in pairs," says Dray. "There's enough room in here for four."

"The She need more room than we do."

"Sure, but I'm hoping there's another reason." He winks at me. Yes, things are definitely looking more hopeful.

A voice calls out, "We're in!" It's Nance, emerging with the news we've been waiting for. Everyone cheers and grabs their packs, and we all gather around the entrance. Up close, the stink of smoke still hangs in the air.

"Okay," says Kāya, "let's see what we've got here. Everyone got a mask?"

I gasp for air. *Crap.* No way I'm going back down there. I can't do it. Then all at once it's clear she was only asking the She. Dread still grips me as we watch them head one by one into the gaping black hellhole.

Kāya stops in front of me. "You okay"?

I startle alert. "Yeah, sure."

She nods, with that skeptical look, and I realize I'm doing it again. If I'm ever gonna deserve her trust, I have to be honest with her.

"Not really."

She pauses, waiting, so I continue.

"That place scares the piss out of me."

"I can understand why. It almost killed you."

"It's not just that. There's something, I don't know, evil about the place."

"Then it's good you don't need to go back in there. We won't be in long. You wait here."

Wait here? "I didn't mean ..." She's already walking away. "You're not scared?"

She turns back. "We're professionals, Tye. This is what we do."

I blush. Such a casual snub, and yet I deserve it. This is what honesty gets me. She turns and heads to the stairway, and I follow. "Uh, where are the masks?"

She glances over her shoulder and stops. "You don't need one. Wait for us here."

Push back, man. "Uh, I'd rather not be alone right now." *Are you kidding me?*

"You've got Dray here with you."

"But I, uh, should show you around a bit."

"That won't be necessary. Why don't the two of you start unpacking the trucks?"

I hold my breath against the lingering fumes as I watch her

descend into the darkness. So this is how it's gonna be. I get them in and now they keep me out.

"We're lucky," says Dray, as I return to him. "Wasn't looking forward to going in there." He must see the grievance on my face, because he turns incredulous. "Really? You want to?"

"I don't know. Not really. But yeah. I mean, this is a real historical site. First I've ever been in. I wouldn't mind having a chance to, you know, look around."

He examines me, then nods, squinting. "I know. I know. This is your dream. But why don't we wait to see if they all come back alive before we decide about that?"

Oh. He's right. There could be all kinds of traps down there. Or worse. Now I'm scared for them. The tables have turned, and if something bad happens, I can't get in there to help. Not without a mask. I start tracking the time.

22

———

INS AND OUTS

WHAT ARE they *doing* in there? My eyes keep coming back to the piles of dirt and cement chunks that mark the entrance, the unburied concrete steps that drop out of sight. Where are they? Time is running out. *Please come back.*

I should be hoping they don't. We'd be free. But a glimpse of the grief I would feel is enough to make me crave being in custody. I need her to be okay. All of them.

Finally, a figure appears, and I ease. The She emerge in single file, each showing relief as they remove their face masks and inhale fresh air. Their eager chatter draws me, and I strain to listen.

Nance says, "Did you see the sign in the conference room? Genhance Laboratories."

"It suggests genetic research," says Aida. "We'll know when we get a look at the labs down there, but it would fit the scale of this operation." The She glance at each other.

Onyx scratches the back of her neck. "If they did genetic research here, that could explain why they buried it. There was violent opposition to that kind of research back then."

"But we're jumping to conclusions," says Kāya. "Let's see what we've got here first."

They notice us by the truck and lower their voices.

"So," I call as they approach, "what do you think?"

They leave it to Kāya to speak for them. "Phew." She rubs her scalp. "This is ... an amazing find. We didn't even scratch the surface."

I beam. "I told you it was—"

Nance interrupts. "Kāya, we're going to need a lot more oxygen, at least until we can get some air flowing."

"We can start by putting the blower at the bottom of the stairs, here, to blow some of the crap out," says Aida.

"Good. Val, get on it," Kāya says.

"If we're going in for supplies, we should pick up a couple of big fans, some more oxygen and hydrogen canisters, and fresh fuel cells. And we need to fix that topside door."

"Agreed."

"I'm not waiting," says Nance. "I need to get down there to explore the lower levels and see what we've got. We'll need to ration oxygen until we can resupply."

"You're right, Nance. You and Aida get top priority. We need a full site evaluation. We'll be here for a while, so we need to dig a latrine." Kāya looks at us. "Make that two. Far apart. Then we'll clean up the area around this doorway."

Looks like I won't be getting back inside anytime soon. But at least she hasn't said anything about getting rid of us, even though they don't need us anymore.

I need to stop fretting and focus on staying useful. I'm good with a shovel, but it's humbling to see the four of them doing the work of eight men. Onyx comes over to help us out, grumbling about how she can't keep up with Kāya, who even turns digging into a competition.

As we work, I feel her out. "Sounds like you know her well."

"Fourteen years together."

"You grew up together?"

"I was twenty-one when I met her. She was twenty-five."

That would make Kāya ... thirty-nine. And in her mid-twenties back when I was drooling over her posters. She age so slowly.

"She was already a big name in the Elite Guard when I made the apprentice roster. I worked and trained under her, and over time we became good friends."

"Only the best enforcers get selected to the Elite Guard," says Dray. "You must have already been pretty good."

She leans in, looking around for eavesdroppers. "It took four years and a lot of help from Kāya to get in. It was a prestigious job, but brutal work. Discovered I didn't have the stomach for it, but I hung in for her. When Kāya decided to quit and study to be a historian, she invited me along, and I jumped at the chance. This is only our second year in business. And from what I've seen so far, this place could be my ticket out."

"Out of what?"

"The world of fighting. Of duty. Of endless competition. I'd rather be a teacher."

Dray asks, "Why haven't you done that?"

She looks down and sighs. "Kāya still needs me. And ... I owe her everything. But now it looks like things are on the right track."

She straightens and looks around, then squints at us. "I trust you can keep this to yourselves."

My heart swells as I realize how much she has entrusted to us. We step on each other to assure her. "Absolutely."

I watch as she turns back to the job. Dray is one lucky freeman. No, we're both lucky to have come across this extraordinary She.

Working together, we finish faster than I expect and move on to making dinner. Dray and I prepare a hearty stew from vegetables and some beef we found in a cooler in vacuum-packed slabs. I recognized the packaging as local. Hillhaven has two bioreactors that produce top-grade cultured meats in their vats, but it's been outside our price range lately. This will be a treat.

The explorers return before we have dinner ready, and the She gather to discuss what they saw. We listen in as Nance reports to Kāya.

"I'm afraid we didn't get far. This place is beyond anything I've ever seen. There are five levels, each the size of the top one, all connected by a central stairway. The whole place was serviced by elevators, which, of course, are out of commission. We decided to start at the bottom, because that's where we expected to find the building's power and utilities."

Aida cuts in. "It would make a world of difference if we could bring any of it back to life. Especially the ventilation."

"Anyway, we were right. The bottom is the utilities level, with a large data center, the environmental control center and the water and power systems. And you're not going to believe this." Nance looks around as everyone perks up. "It's got a geothermal power plant."

"Geothermal?" Kāya asks.

"The place was built to be self-sufficient. Maybe we'll get lucky, and it will still work, but it'll be a major job to get the power plant running again."

The She exchange glances, and Kāya rubs her neck. "Geothermal power. So, that's potentially good for us, but it raises the question of why."

"Yes, it does. It would have been a huge investment. Which means whatever they were doing here had considerable funding."

"Government or private?"

"Don't know yet. We need to get back down there and see if we can find records."

The team spends the entire meal planning out the next day. Listening to the discussion about the deep geothermal power plant, I grow skeptical. I know digging and drilling, and I don't care how advanced they were in the Before, there's no way they drilled pipes down *several miles* into the ground. When I point this out, Aida smirks and says, "Yeah, it would be like constructing a building a hundred stories high." The others chuckle, and I blush as images from the Shell flash through my mind.

Onyx comes to my rescue. "It's good to be skeptical, Tye. History contains a lot of misinformation. In this case, the proof will be in the power." The others laugh, but it's not at me. I admire her anew.

After dinner, the academics drive off, heading to town for supplies. They'll be staying overnight in the "satellite office" and shopping in the morning. Having been there before, Nance knows where it is.

The rest of us turn in early. Dray is still bubbly from the evening's jovial conversation around the campfire. Being included by a group of She without being the target of derision is a novelty.

When I finally lie down, I no longer feel close to sleep. Too many uncertainties about tomorrow.

The rumble of thunder in the distance alerts us. We may have to race to get all these tents down if a storm moves in.

As I lie there in the dark, the thunder becomes more frequent, until Dray says, "What do you think?"

"Hard to tell. But Onyx checked the weather."

"We should check again." He crawls out and heads toward their tent, and I start to follow, but stop outside to check the sky. On the northern horizon, an enormous cloud bank strobes pure white, then black again. The distant rumble intensifies, almost constant now. I watch in awe as pulsing bolts of lightning stream from cloud to massive cloud across half the sky.

My heart leaps as a bright flash illuminates a large figure standing atop a nearby mound. I glue my wide eyes to the spot, petrified, as another flash confirms the nightmare. Someone is up there, not twenty yards away. I want to scream out a warning, but my lungs don't work. Someone big. The figure takes shape in a series of quick flashes, and I see it's a female form, facing north. I know that figure. I ease. It's Kāya.

I follow her in intermittent flashes as she turns and makes her way back down to ground level. "It's not coming this way," she calls out. "It's going to blow by us to the north."

A lucky break for us, but I feel for whoever is in its path. I wave as she makes her way back to their tent, but she doesn't respond. I go back inside and lie down, and the lightning follows me. The tent walls catch each flash as the sky cracks and growls. How am I gonna sleep now?

"Tye?"

It's Kāya's voice, just outside the tent. "Yes?"

"Can I join you?"

I look around, uncertain. "Where's Dray?"

"With Onyx for the night."

For the night? I fluster. There's an empty tent over there she could use, but she came here? To join me? My heart speeds up. "Uh, sure. Come in."

She zips the door closed after her. "It's been quite a day. How are you doing?"

"I'm okay. Tired."

"Not too tired, I hope."

Never too tired for you. "No, I'm fine."

"That's what I like to hear." She starts removing her nightshirt. I watch in the strobing light, heart soaring.

I've prayed for a chance to make things right between us. My mind goes back to the last time we were intimate. I need to know what I did wrong, so I don't make the same mistake. If I can get her talking, maybe get her to open up a bit, she can get to know me and start to see me as a person and not just a convenience. Maybe we can get past this awkwardness and relate on a deeper level, where I would have value in her eyes. She'd come to value my company, my friendship, value ... me. If only I can get her talking. I inhale.

"Kāya, that first night together, back at my place—your place, in Hillhaven, was there something—"

She holds up a hand, a stop sign, stark in the lightning. "Let's not talk."

The words hit me like a body blow. I slump, eviscerated. She doesn't care about me as a person. Why would she? Why would I think ...? Feeling faint, I go flaccid as I fight for breath.

"What?" she asks.

A muffled boom. I stare at the ground, at my bloody heart spattered there. I struggle to get the words out. "I ... I don't think ... I can do this."

She glares at me. "What do you mean? I thought you were feeling better." Her face, menacing and distorted, flashes in the gloom.

I've been fooling myself. I could never be anything to her. My blood goes cold. "I mean, I can't ... I'm not willing. I'm gonna go and sleep in the empty tent."

She kneels, slack-jawed, hulking, as I fumble with the tent fly and topple through into the evening air, where the flashes are stark and piercing. With no will to survive, I stumble off toward the storm.

"*Stop.*"

Shock jolts me like a lightning strike as a pouncing figure lands at my side, towering over me.

"You do *not* just walk away from me!"

Another boom. The world is on a killing spree.

23

THE ART OF FIGHTING

Kāya's eyes flash in the lightning, and in them I see myself, tiny, insignificant. The afterimage burns. *I will not be that.* "Or what? You'll beat the shit out of me? What. Kill me?" I glare up at her. "I live with that threat every day, Kāya. I'm tired of it. I can't live like this. So if you're gonna do it, just fucking get it over with."

I'm beyond fear. I already died earlier; it wasn't so bad. Still, I turn away, not wanting to see death come, and steer myself toward the other tent with no expectation of reaching it. Each moment is my last.

"Tye."

What am I gonna do, run? I stop, heart hammering.

"Tye, what are you doing?"

Her tone is unexpected. It's not an attack, but rather ... uncertain. I try to keep my feet. "I don't know." I take a stand, looking away. A sound from one of the other tents alerts us that they can hear us. She lowers her voice.

"Am I unattractive to you?"

The question throws me off balance. The absurdity of it burps an involuntary laugh from me. I steady myself. "You are the most beautiful She I have ever seen."

"Then why don't you want me? I don't understand. Any man would happily … Is there something wrong with you?"

Wrong with me. Yeah, there is. Most men accept being used. I'm a freeman because I won't. Not anymore. I hug myself, rocking on my feet. *Steel your heart. Steel your heart.* "I'll tell you what's wrong with me." I see her hunch and lower my voice. "I'm a freeman. That's what." I have nothing left to lose. "And you are my oppressor. Your literal job is to oppress freemen, and I'm supposed to be okay with that?"

"It's only one small part of our duties."

Her defensiveness startles and delights me. I press the attack. "And you exploit me because you can. You can force me to do whatever you want. You can demand obedience." A flash shows her scowling down at me, eyes blazing, but I'm committed. "You abuse your power over me, Kāya, and I'm not gonna take it anymore."

She stands frozen, and in what could be my final moments, I savor the deep-throated power in the distant rumbling. Her voice is like a splash of water in the face.

"Okay, okay. You're a freeman. I can respect that."

I'm stunned speechless, yet a response emerges from some deep, hidden calm within me. "That's all I ask, Kāya." I turn my back on her, uncertain, and start toward the empty tent. With each step my confusion mounts. *Respect that?*

"Tye? Can we talk?"

I stop, thunderstruck by the words. She wants to talk? Dubious, I play along. "What would you like to talk about?"

"Back to the tent?"

I hear a plea in her voice, and my resistance falters. "Okay."

I start following her in and hesitate in the doorway.

"I'm not going to hurt you," she says. "I just … want you to understand."

Understand? I strain to see her in the gloom and wait, uncertain. Then I tentatively sit and close the zipper.

Her tone is hushed, like a confession. "For my whole life, men have been throwing themselves at me. Until I was sixteen, they were simply a nuisance. I was a youth champion by that age, so I got lots of attention. I had an entourage of men following me around all the time. Then, when I'd have sex with them, they'd start clinging to me, fighting among themselves, getting in my way no matter what I was trying to do. It became unmanageable. I even had to hurt a couple of them just to get them out of my face. Then,"—a sharp inhalation—"let's just say bad things happened, and I learned that it's better to avoid emotional attachments and simply focus on the art. So that's what I do."

"The art?"

"Of fighting. The path to domination."

We're actually talking. "I'm a fighter, too."

She smirks. "You're not a fighter."

I harden. "I fight for the right to live a free life. As a man, I fight hard every day, against impossible odds. I get beaten down over and over and I come back for more."

"Yeah, but that's not—"

I clench my teeth. "I step into the ring, with my life at stake, every time I speak to you, Kāya. Tell me again I'm not a fighter."

She is still as a statue. Then she eases. "Your life is not at stake here, freeman."

The thunder has faded into the distance. "It feels like it, sometimes."

"I've never come across anyone quite like you, and I'm not sure how to deal with you."

"Deal with me? You deal with troublemakers. I don't want to be dealt with, Kāya."

"No, I didn't mean ... I meant, how to relate to you."

She seems sincere, and I'm drawn in. "I've never experienced anyone like you either, so I guess we're even."

"I don't trust men."

"I can relate to that. I don't trust She."

"And yet here we are."

"Crazy, right?" I lay down beside her. A strange peace rolls over me as we snuggle in, face to face. Her scent floods me and I lose all clarity. I can't see her face in the darkness. Instead, I listen to her breathe and thrill to her closeness.

Her voice is soft. "Can I hold you?"

What's happening here? A moment of hesitation. "Yes."

She gently wraps me in her arms and, with tentative shifts, pulls me to her. Squeezing my eyes shut against the flicker of the distant storm, I melt into her and nuzzle her shoulder, rubbing my lips against her skin, eager to taste her but not daring. As we cuddle, I hear her breathing slow, feel our hearts beat in syncopation as my whole being fills with her close presence.

Her voice licks my eardrum. "This is nice. It's been a long time since I felt comfortable with a man. It's a wonderful feeling, Tye, to know you won't latch on to me like a leech and be difficult ..."

The spell is abruptly broken, and I'm disoriented.

"... to know freedom is as important to you as it is to me. This could be mutually beneficial."

"How do you mean?"

"It turns out we both want to live free of emotional commitment. It's a win-win."

I wince. Is it, though? All I know is that I'm playing with fire. "Yes, I can see the logic."

"I have a request. You are free to say no."

"Go ahead."

"I'm a little on the horny side. Are you willing?"

The scent of her skin flushes all reason from my mind, and my heart defies me. "Now I am."

I'M AWAKENED by movement and find the tent warm with morning sun. Kāya is crawling out through the door. Peeking out, I see the storm has moved on and the sky is clearing.

I climb out into the fresh chill. Kāya and Onyx are laughing as they pull on shorts and running bras. Dray checks me out as I approach to help prepare breakfast, then flashes his eyebrows when I smile. We both had a good night.

"I was worried last night," he says in a quiet aside. "Sounded like a fight out here. Onyx assured me you were in no danger."

"I wish she'd told me that."

Bree and Val emerge from their tent, put on their exercise wear, then loosen up before coming over. Kāya addresses the two of us. "We're on our way out for a run. We've got a free morning until Nance and Aida get back, so after our run we'll come back for a quick bite, then we're going to spend a couple of hours sparring. If you want to go for a run, don't go far."

The four of them head off at a jog, heading up through the trees in single file. Dray and I stand staring after them until they're out of sight. He drapes his arm over my shoulder as we turn back to our task. "I'm starting to like this place."

By the time they get back from their run, panting and glistening with sweat, we've got the campsite cleaned up. My eager eyes dart back and forth, trying to take them all in. After we finish eating, I recognize the outfits they're changing into. It's the same fighting gear Kāya wore against Luce, except with face guards. I tighten.

I restrain myself from yelling out to her, *You can't be fighting*. Both pairs of opponents stake out patches of nearby ground, and I can't hold back. "Kāya, are you sure this is a good idea? You're still healing."

It is Onyx who answers. "It's okay, Tye. I'll be careful."

Kāya adds, "It's been too long already. We can't afford to get rusty. The Spring Ranking tournaments are coming up."

Fine. Be stubborn. I'm not gonna watch this lunacy.

But I can't help it. "They're not fighting, they're sparring," Dray explains when he sees me biting a knuckle. "They're not trying to hurt each other."

If Onyx is being careful, I sure can't see it. She seems to throw herself at Kāya with abandon, get knocked aside, spin back up and go at her again. Then the flow reverses, and Kāya is the aggressor. Their movements are a blur as they bounce around each other, striking out with hands and feet, grappling, throwing each other down. They frequently stop and exchange words, reviewing moves and repeating sequences. Then they switch partners and do it all again.

They're all breathing hard when they wander together back to the trucks. I'm relieved it's finally over, then notice they are all changing into their regalia. And this is new. They're putting on heavy leather skirts, full front-plates, and helmets.

I call out, "What's this for?"

Onyx answers as the others ignore me. "Battle armor."

"What—"

"It offers more protection than our regalia, but it's heavier. Slows you down."

Back in their original pairings but now armed with bokken, they warm up with a series of stylized strikes, blocks and jabs. Then they return to their makeshift rings and salute each other.

With a shout, both pairs of She lunge into battle, and I jump as the cracks of wood on wood split the air. First one attacks with a series of lightning strikes, then the other, with only the occasional whack of wood on armor. The action is often too quick for my eyes to follow, but the swishes and cracks leave me shuddering at the ferocity. I've seen staged sword fights before, but they bore no resemblance to the speed and intensity of this. The stories that used to strike terror into my heart, stories about an Alpha and her bokken, are playing out in front of my eyes.

I used to have fantasies about a group of men with shovels fighting back against an enforcer. I feel sick wondering how long it would take before we were all dead. Six seconds?

I can't watch any more. What has always been a fabled threat now feels all too real. An Alpha has no need to draw her bokken on a man, I remind myself. It doesn't help.

I withdraw to my tent in turmoil. I lie there with my hands over my ears, unable to reconcile the vicious warrior out there with the She who was cuddling me last night.

But before the cuddling ... I shiver. Last night, I lost it. By running out like that, I almost revealed my heart. A dangerous blunder. But then I stood up to her, and she backed down. Curious. Why would she do that?

It was as if my disobedience surprised her but then reassured her. She backed down because she saw me as a freeman and didn't feel threatened. That's the key, right there. It seems crazy, but if pushing her away is the only way she'll let me close, then that's what I've got to do.

24

DELIBERATELY BURIED

WE PREPARE a simple lunch of cold cuts, fresh beans, bread and cheese as the She discuss their plans for the afternoon's expeditions into the dark. When the fighters sit down to eat, Kāya is still over in the truck, where she has been on the radio for what feels like an hour.

"What's going on?" I ask.

"She's trying to register this claim," says Onyx. "There's an outpost just east of the Shell that acts as a remote claim registration office. They're pushing for more details on our location."

"Which they don't need yet," says Kāya, joining us. "We're the only team operating in the area. I wanted them to know we're here, staking a claim. We'll get the details to them when we're ready."

For the rest of the day, the She emerge every half-hour for a short break and fresh oxygen. Though the enforcers are wearing their khakis instead of regalia, I note that they still have their bokken strapped to their waists. Always ready for trouble. We hear their excitement as they compare notes, and I eavesdrop my ass off, soaking up every detail.

"... never seen anything like those labs," says Kāya. "What's with those containment rooms, Nance? What was so dangerous about genetics research?"

"They could have been studying viral pathogens. Maybe trying to develop a vaccine."

Bree cuts in. "Maybe developing a bioweapon."

"Unlikely. No sign of this being a military installation."

They notice me and stop to glare. Bree snaps, "Get out of here, freeman."

"Uh, anybody need a drink?" With no takers, I slink off to a safe distance. A bioweapon? I don't know what all that was about, but I feel more compelled than ever to get down there and see for myself what they're so thrilled about.

During one break, Onyx tells me, "It's like we suspected. This place was deliberately buried."

"Why would they ...?"

"Don't know. But it explains why we can't find a main entrance. The lower levels were all serviced by elevators. Those three doors you saw are for the elevators."

"Elevators?"

"They're like fancy, high-speed lifts."

"Ah." The deepest lift I've been in carried freight down two levels.

"They had to be high-speed in the skyscrapers."

"Ah." I nod, embarrassed that I never considered how people went up into those impossible towers.

They've got a decent map of the layout now. The top level is mostly offices, with a cafeteria area, a media room and a conference room. The second has some living quarters and an energy research lab. Level three houses several bio-labs, and level four, a chem lab, a fabrication lab, and several workshops. Level five is the utilities level. The power system has everyone abuzz.

Aida says, "I studied these deep geothermal systems in school and visited the one they have working north of Provender. We're going to need to prime the pumps. Lots and lots of water. Then we'll need heavy-duty portable power to start the thing up, but from there, it's automated, so it should run itself."

I'm still skeptical. Were the people of the Before that far beyond us? And they still couldn't save their world?

Later, as we sit around the fire, the She relax with cider and swap stories about past exploits. When the topic turns to men, Dray and I both start squirming. Yet it's refreshing to see their openness despite our presence.

Bree leans back. "So, Onyx, how is it that you're so soft on men?"

If it's supposed to be a put-down, Onyx takes it in stride. "I grew up with four brothers. I was the only girl, the star of the family."

"Whoa. Four brothers? Tough break."

"Not at all. It was a blessing. I loved each one of them. Still do. Of course, it's only three now."

The group quiets. "What happened?" Bree asks.

"Ando and a friend were killed by bandits in the outskirts. It was a fight over their bikes, we were told. His bike was his most prized possession." Onyx shakes her head.

"I'm so sorry," says Bree, sitting up.

"I was fifteen at the time. It's why I went into enforcement."

"Fifteen is old to start," says Val. "You wouldn't be an Alpha unless you had a natural talent for it. You must have known earlier."

"Well, yeah, but before then, I never took training seriously. They say every young girl dreams of being an Alpha when she grows up, but not me. I was more into having fun, hanging out with friends. Ando's murder changed that. I was going to end up either in enforcement or in prison."

"I'm lucky you made the right choice," says Kāya.

Dray surprises me when he says, "I lost a brother too. Jamie drowned in the river when he was six. It was my fault."

I gasp. What's he doing sharing something so personal with these She? I break into the sudden silence. "It wasn't your fault. Everyone blamed you, but it wasn't."

"I shouldn't have let him go."

"He was with his friends. How could you stop him?"

"I should have been watching—"

"Stop it, Dray. You weren't even there. There's nothing—"

Onyx cuts in. "It still hurts, though, doesn't it."

Dray sucks in air, meets her eyes and lingers there. "Yes, it does."

"I know." She looks around at her friends. "In some ways, I'm the lucky one. I get to take it out on my opponents in the ring." She returns her eyes to him. "What do you do with it, Dray? With the hurt?"

He glances around and shrugs.

"I'm sorry," she says. "I shouldn't have asked that. It's none of our business."

His whole attitude, over all these years, now makes more sense. How could I not have seen it before? And this She, who barely knows us, sees it right away. A sense of shame fills me, and I shift over to put my arms around him. "I'm sorry, too, freeman."

He shrugs again. "Old news."

An ache of envy. To be able to trust a She with your pain …

Val raises her cup. "To the ones we've lost."

It's a somber chorus. "The ones we've lost." I notice Kāya doesn't join in.

———

THE DAY HAS BEEN DRAGGING ON FOREVER. Since finishing their morning workouts, the She have been in and out, their brief breaks providing the only highlights. Dray and I count down the minutes to their return as we clean latrines, fill oxygen canisters and prepare refreshments and meals. They appear, gushing with excitement, eat, resupply and then, too soon, disappear again.

As Dray fiddles with something in the tank truck, I sit fuming. They're never gonna trust us enough to let us see what all the fuss is about. The whole place is restricted—

My mother's book.

I glance around. I've got at least twenty minutes to myself. An opportunity. The first time I've dared since we got here. I slink into our tent and timidly unwrap the book from the bundle of clothes in my pack. There is an introduction to the section on the Rules. I didn't bother with it before, but it may be important:

The Guiding Principle: We are She. Never again will She be submissive to men, never again treated as property, suppressed and subservient. She will use all necessary force to assert our dominance and ensure the enduring freedom of all She.

This makes no sense at all. A metaphor, maybe? But for what? I read on.

Commentary: The honorific, "She," first introduced in the Manifesto, is used to distinguish post-Inversion females from the smaller, weaker females of the Before, known as women. The distinction was relevant until the last of the surviving women died out some twenty years ago. Today, all living females are She. The term highlights a break with the past, emphasizing the female dominance and leaving no doubt as to who is in charge. Men are to be reminded of this at every opportunity.

The Principle reveals the fears of the ForeMothers, instilled by their direct exposure to the ways of the past and the vicious resistance to change they endured. It was the horrific male backlash against their challenge to the old power structures that led to the creation of the Manifesto—

My heart thumps as a voice jars me. A She, too close. I slam the book closed and jam it under a pile of clothes. The She are back early. I rush out and meet up with Dray at the barbecue, still reeling with confusion, mind blanking on the nonsensical words I just read. I'm grateful to be ignored as we rush to get them fed. Dray is looking forward to an evening together by the fire. We're still cleaning up when the call comes.

"Tye." Kāya's voice is firm. "Over here."

I glance at Dray, and he shies away. *How does she know?*

I approach with pointless caution. I can't run, can't evade her. I feel the remorse rising from me like steam.

She ignores my distress. "I'm sending you on an assignment. It requires I trust you, because I don't want my Bravos harming you, and if you give them cause, they will."

What? This isn't about—?

"Can I trust you not to force their hand? Can I trust you to say nothing about this place to anyone?"

"Of course, Kāya."

She studies me, then nods. "Here's the way it is. We're going to need your flatbed truck and power shovel for some work we've got planned. I understand they've been impounded and are waiting for repairs. You will tell people you've found work in Chesterton and need the vehicles back, and you will pay up front for the repairs."

I hesitate. "But people in town who saw me get arrested will wonder what I'm doing back. Are you sure that's a good idea?"

"You will explain that you found one of your mother's old devices in her twin-dome, and it was confiscated. Tell them you were found innocent of sedition and released."

"You want me to lie to everyone."

She shrugs. "You're a man. It shouldn't be hard."

I sigh. No, it shouldn't.

She trusts me to lie well. It's the only trust I deserve.

25

R & R

We're expecting a cool, wet night tonight, so I'm not looking forward to sleeping in the truck. I do a double take when I see two enticing She emerge. It's Bree and Val in civilian clothes, wearing wigs. Huh. They're gonna try to pass for business travelers.

Dray carries my pack over to the truck for me, complaining all the way. "You're gonna get to have a hot shower, go out for a beer, see the guys again, it's not fair. Why can't I go?"

"They know I'm not gonna try to escape and leave you behind. It's safer to split us up. Besides, wouldn't you rather spend the night with Onyx?"

He pauses, then changes course. "If you're in Sheena's, could you bring me back a jug of beer?" He throws my pack in the back.

"I'll try." I give him a hug. "You behave."

"How am I gonna get in trouble around here? *You* behave."

Bree is behind the wheel, unrecognizable in her afro wig. "Let's go, freeman." Her impatience spurs me to action, and I hop in the back. Dray stands, his outstretched finger pointing at me in the freeman salute that says, *You're devalued by She, but you have value to me.* I salute back with the *you have value* finger-point until the truck starts rolling and I get jostled and have to sit. I watch my dearest friend until I lose sight of him, then turn to see where I am.

Bree warns, "Our bokken are under that bench. Keep your hands off them."

"Of course." I'm sitting behind two deadly beauties who don't seem to like me, probably because my presence puts them all at risk. But how is that my fault?

We cut through the bush on our own tire tracks and are soon out to the old roadbed. It's an easy drive from here.

I should at least try to be friendly. I lean forward. "Val, do you mind if I ask you a question?"

Even stooped, her blond wig brushes the ceiling as she glances back. "That depends on the question."

"How long have you been working with Kāya?"

"Coming up on two years."

"What's she like to work with?"

Her response is cold. "How is that relevant to you?"

"I'm just interested."

"Don't get your hopes up, freeman. She burns through alpha males pretty quick, and you're not even close—"

"No, no, I was—She seems strict about everything. That's got to be hard—"

"Kāya held a position of command in the Elite Guard for many years. You will never find a more disciplined professional."

Bree glances back. "Which is why your arrival in the Shell was disconcerting. But I guess she knew what she was doing." She and Val exchange looks. "Not sure why you're still here, though."

Time to change the subject. "I've seen you two fight, and you're very good. Why aren't you Alphas?"

Bree answers. "You have to earn the gold collar. This will be my year."

"I've never seen a Ranking Tournament. Never been to the city. Provender's a two-day trip from here. And expensive."

They exchange looks like they can't believe anyone could be so deprived. "So, this little town and its backward folk are all you know of the world." Big Val shakes her head, then takes it upon herself to educate me. "If you rank high enough, you get colors. You've got to be in the top one percent of competitors to wear gold."

"What about silver?"

"Top five percent."

"So you *are* very good."

"Bree only challenges Alphas," Val says, then looks away. "Going to get herself broken one of these days."

Bree doesn't look over. "Unless you push yourself, Val, you're never going to get ahead."

"Ahead of working for Kāya? No such place. Happy where I am," says Val. "Besides, one of us needs to have some sense, or who's going to bandage you up?"

Sensing tension, I jump in. "You get injured?"

Bree juts out her chin. "It's a tough business. The attrition rate is high. But if you're determined enough, you come back and try again next year. What doesn't break you toughens you."

I wish male physiology were that robust.

Val scowls at her. "I can hold my own."

Softening, Bree reaches over and touches her arm. "I know you can. I just think you're better than you give yourself credit for."

Val puts her large hand on Bree's, and they touch eyes. I ease back with relief, pleased by their willingness to open up in front of me. We seem to be getting along, so I'm emboldened to go further. "Are you two a couple? You seem close."

"Being close doesn't make you a couple," Val says. "The love we have for one another is not something a man could understand. Love means trusting with your life."

Bree takes over. "When you face deadly dangers every day, you want to know that those around you are always there for you, no matter what. There can be no deeper love than feeling safe to put your very life in someone else's hands. But we can't expect you to know that."

"You don't think men ever face deadly dangers?" I scoff.

"Not if you are where you're supposed to be."

This isn't an argument I can win, so I move on. "You both prefer men?"

Val uses the old cliché. "We have preferences, but we don't always have choices." Then adds, "After a week in the Shell, Bree's better than nothing." She gets a swat for that, and they both laugh.

Bree adds, "We haven't had any men to play with for a while. We intend to have a fun time tonight."

Val says, "There aren't many freemen around. I hope we'll find some at this bar we're going to."

"There aren't many freemen around because She make it nearly impossible to survive as a freeman," I say.

Val turns back to scrutinize me. "You hate She, don't you, Tye."

"No, I don't. I hate the way they treat men sometimes, but I—"

"Noooo," says Bree. "It's only what we do, how we live, how we keep you safe and cared for that you hate."

I rub my scalp. This went into the ditch awfully fast. It's enforcers who hate freemen, but I'm not gonna bring that up. I bite my tongue and sit back.

It turns out they don't need my directions until we get into town. As we pull up to my former home, I notice an unfamiliar jeep parked some distance up the lane. Curious. That's unusual around here. Its lights are off, and from this distance I can't see inside.

"So this is our new home base," says Val. "How about showing us around inside so we can get freshened up? Then you can take us to this bar we've been hearing about."

———

AFTER A FITFUL NIGHT trying to sleep in the back of the truck, I wake up early but stay snuggled in against the chill. The events of last evening cycle through my head.

The repair garage people were surprised to see me, judging by the 'For sale as is' signs on our vehicles. The check from my 'new employer' impressed them enough to promise to get the work done in a week. Dealing with them from a position of power for the first time was exhilarating.

It was strange to be in Sheena's Bar without Dray. Notified by Danner that I was there, Sheena herself was the first one to come over and ask what I was doing back. I had no trouble getting the story out over free drinks. When did I ever get that kind of treatment before?

The night in the twin-dome must have gone okay. Out front in the truck bed, I stopped paying attention when they came past with that second pair of men.

I'm startled by a knock. I must have dozed off.

"Rise and shine." It's Val, with no wig. "The shower is free if you want a hot one."

"Uh, yeah. Thanks."

I sulk as I check around inside. Nothing has changed. It's as if it's still mine, and I pretend it is, luxuriating in the shower with utter disregard for time. When I finally come back out to the truck, the two Bravos are already out there, waiting.

It must have been a very good night. As we pull away, the mood seems lighter, with the two She chatting about their exploits. From the back seat, I try to listen in without being obvious.

I had Bree pegged as a hard-nosed, no-nonsense professional, like Kāya, but I can't imagine Kāya letting loose like that when off duty. Val, in contrast, doesn't seem as hard as she acts. I'll bet she's a heart-breaker, same as Kāya. Broke a couple more last night, no doubt. Even freemen have secret hopes of love—hopes too dangerous to expose.

I notice the jeep as we're heading out of town. I watch for it as we pull onto the hard-packed gravel of Indy Park Road, and there it is, far back. "We're being followed," I say.

The two Bravos turn and scan behind. "What are you talking about?"

"That jeep way back there. It was parked in my old neighborhood, probably staking out Kāya's domes. I'll bet it's the same trackers who followed us into the Shell, then went and told Luce."

Val looks at me. "You noticed them in town? Why didn't you say something?"

"I wasn't sure. But the only reason they'd be out here right now is to track us to Kāya's new site."

Bree studies the rearview mirror. "That's not going to happen. We're going to have a little chat with them."

"More than a chat," says Val. "If they are trackers, they'll require a strong deterrent."

"What are you gonna do?" I ask.

"Trackers are the most stubborn of creatures," says Bree. "I'd feel a lot safer if we took them out of play."

Wait. What does that—

"Agreed," says Val. Then she turns to me. "You can drive a jeep, right?"

"Yes, I can drive, but—"

"Good."

"What are you gonna do?"

"Whatever works."

We crest a small hill, and on the downslope, Bree pulls off the road behind a clump of shrubs and does a quick three-point turn. It is only a minute before the jeep rolls by. They see us right away, but we're on their tail before they can do anything. It looks like we're about to ram into them, but they have the faster vehicle and start to pull away. Bree floors it, trying to keep up. Now we're careening along at breakneck speed, faster than I've ever gone, flying over gravel that would act like ice if we had to maneuver. I cling to the bench with all my strength as we stutter over ruts and potholes, watching death whiz by on both sides.

Val calls out, "They're headed for the Shell, and we can't take you in there. If they reach it, we'll have to throw you out so we can follow. Get ready to jump."

Jump? I'm no She; I wouldn't survive that.

At a sideroad, we see the jeep braking hard to make the corner. I'm thrown forward as Bree brakes in anticipation.

"Get ready," she yells.

I'm gonna die.

The jeep up ahead swerves hard, throwing up a cloud of dust, then slides off to the left, dropping out of sight. Moments later, we arrive to find the jeep on its side in the deep ditch. One of the trackers takes off running for the tree line as the other climbs up through the driver's-side door.

The truck slides to a halt, and the two Bravos leap out and sprint in pursuit. I watch in awe as they fly across the uneven ground in powerful leaps and bounds. One of the fleeing trackers is limping, and Val swiftly runs her down and puts her on the ground. The other tracker disappears into the bush and Bree follows.

Within seconds, Val is sprinting after Bree. The captured tracker sits on the ground, head bowed in resignation. She awkwardly shifts position, and I see she's in handcuffs.

I sit waiting, uncertain, watching to see what the prisoner is gonna do with her captors out of sight. She looks to the overturned jeep, then to the truck. I'm dangerously exposed. But she just sits, not even trying to get to her feet, and as the minutes pass, I gradually ease. Then I start to feel sorry for her. I know what it feels like to be a prisoner. I wonder what they're gonna do to her.

They finally emerge from the bush. The second prisoner, about Bree's size, is now also hobbling in handcuffs. As they get closer, I see blood on her face and a bright red bruise on her cheek. One eye is swollen half-shut.

Val must see the horror on my face. "She should've come peace-fully. She chose not to."

She hauls the seated prisoner to her feet and drags her to the truck as Bree does the same with the other. My emotions swirl as I see the two trackers up close. It's agonizing to see a battered face, and I have to turn away. I glance at the other to confirm she's okay and need to brace to resist her appeal. I quickly look away and remind myself that if she could, she'd turn me over to Luce for execution. Maybe in a different world—

"Out!" Bree orders me. I comply without thinking, jumping down and backing away like the truck's on fire.

"You two. In." The two trackers struggle to climb into the back, and Val checks that their cuffs are secure. Then she and Bree head over to examine the jeep, and not knowing what else to do, I follow at a safe distance, trembling.

"Did you really have to—" I stop as Bree straightens and glares at me.

Val steps in. "Just because trackers can't fight worth shit doesn't mean they aren't dangerous. And right now, these two are a serious threat to us. So shut up and let us do our jobs."

It takes only minutes to get the jeep back on its wheels, and I help with the hook-up to tow it onto the road. Though it's bashed up on one side and has a wobbly front wheel, it's still drivable.

Val hands me the keys. "Take it to Kāya as salvage. We'll find some use for it."

"What are you gonna do with—"

"We're going to take a drive over to Waverly."

"Waverly?" Why would they be going there? It's even smaller and more remote than Hillhaven, about two hours further west. Two hours of wilderness. I lean in and whisper to Val, "Please tell me you're not gonna kill them."

She looks down at me, and her voice is soft as she meets my eyes. "We're not going to kill them."

An intimate warmth of trust flushes through me, and I ease.

In a quiet aside, she adds, "Oh, and freeman. Good job spotting them."

Then her normal voice returns. "Tell Kāya we'll try to be back before dinner."

Still bubbling inside, I snap to attention and give a crisp nod. "Will do."

In breathless wonder, I watch them pull away. They're treating me as part of the team.

I check my pack on the passenger seat. I almost forgot to snatch it from the back of the truck before they left. They wouldn't likely have searched it, but what if they did? It would destroy everything.

And here I am, out in the wilds by myself, with no one around. Opportunities like this are what I've been waiting for. No need to rush back.

26

BOOK OF POISON

It's midmorning as I sit in the driver's seat of the salvaged jeep, parked on the shoulder of the deserted Indy Park Road. With guilty caution, I dig around inside my backpack for my mother's book. It's wrapped in a towel and hidden among my spare clothes. I check around before again marveling at the cover. *The She Manifesto: Notes from a Cultural Historian.* The name Celia, in a larger, bolder font, proclaims my mother's importance back then. A swell of pride. I wonder what ever happened to her. A familiar ache prompts me to reject that line of thought. I open the book and rest it on the steering wheel.

Remembering the confusion I felt the last time, I skip past the section on the Rules and browse ahead until my eyes catch on a heading. *The Inversion.*

The Inversion. The term, though meaningless to me, evokes a sense of dread, of something taboo, unspeakable. Yet here, my mother has written a chapter about it. A powerful reminder that this is restricted material, and here I am, with access to it. Floating on giddiness, I recheck my surroundings, then jump in:

The Age of Man ended in 2038 with the near extinction of the human race. No one knows how or why the Inversion happened, only that what emerged from the ashes was a changed humanity. The Inversion marked the beginning of a new age, the Age of She.

A changed humanity? The Age of She? I am gripped by the sensation of being perched on the edge of a precipice, unable to see the bottom. I read:

The end of the Before world marked our beginning. Over seven billion humans perished within months, and almost a billion more in the years that followed. Those who survived faced unimaginable hardship. Only the hardiest genes survived to be passed along to the next generation. We are the progeny of the strongest of the strong, those capable of surviving when all others died. These are the genes we carry, the genes of strength, the genes of She. You have been taught that the bio-war and subsequent collapse—

There's that term again. What is a bio-war? I hope she explains. Let's see:

You have been taught that the bio-war and subsequent collapse weeded out all the females with weak genes, and all that remained were She. This is in accordance with the law of natural selection. Why weak male genes were not weeded out, no one can explain.

What? Isn't the explanation obvious? The men were protected by She. What does she mean, no one can explain? I read on:

The historical record allows us a detailed comparison between ourselves and our predecessors. One thing is clear. We are distinct, unlike any hominid before us, including Man. Mankind. The very species is labeled for its males, with no regard for the female. But we She are not a derivative of Man. We have moved beyond them into a more enhanced version of human. They remain only Man, inferior to us in almost every way.

I frown. I have no clue what she's talking about here, but I don't like the sound of it. It's just another put-down of men. No wonder they don't want us reading it. Is that really how my mother saw my father? How she saw me? Eyes reluctant now, I continue:

It is as if evolution has taken a mighty leap forward but left men behind. We She are phylogenetically more advanced than the males of our species, which makes no sense from an evolutionary perspective. It is considered inevitable that the male genome will eventually undergo the same leap, returning us to a position of relative disadvantage unless we can maintain control.

But is it inevitable? In what follows, I will propose an alternate possibility, a new theory to explain the mystery of how we made that leap and males did not—

I hear a rustling noise and bolt upright in time to see a murder of crows take to the sky nearby. I examine the front seat for the best place to stash the book in an emergency. Under this seat will do. Now I'm ready to get back into it. I hope it's gonna start making sense soon.

What we know is this: the apocalypse left behind a surviving population that was different. It must be more than coincidence that the Inversion came out of the collapse. Whatever its cause, the Inversion has given us the chance to claw our way back from the brink of extinction and start a new world, with new rules and attitudes. We are guided by a determination to avoid the mistakes of the past, mistakes made by men who led selfishly, with callous disregard for their people.

I squint. Men who led? That must be a misprint. She must be trying to say the men were selfish and disregarded their She. She should have proofread this.

To quote the ForeMothers, "It was men who led the world to destruction, who selfishly ravaged and depleted the very natural resources upon which the population depended, who fought unspeakable wars and thoughtlessly killed the weak and the innocent in staggering numbers. It was men who launched the final war in vengeance, ensuring their own destruction. The nature of the male is demonstrated in their treatment of the planet and all those who lived on it. And though in today's world their behavior is safely constrained, we must never forget that *men have not changed.*"

Indeed, it is we She who have changed, and men have, of necessity, adapted to survive the change in us. But make no mistake. Despite appearances to the contrary, the nature of the male is as it was. And for the sake of the world and all who live within it, we must forever guard against men regaining control.

I blink. This is madness. My mother was mad. I flop back, fog swirling before my eyes. No wonder she left us. She hated us because we were worthless males. She spread vile lies about the collapse being the fault of men, when everyone knows it was the Great Pandemic that caused it. She didn't care enough about us to stay, but I thought she at least ...

I fight a wave of despair and close the book with finality. Now I deeply regret opening it. I am violating the law and everyone's trust, and for what? To learn another horrible truth about my mother? That she hated men? I had such high hopes that she would enlighten me, took all these risks to feel closer to her, and all she's done is feed me poison. I feel myself sinking and don't care.

In my mind's eye, I see the countryside blurring by at top speed, trees and rocks waiting to receive me, wanting me, enticing me with the promise of final peace. I have the keys, and the road is right there ...

I gasp. Dray. Dray needs me. Like handling a hot coal, I drop the book onto the floor beside me, shaking the toxic words from my mind. I squint up into an overcast sky and wish the stiffening breeze could carry away the stench. Why couldn't my mother have been an engineering historian, or agricultural? Why couldn't she have written something useful?

It made no sense, what she said. Guard against men? Did I read it right? Did she really say those things? I must have misinterpreted. Even if I didn't, if I skip over the crazy parts, there's bound to be something useful in there. *No.* I should just get rid of the damn thing. Why did I ever keep it in the first place?

But maybe there's a context that will help it all make sense. I sit gripping the wheel, mind still spinning, and curse my curiosity.

But I'm caught in it now. I've done this to myself. Something strange happened, she said. I've got to know what she was talking about, why she hated us so much.

I gingerly pick up the book but can't bring myself to open it. I can't face it right now. Instead, I carefully repack it.

I'll deal with all this later. Right now, I should get back, before they start wondering.

After babying the rickety jeep along, I'm relieved to make it all the way back. I pull into the encampment and see no one around. Where is Dray? I grab my pack, guarding its cruel contents, and climb out of the battered thing as Kāya and Onyx come flying out of the entrance on full alert. My guilty heart thuds. They ease when they see me, and Dray emerges behind them.

"Tye. It's you," he says. "I didn't recognize the vehicle. Thought it was intruders." He rushes over and greets me with a warm hug. "Where did you get the jeep?"

"What took you so long?" demands Kāya.

I feel the guilt oozing from me and hope she doesn't notice. "Uh, wonky wheel. Had to go slow. Val told me to tell you this was salvage. A couple of trackers were following us, so—"

Kāya cuts me off. "Yeah. Bree radioed in." They examine the damage to the jeep.

I grab Dray by the wrist and lean in. "Were you inside?"

"Just at the top of the stairs to yell down for them. I didn't know who—"

"Nice work, Tye," says Onyx. "This will come in handy once we get that wheel fixed."

"Won't the trackers want it back?" I ask.

"Did they abandon it?"

"Well, yes, but—"

"Then it's salvage, sweetie. Ours now."

"Val said they'd try to be back for dinner."

Kāya gives a disinterested nod.

I have to ask. "Why are they going to Waverly?"

"Nobody will look for the trackers there," says Kāya, as the Alphas rummage through the stuff in the back. "Not for a while, anyway. Buys us some time."

"Won't they just come back?"

"They'll be locked up in the Waverly jail until Luce bails them out. She'll have to find them first."

Of course. Enforcers have jailing authority. No one in Waverly will question the arrests. Or advertise them. A sense of relief washes over me. I knew Val wouldn't lie to my face.

———

It's late afternoon when the Bravos return to a warm welcome. As they catch up on the news, we help them unload the fresh groceries they picked up in Waverly. Aida reports that they're halfway through priming the deep wells and are now charging the system's fuel cells.

Dray and I are about to start preparing dinner when Kāya calls us all together to discuss tomorrow's agenda. To my surprise, Kāya and Onyx are leaving. They're heading to Cedarton to appraise some potential recruits and will be gone overnight. Cedarton is an hour east of Hillhaven and twice the size. Aida says they're hoping to get lucky, though she's not optimistic. For high-quality historians and Bravos, they'll need to go to the city. That's a five-day commitment, and right now, Kāya can't afford to be gone that long. I'm glad about that.

They leave right after dinner, with final instructions and a quick goodbye. Another night without her.

I give myself a shake. I can't start thinking like that. I have no right to expect to spend every night with her. I've been lucky to get the ones I've already had.

And what happened to my pride? I'm a freeman. Am I so ready to throw that away? Crap. It's easy to feed my independent spirit when I'm not looking into her eyes. But I see them even now. When I close mine, there they are, outshining the value of freedom. Maybe it's good to get some time away from her, get my feet under me again.

As a freeman, I'm supposed to refuse to be subordinate to a She. Yes, I refused her once. But I very much doubt I could do it again. As a freeman, I'm a fraud. If she knew that, she'd get rid of me, ship me away.

Because she can, whenever she wants.

And I'm not nearly enough for her, which, let's face it, makes that inevitable.

My being here depends on my ability to convince her I'm not emotionally attached to her. I'll do *anything* to prove to her I'm not desperate to be with her. I'll be the most detached freeman she can find.

27

———————

STORM

THIS TASTE OF POLLEN, this woodsy, dank, earthy smell, wasn't in the air this morning. I expected a blah day with the Alphas away. But now the wind has shifted to the south. I watch the late-afternoon sky and see two layers of dark clouds moving in different directions. To the west, the clouds loom as shredded lumps, like someone has vandalized the sky. Unstable air is a bad sign. I hope the Alphas get back soon. If a storm were to hit while they are on the road ...

Hurry, Kāya.

"Tye. Let's get this done." Dray's annoyance betrays his anxiety. Onyx is out there, too. I turn back to focus on cutting up vegetables for the soup he's preparing.

Bree emerges from the entrance, and I look to her for reassurance. She removes her oxygen mask and checks us, then rubs her scalp, studying the sky. Her face is tense as she shakes her head and disappears back inside.

Two minutes later, she reemerges, followed by the rest of the team. "There's no storm in the forecast," she announces, "but to play it safe, we're going to take the tents down and secure nonessential gear. Let's get moving."

I see grim faces all around as we rush around the camp. We're all worried.

We've packed away the tents, and Dray and I are stowing the last of the cooking utensils when Val calls out their arrival. Relieved, we all rush to greet them. Seeing her face again ... *Steel your heart.* She looks happy to be back, and I can't mask my joy.

It sounds like they had no success, and as consolation I offer to carry Kāya's pack for her.

She turns to confront me, and I'm taken aback. She stabs a finger at me. "You do not serve me."

Serve her? *Crap.* She must have encountered a clingy man while she was away, and now she's calling me out. A freeman would never offer to serve a—I straighten and fire back, in clear challenge, "I am free to do as I please."

Around us, everyone stops.

She glances around, inhales to speak, then hesitates. I hold my breath, bracing. Her beauty stuns me.

"I can carry my own pack," she finally says. The others look away, trying to keep straight faces.

I give an indignant shrug. "Suit yourself."

Her eyes flare. Uh-oh. Did I push it too far?

"What?" she demands, reacting to Bree's smug grin. Bree steps back, raising her hands.

Kāya hesitates, then snaps alert, attention elsewhere. "Storm coming."

We stop and look up.

"I feel it too," says Onyx. "Maybe twenty minutes."

And then I feel it. That unmistakable sudden drop in air pressure. And the distant rumbling of thunder as the sky darkens.

Kāya scowls at me, then steps away and takes charge. "Okay, people. Let's get moving. Bree and Val, prep the trucks. Onyx, Nance, get out the storm tents. You men ever prepped a storm tent?"

"We, uh, know all about them," says Dray.

Him and his damn bravado. Knowing about them is one thing, but we've never used one.

"Good. You can set this one up."

They train us to never stray far from shelter in threatening weather. And besides, freemen can't afford such specialized equipment. We better figure this out fast, because the breeze is starting to strengthen. "Should we take shelter inside?"

"No air down there," says Bree. "You want to suffocate again?"

I gasp a silent no.

Onyx adds, "We'd quickly burn through our oxygen, and we'd be stuck down there."

"Coming out of the west," calls Bree.

As we work, the Bravos chain the vehicles together, front and back, and hook them to the largest nearby tree trunks. Next, they collapse the roofs and lock them down to present a minimal profile to the wind.

The storm tents turn out to be simple and quick to set up, as emergency equipment should be. When rolled out, they look like squashed teardrops, fourteen feet long and five at the widest. They narrow to a point at the end facing the wind. At the wide end, the ribbed tents are less than two feet high, tapering to ground level at the windward point, which is anchored to the ground with a long spike.

Onyx shoves a hammer at Dray. "Here, cutie. Hammer that in. I'll go help Kāya."

He finishes and stands to admire his work, then squints into the wind, looking to see where else he could be useful. I grab his sleeve. "Look at the aerodynamics on these two-sleepers. The wind won't even notice they're here, except to press them more firmly into the ground." The now-dark sky rumbles, and the wind builds to a dull roar as it rips through the nearby trees. My pant legs flap against my shins as I try to keep my hair out of my eyes, but unless I'm facing the wind, it's pointless.

Aida beckons us from one of the trucks and tosses packs to us. "Get these supplies into the tents. No telling how long we'll need to hunker down."

Moments later, Onyx returns. "This grove and these hills will cut the wind a bit. We should be good up to about one-sixty. Let's hope we don't get a cluster of tornadoes."

The wind is howling now, and the thunder is getting closer. A clump of leaves blows by, still attached to their branch, and I hear a *thunk* as something hits a truck. These tents may be amazing, but they don't have armor glass. We'll either be lucky tonight, or we won't. The trucks creak on their suspension as I track Kāya doing final checks with everyone. My heart is in my mouth as she fights her way over to where the rest of us are crouching.

"The others are secure," she shouts above the roar. "Let's get zipped up before the rain hits."

"Okay," shouts Dray, "so, which one do you want us in?"

"Dray, you're with Onyx in this one." She gives Onyx a quick hug.

Onyx slithers in, feet-first, and props up on her elbows, then looks up at Dray with that smile. A grin spreads on his face as he holds his whipping hair out of his eyes. Then he scrambles headfirst beside her into the tent.

Onyx hollers up to Kāya, "This is going to be fun." She wiggles back inside and pulls down the zipper.

Kāya gestures for me to get into the last tent, and I cringe at the terrible timing. This is gonna be awkward.

"Hurry. Get in," she says, shielding her face from a gust of wind.

"This is gonna be awfully close quarters," I say.

"Do you have a problem with that?"

"Um, do you?"

She looks away in annoyance, then grabs me by the arm and collar, drives me to my knees and throws me in.

"What the hell was that?" I protest as she pushes in behind me and closes the flap.

"You want to stay out there, just let me know," she snaps.

A flash of lightning momentarily blinds me, but it's the boom that jolts me. Then it's like someone throws a bucket of water at the tent. Then another. Then it's a steady drone.

I scramble to find my wits, then say, "No, I'm good."

"Suit yourself," she says, and even in the dim light I see the smirk. She unstraps her sheathed bokken and reverently lays it beside her.

"You take that thing everywhere," I say.

She stops. "Kaybo is a part of me, and you will treat her with respect."

"Uh, yes, of course." She's given it a name?

She rolls over and retrieves her pack. "We could be here for a while. I hope you've got something to read."

"No!" bursts out. "Uh, no. Nothing. I'll ... catch up on my sleep, I guess."

She turns and studies me. "Something wrong?"

"Not at all. I ... Nothing."

She sighs and turns away, then settles back and starts reading.

I ask, "How can you even see the page?" She chuckles, not needing to answer. Enhanced senses. It's so unfair. Like everything else about her.

It's not long before I start to feel a chill. Unrolling a blanket, I peel off my clothes and climb under as the storm intensifies.

"Good idea," says Kāya, laying her book aside.

She struggles to wriggle out of her khakis in the cramped space, and as her scent fills the tent, I lose track of whatever I was fretting about. All at once I'm grateful for the flashes, the booms, and the relentless thunder of torrential rain hitting the tent. It drives us both to seek the reassurance of human contact. We cuddle together against the roar, feeling the ground shake as the wind buffets our tiny shelter. All at once I realize that against this greater power, even *her* strength is nothing. She's as helpless in here as I am.

Her eyes close, and I watch her in the dim light. "Kāya?"

"Yes?"

"There's something I need you to know." I draw my face close to hers and, as gently as I can, touch my fingertips to her now-healed cheek. "About the fight with Luce. I'm so sorry, Kāya. I didn't understand what was going on."

She pulls her face away. "You're not expected to understand, Tye. You're a man."

I bite my tongue, holding back, then reconsider. A freeman wouldn't hold back. "What is it you think a man can't understand? Maybe if someone had explained it to me—"

"She have responsibilities, hard decisions to make."

"Freemen have responsibilities."

"You're responsible for yourselves. That's not the same as being responsible for the safety and the lives of others."

"You mean, like when we're looking after the children? True, I can't carry nearly as much as you. But that doesn't mean I can't understand what it's like to carry a heavy load. What is it you think I can't understand?"

She squirms. "The social rules of the dominant class, for one thing. They're complex and unforgiving, and they need to be, or else our society would collapse into chaos and violence. And by the way, men would not fare well if that were to happen."

I concede the point. "But how could my knowing history lead to that?"

"Look, I've encountered men who learned history, and some of them became ... unhinged. It seems to be an effect. We certainly don't want it spreading."

I flash back to my distress from reading just a snippet of my mother's book. "What is it about knowing history that would cause that?"

She throws up a stop hand. "The whole history thing is complicated. I get that you're frustrated about being kept out, but please understand. I'm trying to protect you. There are things I'm simply not comfortable with you knowing. Not yet. Maybe someday. I know that's not fair, but ... I'm asking. Let it go for now."

I relent. "Maybe someday. Until then, you've got a horny, unmanageable freeman to deal with."

"Unless I throw you out." She reaches for the tent-fly zipper. It's vibrating like a nervous hand as the tent shudders in the gusts.

Kāya being playful like Onyx? I jump to encourage more. "You threw me in, so why not?"

She grins. "But that would be too easy, and I've always liked a challenge."

"Oh, I'll give you a challenge."

"I'm sure you will."

She's playing with me. My heart bubbles as I savor her contented face in the dim light. I snuggle in and feel enclosed in her warmth, the dull roar now thrumming, as waves of heavier rain roll through. I'm out in a tiny tent, in the middle of a wicked storm, and there is no fear in me. I smile to myself in amazement, energized by my boldness.

"Kāya? Can I ask you a question? That first night. What happened? Why were you upset?"

The seconds drag, and the buffeting seems to intensify.

I exhale when she speaks. "You caught me by surprise, is all. I wasn't ready."

"Ready for what? All I did was ask you to guide me."

"Yes, but … it caught me off guard. I was expecting passive-aggressive, and then … you were too considerate, too attentive to my needs, too …"

"Too what?"

She sighs. "Too easy to like."

I look away, baffled.

"I didn't know where things were going, what my duty might require of me. I didn't want to get attached to you."

It's now clear. I heard Onyx right.

"I still don't trust you, Tye. Not in that way. Or maybe it's me I don't trust. Either way, this is hard."

Yes, it is. Now, for sure, I can't be honest with her. "That's okay, though, because I still don't trust you either. Not in that way." What am I even saying? How do I pretend not to care about her? Oh, yeah. *Steel your heart and stand apart. Steel your heart and stand apart.* I can do this.

"At least in this regard, we're on the same page."

I'm not sure how to respond, so I stay quiet. She relaxes back, and we lie side by side in the din.

No, I can't do this. I've got to at least try to connect with her. But what's safe to talk about? I remember back to Onyx breaking the ice that second night. "Uh, how about that weather?"

I wait for a laugh, but she gives me a puzzled frown. "You mean the storm?"

"Never mind."

"What about the storm?"

At least it's an opening. "What's the worst storm you ever got caught in?"

I bounce along on sunlit clouds as the conversation flows. I watch her mouth as she speaks, her lips tantalizing, and wish with a powerful longing to feel their warm softness against mine, to taste them, to melt into them in an intimate joining. But a kiss is too much to hope for. A ridiculous notion. Even hinting at it would be a terrible mistake, and she'd push me away for sure. No, I should be grateful she's even willing to tolerate my close presence like this. After a time, we fall into a comfortable silence, and I find myself soaking in the warm tub of her closeness.

I swoon as her hand starts to explore my skin. There will be no kissing, but things could still get wonderfully hot. I mindlessly match her enthusiasm. Then, her hand stops, and she whispers in my ear.

She's telling me what she likes. In unison, my heart and loins burst into flames. "I would love to help you out with that," I say.

As the elements pummel the tent, its tough fabric slaps and flutters against my back, but I'm beyond it. Our dark, roaring cocoon is the whole world.

28

———

HARD CLASH

THE MORNING SUN shines through the still-dripping trees as I crawl out into the cool air. The tall grasses in the field have been flattened, and small broken branches lie scattered around, but there is less storm debris than I expected.

Nance and Aida have a camp stove going and are boiling eggs and warming toast. No sign of Onyx and Dray. Their zipper finally opens and Onyx wriggles out. She stands, stretches, and looks around, and I enjoy every moment of it.

Dray straggles out looking bleary-eyed and nods in appreciation when Nance offers him a mug of coffee. The She have a hearty but hasty breakfast of eggs, cheese, fruit, and granola. We gratefully join in. As Dray and I collect and wash up the plates and implements, the others open up the trucks. Then Kāya calls us together.

"Okay, everyone, here's the way it is. We need to make up for lost time, so we're going to skip training this morning. You all know what's at stake. As is, this is just a buried collection of artifacts. But if we can bring this facility back to life, it will be monumental. The first step will be to get the ventilation system running and air out the place."

"If we can get the utilities operational," says Onyx, "we'll be able to spend all the time we need inside."

Nance chimes in. "The digital archives alone will prove invaluable if we can get at them, and we need reliable power for that. Right now, we can only deal with things piece by piece, but can you imagine having the whole place available to us?"

Every face shows excitement. I wish I could share it.

Kāya continues. "We'll either have power by the end of the day, or it may be a long time before we can take full advantage of what we have here. Aida, please walk us through the plan."

Aida is all business. "Tye's suggestion about priming the geothermal system from the local aquifer was a good one, and we've finally got the levels to where we need them. We've tied our portable power to the control systems, and so far, everything checks out. If all goes well, we'll try firing it up this afternoon. The equipment looks to be in excellent condition, but considering its age, there are no guarantees. We'll go over work assignments on site."

"How can we help?" I ask.

Kāya looks at me. "You can start taking down the storm tents. Let's get the others back up."

Not what I had in mind. The She carry their excitement inside, and we are left to clean up, as usual. When we're done, my frustration is still simmering. This is historic, and I can't be a part of it.

The team is going back down after their second oxygen refill when Onyx stops to check in with us. When I complain about feeling left out, she thoughtfully nods, then looks around.

"You two are an important part of this team right now. You are our eyes and ears up here while we are all indisposed. In fact, we should have a better way for you to notify us if there's trouble. Let me show you how to use the radio in the truck, and I'll take a radio down with me."

"Are you expecting trouble?" asks Dray.

"I'm always expecting trouble."

"Luce," I say.

"It's only a matter of time before she finds us. We need to get into the city before then to recruit a bigger team. And Kāya wants to request an exemption from the High Council to allow you two to be here. Until then, we're exposed."

Dray speaks with resolve. "Onyx, when trouble comes, I will fight at your side."

She straightens and looks down at him. "No. You won't."

He stoops and picks up a shovel and, with a quick jab, slices the head off a wildflower. "Yes, I will. I'll have your back. I'm gonna protect you, Onny, and you can't stop me."

I cringe as she narrows her eyes at him. "You're good with that thing," she says.

"I'm a digger, so I get lots of practice. Yeah, I am pretty good."

"You're dangerous with that shovel, are you?"

"I could be, if I had to be."

"Dray. Sweet man. No, you couldn't." She looks around, picks up a two-foot stick as thick as her thumb and holds it up beside her. "Using your shovel as a weapon, hit this stick as fast and hard as you can. Kill it."

She's testing him, but she doesn't realize he has real skills with that shovel. I've seen him use quick jabs to clear mud from an old bottle without breaking it.

"Go ahead, Dray. Hit the stick. Try to surprise me."

I can see he's tempted by her taunts.

"Do it, loser."

He lunges with a quick thrust—that never lands, because the shovel is no longer in his hands as he spins in the air and lands hard on his back.

I rush over in alarm, and Onyx puts out a hand to stop me.

She leans over him, examining him with concern. "You okay?"

To my surprise, he seems to be. "What the hell!" he cries.

"Dray. Men are not built for fighting. Your skills don't matter. I can't have you thinking they do and going into harm's way. Do you understand?"

He climbs to his feet, dusting himself off, flustered. "Was that necessary?"

"Your nervous system is weaker, your reaction time slower. Any

She has that advantage, and an enforcer's advantage is magnified by training. I saw your muscles load to strike and was moving to intercept before you even launched."

He sags.

"The point is—Dray? Are you okay? What's wrong?"

He stares at a freshly crushed wildflower by his foot. "Well, now you've demonstrated my utter uselessness. I get it. Can I just be alone right now, please?"

"Dray, don't be like that. I'm trying to protect you."

"Protect me? By showing me how feeble I am?"

"Yes. Exactly. You need to remember that, because the minute you think you can challenge a She will be the minute you get hurt. Please tell me you understand that."

They exchange a long, pleading look, and his forlorn face softens. Then he sighs. "I get it, Onny. I guess I needed a reminder."

As she gives him a hug, she questions me with her eyes. I throw up my surrender hands. "No reminder needed here."

As she heads off, Dray calls out, "You better take care of *yourself*, then."

Without breaking stride, she glances over her shoulder, then puts on her mask and steps down out of sight.

———

During the next break, the excitement is infectious. They're doing final checks of the power system, and everything looks good. They are about to bring an ancient facility back to life, and it could provide a whole new window into the Before. A window I can't look through.

"Kāya, please. Why can't I watch? I'll stay out of your way."

"Stop it, Tye. You know why."

"But this could change everything, and how can I not—"

She points a warning finger in my face. I look down, pouting. When I glance up, she's mimicking my pout, and I can't help but laugh. Then she gazes down into my eyes and, as always, I surrender.

Her voice is soft. "It really is unfair, isn't it."

Hope churns in my heart. She sees?

"I think I'm starting to get you, freeman."

You've always had me. I clench to contain myself. "Well, you're still a total mystery to me. Lucky for you, I like mysteries."

She looks away and goes still.

"Kāya?"

"Mysteries can be dangerous. Tye, I wish I could let you in. I really do. I just … I'm not sure what to do with you."

"What do you mean, do with me?"

"You found this place. You've been inside, almost died in it. If anyone deserves to see it, you do. But it's a historical site, and you're a man, and … I just can't take the risk."

"What risk? You think I'll go mad?"

"It's a lot bigger than that, and you know it. We don't know how learning history might affect you, but I can't ignore the fact that you would become a sedition risk." She turns away and looks at the sky. "I made a terrible mistake, letting you back in a second time, and I don't want to—"

"No, you didn't."

"You almost died."

I bow my head, then change tacks. "I don't even care about history anymore. I'm just curious to see what's down there. I won't even—"

"It's a historical site, Tye. History is what's down there. You know that. Look, I'm getting tired of this."

You think you're *getting tired of it?* I don't get a chance to sort out my arguments before Val appears at the door. "We're all ready."

I can't hold back any longer. "What's happening?"

"We're about to test the power system." They withdraw down the stairs.

They'll be turning on the lights, feeding electricity to all the devices. Bringing the whole place, full of magical technology from the Before, back to life. What was a dark, scary cavern to me will now be—what? Something spectacular.

This is historic. And I'm missing it.

Dray sees my agitation and grabs my arm. "Come on. Let's get the last tents up."

They've left us behind again, and I fume. Dray's annoyance barely registers as he tries to keep me on task. They're doing what She have always done to me: restricting me to an irrelevant life as an inconsequential man. It's cruel and hateful. They might as well cut off my legs and make me crawl everywhere. Job done, I gaze at the entrance, aching with curiosity.

The dark stairway brightens. Power! I'm drawn like a moth.

My anger turns to icy resolve. "I'm gonna see what all the fuss is about."

"You mean, going in? No, you can't do that."

I'm giddy with excitement. They'll be pissed. So what? She's not gonna hurt me. I've had it with being shut out. Besides, they'll be in a good mood. They probably won't even care.

"Tye!"

I wave him off.

My heart races as I descend the stairs, now with lights on at each landing. I gasp and cough as I peer in through the propped-open bottom door and see the wide hallway brightly lit. The entire spacious length of it. Is this the same hall I was in before? Look at this place. I stand shivering in awe.

Along the hallway, dark doorways beckon, promising more lights to be turned on. There is no one around, so I continue in, marveling at how bright and open everything looks. I cough again and realize I still can't breathe down here. Okay, just a quick peek.

I cough again, then hear someone running up the central staircase. I make a quick decision to stand my ground. It's Val, her mask obscuring her face.

"Thought I heard you up here. What are you doing, Tye? Out. Now."

"I just want to see what it's like down here with the power on."

"Now you've seen. Go on. Out. We'll be up in a few minutes and tell you all about it. Go!"

She stares me down, and through her faceplate I see her annoyance grow. I can't win this. Not when I can hardly breathe. I shake my head and turn to make my way back up into the fresh air.

Dray is boiling water for coffee, expecting the She to take a break soon. He looks at me with scorn. "I don't know what you think you were gonna accomplish."

"Screw off, Dray." It's a whole new world down there. He wouldn't understand.

The She straggle up in pairs, talking excitedly.

I'm nursing a mug of coffee, scowling, when Kāya approaches me.

"You came inside? After I specifically asked you not to?" We glare at one another. "What is it with you? How do I make this any clearer? You do not go in—"

"I don't take orders from you." My voice is more authentic than I expect.

She goes rigid, then looks at me askance.

I continue. "I have a *right* to see what's down there—"

She bites off my words. "You have no such right!"

"Hey! I found this place! I was in there before you even knew it was here. And now you won't even let me look?"

"Tye, we've talked about this. Please don't—"

"Sure. Share your wealth of new history with all She and leave the men out in the cold, like always."

"I'm done with trying to explain this to you. Now you will—"

"I don't need you to teach me history. I can learn it on my own."

Her alarmed eyes alert me. No, shouldn't have said that. *Change the subject.*

"What do you—"

"You wouldn't even be here if it weren't for me. You'd be stuck out there in the Big Death, scratching for—"

"Tye! Stop right there!"

They're all looking at me now, and it's like I draw power from the attention. "No! I'm not gonna stop. Not until you stop treating me like some child who's gonna—"

"*Enough!*"

Her real voice sends a shock wave through me, and for a moment

I'm paralyzed. But I shake myself free and my face flushes. "I do not serve you!"

Dray's voice is angry. "Tye!"

"*What!* I'm sick and tired of being held back, left out, oppressed by greedy She who think they can come in and take whatever they want. *You don't control me—*"

Her reddening face twists in rage and my blood goes cold. There is a sudden flash, and my cup explodes in my hand. The world expands and I'm not in my body, yet I see her standing there, bokken poised, eyes wild, voice real. "How *dare* you—"

Onyx is on her in a second, staying her arm. "Kāya! Whoa, easy. Kāya?"

Kāya turns on her in anger, then goes still. Her weapon drops from her hand as her face distorts in anguish. She puts her fist to her mouth, turns and runs off as I watch in horror.

29

—————

LETTING GO

I MUST HAVE BLANKED, because Dray is confronting me, and I don't know where he came from. I can see his anger, but I feel nothing.

He's yelling something. "*Guns, Tye. What's wrong with you?*" He punches my shoulder.

Ow! That hurt. I felt that, but my head still won't clear. It's wrong. It's all wrong. Gravity drags me down by the throat and I'm on my hands and knees, about to puke. Dray says something I can't follow as my body tries to hurl the life out of me.

He tries to help me to my feet, but I'm not interested. I glance over and see the She milling around together, heads down, talking in hushed tones. Neither Onyx nor Kāya are with them, or anywhere in sight. Compelled by the need to hide, I struggle to my feet and don't resist as Dray helps me to the tent, where I crawl in and collapse. Lying there, I bob and tumble in a boiling cauldron until the world finally fades and I embrace the darkness.

When the world returns, it's dark outside, and it's not a world I want to be in. I withdraw back into my own empty depths.

I stir awake at the sound of a zipper opening. There is daylight outside the tent as Dray pokes his head in. He has a bowl in his hand.

"You slept through dinner and breakfast, so I brought you something." He climbs in and sits beside me. "You need to eat."

"Not hungry."

"At least have some water." He holds out a canteen for me, and after a moment I become aware of what feels like a mouthful of sand. I accept his offer.

"Are you gonna be okay?"

The concern on his face draws me in, and I'm moved to reassure him but can't. I sag back.

"Tye? What happened? What was that all about?"

What happened? I can't bring it into focus in my mind.

"Look, I know you don't want to talk about it, but you need to. You need to get your head sorted out, or someone is gonna remove it. I don't want to lose you, buddy. Please talk to me."

"What ... what's going on out there?"

"It's not good. You ruined their celebration. They think you're nuts. They're talking about sending us to re-education."

I moan. He doesn't deserve this. "I don't know what happened. I guess the frustration has been piling up for a while and then ... I just lost it. I lost it. I'm such an idiot."

"You've got to say something. You've got to talk to them, convince them we're not a threat. Can you do that? Please, Tye. I ... Please."

"Yes, of course I'll ... talk to them." What could I possibly say? I'd rather get shipped off to re-education than face any of them. But I can't do that to him. He's been happier than I've ever seen him, and I'll never forgive myself if he loses Onyx because of me. He'll hate me.

"They'll be coming up for a break soon." He puts a firm hand on my shoulder and glares at me. "It's your chance. You owe them all an apology. Especially Kāya."

When they emerge, I approach the group, forcing myself to the edge of the cliff with every intention of jumping. But Kāya is not with them. I serve a snack of toast and jam with coffee, offering sincere apologies to each as I go. They all remain tight-lipped, merely nodding. I do my best to explain my simmering frustration and my envy of their discoveries, and how that doesn't excuse my outburst. I ask Onyx to please convey my remorse to Kāya, but she's noncommittal. "I'll see if she'll come up for a minute so you can tell her yourself."

When they all go back down, I follow to the entrance and sit on the top step, hoping Kāya will come out, fearing she will. I clasp my hands, trying to steel myself for the encounter, wondering if it's even possible for words to make things right. They've got the blowers on. I cough as the dusty breeze carries its spite up from below.

An angry yell of refusal echoes up from the depths. It's faint, but I can clearly make it out. "I don't want to see him!"

My heart collapses.

I sit vacant until the impulse to flee overtakes me and I dash for the refuge of the tent.

Dray follows. "Did you see Kāya?"

"No."

He is insistent. "You need to—"

"She won't talk to me." I clench myself but can't stop the tears. I sit in the awkward silence, waiting for a hug that doesn't come. Instead, a face of stone turns away from me, and he's gone.

I collapse back onto my bedroll. The light slowly settles, and I float, beyond time. Yes, there is relief in oblivion. Peace.

Dray's voice jars me. "Onyx has a job for us. She wants us to take the wrecked jeep into town to get fixed."

My mind spins, struggling for traction.

"I think she wants us out of the way for a while. Our story is that we're dropping it off for an employer and will come back for it when it's ready. You'll follow in the other jeep and pick me up. Can you get yourself together?"

They're sending us out in the jeeps? Alone? "Uh, yes." This is good. There is sudden urgency in my need to get out of here. The sooner the better.

As I try to organize myself in a fog, a point of clarity jumps out at me. There is one thing I definitely can't leave behind to be discovered. I grab my pack.

I'm in no shape to drive, but being in separate vehicles will make it easier. Dray leads in the wreck. All I have to do is follow.

After ten minutes of focusing on the trail, my woozy mind is starting to clear. The mid-morning sky looks angry, with jagged ridges of cloud slashing into the blue. I wish they were storm clouds. I picture the wind lifting me up and hurling me away, releasing me. Kāya is right about emotional attachment. Best to avoid it. Too close to the edge, I grip the wheel.

The driving gets easier when we get out to the old roadbed. Mindlessly following in Dray's tracks, I check my pack on the seat beside me. Close call. I almost left it unguarded. I survey the surrounding wilds, and the solitude is welcoming. And here I am, driving a jeep, alone and free, like a gull floating on the wind.

I am suddenly overtaken with a sense of giddy guilt. *I've gotten away with it.* I have been in the midst of enforcers for days, Alphas and Bravos, with prohibited material in my possession, and they don't even suspect.

And now I have nothing to lose. This book holds the secrets of history. If they're gonna send me away anyway, I may as well at least know why. All I have to do is get past the parts that will drive me insane. I can do that. I can read with a critical eye and block out the obvious lies. I can't have the strength of She, but I can finally have the knowledge of She.

First, I need to get away from Dray for a while so I can read. I slow to a stop, and Dray stops to check on me. "I've got to take a leak," I call out. "You go on ahead, and I'll catch up with you at the garage."

He scowls with suspicion, and I wave him on. "Don't worry, I'll be right behind you." He shakes his head and finally pulls away. I stand behind the jeep until he is out of sight.

Back in the jeep, ripe with anticipation, I rest a trembling hand on the illicit book and—was that disappointment on his face? No. He was just—A flash of Kāya's rage pumps terror through me, replaced by a burn of shame. She trusted me. They all trusted me. Enough to let me drive the jeep into town, alone.

And I'm violating that trust.

Kāya is angry with me, with good reason. But if she were to find out that I've been hiding this from her, she'd *hate* me. I'd be just another lying man in her eyes, and she'd be right. This is stupid, stupid, stupid.

But she already hates me. And I have all the answers, right here. Ignorance is bliss, they say, but ignorance exposed is torment, a gnawing hunger. And everything I learn raises new questions and makes me hungrier. I must know. I must.

But what if I let slip that I know? What if Kāya were to forgive me and then find out …

I sit convicted, vacant, absorbing my surroundings, the unspoiled beauty of the wilds, the taste of pure, clean air, the peace of innocence …

A peace that is out of reach. Closed off to me. Because I'm *guilty*. I'm *violating her trust.*

What am I doing?

The fever breaks. I push the jeep up to speed, now desperate to catch up to Dray, to be above suspicion. But by the time I get to the turnoff to town, he's not in sight. He must have already crossed the bridge. All at once it doesn't matter. It's clear what I must do.

As I approach the bridge, the flowing water below calls to me, and I brake to a stop. I spent a lot of time on this bridge as a kid. The view to the east hasn't changed. The river narrows at the turbines, then widens upstream at the reservoir inlets, bordered by whip willow and birch groves.

The river tugs at me, drawing me, and I find myself at the railing looking downstream. Peering down at the water, I'm a child again as the familiar swirling patterns trigger an earlier time. A time of wishes that could come true if only … I kick a wishing stone off the roadway into the rolling water below. I stood right here as a kid, staring into the flow, with that vague yearning, that unformed ache for something I could not yet name. I remember wondering where all the water was coming from. And where it would take me.

Life has a way of taking us to unexpected places, no matter which course we set for ourselves.

I go cold. *Was that your excuse? Why should I listen to anything you have to say? It's my turn to leave you behind.* I dig her book out from its nest in my pack and clutch it to my body as a truck rolls by. All clear now.

An unfamiliar certainty steadies me. I pull back and hurl the book to the wind. *Good riddance.*

Its pages don't flutter as it arcs through the air. It tumbles end over end until it hits the water. The splash quickly washes out, and I lose sight of its dark shape in the cleansing flow.

A crushing weight lifts. I fill my lungs and grip the railing to hold myself from floating off.

Gone now. My last tie to my mother. My last stubborn defiance. My quest for knowledge of history is over and done. And what remains?

The ache is still there, the old yearning, except now it has shape, color. Aquamarine. Faint hope is still hope. I'm surprised how much it feels like freedom.

———

I LET Dray drive the good jeep back so I can focus on my plea for forgiveness. I relive the nightmare. What did I think I was doing, defying an Alpha like that? Oh, yeah. She wanted me to be independent. She wanted ... I can't blame this on her.

A pair of deer bound off into the bushes as we approach. Also skittish, I turn and check behind us. There's no one in sight.

"I'm worried about you, Tye." He doesn't take his eyes off the trail. "It's like this place has changed you. Or maybe the oxygen deprivation did some damage or something. But you need to get it together, freeman, or we're screwed."

In the passing woodland, a flock of starlings bursts into the air. "I know." I've always found comfort out in the wilds, but now the whole area carries a burden of remorse. Kāya could very well send us away.

The silence drags until Dray speaks. "I hope you got that nonsense out of your system."

"What nonsense?" I check behind us again and see no sign of being followed.

"Thinking you have a right to learn history."

I examine my hands. "Yeah. All cleaned out."

"She's trying to protect you, Tye."

"That's easy for you to say. You didn't feel the wind of her blade on your face."

"She left you with a face, didn't she?"

There is that. It's not much, but it's something.

30

DEADLY CHALLENGE

I BUSY MYSELF with my chores around the encampment, anxious the whole time, ready to throw myself at her mercy at the first opportunity. But she doesn't come up for breaks, nor does she appear with the others for dinner. In fact, none of them stay to eat with us. Bree sneers at me as they take their food and head back inside. Without supplemental oxygen.

As the last one disappears, Dray drops his head, pensive. Being shut out of the facility is one thing, but now we're being shut out by the team, and we both feel the weight of it.

"Looks like the air is breathable down there now," I say, trying to break the tension.

He shrugs and pokes at his portion of vat-grown ham. I know what he's thinking. We won't see much of them from now on.

Evening falls, and only Bree and Val come up to sleep outside in their tent. It's their job to guard the place, so we shouldn't be surprised. But it means that the air quality has improved enough to let them sleep inside. In where we can never go. Even if I hadn't mucked everything up, our usefulness here has ended.

I spend a restless night trying to imagine how they'll go about sending us away. Will they take us into town and deliver us to the authorities for deportation? Or take us to the Waverly jail to await prisoner transport? And to where? West, obviously, but what is out there?

All morning, Bree and Val take turns topside, spelling each other off. Neither will talk about what's going on inside, and I don't press. It doesn't matter anymore. Every time one of them goes down, they take food supplies in with them, so I guess they've got the kitchen working now. Soon they won't even need us for preparing meals. We'll be … irrelevant men again.

"I don't know why we're still here," I say, as Dray patrols the encampment.

His tone is sharp. "Once Kāya gets clearance for us from the High Council, everything will be fine. Until then, we lie low and help out where we can. Is that clear?"

"Don't go gettin' all She on me."

"Then get your head on straight."

His icy words are like a stab to the heart. My best friend has turned against me. I wander off in a daze, unable to deny that it's my own fault. I've turned everyone against me, all because of my stubborn, impatient curiosity.

I find myself wandering through the trees in the general direction of the trail, with no intention of running. I just need some space.

Sitting mindless on a pile of rubble, I feel it before I hear it. A vibration in the ground. Is that a vehicle approaching? Alarmed, I climb a nearby mound and look toward the trail. Oh no.

I sprint back toward the entrance, making a beeline across the raised ground topping the facility. The vehicles will have to wind their way around, following the tire tracks.

I dash to the entrance and yell down the stairs, "Bree! Val! Come up! Someone's coming!" Then I remember the radio in the truck, and hurry over to make the call down. I'm still fumbling with the damn thing when the Bravos come bounding out, looking around.

I cry out a warning. "They're coming up the trail. They'll be here any second."

The alarm on their faces transforms into determination.

Bree curses. "You're sure you weren't followed back here yesterday?"

"Positive. I was watching the whole way."

Bree takes the mic from my hand and calls down, "Kāya. Onyx. Company!" She turns back to me. "How many vehicles?"

"Uh, not sure. A few. I only caught a glimpse."

We can hear the approaching vehicles now. The Alphas rush out in their work clothes, and Kāya glances my way without acknowledging me. Then she takes charge. "Bree, Val, Onyx. Battle armor, now."

Bree is already changing. The other two rush to the trucks as a jeep rolls into the clearing, followed by three trucks. I see a pair of trackers in the jeep, though not the ones we encountered before. They're easy to identify in their tracker leathers.

Val is the second one armored, and when she returns to guard the entrance, I lean in behind her. "Luce hired more trackers already?"

"Shows how eager she is to find out what we've got here."

"Why?" I ask. "They already took your last claim."

Onyx, now armored, forms up with the others. "Which was meager at best. Luce is getting greedy, looking for the big score."

"I'll bet she has a spy in the registry office," adds Bree.

Kāya calls for attention. "Plan A, everyone. Let's play it safe."

Play it safe? The best way to do that is to give us to Luce this time. My heart sinks. I can't blame her. The last site was nothing compared to this one. This facility is far too important to trade away for the lives of two men.

In his oblivious way, Dray likely doesn't realize we're about to be sacrificed, and I'm not gonna tell him. He thinks Onyx will protect him. I care about him too much to destroy his hope like that. Let him bask in the glow of his own foolish heart for as long as he can.

All three trucks empty out, and when I recognize the one taking lead, I prickle. *Luce.* The monster who hurt Kāya. Who will kill us as soon as she gets the chance.

Bree herds us forward. "Kāya wants you two front and center."

This is it. To my surprise, I'm okay with it. I'll be her bargaining chip if it will protect her. There's no other way I could ever make amends for what I did. Perhaps my sacrifice will earn forgiveness. To see that in Kāya's eyes, to see acceptance on her face one last time ...

Our enforcers surround us, all but Kāya in battle armor, and we find ourselves facing a forest of fighters. Jaw clenched, I straighten in defiance.

Still in her working clothes, Kāya steps forward. "Hello, ladies. You look lost. Did you make a wrong turn?"

Luce notes the battle armor on the others. "I see you are expecting trouble. Guilty conscience?"

"Expected you days ago. Your desperation makes you predictable."

Luce ignores that. "What are you doing here, Kāya?"

My clenched fists throb like hard hearts as I glare at her.

Kāya's voice is calm but firm. "I've staked my claim. My discovery, my first right of salvage. What are *you* doing here?"

"I seem to have lost a jeep. I want it back."

Kāya looks around. "Sounds like you should keep better track of your stuff. You won't find it here. Go look elsewhere. Now, *move along*."

"I see you have chosen to defy me."

"Defy you how?"

"Don't play stupid, Kāya. It's beneath you."

"We are well outside the restricted zone. There is no prohibition against men here."

"Tell me this is not a historical site."

Kāya sets her jaw.

Luce continues. "Tell me you have not allowed men to enter a historical site."

"Here's the way it is. I don't have to tell you shit. You are trespassing. Get off my claim."

"I'll take that as a confession. This affront to the rules cannot go unpunished. You leave us no choice but to inflict justice and put down this threat to our community."

Luce looms like a building teetering to fall on me, and my mousy resolve scurries away.

Kāya severs the tension. "Cut the crap, Luce. You're not among Quo here. Nobody buys this righteous act. There is no threat here. These men are here under strict supervision, and you have no evidence to the contrary."

"All the evidence I need is right here in front of me. These are the same men you sheltered in the Shell, and now they are here. It's obvious they know too much. That knowledge must die with them, before they have a chance to spread it."

"You know fucking well that under the Madeline Amendment, killings are to be avoided except—"

"You dare to speak of the Charter in front of men?"

"—except under the direst of circumstances, and even if your accusations were true, which they are not, this would not qualify as dire. The fact is, these men know nothing of history, and are merely here as errand boys."

Errand boys? I try to keep my face neutral. I'm just a bargaining chip.

Luce says, "Careless talk, disregard for the rules—Kāya, your recklessness makes you a threat yourself."

"Like I said, there is no threat here."

"But I'm a reasonable She. Give me the men, so that I may cleanse this transgression, or I will take this site."

That's my cue. Wait. The men? "No! Just me." It comes out as a croak and Val, standing behind me, slaps the back of my head. "Shut up, Tye."

Kāya chuckles. "You must think me a fool, Luce, to try that again. We are not in the Shell, and these men—they're standing right here —are on neutral ground. This is their tent. *On neutral ground.* You have no basis for complaint. Now turn your Quo ass around and *get off my site!*"

Luce scowls down her nose at us. Her Bravo leans in and whispers to her, and she straightens. "We have enough circumstantial evidence to take action."

"If you choose to take illegal action, you will be held to account."

"I'm not interested in your excuses, Kāya. No more talk. We settle this now."

I hunch, shaking. It's happening.

Kāya looks back at us, smirking, then back at Luce. "You waiting for something?" Luce's face goes red, and Kāya continues, "You really thought you could provoke me into challenging you again? No. Now *go*."

A ray of hope.

Luce pumps up, upper lip curled back, blowing livid breath through her teeth. She hunches forward and squints at Kāya, her voice icy. "You have already challenged by your actions." She straightens and bellows, "To all assembled. Let it be known that this is a capital challenge. Any interference will be met with lethal force."

What?

I hear gasps and protests around me.

Kāya seems uncertain. "*You* are challenging *me?*"

"You heard me."

"On what grounds?"

"Your unwillingness to engage in dispute resolution."

Kāya's shoulders droop.

Flummoxed, I lean into Val. "What dispute? There's no dispute."

"There's a dispute if Luce says there is. She's got Kāya boxed in a corner."

"But that's crazy."

She shakes her head in disgust. "Any law can be twisted and abused, in the wrong hands."

I step forward, voice stronger this time. "Stop this! You can take—"

Val smacks me again, and this time I see stars. "Shut up, Tye. Not one more word."

"But—" I freeze, seeing her hand poised to smack me again, though she never takes her eyes off the wall of adversaries in front of us.

Kāya studies her challenger. "I don't want to kill you, Luce."

"Oh, I think you do."

"If you're making a capital challenge, I claim the right of arbitration."

"What? That's the coward's way out. Real She fight."

"The High Council needs to have a say in this."

"We're not in the big city out here. Local jurisdiction rules apply."

"This is not a local issue. This is far bigger than the two of us. You are obviously here to take this site by force, and you don't even know what this is. The High Council will be furious you didn't include them when they see the scope of what we have here. And they will see your actions for what they are. A high crime."

I've got to stop this. I glance at Dray beside me and see him huddling behind Onyx. Then I remember her lesson. I can't expect him to help me here ... Help me do what? My mind spins like tires in mud.

Luce scowls, chewing her lip. "So, what is this place?"

"Way beyond you, is what this is. And none of your fucking business."

Her Bravo leans in to tell her something, and Luce juts out her chin. "I'll give you twenty-four hours. We either have a ruling by then, or we settle this in the traditional way." With that, she turns and signals her team, and they all return to their vehicles.

Kāya calls after her, "Rules of engagement, Luce. You and your people will keep your distance until then."

Luce glares at her without responding. I turn to rubber as the intruders pull back out to the far edge of the clearing.

Twenty-four hours. Midafternoon. I can't stop myself and the words burst out. "Please tell me you're not gonna fight a capital challenge."

She ignores me, but Val says, "A fight to the death? Kāya, this is crazy!"

"She's not getting this site," says Kāya through clenched teeth.

I gasp. "No! You can't be serious! Kāya! You can't!"

"You stay out of this." Kāya turns to Onyx. "I'll send off a message to the High Council."

"Looks like they'll be setting up camp right here," says Onyx. "You do realize there's no way an Arbiter could get here that soon? It's a good two-day trip."

Kāya nods, her gaze far away. "Then it's up to me."

31

PREY

AN HOUR LATER, six tents have been erected at the far edge of the clearing, about eighty yards into the meadow. They have clear sight of the entrance. I'm still protesting Kāya's plan. Bree, sick of it, heads back inside to find Val, who's supposed to be starting her shift on guard duty. Dray and I are loading a packed tent into the truck when a noise behind us alerts me. I turn and freeze, looking up at unknown enforcers, a towering tidal wave of menace rolling toward us. Four of them, all in regalia. Frantic, we both look around. We're alone up here, and we'd never make it the forty yards to the entrance. Dray yells out, "Bree! Val!"

The intruders survey the area to confirm we're alone, then spread out as the tallest one speaks. "Look what we've got here. Stud service. I could use some action." Pointing at Dray, she says, "I'll take this one first."

There's nowhere to run. They're right on us. Heart hammering, I see Dray drop to the ground and scramble underneath the truck, and I'm right behind him. We squeeze together like trapped rabbits, as far from the edges as we can get, faces in the dirt as we try to track their movements.

We hear them joking together as we watch their feet surround the truck. "You're going to share, right?"

"A little medicinal help and he'll be up for all of us."

They're squatting down now, and as taunting faces peer in at us, we instinctively try to back away but have nowhere to go. Dray shrieks and clutches for me as he starts sliding backward, dragged by a hand on his ankle. We both scream for our lives as I cling to him and get dragged with him into the open. Four huge predators leer down at us. "Leave us alone!" I cry. I try to scramble away but run into boots. They have us closed in. I scream again as powerful, shielded arms and grabbing hands reach down, and I squirm but can't evade them. We're both lifted from the ground, and a large hand clamps over my mouth. My captor leans in and sniffs me. "Ah, I love the smell of fear on a man."

I stop struggling and go limp, as caught prey does, and after I've gone quiet, the hand lifts from my mouth and I gasp for breath. My mind goes calm, and I recognize this state. It's the calm before death. I've been here before, and all I can do is to die well. As a freeman! The strength of my voice surprises me. "You're making a big mistake. We are not studs."

More laughter. "You think we don't know studs when we see them?" The big brunette must be six-ten. Holding Dray's arms behind his back, she examines him. "This one is going to be tasty." I see the horrified anguish in his eyes, and my heart breaks. He tries to knee her and takes an open hand across the face that knocks the fight out of him.

Rage flares within me. Pulse pounding, I shout, "*No!*" It catches them all by surprise. "We will *not* stud for you! If you try to force us, we will resist!"

Startled, the raiders exchange glances, then grin. A smug one says, "Men? Resist? *Ha.* When your hands and feet are tied and my juicy gens are in your face, we'll see how resistant you are."

I turn to stone, grit my teeth, and throw my hatred into her eyes. "You will be *dismayed* by the strength of my resistance!"

Her expression turns from surprise ... to puzzlement ... to outrage, and as she starts toward me, I brace for a blow. She abruptly stops.

A ground-shaking roar close behind me makes me jump out of my skin. *"Let them go!"* The grip on me releases, and I wheel around and there is Onyx, prowling ferociously forward, glaring at the raiders as they back away.

"Back off, now!" she roars in that deep, deadly voice.

They start backing away, then stop. The tall one speaks. "There are four of us, Alpha. You are not in charge here." All four draw their bokken in unison and hold them in attack position.

"Challenge accepted," says Onyx, her bokken still in its sheath. She steps towards them, there is a yell and a flash of wood, and two quick cracks split the air. Bokken clatter to the ground as two Charlies stagger back clutching their hands, howling in pain.

Onyx snarls. "I demand justice for this violation. Who wants to die first?"

The other two turn and flee toward their encampment, where an audience has assembled. Several enforcers have started toward us, coming to the aid of their companions.

Onyx bellows, "Luce!" Without waiting for a reply, she yells, "Keep your barbies away from here or you will *lose* them!"

The injured two back away, whimpering, then turn and run, leaving their weapons on the ground. I sink to my knees, faint, then look to our savior with awe. Onyx glares at them as they all withdraw, then rushes to Dray, who is sitting on his ass, stunned. She kneels and tenderly checks him over, then helps him up as Val comes running out.

"Was that you yelling? What happened?"

"Where have you been? You were supposed to be out here. I had to chase off some intruders."

"Sorry, Onyx, I—They're not supposed to be over here."

"No shit."

"Onyx, I'm so sorry."

"Just keep an eye on the rabble out there. I'll get Dray back to his tent."

When Onyx sees how shaken he is, she wraps a concerned arm around him and helps him along. I flop down as they clamber inside, calming myself by replaying the vanquishing of our assailants, the shock on their faces.

I hear her approach, and she crouches down to confront me, eyes narrow.

She hasn't said a word to me since ... Shame floods me. "Onyx ... I ..."

Her demeanor changes. "That was bold, what you said to those punks. You may not be built for fighting, but you have the heart of a warrior. Now I know what she sees in you."

What? I wipe my eyes.

"And why you piss her off."

I wince at the unwanted confirmation.

"You are fucking infuriating. The question is, are you worth the aggravation? And that will be up to her."

"Onyx, I messed up so badly ... what can I do?"

"Don't ask me. Oh, one thing, though. You could stop humiliating her in front of everyone."

I moan. "I never meant to do that, honestly."

She pins me with her eyes. "Then stop."

I nod my hanging head as she scans the tree line and the enemy encampment.

"Onyx, thank you. For saving us. I knew you were good, but— whew."

"I was trained by the best." She examines me, then sniffs the air. "You probably don't know this, but Kāya has long been feared throughout the region, the youngest ever to achieve the rank of Swordmaster. Some of these youngsters weren't even born back then. Might not remember her."

"When you say sword, you're talking about these wooden bokken, right?"

She glances around and motions for me to follow, and we go back to join Dray in the tent. We sit hunched beside him. He looks feverish. "How are you doing, buddy?" I ask.

"Oh, you know." He doesn't look at me.

Right. Not good. "We're here. You're safe. Get some rest. Onyx was just telling me about the bokken."

She rubs his upper arm as she talks. "I'll give you some—sanitized—history if you promise not to tell."

"Wait. Are you sure? We don't want to get you in trouble."

She looks away, fuming. "Those young punks can do that, and I can't even talk about harmless stuff like this. It's ridiculous. The prohibition is overly broad. I doubt I'm going to tell you anything you don't already know."

I stroke Dray's hair. "We won't tell a soul, will we, freeman."

Dray's eyes are unfocused, like he's somewhere else. He's still struggling for air.

"I know. It's okay." She puts a hand on his cheek, and he settles back. "In the Before, they had weapons that could kill from a great distance."

"Yes, we've ... heard about guns." I blush, feeling dirty.

She nods, then chooses her words carefully. "After the collapse, on the brink of extinction, we could no longer afford such disregard for human life. One of the first decrees from the ForeMothers was to destroy all those weapons and ban the construction of new ones. But the laws still needed to be enforced, so enforcers were solely authorized to carry weapons. The blunt-edged bokken were adopted to keep the death toll to a minimum. Even so, in the hands of a skilled fighter, a bokken is a deadly weapon."

"Those enforcers were out to kill you?"

"No, no. That would be unthinkable. Just some young hotshots out trying to prove themselves."

"But when you fight, someone gets hurt."

"If no one submits."

"Then why does Luce want a capital challenge with Kāya?"

"Because she's a greedy fool? I don't know. It seems her hand-to-hand victory has given her false confidence. Luce must suspect the value of this place and want undisputed ownership. It's a corrupt purpose for a challenge. I hope the Arbiter will see that, if she gets here in time."

"Kāya would win anyway, right?"

"Nothing is certain in the ring."

"Then we must *stop* this."

A grin. "The heart of a fighter. It's a good thing; you have a hell of a fight on your hands."

"What do you mean?"

She leans over and checks outside to see that no one is near, then speaks in hushed tones.

"Kāya is hard on men. She fears that if she loves, it gives a man too much power over her. She's determined to never let that happen again. She has to be the one in charge."

"What happened?"

She disregards my question. "What you need to understand is, for someone with her power, a loss of self-control could be disastrous, and she knows that, and it's a heavy responsibility. She always maintains tight control."

I raise an eyebrow.

"Except when it comes to you, it seems. I've never seen a man push her buttons the way you do. She hates that. And it should scare the crap out of you."

"Believe me, it does. I'm not doing it on purpose."

"Then, on purpose, *don't* do it." She looks down and studies Dray's face. His breathing has evened out, though I doubt he's sleeping. "I understand her need for control. I wish I had her self-discipline. That's why I need her. Being with her keeps me in line."

I take Dray's hand and hold it. "I used to think that was my role with him, but it works both ways, doesn't it, buddy."

Without moving, he mumbles, "Yup, does." I feel a light squeeze on my hand, and relief washes over me.

"Yes, it does." Onyx's soft voice is thoughtful.

We sit in silence until restlessness overtakes me. "I'm gonna stretch my legs."

"Me too," says Onyx. She tenderly brushes the hair from Dray's face. "I'll be just outside."

I climb out into the fresh air, and Onyx follows. "We were taking the other tents down. I should probably get back to it."

She follows partway, then stops. "I'm going to stay nearby while he rests."

I nod. "Please do."

She leans in and whispers, "What's going on with him? He wouldn't tell me."

I go up on tiptoes to whisper back, "He just got threatened with gang rape. It's messed him up a bit."

She stops without looking at me, and her shoulders slump. "I wondered."

I take a long breath. "He still has nightmares about it. Bad ones."

"I've never seen him have one."

"Glad to hear. I thought you'd be good for him. But this could be a setback. It'll be spinning through his mind again. They threatened to dose us with chemicals, Onyx. You know, the ones that make a man rigid so he can be repeatedly used."

She sways back and forth, biting her knuckle.

I continue. "Most survivors are never able to see She the same way again."

She seethes as she glares in the direction of the intruders' retreat and struggles to keep her voice low. "These thugs make all She look bad. And that *really* pisses me off." She turns to me with renewed concern. "Are you two going to be okay?"

"Well, we just had a She stand up for us. That might be a first."

She leans in and kisses me on the forehead, then holds my eyes. "He needs you here with him, Tye. Don't mess this up."

Easy to say when you're not the one running blindfolded through the woods.

32

REFUGE

The angle of the sun tells me it's late afternoon. There are storm clouds on the southern horizon, and I wish they would come this way and blast Luce and her monsters out of here. But storms never come when you want them.

With Onyx in the tent tending to Dray, I return to the one we were dismantling, but I'm too busy watching for danger to be productive. Val is making her presence known to the enemy, patrolling back and forth, and her proximity gives me comfort.

A disquieting thought intrudes as I gather up tent poles. The fact that they want their tents down means they're not gonna sleep out here where they'd be vulnerable to a midnight raiding party. But what about us? Are they gonna leave us out here alone?

"Tye." It's Onyx, and Dray is climbing out of the tent after her. "Come on. We're going inside."

I hesitate. "Inside? Are you sure?"

She glares at the enemy encampment, then at the entrance. "I'm not leaving you out here."

My heart aches with admiration. I nod to Dray, trying to hide my envy.

As we approach the entrance, my chest tightens. I cling to Dray, who clings to Onyx as we make our way inside and down the switch-back stairway, a dusty breeze in our faces. "You really have running toilets down here?" Dray asks, and Onyx laughs and assures him they do.

Bree appears below us, alerted by our noisy descent, and calls for Kāya. My stomach twists.

We reach the bottom just as Kāya rushes up and stands beside the portable blower fan, blocking the door. I shrink back, ready to retreat, and whatever hope Onyx had given me shatters under the blow of her words.

"Onyx, what are you doing? Get them back outside where Luce can see them."

"They can't stay out there."

"They need to. I can't have them in here."

I call out to her, "Kāya, I need to apologize for—"

The dismissal is harsh. "Not now, Tye."

My face flushes, and I fight back tears. She's done with me, all right. I have no one to blame but myself.

Onyx confronts her. "If they stay out there, Luce will take them. Her goons already tried."

Kāya spins on her in alarm. "What?"

"Four young punks came over and grabbed them. I took care of it."

Eyes squeezed shut, Kāya clenches her fists, then slams them against her thighs. "How *dare* they disrespect me like that!"

I brace.

"To attack men in my custody, *right in front of me.* In front of *me!* Show me who did this! They'll face my justice!"

"They paid for their violation," says Onyx, holding out the two captured bokken.

Kāya snatches the weapons. "I'll find them myself."

She storms toward the stairs, but Onyx grabs her by the arm and yanks her to a stop, then leans in and confronts her, eye to eye. "I took care of it."

Two statues, face to face, cold as rock, glare at each other.

"I know," says Onyx. "It's not fair that I get to have all the fun."

Kāya eases. "I'm sorry, Onny." She takes a deep breath to compose herself. "I just can't *believe* ... It *appalls* me that this new crop of enforcers can have so little discipline and self-respect."

"Tell me about it."

It's not until I sigh in relief that I realize I'm breathing without a mask. The air still smells dusty, but no worse than the upper entrance.

Onyx says, "They didn't seem to know of you, Kay, so it wasn't the disrespect you think."

"Even so, it was still a disrespectful violation of the rules."

Onyx nods in agreement, then rubs the back of her neck. "Maybe it's a good thing that your old reputation hasn't followed you out here. Yes, there are perks to being feared. People defer to you. But there are drawbacks too. I thought we wanted a fresh start."

"I am well aware of the drawbacks," snaps Kāya. Her shoulders slump. "So that's what we're dealing with, is it? A bunch of undisciplined young punks? It's probably all Luce can afford."

"Or the only losers willing to join a criminal gang. Which means we can't trust them." Onyx is emphatic. "I am not leaving the men out there, Kay."

"Then send them back to town."

"That would be like handing them to Luce. She'd use them as hostages. And we can't send anyone with them. We need all of us here."

Kāya's jaw clenches as she rubs her head.

Onyx shrugs. "I'll stay out with them if I have to."

Kāya examines her eyes, then turns away. "No. I don't want you..." Her head falls back, and she rubs a hand through her brush-cut hair.

Onyx reaches out and touches her arm.

"Onny, what are we doing? They can't be in here. They could cost us everything. I made this mistake already. How can I make it again? It makes me no better than those punks, violating a law I'm supposed to enforce."

"A law you don't even agree with, I thought. Do you honestly think these men will pose a danger? Given what we've now learned?"

They just learned something?

"It's not a choice," says Kāya. "Luce is here now. It gives her justification."

"Of course it's a choice."

"Not a legal choice. It kills any chance we have with arbitration. They'll have no choice but to rule against us. We'll lose this place."

Tight-lipped, Onyx glowers at her.

"Onyx, we're enforcers. A ruling against us would end our careers. We have a duty here."

Onyx stares down the hall. "What about justice? Fairness? Compassion? If you leave them out there, they'll be killed. Is it time to get rid of them, Kay?"

Kāya's face falls. "No. No, of course not."

I tremble as she rubs her forehead. She still hasn't looked at me. Finally, she takes a deep breath. "Okay, then. Arbitration is out. I need to face Luce before the Arbiter gets here."

What? No. That's not—

"That's not what I'm saying," says Onyx. "There's got to be—"

Kāya cuts her off. "There is no other way. Now, where are we going to put them?"

Onyx tries to offer a compromise. "We can let them sleep at the bottom of the stairs, where they won't see anything."

"It won't matter to Luce, or to the Arbiter. All they'll see is that the men are inside." Kāya's head falls forward. "We might as well make them comfortable."

I've always tried to avoid being a burden. But this ... this is too much. Our being here could cost her everything—this place for sure, and maybe even her life. I look down a brightly lit hallway that has no resemblance to the suffocating black tunnel I remember, a welcoming entrance to an entire world of history that I now, finally, have access to. And I kiss it goodbye.

"No. No, we can't stay here. We need to go. Come on, Dray, we need to go." I grab his arm and pull him back toward the stairway. He resists.

"Tye, she said we could stay."

"We can't stay. We've got to leave, *now*."

Onyx intervenes. "Tye, what are you doing? You can't go back out there."

"It's more dangerous for us to stay."

Dray pulls his arm free. "What's wrong with you?"

"Luce is here because of us. She'll keep pressing as long as we're here. They'll lose this place if we stay. If we go, Luce has no justification for being here." I yank his arm. "Dray, *a capital challenge*. Would you stay if Onyx might die because of you?"

His shoulders droop, and he turns to her with pleading eyes. "Is he right, Onny?"

She opens her mouth to object, then turns up her hands in a shrug.

"Onyx, would you trade Kāya's life for Dray's? Because that's what you're doing by bringing us in here," I say.

"No, that's not ..." She deflates.

Kāya steps forward. "Here's the way it is. You can't leave."

"We can't stay," I snap.

She crosses her arms and looks down her nose at me. "So, what's your big plan?"

"We've been hiking these wilds for years. We know our way around. Don't worry, we'll find the highway."

"They'll be watching for you. They'll never just let you leave."

My eyes falter, and I look to Dray. "We'll sneak out after dark. When the Arbiter gets here, tell her the errand boys finished their deliveries and left. Tell her they were never inside."

"You want me to lie to an Arbiter," Kāya says.

"Then tell her you protected history and we never learned one bit of it. Because that's true."

She winces.

"Kāya, I didn't mean that as a complaint. You've been right all along. I'm sorry I've been such an ass. We can't be here. I wish you all the success in the world, Kāya. And Onyx? We love you. Don't let her fight, okay?"

As I turn to leave, Onyx grabs my arm. "They're watching, you know. They'll come after you."

"We'll hide in the bush."

She gives me a matronizing smile. "They've got two trackers over there who can track a rabbit through a swamp. You really think you can hide from them?"

Crap. I forgot about trackers. I look at Dray and see the fear in his eyes.

Guns. I've done it again. Another bold defiance, another bad decision. Kāya's right. Again. I try to hide my face, but she comes right up and looms over me, and I draw back. But she confronts me with her full face and grabs me with her eyes, and ... those deep aquamarine eyes ... I'm suddenly lost.

"You're thinking about sacrificing yourself to Luce in the hope of preventing the fight. I know you are. It won't work, Tye. Luce wouldn't be satisfied, even with killing both of you. It's not you she wants. It's this facility. You men are merely her justification. So, can you see how it would be a pointless death?"

I nod, helpless.

"Good." She steps back from me. "I am responsible for your safety." She looks at Onyx and nods, and Onyx eases. Eyes on the floor, I recover myself. I refuse to be a burden to her.

"We're freemen, Kāya. You're not responsible—"

"I brought you here. I let you in. I *am* responsible."

I shrink in the glare of her authority. She corners me again.

"And if you want to be part of this team, you will start acting like it."

My mouth falls open, and I stare, blinking, but she has turned away.

"Onyx, since you're not busy, you might as well show them around."

"You sure?" says Onyx. Not looking back, Kāya waves her off as she walks away.

Onyx puts a protective hand on Dray's shoulder and checks me. "Are you done?"

Speechless, I nod.

"How about you, Dray? Are you ready for the grand tour?"

He almost giggles. "Sure."

The grand tour. My dream come true. This is what I've been fighting for, demanding, and I'm finally getting my way. I should be thrilled, but I'm too dazed. I'm putting Kāya in jeopardy, and yet ... *Show them around*? *Part of this team*? After what I've done?

I shake myself and hurry to catch up with Onyx. "She's letting us look around?"

"Nothing to lose anymore. If she wins tomorrow, she dictates the law around here, and we won't have to worry about being charged."

I wait for the rest, but it doesn't need saying. If she loses, none of this matters. Kāya is granting me a final request.

And I don't want it anymore, not at such a cost. If I could, I would trade it for her safety in a heartbeat. But clearly, I can't.

Stomach in knots, I follow Onyx down the hall, but she's in such a huff I take notice. It's hard to pay attention to anything else. When we enter the cafeteria, there's no one around, and she pulls Dray aside. "I need to speak to your friend for a moment. Don't worry, cutie, this has nothing to do with you."

He nods with perfect understanding, and she gets right in my face. I blanch.

"Sometimes I wish I were a man," she says, "just so I could beat the shit out of you." I tighten and pull back. "But the most aggravating thing is, it's hard to stay pissed at you because your heart's always in the right place. You know, I thought growing up with four brothers prepared me for dealing with men. In your case, I was wrong. I give up. I'm not protecting you anymore. And I won't let you take Dray down with you. Do you understand?"

My head falls. "Perfectly. And you're right. I deserve this."

"Oh, shut up. Can't I just be mad at you for five minutes?"

Dray says, "Good luck with that. I've been trying for years."

She shakes her head with a grin, and my fear recedes. There's that humor they share, with its power to snuff a fuse. Grateful, and again envious, I gather myself back together. The look on Dray's face is so smug I have to fight the urge to smack him. But I can't blame him. How can he—how can *we* be so lucky as to love someone like Onyx?

She looks around. "Since we're right here, let's start with the kitchen. You won't believe this place."

We follow her in, and my mouth falls open. With the lights on, it looks entirely different, otherworldly. The walls, cabinets and countertops all gleam silver. Several cabinets are open, and there are dishes on the counter and in one of the sinks. The cabinets are full of matching white mugs and clear glasses, all within easy reach. Everything in here is sized for a man. No surprise there; a kitchen is a man's place.

For the next half-hour, Onyx takes us on a whirlwind tour of the lower levels, each a mysterious new world of its own. The bottom three levels are laid out differently from the top two, with one central hallway dividing the workspaces on both sides.

Even after exploring the fabrication lab, I have no idea what they did here. Onyx tells us some of these machines made things on their own. I sometimes wonder if she's making stuff up.

In one of the workshops, I see things that at least seem familiar, like a drill press, a table saw, a welding table, and metal filings still waiting to be cleaned up. While the tools have recognizable elements, I can't see how to use any of them.

Sub-level three, with its brightly lit main hallway and labs, has no trace of menace. Glass walls and doors line one side of the hall, and large windows the other, exposing everything in the surrounding rooms. All other surfaces are white, making the whole place seem to shine. It's a complete inversion of that black nightmare from before.

We follow Onyx down the hall, watching through the line of windows as Val pokes around in one of the labs. She seems to be taking inventory of what's here.

Just this one lab is huge. Half the space is filled with large desks, and half with long white tables. All are covered with—stuff. Big storage cabinets sit under most desks, and smaller ones hang above.

Closet doors line the wall on the left, while along the far wall are several huge cabinets that look like oversized refrigerators. It will take years to search through all this stuff.

Onyx points to a door. "Nance and Val should be in here. This is a bio-lab. They're busy documenting the place, so try not to get in their way."

I follow Onyx through the door and freeze. *Ghosts.* They're all around me. Big, white—No. Not ghosts. The room is lined with—with deflated balloon men all watching me through vacant eyes. Onyx pays no attention to the strange white figures, and they show no reaction to her passing.

"Outfits of some kind," says Dray, behind me.

Onyx looks back and grins. "That's right. Biological isolation garments. To protect the people working in here."

Right. That's what I'm looking at. This was some kind of changeroom.

We continue through into a large room that contains a smaller room with glass walls. A glass passageway with doors at each end acts as an entrance to the inner box. Within the inner box is a long work-table covered with strange devices, large and small. There are clear boxes with black hands reaching into them. Some weird kind of gloves? I'm tempted to reach in as I try to imagine holding something inside the box from outside. Curious.

Aida sees me looking perplexed. "This is a negative pressure lab," she says, "meaning that the air pressure inside is lower than that outside. If a leak were to occur, nothing would spill out, because the air is sucking inward. It's quite ingenious."

I have no clue what she's talking about.

She continues. "They used places like this to study the most dangerous pathogens, stuff they didn't want getting out into the open."

"Like what?"

"Lethal toxins, dangerous microorganisms, stuff like that."

"Like viruses?"

"Yes."

"Are we safe in here?"

She shrugs. "Don't lick anything."

Was that a smirk? Suddenly not so curious, I cautiously retrace my steps.

I'm getting used to the boxy spaces, with all the square corners and long, straight lines, but the endless variety of mysterious forms and objects is starting to feel oppressive.

My interest picks up when we get back up to the living quarters on level two. Onyx explains that no one lived here, but these beds were available for emergency use. Eight small bedrooms line a wide hallway. I recognize the travel bags in some of the rooms and note that two of the beds have no mattresses. We could bring our bedrolls down if they let us stay. The bedrooms are serviced by two large washroom areas, each with multiple sinks, closed-in toilets, and a communal shower room. Something else to look forward to.

As we climb the stairs to the top floor, my heart jumps at the sounds of fighting. I know the clash of weapons when I hear it. We turn to Onyx in alarm, but she seems unfazed until she notices our trepidation.

"It's okay. They're only training."

Indeed, we find Bree and Kāya sparring in the large conference room, where they've pushed all the furniture to one side. In battle armor, they're jumping around, whacking at each other, until they see us at the door and stop. Breathing hard, they remove their helmets, and Kāya dismisses Bree, who eyes us with resentment on her way past.

"How's the tour going?"

"Amazing," says Dray.

Ignoring me, she addresses Onyx. "Any problems?"

"Nope, smooth as silk. We've done a quick run-through."

They chat as we follow down the hall to a large office, where Kāya steps through another doorway into an inner office and strips off her battle armor. I see one of the mattresses from downstairs in the corner, with her travel bag and other belongings strewn about. This must be where she has settled in.

"It's still early, but we should think about dinner in a couple of hours. Did you show them the kitchen?"

"Sure did. They could likely use some help with working the induction cooktop. Do you need me for anything else right now?"

"No, that would be good." Kāya turns her back on us, and I reluctantly follow the other two out.

But in the hallway my feet stick to the floor, and I can't move. They both look back. "I'll catch up," I say, waving them on. Onyx hesitates, then gives up.

I can't take it anymore, being closed out like this. I'd rather face her rage.

33

———

MYSTERIES

I REENTER WITHOUT PERMISSION, and when I close the door behind me, she swings around to confront me. "Kāya, please. Just hear me."

Her eyes narrow but she says nothing.

"Yesterday, when I ... mouthed off at you, Kāya, that was so wrong of me, I ... I don't even know ..."

She turns her back to me.

"There's nothing I can say to ... I'm so sorry. I'm so ... sorry. Kāya ..."

"Stop."

The air goes out of me.

"It's not you I'm mad at, Tye. It's me."

My world tilts. Before I can recover, she goes on.

"I'm the one who should be apologizing. I just ... haven't been able to face you."

My mouth falls open. "I don't understand."

"I ... lost control. That should never have happened."

"Kāya, I deserved it."

She wheels around to face me. "No. You didn't. I could have killed you."

"I don't believe that."

She stills, scowling.

"I still have my face," I say.

"What?"

"Nothing. I mean, yes, I know what you're capable of, but ... Kāya, I'm not like this. I don't know why I seem to have this need to provoke you all the time, but please understand that ... I honestly have profound respect for you."

She looks away. "Those things you said ... you weren't wrong. It really is unfair. And I thought you explained it well when you said we were natural enemies."

"I said what?"

"You being a freeman and me, an enforcer."

"Oh, right. Uh, I didn't mean actual enemies, more like rivals."

"I know what you meant. Let me finish. What I did to you was reckless and wrong, and I'm sorry. That will never happen again."

My eyes sting and well up. I should leave it alone, but I can't. "Then stop practicing. For the fight. Kāya, please don't fight Luce."

She sighs. "There is no other way. Your being here—"

"You could just give her the damn place. Please, just let it go."

"Let it go?" Her voice is incredulous.

"Kāya, we can find somewhere else. Now we know what we're looking for. There must have been more places like this. I'll find something."

"Okay, first, you have no idea how uniquely important this place is, and how could you? That's not your fault. And second, I'm not gonna just give it to her. She has no right to it."

"Might makes right. She brings superior force."

"With criminal intent. I won't let her steal it. I'm going to stop her right here."

"Please don't fight, Kāya. Please."

"How can you ask that of me? Our futures are at stake here. All of them."

"Kāya, your *life* is at stake! Nothing is worth that."

She turns away, then pulls herself up and faces me. "You need to understand something, Tye. This is what I do. I've spent my entire life preparing for this. What is my life worth if I can't protect those I love? If I'm not willing to fight for the future of my people? Because that's what's at stake here. End of discussion." She leans back and crosses her arms. "Now if you'll excuse me, we both have somewhere to be."

The bottom falls out of my heart, and I flee from the room. Heroes like Kāya, like my mother, are everything to you—until you lose them. And there's nothing I can do to stop it.

———

THE TEAM HAS GATHERED in the cafeteria. Over coffee and buttered nut bread, the talk is somber, mostly about strategies for dealing with Luce. I've had to accept that the only way to resolve this is for Kāya to fight. No one seems to have much faith in arbitration, given our "situation." Their stupid rules have never made sense to me. Luce's challenge couldn't have come at a worse time, they complain. It has blocked the recruitment of needed help, including both historians and enforcers. Of course, none of that matters if Luce takes the place from us. And if she kills Kāya ... nothing matters.

I can't think like that. Kāya is the best of the best.

I wish I'd never seen Luce beat her.

Though no one has mentioned it, it's clear to me that if Luce wins, Dray and I will die too. Learning history now seems irrelevant.

Cleaning up after the coffee break, I notice Kāya step out to the washroom around the corner. When she comes back out, I'm waiting in the hall. "Have you got a minute?"

"Uh ..." She looks for an escape.

"Please." I grab her by the arm, pull her into the empty office beside us and close the door, then realize what I've done. I've touched her uninvited. I quickly pull away. "Sorry."

"What is it, Tye?" She's impatient.

I jump right in. "Onyx showed us around the whole place. I saw all kinds of amazing, wondrous, mysterious things, but ... What's the big deal? Why shouldn't we be seeing this? I don't understand."

She puffs out her cheeks. "This isn't the stuff we're worried about."

"Then what?"

She gives one of her exasperated sighs. "We're back to this, are we?"

"Kāya, you're in trouble because you have men in here. Why does such a law exist? It makes no sense."

"I wish you'd stop pestering me about this. You know I can't—"

"I'm not asking you to reveal history. I just need to understand this law. Please. Why is history forbidden to men?"

In frustration, she blurts, "Because it exposes She to danger, okay?"

I furrow my brow. The words snag something my mother wrote. Something ludicrous about men taking control. Is that what they're afraid of? "So, me knowing history exposes She ... What danger are we talking about here? You're afraid all the men will suddenly go crazy?"

"I'm starting to think it already happened to you. When did you learn history?"

I gasp. "No. No, I didn't learn ..."

She raises her eyebrows at my defensiveness.

"I mean, I ... Do you think I'm crazy?"

"Tye, I'm teasing."

"I don't want to expose you to danger, Kāya. Maybe if I knew what the danger was, I could prevent it and keep you safe. That's all I want."

She hides her mouth behind her fist. "I'm not sure anymore how real the danger even is."

"Anymore?"

"We've ... learned some things."

"Men used to be more dangerous? In the Before?"

"We've always known that."

I didn't. Is that what my mother's book was about? "Did these devices give men special powers or something?"

"Something like that."

"Okay, so I can see why you wouldn't want men to have them. But they're so rare now, and can't be replicated, so how hard could it be to control access? And that doesn't explain how knowledge of history itself is dangerous."

Her impatience heats her voice. "The threat of insurrection, remember? You know that."

Sedition to incite insurrection. Right. I suck air. "So we men get together and cause a ruckus. So what? There is nothing we can do. You can crush us."

She squints and goes quiet.

"So, what's the threat?"

No response.

"What would happen if my anger drove me mad enough to retaliate against you? What would you do?"

I expect her to say she'd smack me down. Instead, a flash of anguish drains the blood from her face, and she abruptly turns away, clutching herself. I freeze. I've triggered something. A bad memory? Some past retaliation? I wish I hadn't said that.

"Kāya? Are you okay?"

She snaps upright and grinds her palms together but says nothing. I try to clarify. "All I'm saying is, even if I wanted to, which I don't, I could never do you any harm. As you have repeatedly demonstrated."

Eyes down, she stretches her neck. Her voice is icy certainty when she says, "Yes, you could."

I shiver. "How?"

Eyes squeezed shut, she puts prayer hands to her mouth. "Get out, Tye. Right now."

My instincts demand that I heed the warning. Incredulous, I back toward the door, but then stop. I can't leave her like this. It's a desperate stab in the dark. "Kāya. I'm not him."

A look of shock subsides. As she studies me, her intensity sucks the air from my lungs. Finally, we breathe.

"No," she says. "You're not." She brushes herself off and composes herself. "I've got work to do. Shouldn't you be helping Dray?"

———

I'VE BEEN TRYING to process what happened with Kāya, but all I know for sure is that somewhere along the line she had a bad experience with a man. How bad could it have been? I mean, she's an Alpha. I give up and focus on preparing food.

We have no idea what they're up to, but the team's She have all been together for what seems like hours. Dray and I have managed to figure out enough of the kitchen to prepare a meager dinner for everyone. Then, when nobody shows up in the cafeteria, we decide to deliver it. I take the first tray and head off while Dray prepares another. I find the conference room door cracked open and a lively discussion going on inside. I pause outside the door and listen.

There's Aida's voice. "Can we at least agree that this changes everything? I mean, when this gets out, it will shake our world. It directly challenges some long-held and cherished assumptions."

I still my breath to hear. A tingle of anticipation quickens my pulse.

Nance adds, "People have been searching for years for confirmation of the Celia Hypothesis, and now we have it. No question this will cause a stir."

The Celia Hypothesis? Where have I heard that before ... Yes, Kāya, at the old site. But what does my mother have to do with this? Now I'm riveted to the spot.

"And it's about time." It's Onyx. "This world needs a good stir."

Bree counters, "We don't need sedition coming from our own ranks. We have to—"

I alert to the sudden silence.

Without warning, the door swings wide, and Kāya is towering over me, glaring down.

"What are you doing here?" she demands.

How did she know—Her senses. "I ... uh, I brought you some dinner. Dray is coming with another tray."

"How long have you been standing here? How much did you hear?"

"Enough to know you made a big discovery, not enough to learn any history."

She gives a satisfied nod, then takes the tray from my hands. "Thank you. Now go."

"What is the Celia Hypothesis?"

Bree jumps from her chair. "I'll deal with this." She strides at me. "Leave, Tye. Now!"

"You're talking about my mother."

Bree's voice is surly. "Are you going to leave peacefully, or—"

"Bree. Stand down." Kāya sets the tray down as Bree fumes, then she turns to me. "Your mother is a brilliant historian. Her work is no concern of yours."

"My mother was crazy. She learned too much history, didn't she. It drove her mad. You think the same will happen to me."

With a puzzled frown, Kāya says, "Where did you hear that?"

"You told me yourself."

"No, the part about your mother being crazy."

Uh-oh. "I ... don't know. Somewhere. But it's true, right?"

"No," says Nance. "The opposite is true. She sees more clearly than most."

I'm taken aback. What about all the nonsense in her writings? I dare not ask out loud. Dray's arrival with the second tray rescues me.

He hesitates, looking from face to face. "What's going on?"

"Tye was just leaving," says Bree.

I ignore her. "What will happen to men when you shake up the world?"

They exchange looks around the table until Nance says, "We don't know."

Bree says, "Nothing will happen, because men aren't involved."

"We're going to need to revisit Rule Six, Bree," says Nance. "Our discovery makes it hard to justify the history prohibition. I mean, what are they going to do? Reinvent gene editing with today's technology?"

Reinvent what?

Bree reacts. "You think men won't be angry? How can they not hate us when they find out?"

Onyx says, "You think we can't handle them?"

"Not if they all rise up together. They could tear our whole society apart. The fact is, we just don't know how men will react."

I jump in. "You're worried about how men will react to your new discovery? Why don't you find out? You've got a couple of men right here. Use us as test subjects and see how we react."

Kāya shakes her head. "Tye, I'm not going to risk—"

"Risk what? My life? Your life? Tomorrow, Kāya, you will fight to the death. And I'm supposed to stand back and be careful? Please. Use me to learn what you need to learn. If I go crazy, then put me down. I'd rather die by your hand than by Luce's."

The She exchange nervous glances.

Dray's voice surprises me. "He's already crazy, so what's the big deal?"

His support bolsters me. "Show us history. Throw it at us and see if we survive. You'll have your answer."

Stony silence. I breathe again when Aida speaks. "It's not a bad idea. The stories of men going mad when exposed to history were meant to scare off men, but even some She have come to believe them. Before we go public with any of this, it would be good to have evidence that the old fears are unfounded. There will be strong resistance to change, and we need to be ready to counter it."

Val says, "I just think we should take more time to digest this."

Aida says, "Time is the one thing we don't have."

Kāya stands. "Thank you, freemen. Please leave us now."

It's her 'end of discussion' tone, and I won't push her again. She's got enough on her plate right now. I wrap Dray's arm in mine and escort him from the room.

"I never cared before," he says, "but after seeing all this historical stuff, I'm starting to wonder. What's so bad about knowing history?"

I grip his hand. "Welcome aboard, my friend."

34

———

TEST SUBJECTS

Back in the kitchen, we're cleaning up when Onyx arrives to check on us. She's showing us how to prepare an automatic coffee machine when Val appears at the door.

"Onyx, you're to report to the media room with the men."

"Got it," says Onyx. I can see she's unsettled.

"What's a media room?" asks Dray.

"It's like a library, I guess. Where you get information. Come on. You'll see for yourselves."

Back in the main hall, we walk past open doors and glance in. They seem familiar now, yet Dray stops to reexamine one. "Onny, here we are, inside a historical site, and things are strange and amazing and all, but I still don't see what's the big deal about us men being here. What is it you She, with all your power, are so afraid of?"

She looks at me like I put him up to it. I plead innocent, and she turns and continues down the hall. "You'll find out soon enough."

Our destination is next door to the huge conference room. When we reach the room, everyone else is already in there.

The "media room" is larger than the offices, with a long table against the right wall and three rows of three chairs in the middle. On the left wall is a huge picture of a man dressed in odd clothing, his mouth open, as though in mid-speech. The picture seems to be glowing like a movie screen, except there is no projector, and no screen. It's like it's painted into glass. I'm drawn to examine it but notice the tension in the hushed voices around me and pause to try to hear what's going on.

Kāya confers with Aida, then calls for attention. "Everyone, take a seat."

When we've all settled, her attention turns to me and Dray. "I see no point in putting this off. After considering your offer, I've decided to take you up on it. We need you to be test subjects. Are you willing to do that for us?"

Nance adds, "We need to see how you react when exposed to ... certain information. Some of us,"—she glances at Bree—"need to be reassured. From there, we'll be able to make informed recommendations."

"Yes, we're willing," I blurt, then check with Dray. His response is part nod, part shrug.

"Good," says Kāya. "So, we're all agreed." She addresses the others. "Our time is limited. We have enemies outside. We don't know what tomorrow will bring, but I'm going to do my best to end this travesty quickly." She looks to each of her enforcers. "If I fail, you will implement Plan B."

"You won't fail," says Onyx.

"What's Plan B?" I ask.

Kāya ignores me. "Reviewing this material will help us stay focused on what's at stake here, what we're fighting for."

"Yes," says Nance. "All the physical riches we've encountered are only a small part of what we have here. This is without doubt the greatest historical find in a generation. This will define our careers. If we can hold on to it."

Aida adds, "And there's a lot more we haven't seen yet, an entire digital archive. A complete historical record of the years leading up to the collapse. It is crucial—I can't emphasize enough how important this is—that we protect this archive. We simply cannot trust it to Luce."

"In fact," says Kāya, "we *can* trust her to plunder the place and spoil the records. We can't let that happen. We must see to it that this knowledge is made available to everyone."

Onyx jumps in. "The artifacts alone will have an enormous impact. As soon as we show our salvage, people will be fighting to see the source. Think about it. It's a safe location outside the Shell. Once we've cleaned the place up, we can open it to others, and people will pay for the privilege of seeing it."

"Like a museum?" I ask.

Onyx is beaming, a faraway look in her eyes. "This will become a center of study, a history university. Scholars of all stripes will descend into this space and scour every inch of it for knowledge that could benefit the entire world."

Dray joins in. "And you might not even need to keep it from men."

Bree scowls. "Are we really doing this?"

Aida speaks up. "Bree, Rule Six followed from those dark times when men refused to accept what was then a new reality. The rule brought peace and stability."

"Exactly," says Bree.

"To modern men," adds Nance, "it is *not* a new reality. It's normal. That changes the equation. In that light, this is an important test. Think of it as research."

"Yes," says Aida, "there is concern about the effect this information will have on men. I say we watch these two and see how typical men react."

Bree remains unconvinced. "I still think it's a mistake."

I stand and move to front her. "Bree. I respect your concern. But we are freemen. We choose to take this risk, and it is our mistake to make. No fault of yours."

Dray grins. "Well put, freeman."

Bree reddens until Kāya intervenes. "I'll be honest, Bree. I don't know how they'll react. But unless knowing history throws men into a suicidal rage, the old fears are unfounded. We have the opportunity, right now, to put this to the test."

A suicidal rage?

She continues. "I take full responsibility. If suppression is needed, I will do it." The She all turn to look at us.

"Suppression?" I ask.

Kāya looks me in the eye. "Here's the way it is. I will do whatever is necessary to prevent you from harming anyone."

Uncertainty grips me. "So, if you show me history, you might need to kill me?"

She shrugs. "Do you still want to learn?"

There's no way I would fly into some suicidal ... Could it really be so bad? But look how I felt after just a small taste of it. And when I lose it, I lose it. I pull my hair back tight on my scalp. No. She looks a little too smug. I think she's playing this up. Besides, I'm not gonna back out now. "Do what you need to do."

Kāya quizzes Bree with her eyes. Bree sighs and looks away.

Onyx jumps in. "Dray, you don't need to do this. We can go down to the power lab until they get this sorted out."

Dray shakes his head. "I'm gonna stay, in case I need to bail out his ass again." He leans into me. "Let's learn history, freeman. I got your back."

Onyx notices Kāya watching her, and turns to say, "I'm not worried. They'll be fine." She's trying to convince herself. That's not reassuring.

Dray puts his hand on my shoulder. "Some adventure, huh?"

"You don't have to do this."

"You think I'm gonna let you keep secrets from me? Besides, somebody's got to keep you in line. And like I said, all this has made me curious. Now I want to know, too."

"Okay, then," says Kāya. "How can we prepare these two for this?" She examines each of us in turn, then says, "You'll be disturbed by what you are about to learn. You will find it uncomfortable, upsetting. You will find it unfair. You will have questions. When we're done, we'll do our best to answer them. You ready?"

I steel myself. Of course I'm ready. I've been waiting for this my whole life.

35

MEDIA ROOM

I NOTICE Aida wearing a band around her left forearm that seems to be glowing. On it, I see the same picture as the one on the wall. "What's that?"

"It's called an e-band," says Aida. "This image on it is being shown up there so everyone can see."

I shiver. This is the magic I knew was here. I'm finally seeing it.

Aida looks around the room. "We've decided it's a good place to start." Kāya nods, and with a touch, the portrait on the wall comes to life. I jump. The man is talking, right in front of us. Aida gestures, and the picture changes. It's the same middle-aged man, but now he's seated across from another man.

The picture changes, and we see the head and shoulders of a pale-skinned, clean-shaven man with a short-cut She hairstyle. He speaks directly to us. "With further easing of restrictions expected, human genetic engineering will soon be coming out of the closet and jumping into the mainstream. To give you a quick preview of what that's going to look like, we're here at Genhance Inc. with CEO Derik Henley. Thank you, Derik, for meeting with us."

Val interrupts. "This was shot here."

Her voice shakes me from my spellbound state. "What is this we're looking at?"

Val says, "You've never seen a television?"

"This is not a television."

Nance helps out. "This is a Before version, called a wall-screen, and we're watching what was called a video clip. The images are re-created from data stored in a computer database."

Don't know what any of that means. "It looks so real."

"Yes, it does. A lost technology, unfortunately. Computers have a limited life span, and we don't have the technology to make new ones. Best we can do is throw together salvaged parts until we can get one working. And working parts are getting harder and harder to find. Thanks to the durability of DNA data storage, we have lots of intact data, but it's rare to come across a computer in working condition that can process it. You are witnessing a momentous thing here."

No shit. It hits me that I'm looking at the faces of people who lived in the Before, hearing their actual voices, as if they are right here with us now. A sense of awe stirs me. I'm in the presence of magic.

"Can we get back to it?" Bree sounds impatient.

I close my gaping mouth. Swirling questions leave me dizzy, so I bite my tongue. We settle back, and the picture starts moving again.

The first man, Derik somebody, says, "Thanks for coming in, Abram. We're delighted to have you here. You know, our work gets a lot of bad press, and we're happy to get the opportunity to set the record straight."

"Derik, your work here scares a lot of people. What do you say to those who fear the creation of monsters?"

My excitement flips to uncertainty. What is this about?

"They've completely missed the point. We're making the opposite of monsters. We're making angels."

"Help our viewers understand what you mean by that."

Yes. *Please.*

"Have you seen our girls? The very embodiment of angels."

"Of course, of course. Celebrities from birth. The early results are remarkable. But mistakes happen. And no one knows what the long-term effects of these enhancements will be—when they reach puberty, for example."

"Did his matria do something to their daughters?" I ask, and get shushed from every direction.

"We've gone through years of painstaking research to reach this point, including animal and human studies from around the world, and have seen no reason to expect problems later. As you know, we started out working to delete genetic defects. Our success led to a demand not just for healthy babies, but for enhanced babies. What parent doesn't want their children to be bigger, stronger, more beautiful, to go through life with all the advantages? There's no question that designer babies are the next big thing. The demand is exploding."

"But doesn't this leave normal children at a huge disadvantage?"

"Yes, parents fear their children being left behind, which is why it's going to be impossible to keep up with demand."

"But realistically, most parents can't afford to have their children genetically enhanced. Doesn't that leave *most* children behind?"

"We expect costs to plummet as the technology improves. Over time, the entire population will be elevated. Imagine the possibilities."

Aida motions, and the image freezes. "Questions?"

I'm squirming in my seat. I don't know where to start.

Dray narrows his eyes. "Why are men doing the talking? Where are the She in charge?"

I turn to Onyx. "Genetics has to do with how we're made. Like our human blueprint, right?"

"That's right. It may be difficult to believe, but in the Before, humans had developed the technology to rewrite that blueprint, to take the human template and alter it."

It's true, then; they had miraculous powers. I find myself trembling.

Dray frowns. "Why would they do that?"

Aida answers. "At first, it was to help people, but then later, they decided they wanted to make better people."

"Better than what?"

Bree cuts in. "Better than the people who were ravaging the world back then."

"We're getting ahead of ourselves here," says Kāya. "Let's get back to the interview."

On the screen, Derik starts speaking again. He's a ruggedly hand-some man with flawlessly trimmed facial hair and a smug certainty that makes me distrust him.

"With gene editing, we can make narrowly targeted changes. You want your child to be bigger, stronger, more beautiful? You can have any of those today. We can even add in genes from other species to confer specific advantages. Want your child to always land on her feet? There's a feline gene for that."

"At what point does an altered genome stop being human?"

Stop being human? My skin crawls. What are these people doing?

Derik answers, "Are better humans still human? I guess that's an argument for philosophers. All I can tell you is, judging from our girls, the men of the world are going to be very pleased with what's to come."

Aida pauses the image, and they all look at us. She chuckles. "That seems a little ironic, doesn't it?"

"And we have a whole library of this stuff," says Nance. "We are about to rewrite history."

Bree shakes her head. "Of all the times to have men around."

I shrink and shield my eyes from the glare of the screen.

"Well, we do," says Kāya. "And how they handle this will help you decide how to move forward." She directs that to Nance and Aida. Why leave it to them? My heart thuds. Tomorrow's fight. In case. "Let's continue," she says.

They're watching to see how we handle this. They all turn back to the screen as the picture starts moving again. Mind spinning, I have trouble following the rest.

The interview ends and Aida does something. A new picture pops up. We all watch as a pair of people in white overcoats, a She and a man, stand side by side in what looks like one of the labs downstairs.

The odd thing is, the man is a good half-foot taller than the She. They're being asked questions about their work and seem excited about it. Are those white coats some sort of uniform?

Dray whispers to me, "Look how tiny she is."

I notice Onyx watching us and return my attention to the screen in time to hear the She say, "We know that weaponized viruses are the state of the art in biological warfare. The virus is the ultimate weapon of mass casualty. It provides a low-cost delivery system, can be adapted to a wide range of forms and functions, and leaves infrastructure untouched. Once again, it's the promise of mutually assured destruction that keeps these weapons from being used."

Warfare? Mass casualty? Weapons? She speaks of madness so casually. What kind of people are these?

The small She is still as she speaks, with only her bottom teeth visible. Still, her enthusiasm comes through. They say my voice is high-pitched and childlike, but hers is dramatically so. "We're talking about turning the threat upside down and using synthetic viruses for good instead of evil. Imagine a virus built to have no effect on its host but designed to find egg cells and edit their genomes in highly specific ways. A completely noninvasive way to enhance offspring."

The man adds, "Viruses have played a huge role in evolution, editing genomes since the beginnings of DNA. But the edits have always been random. For the first time, we can take control of those edits, make us better than we are."

She takes over. "You know, a lot of people think it's dangerous, what we're doing. But wouldn't it be more dangerous to do nothing? To let mankind destroy itself with its fatal flaws? We can make a difference."

Mankind. Fatal flaws. This is what my mother was writing about. Maybe it wasn't all madness. I look around to see if this is making sense to the others, and they all seem to be taking it in stride.

Onyx presses her hands together in front of her nose, staring at the floor. Kāya puts a hand on her shoulder. "Onny?"

"There's an ancient quote: 'The road to hell is paved with good intentions.' They had no idea..."

"They were reckless. Men may have started the wars, but women helped trigger the crisis."

Dray cuts in. "What do you mean, 'women'?"

The two Alphas look at him, then at each other. Kāya's voice is soft. "That's what the females of the Before were called."

"Oh," he says. "What were the men called?"

I realize I already know. *Men have not changed.*

She blushes. "Uh, they were just called men." Then she notices me rubbing my temples. "Are you okay?"

"What? Oh, yeah. I'm fine." I check with Dray and see his bravado face. Not a good sign. "How about you? Are you okay?" Onyx watches intently.

"Couldn't be better," he says. "Let's do this."

We're in over our heads. I can see that now. I grab his hand. "Dray, you're a hero to me. You know that?"

"Yup, I know."

We hold each other's eyes, and I give him all the reassurance I can muster. Why did I put him in this situation?

36

THE NEWS

As Aida fiddles with her tablet, the media room is full of restless motion. It stills when she turns to address us.

"I've assembled a series of news clips that I think tell a coherent story. I'm going to go through them chronologically." She selects the first.

A—*woman*—sits behind a desk, surrounded by a swirl of images and words. She has thick, flowing hair in the masculine style, and an open neck adorned with jewelry. She sits at what looks like a fancy glass table, so we see her from the waist up. I catch my breath as she seems to float above a city—No, now she's immersed in—Now she's got pictures in boxes and words flying all around her—It's too much to keep up with. I close my eyes and try to focus on her voice.

She's talking about an unusual summer flu that everyone is catching, calling it the most virulent strain on record. I remember catching the flu in boarding school. Only the boys got it. It was brutal. I open my eyes in time to see flashes of images, from individuals and couples walking, to crowds of people, some wearing face coverings. Surrounding them all are huge square structures and roadways packed with colorful shiny vehicles. The Shell when it was a living city. The imagery is astonishing.

Aida selects the second clip, and this time we see a man. He looks my age but well kept. He seems clean and tidy, and his makeup is flawless. Whatever he's wearing has straight, sharp shoulders and a tight white collar, and I struggle again to focus on the words. A global pandemic called the "wildfire flu." Huh. I thought it was called the Great Pandemic. Up to eighty percent of the population exposed before the first symptoms even appeared. Impossible to counter. Images zoom in and out from points on a spinning globe to show scenes from different-looking cities.

"Is this when everybody died?" asks Dray. Now he's getting it. Nobody reacts, and the clip continues.

"Officials are describing it as a worst-case scenario for an airborne transmission event, with rapid spread and a long incubation period. Though casualty figures are not available, there are few reports of flu-related deaths. Nevertheless, we are still in the preliminary stages, and there are rising fears about the long-term effects of this infection. The flu-like contagion arrived with no warning, from no traceable source, transmitted by an unknown virus with an infection rate exceeding that of any known pathogen. All these anomalies are leading some to suspect the virus is man made."

Men made a virus? *Men* had the power to create something that could kill everyone? I notice that my mouth has fallen open. No wonder She fear us and don't trust us. No wonder my mother hated us. I squirm in my seat.

The next clip is hard to interpret, even listening closely. "Investigators are confident the viral genomics technology involved is American weapons-grade biotech, though the Pentagon denies any involvement." I'll need someone to explain that to me later.

If men did this, why would She worry about *us* being angry? They're the ones who should be angry. I'm angry at myself just for being a man.

The next newscast surprises me. Most infected people fully recovered? I'm confused. "So, it wasn't the pandemic that killed everyone?"

"Keep watching," says Aida. "I'm going to skip ahead about six months."

A woman again. She's talking about widespread reports of expectant mothers carrying abnormally large female fetuses. "The size difference is often noticeable by the second trimester and pronounced by the third. Questions are being raised about whether these abnormalities are related to last summer's pandemic."

I see images of hospital rooms and hallways, pregnant women being examined, and strange pictures I can't interpret. Another clip starts. *Breaking News: Mothers are dying in childbirth. The world watches in horror as casualties mount.* I gasp and clasp my hands over my mouth as I watch in dismay.

"All over the world, the increased size and nutritional drain of the female fetus is proving harmful to the mothers trying to deliver them. Where good medical care is available, female infants are now being removed premature, by cesarean section. Without care, however, natural childbirth is proving to be fatal for a devastatingly high percentage of women delivering female babies. The time frame leaves little doubt we are seeing the tragic aftereffects of the recent pandemic. We can only wait in fear for other long-term effects to show themselves."

Fucking hell. Shocking, obscene images of pregnant women in crisis burn into my head, and my face is wet, but I've gone numb. Bree stares off at nothing, and Onyx tries to calm Dray as he hyperventilates. The other She sit in silence, watching us.

"Time for a break," says Kāya softly. "Let's get some air."

Clutching each other's hands, Dray and I mindlessly follow as the four enforcers lead us up to the top entrance and confirm the area is clear. But the enemy is right over there, watching us, and I don't even care. I'm grateful to be out in the open, and can see everyone feels the same.

Nance is the first to say it. "I really needed this fresh air."

"I was suffocating in there," says Val. "Not as bad as the first time through, but still bad."

Onyx rubs Dray's shoulders. "This is hard even for us. History is brutal. Reading about it is one thing, but seeing it right there in front of you, being immersed in it ..."

Nance says, "There's more. You men sure you want to go through this?"

I close my eyes. I did this to myself. I don't know if I'm strong enough for this.

And yet how can I stop now? I'd never forgive myself if I did. I look out at the enemy encampment. This could be my last chance. "I'm sure."

Dray stares at the ground, head shaking.

Onyx is studying us. "Are you—"

"Heads up, everyone. We've got company." It's Bree, voice urgent.

We all jump to our feet.

The enforcers all bunch in front of us as six adversaries approach. Kāya steps out to confront them, and they stop at a safe distance.

A rush of hatred pulses through me, catching me off guard. I quake, resisting the impulse to charge at them in fury. I imagine landing blows, driving them back with my fists, bloodying them into retreat. The image collapses as quickly as it came, leaving a fever of helpless shame. Great Mother, was that the suicidal rage? Please, no.

The Bravo in front stands firm, but the others—I recognize frightened fidgeting when I see it. The Bravo calls out, "Luce wishes to remind you of the rules of engagement. With a capital challenge pending, there must be no secondary fighting, and no other challenges are permitted."

Kāya responds with impatience. "We don't need to be reminded. You remind Luce that she has already violated these rules with her little raiding party, and she will be held to account."

As they back away and withdraw, Onyx bellows after them, "Six of you to deliver a message? Luce is the treacherous one, not Kāya."

When they are out of earshot, Nance poses the question for me. "What the hell was that all about?"

It's Bree who answers. "They're vulnerable out there in tents. They don't want us raiding them in the middle of the night to thin out their numbers."

That's a great idea. I look to Kāya, and her stoic face brings a blush of shame to mine. It's fortunate I don't hold power.

Onyx says, "It's something Luce would do. She disgraces the gold collar. Ever since she got thrown out of the Guard, she has been ruthlessly building a business empire out of scavenged goods. I'm sure her goal is to make a triumphant return to the city and thumb her nose at the High Council. She has always abused her power, throwing her strength around with little regard for those she harms. She takes whatever she can get away with."

I have to ask, "Are we safe tonight?"

"Even without the rules of engagement, we have two locked steel doors between us and them, so yes. Tonight, we can rest easy."

I can't imagine resting at all.

———

BACK IN THE MEDIA ROOM, Aida selects the next clip.

"This picks up just after we left off," she says, "with mothers around the world dying in childbirth. People were justifiably outraged. They assumed that the pandemic was a biological attack."

"Wasn't it?" asks Dray.

"I suppose it was, in a way. And they feared the motives behind it. To punish and deter the attackers, they struck back."

She starts another clip. A different woman, stern and formal, sits at a plain desk. A stream of words flows by on the screen below her, a message from the Emergency Broadcast System. With the country under attack, a national state of emergency has been declared. A deadly viral epidemic is in progress, and all citizens are ordered to stay indoors and follow quarantine protocols until otherwise directed.

"Are we back to the pandemic?" asks Dray. "I thought we were going forward in time."

"According to the timestamp," says Aida, "this is from nine months after the pandemic."

"Another pandemic?"

Val cuts in. "Fuck. Can't you just be patient and let the information play out?"

What follows is a report about other nations retaliating for the previous attack by striking back with lethal bioweapons of their own.

"What?" Dray says. "Other people deliberately caused pandemics too?"

"Men and their revenge," says Bree with a sneer.

"What do you mean, men?"

"Oh, come on. You see it on every playground. Girls settle things on the spot. When boys lose, they look for revenge. We have to kick their butts a dozen times—"

Dray cuts in. "Which you do."

"—before they accept defeat. It's just the way men are."

"Why are you blaming men?" says Dray.

"Because men were in charge of—"

Kāya cuts in. "Bree. That's enough."

"Are we going to tell them or not?"

My ears prick up. Tell us what?

Kāya confronts her. "Are you challenging me, Bree? Because I keep feeling like you're challenging me."

Onyx steps in. "Kāya, stop it. We're all a little stressed here. We *are* going to tell them, right?"

I clench my fists. *Tell us what?*

"Look," says Kāya, "I—Let's just go easy with it, okay? I'm sorry, Bree. That was out of line. You're free to question me whenever you need to. I just need this to go right."

"Okay, everyone," says Nance, "let's take a breath. Every viewing, seeing this play out right in our faces, is a bit of a gut punch for all of us. And it only gets harder, so Kāya's right. Let's take it slow and easy."

"Thanks, Nance," says Kāya. "Are we good, Bree?"

"I'm with you, Kāya." The two clasp hands.

"Are we ready to continue?"

Nods all around. Except from me. Playback resumes.

The next series of clips hammer us with a battering audiovisual assault. I've always thought of ours as a culture of violence. But for the most part, it is strictly nonlethal violence. Violent deaths are exceedingly rare and cause for public shock and outrage. In our sparse population, each death carries a heavy weight. Now, for the first time, I see "war." War on an unimaginably vast scale. Global war. The death counts and images accompanying the reports are unfathomable. Cities in ruins, enormous ships erupting in flames, sleek flying machines streaking overhead, exploding, plummeting, ground vehicles blowing to pieces, huge explosions, fires, chaos. I'm dizzy trying to make sense of what I'm seeing. I peek out from between my fingers at images from a nightmare, and want to run from the room, but hold myself down. It's not real. It's only history. It's not real. I can't take any more. No. I have to see this through. I feel sick.

I'm not the only one. Kāya looks exhausted, and Onyx distressed. Val stands and starts pacing the back of the room. How much more do we have to take?

I contract in horror as I learn of bioweapons, and how by their very nature they are impossible to control once released. Attacking nations overrun by the backflow from their own weapons. Populations decimated by waves of lethal pathogens. And through it all, the ongoing fighting everywhere. A haggard speaker drops her gaze to her desk. "Madness. Utter madness. Apparently, mutually assured destruction was not enough of a deterrent in the face of man's need for vengeance."

"There," says Bree. "What'd I tell you?"

Everyone ignores her. We've all withdrawn into ourselves, trying to make it through. I can't take it anymore. "Stop. Can we please stop?"

37

THE END OF THE WORLD

MY MIND HAS GONE NUMB. My dreams about the shining cities and miraculous devices of the Before, my entire fantasy image of that glorious world—all shattered.

We sit staring at a blank screen, grateful for the silence.

Nance pulls us back to the present. "Remember, this happened long ago. The world is still here."

"Not that world," says Bree, voice bitter. "We would have inherited an advanced, thriving global civilization. Men took it from us."

"They didn't take it from us," says Onyx. "We didn't even exist back then. They took it from each other."

"It still would have been ours."

Dray says, "What do you mean, we didn't exist?"

"You men existed," says Nance. "We She did not. Not yet."

"What are you talking about?"

She turns to Aida. "We need to make copies of these reports. Let's get them all filmed and transcribed. This will be a rich addition to the historical record."

Dray says, "I think I know why you didn't want men to know about this."

"Oh?" says Onyx.

"Yes. It's the fault of men that civilization fell. You didn't want us to have to live with the guilt and shame."

"Uh, well—"

"One thing I still don't understand, though. Why the hell were men put in charge when all that was happening? Why didn't the She do something to stop them?"

Aida interrupts. "I've got something else here. A lab log."

"A what?" asks Onyx.

"A record of the work being done in the lab downstairs. Most of it is advanced genomics. I don't have a clue what it means."

"Nor would anyone else," says Nance. "Not a useful field of study without the needed tools."

"Then why bring it up?" asks Kāya.

Aida says, "There's something at the end you'll want to hear. A diary entry, audio only."

No pictures. That's a relief. Kāya nods, and we all settle in to listen. It's a male voice, dripping with fatigue.

"This will be my last log entry. We're clearing out today. Not many of us left anyway. Nowhere to go. But we can't stay here. The locals already firebombed the top floor. Then when they saw the smoke, they got scared and demanded the smoldering fires be buried. Cox says it's a good idea. We can't let them get access to the labs. He's threatened to bury us in here if we stay.

"The people would have lynched us if they could. Can't say I'd blame them. There was never any official plan to use military-grade viral stock. But we had a sample, so ... It was supposed to be administered in tightly controlled conditions and followed up with high-end medical supervision. Thought that was overcautious. Obviously not. Doesn't matter anymore.

"It wasn't just me. Once the viral package proved viable, we all thought, why not? Imagine. Improving the entire human race in one generation. Never expected a fucking insane backlash like this.

"Yeah, we probably should have waited. But even improving half the human race would have been better than nothing. If we'd waited until we'd solved the Y chromosome problem, we'd also have enhanced male fetuses. But then, twice as many mothers would have died. Irrelevant now.

"No point in secrecy anymore. Yeah. Fuck you, Cox. I'm leaving the system unlocked, in case … in case what? I've got to believe this isn't the end of humanity. Just because civilization falls doesn't mean it's the end of the human race. We were around long before there was any civilization, and we … Surely some will survive …"

No one dares speak. There is urgency to our eye contact as we silently connect with each other, as if unable to carry the burden of shame alone. The voice resumes.

"If you're listening to this, welcome to the birthplace of death. Forgive me if I'm a little delirious. I want you to know it wasn't supposed to happen like this … But you, my imaginary friend, can judge us as you see fit.

"If you're listening to this, it means humanity is not extinct, that some of you have managed to carry on. If so, you must be a changed humanity. A better one. I hope that's true. A germline edit to the DNA of egg cells is heritable. A permanent change. The Eve-2 genome would pass down from generation to generation, reshaping all women.

"If you're female, you're welcome. Your Eve-2 genes will make you bigger and stronger and more beautiful than nature could have achieved. And if you're male, you're welcome. I can only imagine what it would be like to be surrounded by a world full of perfect women. Yes, now there's the future I'll dream about.

"Well, I've got to go. Go off somewhere and die, I suppose. I only wish I could have lived to see our angels grow up. They could have made such a difference. Maybe saved us from ourselves. Too late now. So determined to kill each other … we finally succeeded. How can beings smart enough to rewrite their own DNA be *so fucking stupid?*"

It ends there, with that agony of bitterness in his voice. The last words echo in my ears, exposing me, humanity's son. I look at Dray and find him absent, though we share the attention of all the She. They're waiting for something. Remorse? Contrition? No. I'm misreading them. I close them all out, and puzzle pieces start falling into place. A storm receding. A picture coalescing. Something shifts, and I look up.

"So," I say. "The first pandemic didn't kill everybody—it *changed* everybody."

"Not everybody," says Nance, her voice gentle. "Every female. The Eve-2 genome only expresses in females."

"Women were smaller," says Dray. "Weaker, too?"

Nance shrugs.

"Smaller and weaker than men? How small?"

"The average height was five-four."

Smaller than me. They were the size of young girls.

The world cracks open and spills an alien world history into my lap, filling the once-troubling void with something far more disturbing. Countless generations of large men and smaller—*women*, stretching back to the beginning. Men who abused their power. Women who suffered as I have. Protective anger wells up in me. They didn't deserve that, just for being smaller. Those men got what they deserved.

I gasp. I'm one of them.

I notice the eyes on me and try to pull together. *Don't go crazy. Breathe.*

Kāya's voice draws me. "Tye?"

"I'm okay. I'm okay. I think I see. That's why men were in charge. She who can—whoever can enforce the rules dictates the rules."

Dray adds, "Might makes right. When push comes to shove, the strong get their way. That's it, isn't it. Men were bigger and stronger, so men ran things."

"Um, something like that," says Val.

"Bigger and stronger," says Dray, mulling it over. "Imagine. No more bullying, no more abuse."

I grasp his arm. "Dray, don't you see? Men used to be the ones doing the bullying and abusing. That's why—"

"What? No, that's ridiculous. Men aren't like that. We're gentle and cooperative. We're caregivers."

I rub my face. "Obviously, that wasn't always the case."

Nance nods. "I've read and seen a lot more history than you have, Dray, and I'm telling you, the behavior of men wasn't pretty."

Dray counters, "But our genetics weren't altered. We're the same as we've always been."

I sink as my mother's words fall into place. *Men have, of necessity, adapted in order to survive the change in us.*

Aida steps in. "It is in our human nature to seek advantage. The strong seek advantage by pursuing domination. The weak seek advantage by pursuing peace and cooperation. It is no longer to your advantage to be aggressive, so you've adapted."

Dray hunches in his chair and runs his hand through his hair.

I sit up. "Nance, the other day when you were talking. About my mother. What is the Celia Hypothesis?"

She looks to Kāya, who nods, then takes a moment to choose her words. "Years ago—you were probably still a child—your mother wrote a book, a scholarly work that became quite influential. She rejected the idea that natural selection could account for the sudden, dramatic change in us, and proposed instead that human intervention was involved."

The breath leaves me. That's what the book was about. "And she was right."

Onyx steps in. "These days, all historian trainees study her book in school."

Nance continues. "It was a pretty wild idea back then. We knew from the records that they had achieved the capacity for genetic engineering, but it was considered preposterous that it could be done on a global scale. Or that, in a patriarchal world, they would choose to enhance only the females. But after painstaking study, and rejecting all other possibilities, your mother hypothesized that the She genome was not the result of a random mutation, but rather, engineered."

"Is that the 'Eve-2' genome they were talking about?"

She nods. "The idea that we She were somehow 'unnatural' did not go over well. There was strong opposition to her thesis—a violent backlash, in fact. So much so that she received serious death threats and had to move into hiding. Her family would most certainly have been subject to those threats as well. The fact that few of us even knew she had a child speaks to how well she protected you."

I grunt as my gut contracts. Nance crouches beside me and takes my hand. I can't look at her, couldn't see her if I did.

"It must have been very hard for you," she says.

The dam bursts and I gush out. It's all too much. Too much.

At a certain point, I feel the hands on me, and the rhythm of breathing returns.

There is a long silence.

"Tye?" It's Kāya's voice.

I fill my lungs and look up at her. I notice Dray's hand on my shoulder and reach up to hold it. "This is a lot to take in."

Her voice is gentle. "I tried to warn you. Are you okay?"

Being numb now, I can't tell. "I need some time." I glance at Dray. "We both do."

Kāya nods reassurance to Onyx. "Take all the time you need. Both of you. Let's take a break for some fresh air."

38

AFTERMATH

THE DAY IS TURNING to dusk as we emerge into the evening air. Seeing the sky again, and the trees and the birds, helps me settle, reassured that the world is still here. But the images won't leave me. Huge rooms filled with sprawling, dying people. Streets crowded with rampaging masses, smashing and burning everything around them. A shining city in flames, billowing black smoke. Streets littered with bodies, men in bulky gear running from corner to corner, smoke and sparks puffing out of their weapons.

All dead now. Like that entire world, all long dead and gone.

I become aware of the enemy across the field. Luce is out there somewhere, preparing for battle. She will take this place by force, kill us all, if she can. With our tiny population, each death has the same impact as thousands of deaths in the crowds of the Before. Yet Luce kills without hesitation to benefit herself. How is she different from the violent men of the past? She doesn't have their war machines, but if she did, what would she do with that much power? How far would she go? And her enforcers. Are they not soldiers following corrupt orders, like the men of the past?

Perhaps, deep down, we are not so different, men and She.

I look around at the team, my She, with sudden certainty that there were good men too, in the Before, just as there are good She now.

We sit, some on the trucks, some on the ground, each lost in our own thoughts. Most of the team has, in turn, come around and checked with us, offering encouragement. Am I okay? I don't really know. My head has stopped spinning, if that's what they want to know.

And I feel no rage. If anything, I have lost control of my heart. It opens too easily, each time someone shows concern. Maybe I am crazy.

Nance sits beside us, and there goes my heart, opening to her. "That Before world," she says, "and all the people in it, perished long ago. We who came after are the descendants of only the strongest of the survivors. You are strong, Tye. And not because of the Inversion."

There is that word again. "The inversion?"

"The inversion of the physical order. The onset of the She dominance."

"We are what we are," says Onyx. "We had no say in it, any of us."

"No," says Dray. "No, we didn't."

"It's all a long time gone," says Nance. "Remember that. We live in a different world."

And my world will never be the same. "So ... what do we do now?"

"We learn, we love, we carry on."

Historians are a tough breed. I love that about them.

I'm still not accustomed to seeing Dray deep in thought. It's unnerving. He looks up when I sit and put my arm around his shoulder. "Some adventure, huh?"

"I didn't need to see all that," he says. "Maybe the She were right to keep it from us. Maybe that was for our sakes."

Horrific images continue to play out in my mind. Vehicles and entire buildings exploding in flames, charred and mangled bodies, weeping survivors. *And men were in charge.* All that responsibility. And obviously, their failure was catastrophic.

I try to shake it all from my mind but can't. Then I see Kāya and

Onyx exchanging quiet words and flash to our current jeopardy. I'm facing my own catastrophe here and now. What am I doing dwelling on the past? I need to put it behind me. We all do.

I seek out Nance and quietly implore her, "There must be a way to stop this fight."

"I wish there were," she sighs. "Some of our laws and traditions seem ridiculously primitive. But until we can change them, they are what they are."

"But why fighting?"

"When it comes to power, physical dominance is primal, built into our animal natures. It's what takes charge during times of chaos and lawlessness, which is why it's the basis for our oldest traditions."

This is what Mom meant by *the survival tactics of feral children.* "From just after civilization collapsed."

"That's right. But as order is established, other forms of power become important. Knowledge and ingenuity become valued and take on power. That's where academics come in. Then, as communities form and commerce develops, the many aspects of social power emerge."

"Social power?"

Nance explains. "We're social animals. We don't need strength to do something if we can persuade others to help us. We don't need to fight if we can enlist others to protect us. We don't need to grow our own food if we can trade for it. That's social power."

"So, social power is a kind of power for the weak."

"Exactly," says Kāya. I hadn't noticed her listening.

Nance rolls her eyes. "Make no mistake. Social power is a far greater force than either physical or intellectual power."

It's Kāya's turn to roll her eyes. But I'm intrigued. "How is that?"

"There is strength in numbers."

Aida, also listening now, adds, "That's why it's illegal to form an army. As a society, we cannot afford to risk the onset of war. Luce is already at the legal limit."

"And who enforces that? Who polices Luce?"

Kāya says, "Out in the Shell, she's the law, and I'm sure she doesn't want the real law constraining her. Which leaves it up to me."

And here we are again, back in my world of powerlessness.

———

OUTSIDE, darkness has fallen, though the evening is still young. With the outer and inner doors closed and locked, everyone prepares for an early night. Dray and I are still waiting for room assignments when I hear Onyx invite Dray to join her. She and Kāya are both in offices on level one, to be near the entrance, just in case. Onyx says she wants to make sure he's okay. I'm glad he's in good hands.

I don't realize I'm holding my breath until Kāya says, "Tye? With me."

The sign on the door says *Derik Henley, CEO, Genhance Laboratories*. Even with her mattress in the corner, the inner room of the suite is spacious. Curiosities line the shelves, though they now seem tainted. It takes me a while to settle, and I'm relieved when she doesn't seem to be in her usual rush.

In fact, she seems preoccupied as we lie together. Maybe we'll just cuddle tonight. I'd be fine with that. "You okay?" Stupid question. How could she be?

Her eyes are downcast. "Onyx just told me she's quitting enforcement, after we clear up this mess with Luce."

"She's quitting?"

"Not happy in the role anymore, she says."

"And you are?"

"It's who I am."

"Kāya, your role doesn't need to define you. You can be whoever you want to be. Onyx can be a wealthy and successful historian now if she wants, and so can you."

She sighs. "I'm an enforcer, Tye. It's who I've always been. I can be both."

"She's gonna stay on as a historian, isn't she?"

"I hope so." She remains pensive. I stroke her arm, and after a minute she snuggles down and looks at me. "I knew I didn't need to worry about you. You're okay, right?"

"I'm okay. Just worried about you. Is there anything I can do to help?"

"This is helping."

"Kāya—" *No. Let her rest.* The last thing she needs is more opposition from me. I have to let her do what she needs to do, even if it means ... I squeeze my eyes shut. I have her here with me right now. That has to be enough.

There is so much I want to say to her, but ... I can't. My dilemma comes into stark relief. I lie and deceive her every day, pretending not to feel how I do. How could I ever deserve her trust? Sinking, I reach for a handhold. "Thank you for letting me be here. For showing me ... everything. I know I don't deserve your trust, but I ... I wish ..."

She starts to say something but holds back.

I fill in the blank. "Yes, I know. You can't trust men."

"Tye, in my experience, when you have the power to control a man's life, he will say *anything* to stay on your good side. How can you trust what he says?"

I wince. "No, I can see ... Huh. Stay on your good side? And how well have I done with that?"

She hesitates, then chuckles, then laughs. "You suck at it." She ruffles my hair.

The irony twists in my gut. I lie to earn her trust, which is exactly why she can't trust, but I do it so badly that ... I don't want to think about it. Not right now. It doesn't matter right now. All that matters is that tonight we're together and safe. I can't think about tomorrow. She's right here, right now.

"Is that why you decided to become a freeman?"

I chuckle. "Because I suck at being agreeable? Maybe. But mostly so I could choose for myself who I want to be, instead of being forced into a role I didn't want."

"And what role *do* you want?"

"You mean, like, who do I want to be?"

"Yeah."

Someone you can respect. Someone who can reveal his heart to you ...

Careful. I dig deeper. "I want to be someone of value to those he loves."

She nods, tight-lipped, and we fall into a comfortable silence.

With a sigh, I snuggle into her and immerse myself in her scent. Her powerful body eases as I caress her, savoring each texture of skin, memorizing each curve, each scar. It's not long before her hand seeks my attention and gets it. When our bodies finally entwine, our passion grows from the tenderness of a long goodbye to the intense heat of a last chance. When we finish, there is nothing more I can ask of life.

"Wow," she says, panting. "That was just what I needed." I fill my senses with her closeness and warmth to keep the heartache at bay.

We doze in each other's arms until she rolls away and sits up. "Thank you, Tye. That was nice, but I'm going to go now."

"Go where? This is your room."

"I need to be with Onyx tonight. I hope you understand."

What? My mind spins, trying to ...

Tomorrow's fight. This could be her last night, and she ...

My jealousy flashes to shame as I recognize it. "Yes, of course." Of course she needs to be with her partner tonight. Watching her go, I wonder how often they've faced death together. It's ludicrous to think I could ever replace Onyx. The depth of their relationship is beyond me. It would be like ...

All at once I need to see him. This could be our last night, too. *He's* the one I should be asking for forgiveness. I've been such an ass. When I see her face, I lose myself and the rest of the world disappears. He deserves a better friend, and I need to tell him—

He's at the door. I feel relieved, but then I see the helpless look on his face. Our eyes lock, and I show him my desperation.

"Storm coming," he says, mouth tight.

The forecast calls for clear and calm. "I know." I lift the blanket, and he climbs in.

39

SIEGE

C OMPLETELY ISOLATED from the outside world, the night seems endless and sleep impossible. Yet when Dray wakes me, I'm disoriented. The hall lights are on, and I hear activity in the cafeteria. We quickly dress and join the others over a breakfast of eggs, vat-grown ham, yogurt, and dried fruit.

The team again reviews plans. I listen, heartbroken, as they casually discuss worst-case scenarios. If Kāya loses—I struggle to breathe —Onyx will immediately challenge Luce for violating the capital challenge rules of engagement. Luce is allowed twenty-four hours to recuperate, but if Kāya can at least do some damage, Luce might withdraw. If not, it will be up to Onyx to at least hurt her, to give Bree a better chance with her challenge.

The Arbiter should arrive before then. It will be up to those holding the site to argue that taking in the men was a humanitarian act, given the illegal threat from Luce's forces. If worst comes to worst, the academics will demand that the Arbiter take custody of the site on behalf of the High Council and all the people of the region. At all costs, they must keep the facility out of Luce's hands.

After breakfast, the enforcers go through a light workout, limbering and stretching, rehearsing attack and defense techniques.

It is late morning when they towel down and gather to meditate together. Onyx cautions Kāya about her hatred of Luce, and how those emotions can push her out of the 'flow.' Whatever that means, it sounds bad. Kāya acknowledges this with a nod and proceeds to calm herself.

It is to be a midafternoon fight. I'm in the kitchen preparing a light lunch when I hear voices calling out. Alarm seizes me. Something is going on. We rush out into the hallway and at the bottom of the stairs see Bree and Val putting on their battle armor. In front, Kāya and Onyx stand in regalia. Where is their armor? Then I remember. Battle armor is for battle, not a challenge fight. They prefer the advantage in speed and flexibility afforded by not wearing armor. Then I hear it. Someone is hammering on the top door.

"That's not twenty-four hours," I say.

Kāya glances our way. "You expected Luce to keep her word? Everyone ready?"

And then they're gone, and we run to catch up. All four enforcers huddle on the top landing, then take up defensive positions. Onyx opens the door, poised to strike. Whoever was hammering must have retreated as the door opened. The team moves out in formation, except for Bree, who stays behind to block us in.

Looking past her, I can see a wall of enforcers out front and hear myself whimper. Bree holds a finger to my lips and glares at me until I still myself. I watch in horror as Kāya strides out to face them. Val and Onyx follow behind, side by side.

"Go!" I say to Bree. "We'll be good."

She checks my eyes and nods. Then she's gone, joining the others to complete a diamond formation.

They hold formation as Kāya stops ten yards from Luce, who is fronting over a dozen enforcers, all now in battle armor. More must have arrived this morning. As my quick count reaches twenty, my fear turns to outrage—twelve is the legal limit for a fighting force. This is more proof that Luce hires criminal mercenaries.

Kāya addresses Luce. "I see you've assembled an army. Are you now so brazen in your disregard for the law?"

"This is no army. Some are here merely to witness."

"Then why are they armed?"

"Enough talk. Your time is up, Kāya. Give me the men and I will cleanse this transgression. Or you could sign over this claim. There is no need for you to die."

My heart falls through my feet. This is it.

Kāya responds, "Unless you withdraw *now*, there *is* need for you to die."

"This is pointless," says Luce. "You must know no Arbiter is going to side with you. History is not for men to know. This is not in question. And I will not wait. Either hand over the men right now, or by righteous might we will take this claim."

Kāya snarls. "I accept your capital challenge. We fight!"

Eyes riveted on Luce, I feel my heart pound in protest. I thought I knew hate. But this has a taste to it, a weight, a pressure. This is new, this desire to kill.

"Again you disappoint me, Kāya. I hoped to be able to spare you."

"You hoped to avoid facing me. Your era has come to an end, Luce. The lawless frontier has dried up. There's a big change coming, and neither you nor your Quo extremists can stop it. But I can stop you. Let's finish this."

"Oh, we will. But my offer of challenge has expired. We are taking full-scale enforcement action now." Luce raises a hand, and all her fighters step forward and raise their weapons.

What?

Luce continues. "If you give us no choice, many will die. Be reasonable. The men cannot be saved, but your team can. You are badly outnumbered, Kāya."

Despair grips me.

"Is that how you count it?" says Kāya. "Here's the way it is. We are two Alphas and two Bravos against one and one and a bunch of momentary distractions. Bad odds for you."

I see Luce's forces exchange uncertain glances. Paying no attention, Luce announces, "Any She who surrenders will be spared."

In response, all three of Kāya's enforcers take a stand with her, their weapons raised. Onyx stands on her right flank, Bree on her left and Val behind. Kāya counters, "And any She who declines to take part in this criminal act will avoid prosecution."

"We have every justification!" bellows Luce.

I grind my teeth. *Nothing justifies your crimes.*

Kāya calls out, "How many will you doom with your lies, Luce?"

"Enough! This ends now!"

Kāya draws her bokken and points it at Luce.

In the tense silence that follows, my panic builds. *I can't watch. I can't handle this.* I squeeze my eyes shut. Then my ears jump at a loud patter of cracks and bangs, and my eyes shoot open. Luce's forces have attacked in a pack. Several attackers lunge at once, and bokken clatter as their thrusts are parried. The one in front of Kāya goes down, wailing, and the rest jump back out of reach. The team spreads out in a semicircle, protecting the entrance. They hold position, maintaining a solid front, passing up opportunities to move forward in pursuit.

The attacks become sporadic as the two sides hold their ground. It is clear the attackers are desperately trying to stay out of reach of the Alphas, yet a second goes down before Kāya. The others are holding the attack at bay, with both sides lunging, striking, and block-ing. Yells, grunts, and cries fill the clattering air as the combatants lunge, thrust and parry, slash, thrust and parry in a mesmerizing dance of war. There is a howl of pain in front of Onyx as a fighter falls into a fetal position. Another attacker drops back, clutching an arm, and another, hobbling.

"Rally!" yells Luce, and the attackers withdraw, taking their fallen with them.

Kāya checks her team. They all seem okay. "You are magnificent," she says, catching her breath. "Every one of you. We've got this."

Several minutes later, the attackers return, and I notice a new strategy. They attack again, but four of them isolate Onyx and sepa-rate her from the rest. I watch in terrified admiration as she fights off several of them at once. One withdraws, clutching herself. Out of nowhere, another leaps in from behind and spears Onyx in the back.

Her eyes go wide, and she bites off a cry as she goes down. There behind her is Luce, a murderous leer on her face before she disappears back into the fray. Dray screams, then dashes out, and I follow without thought, running toward a wall of killers with weapons held high.

Alerted by his scream, Kāya beats us to her fallen friend, another attacker collapsing in her wake. Within seconds she has cleared the area, the attackers dodging back to stay out of her reach. She struggles to drag Onyx toward the entrance while fending off attacks, then lets us take Onyx and grabs her weapon with both hands. Then she is gone into a clatter of war, and getting Onyx to safety is all that matters. Val is limping as she and Bree close ranks to guard us, freeing us to retreat down the stairs. We are met by Nance and Aida partway down, and, seeing us struggling under the weight, they take over. We follow as they get Onyx to a couch in the second office. She's fighting for breath, clearly in agony. Dray strokes her face, telling her she's gonna be okay, while Aida examines her injuries.

Moments later, Val bursts through the door, limping, chest heaving. I rush to the lower stairs, yelling for Kāya as the noise of the fight echoes down to me. Frantic, I start climbing. Suddenly Bree is flying down at me. "Get inside!" she yells. Kāya, right behind her, scoops me up and throws me in through the door, then slams it shut behind her. Seconds later, there is a clatter of blows against the door, that beautiful, locked one-way door.

As they catch their breaths, Aida quietly reports, "A deep puncture. It's bad. Likely a kidney. Heavy internal bleeding. She'll go into shock soon. She needs immediate trauma care, Kāya. We can't help her here."

Kāya's panting slows and she slumps, then sharply inhales and forces her eyes to Onyx. She moves in to take over from Dray. Onyx tries to speak but can't. Kāya caresses her head and smiles into her eyes, and with a tenderness I've never heard, says, "Relax, my love. The fight's over. We won."

Teeth clenched, Onyx stiffens, gasping.

Aida says, "We've got to get her to—"

Kāya flashes her an angry look. She knows we can't get her anywhere. We're trapped down here. "What can you do?" she asks.

Aida wipes her face. "I'll give her something for the pain, but—"

"Do it."

Aida dashes off, and Kāya resumes her caresses as her head sinks. I run to get blankets and get back as Aida does. I'm numb as I watch the injection. It is only moments before Onyx eases down and closes her eyes, clasping Kāya's hand with pale knuckles.

"You fought well, Onny. I'm so, so proud of you."

Onyx's breathing slows.

"Onny, I've been so very fortunate to have you at my side."

As we watch, Onyx's grip loosens. Kāya's head falls.

Aida puts a hand on her shoulder. "She'll be out for a while. It's best we keep her quiet and warm."

"Will she make it?"

Aida gives a helpless shrug. "She needs trauma care, Kāya. All I've got is first aid."

I help wrap Onyx in blankets as Dray puts pillows under her feet. Kāya is on her knees beside Onyx, clasping her hand, eyes locked shut.

I drift, disembodied, to the corner of the room, and note Dray's vacant eyes. I should go to him, but I imagine him crumbling to rubble at my touch, so I hold back. I watch the She coalesce around Kāya, their helplessness thick and heavy, thick and heavy, and I'm buried again in that mudslide, back when that excavation went wrong, caught immobilized, cursing my fate and weeping for my lost life, and if it weren't for Dray being there to dig me out—

He collapses to his knees, and I find myself at his side with nothing to dig with. I instinctively look to Kāya for help, then falter, abandoning all hope when I see her pain.

———

I SIT WITH DRAY, holding him, searing in my own helpless despair.

Bree and Val guard the entrance, listening to the sounds of Luce's enforcers trying to pick the lock.

"Kāya, I think they're close," says Bree.

I see the heroic effort it takes for Kāya to turn away and straighten. Then she inhales deeply, her face hardens, and she climbs to her feet, all warrior.

How is she doing that?

She quickly appraises the situation. "The door opens outward, so we have the advantage," she says. "They can only come through one at a time. We attack through whatever opening they give us, and they won't be able to get the door all the way open. Bree, you go low, Val, high. I'll take dead center."

Minutes later, the door pulls back and the three of them lunge forward. The attackers fall back, and Bree pulls the door closed and re-locks it.

"They've only got one play," says Val, "and that's to push us back so they can get the door wide enough for a team to come through. I'll bet they're out there drawing straws to see who has to come through first."

Kāya says, "The unfortunate one will try to bowl her way through. We must meet her as a wall of spikes. We've got to stop her in her tracks."

When the door opens again, her strategy works. With a cry, the poor Charlie drops hard in the doorway, impeding the attackers but also blocking the door from closing. Kāya grabs her and hauls her clear as Bree slams and locks the door again.

The disabled attacker lies gasping on the floor. After dragging her out of the way, the defenders return to guarding the door. Aida, the closest thing we have to a medic, goes to check her over, and asks me to follow with her first-aid kit. I'm grateful to have something to do. In the lull, Kāya withdraws to return to Onyx in the second office.

As Aida kneels to examine her injuries, the Charlie gasps, "Please. Please tell Tika—I love her." She writhes, struggling to speak. "My daughter—tell her to be strong. Tell her—I'm sorry."

A moment of confusion prompts me to look again as Aida

removes the attacker's helmet. This monster. This enemy. Just a She. Worse. She's someone's mother.

"Tell her yourself," says Aida, who then calls out to Kāya. "Looks like her armor saved her, but she's not going to walk for a while. Or use this arm. You hit a collarbone. She's going to need care." She beckons for me to hand her the kit, and I kneel beside her as she holds a vial to the wounded She's mouth. "Here, drink this." She gulps it down. Aida calls out, "None of her injuries look life-threatening. She'll live."

With sudden fury, Kāya fills the doorway, bokken in hand. "*No she won't.*" The prone Charlie spasms in horror as Kāya charges at her, weapon poised to strike.

40

NO WAY OUT

"*No!*" I leap into Kāya's path, then fall backward before the helpless She, hands out in surrender, shielding her as best I can. "Stop! Kāya, stop! Don't do this!"

Kāya's real voice roars, "*Get out of my way, Tye!*" She reaches down with her free hand, yanks me right off the floor and tosses me aside, but I scream, and she hesitates. Aida grabs her raised arm with both hands, and Kāya's face snaps to her with fury.

Aida cries, "Kāya! Please! That's not who we are."

She freezes, and I call to her, pleading, but she doesn't seem to hear. Her face goes flat, then she looks at the floor and sags, dropping her arms.

Now the injured Charlie on the floor is sobbing.

Kāya's eyes have gone vacant. I take her by the hand and lead her back to Onyx. She eases herself to the floor beside Dray, hides her face in her hands and weeps. I can't bear it and turn away. I drift back and flop down on the floor beside the whimpering She, drained.

Bree approaches me. "Why would you do that, after what they did to Onyx?"

It would destroy me to see Kāya kill in cold blood. I could never love again. I look up at Bree, and my eyes finally focus. "Only men seek vengeance, did you say?"

Bree hangs her head, then returns to join Val, guarding the door.

I follow Aida back to the others. Kāya sits on the floor beside Onyx with a hand on her shoulder, Dray with his head leaning against her leg. Aida kneels beside Kāya and wraps her arms around her, murmuring something I can't hear, but Kāya settles. Then, so Dray can hear too, she explains Onyx will be out for hours and may never regain consciousness.

Dray is inconsolable. I can't break through to him, and even if I could, what could I say when my own heart is bleeding out? I try to rub his neck, and he pulls away and again buries his face in his hands. He needs space. My helplessness chokes me. I stand and back away, desperate for something useful to do.

I step out into the hall and look around. I need to move. To be anywhere else. As I pass her, the injured She cries out.

"Please!"

I stop and look down at her.

"Stay."

Her desperation moves me to approach, and I can see she's still terrified. Uncertain, I sit beside her. She eases onto her back and closes her eyes, good hand guarding her damaged collarbone.

I examine the prisoner. Her chestnut hair is standard enforcer style, cropped short. Her dark eyebrows match a russet-brown skin tone, and her eyes are narrowly set in a face that would be appealing if it weren't creased with pain.

Like Onyx's face before the injection. My heart hardens toward the prisoner. How can such a lovely creature do such vile things? The image of fury on Kāya's face rings through me like a gong, and I forcefully shake it from my mind. When I look again at this one, I can't help but see a little girl somewhere longing for her return.

After several moments, her breathing steadies. She opens her eyes and checks that I'm still there, then looks around. "What is this place?"

Why would I tell you? Instead of revealing anything, I throw out the most outrageous thing I can think of. "Welcome to my home."

Her eyes flare. Confusion? Fear? All at once, my snarky words seem cruel. She's frightened enough as it is. I add, "You're safe here."

She squints, trying to read my eyes, then checks the guards at the door. "Where are the others?"

"They're busy."

She sinks back and closes her eyes again. After several moments, she says, "You don't need to guard the door. They're not coming back."

A trick? "What do you mean?"

"Luce knew a frontal attack was a long shot."

"She knowingly sent you to die? And you let her?"

"Somebody had to ..." She grits her teeth and curses, shaking her head as tears run down her cheeks. "How could I be so ..." She slams her fist on the floor beside her, then, eyes squeezed shut, breathes hard to calm herself.

"Hey," I say. "I know all about being used."

Her wet eyes find mine, then drop. When she speaks again, it's with new conviction. "The backup plan is to starve you out. Come at you again when you're weakened."

That seems to make sense. Her eyes hold steady against my suspicion.

I believe her.

———

WE'RE TRAPPED IN HERE. I've spread the word, and the She take inventory of our available food. If we ration, we could last for a while, but Luce will easily wait us out. And Onyx can't wait, even under Aida's care.

The injured prisoner lies against a wall, twenty feet from the locked door at the bottom of the entrance stairs. The team stands thirty feet away, discussing various attack strategies. I have no doubt Nance and Aida could put up a good fight, but the academics need to be kept safe and neutral, as noncombatants, to ensure they survive. It may fall to them to appeal to the High Council. The enforcers are now three against at least a dozen who have the high ground.

They could get up the stairs, but the top doorway is a choke point where Luce's forces would have an overwhelming advantage. They could try to lure the attackers in, a couple at a time, and thin them out that way. Kāya suspects Luce will call for reinforcements.

"The Arbiter should be here by tomorrow," says Val. "Maybe she—"

"No chance," says Bree. "Luce is right. No Arbiter would side with us once she hears we have men down here."

Kāya's mouth is tight. "She'll at least get Onyx to medical care."

A moan draws our attention, and Kāya looks to the injured prisoner, then goes over. I nervously follow, but Kāya just sits and questions her about Luce's forces and strategies. The prisoner is forthright and thorough.

It turns out she's a young mercenary who signed on with Luce only days ago, hoping to prove herself and make some quick money. Then she discovered that she and other newcomers were surplus, that Luce already had twelve fighters, all loyal to the Quo. Luce assured the new ones they would only be used as substitutes but would still get paid. But the substitutes were sent into battle first, against Alphas—against Kāya—and she realized she'd made a terrible mistake signing that contract. Most of Luce's regulars were a disgrace to the profession, and the newcomers were all expendable, and trapped. When she pulled the short straw on the breach, she decided it was better to die with honor than be killed by extremists for desertion.

"And something you need to know," says the prisoner. "Luce canceled the Arbiter."

"*What?*"

"She radioed back and told them the dispute was resolved and arbitration was no longer needed."

Kāya's shoulders drop, and the air goes out of me. When she rises to leave, the prisoner calls to her.

"Kāya."

She stops.

"It was Luce who took down your second. She boasted of it."

Kāya nods, jutting her jaw, then turns away. "I know."

"Kāya."

She turns back.

"I watched you fight. As a child. I watched you whenever I could. Growing up, you were my hero." Though her face is calm, tears roll down her cheeks. "I'm glad ... you stopped me. If I live—if we—survive this, I will stand with you, if you'll have me."

"What's your name?"

"Mara."

Kāya kneels and takes the Charlie's hand in hers. "Mara, if we live through this, I would be honored to have you stand with us." She rises and heads back toward the others.

I catch up with her. "I believe her, Kāya, but I'm surprised you do. She tried to attack us."

"She was doing her duty. With courage, honor, and sacrifice."

"Duty sucks, huh?"

She stops and looks at me. "Duty—" She turns away and wipes her face. "Duty is something a man could never understand. Make sure she shares in our rations."

The team goes back to discussing our predicament. They go round and round, refusing to accept the obvious. Our situation is hopeless.

After a while, Nance comes over to where Dray and I are sitting with Onyx. "Dray, you need to stretch your legs."

"I'm not leaving her."

"You've been sitting there too long. And we need to dress her. So go on. Take a break. She'll be here when you come back." When he balks, she turns to me. "Tye, help him up. You two need to go for a walk."

I don't make any headway with him until the team comes in and gently crowds us out of the room. "It's their turn," I say. "They need time with her, too."

He reluctantly concedes and lets me lead him by the hand. We find ourselves wandering the corridors like corporeal ghosts, drifting rudderless, unseeing. Finally, Dray says, "This can't be happening. She can't die. She can't. She's the first She who ... I hoped ..."

"I know, I know."

"You know what she said to me? Just before—" He chokes. "She said she should have killed those young hooligans for me. I told her she was crazy. I said, never do that, I don't want to see *anyone* get killed. She said she was gonna keep me safe from now on. Me. Why would she say that?"

Rubbing his arm, I think of Kāya. No way she'll sit down here and let Onyx die. She'll go out fighting. I know she will. I'm gonna lose her. I gasp to hold it in. Dray glances at me, and I avoid his eyes.

And the moment she falls, we all do. It's so clear.

We've come to the end of the road, and I can't help but feel responsible. I pushed us into this. Had I known it would cost the lives of others, I would never have pushed ... Would I?

Now I know history, and what good does knowing do me? It won't keep me alive. What was the point of all this? Now Luce will plunder the whole place, and everything will be lost.

We continue wandering, past open doorways that no longer interest me.

Dray moans. "I didn't even get a chance to—" He stops, clenching, and looks me in the eye. "It's us she wants, that Luce."

"She says that, but—"

"If we surrender, she'll spare the others."

"No, she won't. She doesn't care about us. She wants this place."

"There's got to be something we can do."

"Like what?"

We both stand in silence.

"There's no way out, Dray."

He embraces me, and our tears mingle on our faces.

"You'll think of something," he says.

For the first time, his oblivious optimism angers me. I don't hold back. I sob right at him.

41

———

IMPOSSIBLE

I can't face the She right now. Our world has fallen, as the Before world did. I relive the desolation in those eyes on the wall-screen and feel a kinship with the doomed.

I just need to keep Dray moving. Our aimless wandering takes us down a corridor, and as we approach the end, I recognize it. This is where I first came in. I get a tickle in my chest.

I stand under the vent opening, looking up.

It catches his attention. "What are you doing?"

"A way out," I say, examining the hatch from below.

His mask of misery takes on an air of derision.

"I'm serious," I say, trying to peer into the vent. There it is, still in place. My heart leaps. "The safety line's still there."

Dray scoffs, "So what? What are you gonna do? Climb all the way up through that?" He turns away in scorn.

He's right. It's ridiculous. I'd never make it. Claustrophobic memories of the dark enclosure pulse dread through me. Impossible.

"We need to get back," he says.

I look down the long hallway toward ... what? I see again the face of the doomed news reporter, and my mind reels from our shared helplessness. There's got to be *something* I could ...

I look back up at the opening.

It's stupid. I'm not suicidal.

I look away, and a Shellful of loss rips through me as I see my entire world on the brink of collapse. We're all gonna die. Everyone I've come to care about.

What is my life worth, she said, *if I can't protect those I love?*

I suck air through my nose. That's it, then. I rush to the nearest office.

"Dray. Help me drag that desk over."

He squints at me. "Why? The vent? You're not gonna get out through there."

"That's exactly what I'm gonna do."

"That's crazy. There's nobody to winch you up. It's too small to—"

"Dray. I'm doing this. I have no choice."

He shakes his head, wrinkling his nose. "Even if you got out, what would you do then? The place is surrounded."

"They're all over on the entrance side. Can't see this from there."

He won't even look at me. "Why do you always have to go nuts on me, just when—"

"Fine. I'm crazy. Now help me. Please."

He turns cold. "Fine. Just go. You'd rather die alone, go ahead."

"Dray, it's not like that. Come on, freeman. I've got to do something."

His voice teeters on the edge of breaking. "Friends are there for each other. At the end. I thought we were friends."

I fight to pull breath. "I *will not* sit here and watch Onyx die—watch *you* die. Not if there's *any chance* I could ... I'm going for help."

"Who's gonna come and help us? Against an army of enforcers?"

He's right. I fluster. "Maybe I can at least find a medic willing to come. Medics are neutral."

He takes interest, then nods. "Yeah, they couldn't stop a medic from coming in." His eyes well up as he studies mine. "You'd do this for me?"

"Not if I had any sense. Don't tell Kāya about this."

He wipes his sleeve across his eyes. "Don't worry," he says. "I got your back."

"I know you do."

We drag a desk over, and he climbs onto it with me. Holding my arm, he gives me a lingering look, then his face hardens with a sharp nod. "You got this, freeman."

"I'll be back soon," I say, blinking to clear my eyes.

He locks his fingers together and hoists me up. I pull myself in far enough to grab the safety line, then look back at him and see my own resolve mirrored on his face. I point to him, and he points back. *I love you, man.* "Now get out of here." I turn and wriggle the rest of the way in.

I find myself tightly enclosed and fight off a moment of panic. But it's easy enough to slide along on my back until I reach the vertical shaft. This is the tricky part. Cautiously pulling myself out over the narrow void, I struggle to get upright, then use the right-angled junction as a toehold while I catch my breath.

Okay, I've made it into the vertical shaft okay. Except I can't seem to get any further. The shaft really is too tight to climb. Dray was right. I'm such an idiot. I can brace myself with my toes but can't use my legs at all. The rope is right on my cheek as I try to haul myself up through the darkness. My arms quickly tire, and I've only gone a few feet. What have I gotten myself into?

How far does this shaft go down beneath me? Does it go all the way down to level five? I try not to think of what would happen if I fell. I focus instead on how grateful I am to be able to breathe in here, with the huge fans below sucking in air. I grit my teeth and start hauling again, inches at a time, taking turns bracing and pulling.

If I can get to the road, I can hitch a ride into town. I'll head straight for the clinic. There's got to be one medic willing to come. When I tell them the life of an Alpha is at stake, I'm sure they'll drop everything for a chance to be the hero. And if I can draw enough attention and expose Luce for what she is, maybe people will come out in support. All I've got to do is get out and get on my way.

After what seems like forever, I look down and am dismayed by how little progress I've made. I resolve to keep my gaze up, heading for that small patch of diffuse light above me.

I figure I'm halfway there now. Breathing hard, I stop for a rest. When I try to start up again, my trembling arms don't want to move. The realization hits hard. I'm not gonna make it. I have a flashback of being trapped on the stairway, and fight for air. *No.* I'm gonna do this. I'm not gonna let Dray die here. My hands are burning, and the rope slides through them as I pull. Thankful for my shoveling callouses, I squeeze harder. Another inch. I'm not beat yet. My arms ache and tears wet my cheeks, but I will not stop.

I pause for breath and try to shake out my hand. The energy drains out of me like through a severed artery. It's hopeless. This is impossible. What was I thinking?

I bang my head on the wall of the vent. I know exactly what I was thinking. Onyx needs me. Dray and Kāya need me. Onyx's death would crush us all. And I'd rather die than watch loved ones be killed. I see Kāya's face, fearless, fierce. I feel the strength in her firm arms, and fire flares through me. I cry out, and my weak imitation of her battle cry is amplified in the narrow space, invigorating me. I throw myself into her rescue, one hand after the other. *I'm coming, Kāya! Onyx, hold on, I'm coming!* My arms and hands scream, but their protest is drowned out by the roar of the flames within me. *I'm coming! Hang on. Pull, Tye, pull! Again! Again!*

Gimme your pain, Onyx. I'll take it. Dray, I'll take yours, too. Kāya, I can take it. Give it to me. I challenge the universe with cold rage. Reaching up into the icy numbness of the void, I haul down stars from the heavens, crushing their burning embers in my hands, greedily reaching for more, and more, until the sun itself threatens to engulf me. The void has become brighter. There's light all around.

I find myself groping for the rope as it curves over the bend at the top of the vent. Almost there. Almost ... Using my toes, I wriggle up until I'm folded over the bend. Through the tiny patch of daylight, the ground beckons, and I embrace it, letting myself drop the final two feet face-first.

And I'm in the open world. I lie on my back gasping, gazing up at the underside of a tree, arms and hands spent and useless, and close my eyes. When I look again, the shadows have shifted. Guns. How long was I out? I scramble to my feet, and pain sears me. I look at my hands and try to work them but get nothing. I look around, scanning for enemies, and trying to get my bearings.

North. Head north. I must get to Hillhaven. I head off at a trot.

After what seems like miles, I slow to a walk to catch my breath and realize I neglected to bring water. My throat is parched. And the sun is getting low in the sky.

Facts are facts. I'm just a man. My male body can only take so much, and I'm already way past my limits.

Even in the Before ...

The world shifts. I'm not just a man. I'm a freeman who knows history. And I have amends to make, on behalf of all men. I'm gonna save my friends or die trying.

I freeze, bristling, at the warning hiss of a feral cat. A glimpse of movement and it's gone. Then I see why it's angry. I've interrupted a meal. Some small rodent I don't care to identify. The big eat the small. It's nature's way. The strong eat the weak. The cat's only hiding because I'm above it on the food chain. Not at the top, though. If She were cannibals, I'd be dinner.

What? Where did that come from? Did I really think like that? With sudden shame, I see I've been as hard on them as they've been on me. I picture the team, huddled together, brainstorming.

The team. Not like cats at all. Cats are solitary predators. Their size and strength are all they have. But Nance said we humans are social animals, capable of working together to do things we could never do on our own. Size and strength are *not* everything to us. *There are many forms of power*. The idea of social power has been swimming around in my head since she mentioned it. Strength in numbers. It seems so obvious now. Social power, the refuge of the weak, is the greatest power in the human arsenal. All I need to do is persuade enough people to come to our rescue—

I stumble and have trouble straightening. First step: don't die out here in the wilderness.

It will be dark soon. I'm fighting the urge to collapse when a rumbling sound startles me. I fall to the ground and listen. Vehicles. They found me. It was all for nothing …

But no, they're coming from the wrong direction. I struggle off the trail and hide behind a rock as the first vehicle, a jeep, comes into view. Then a truck. Then another. Three trucks full of enforcers. Luce's reinforcements. My heart sinks.

I peek out as they crawl along on the rough trail and see emblems on the hoods and sides. Two clasped hands surrounded by a circle of six stars, all in gleaming gold on a mahogany crest. I recognize that. It's the emblem of the High Council, the stars representing the Six Cities of the Eastern Territories. What are they doing here?

And then it hits me. *The Arbiter*.

I gawk. I thought Luce canceled the arbitration.

Doesn't matter. She can help Onyx. I need to convince her. If I can't … I need to at least try. I stagger out onto the trail as the last truck rolls by, yelling and waving my arms. It takes a few seconds, but the tailing truck pulls to a stop and four enforcers jump out and approach me on alert. All Alphas. I blanch.

I stop and stand, hands in the air, and let them check the surroundings. The other vehicles have stopped now, too.

"What are you doing here?" The demand is accusatory.

My voice is hoarse. "I need to speak to the Arbiter."

"Who's with you? Where are the others?"

They're expecting an ambush? "No. I'm alone. Please! I must speak to the Arbiter."

"The Arbiter is on an important mission. She has no time—"

"Lina. What's this?"

That voice. I follow it and see a tall, brown She in purple robes step down from a truck. She is staring at me as she approaches. She comes into focus. Shock wallops me, and I reel back, the blood draining from my face. My vision blurs.

"Celia, this man came out of nowhere. He claims to be alone."

It *can't* be her … Lightheaded …

"Does he now?" She examines me up and down.

I lose contact with the ground, and a little child's voice comes out of me.

"Mom?"

The world spins and goes black.

42

REUNION

I COME to with a jerk as something assails my nostrils. Smelling salts. I'm lying on my back, and someone is holding my head. It's an angel, one of two kneeling here, gazing down at me. The brown one is my mother. The world grays, and I struggle to stay afloat in the clouds.

"His lips are parched. Someone, give him some water." It's my mother's voice. I urgently seek her face. It's my mother's face. I'm suddenly lost in time, disoriented.

My mouth feels rusty. Awkwardly clutching at the canteen, I take a swig and immediately feel nauseated. So, I'm not dreaming.

"And his hands. They're a mess. Get them cleaned up."

I stare at her. "You?" I croak, eyes struggling to focus. "How?"

"He's clearly delirious," she says. My mother motions for the others to step back and helps me sit up.

Her deep brown eyes are guarded in a way I don't remember, but it's her. I'm certain. I can't look away and I can't seem to form words. I clutch at her arm, and she lets me, and it feels solid, real, and my mouth is gaping open and my tears start to flow and I plead, "Mom?"

She blushes as she looks around, then helps me to my feet.

"He's still out of it," she says. "He'll come around." She whispers, "Just shush for now. Let's get you—"

"What are you doing here?"

"I'm here on the business of the High Council. What are *you* doing out here?"

A medic starts wiping down my hands, and—*A medic.* All at once I remember why I'm here. "We need to get back. There's a severely injured Alpha there who needs a medic, right now!"

"An Alpha? Who is it?" All movement around me stops.

"Onyx. Please, we need to hurry!"

Her tone turns abrupt. "Where? Where is she?"

"Back at ... where you're going."

The other Alphas are already dashing back to the trucks, and my mother half drags me to hers. "I'll interrogate him on the way," she announces. "And how do you know where we're going?"

"We called for you."

She hoists me into her passenger carriage as the vehicles in front pull away. As soon as we're seated, she signals the driver to go and seals the compartment. "Okay, now tell me, Tye. Why are you out here?"

"I came looking for you."

She straightens, scowling. "How did you know?"

"I didn't."

"Then—"

"I came looking for help. Can't you tell them to go faster?"

"One of their own is in trouble. Believe me, they're going as fast as they can. Now tell me. What are you doing here?"

"How do you know where you're going?"

"Our trackers are leading us, but all the vehicle tracks make the route obvious."

Yeah. The wilds can't hide this much traffic. I glance over my shoulder, and through the partition see two other compartments. Several Alphas are squeezed into the rear seats, behind a pair of colorfully robed Councilors in the middle compartment. My mother is the only one wearing a blood-red sash. "They're all Alphas?"

"Yes. A kleek—a team of six—from the Elite Guard, supported by another from the Council Guard. Arbitrations can be ... tense. Now, what's going on?" She sees my unease. "We have privacy here. You can speak freely."

"Remember that place you searched for near here?"

"I do."

"I found it."

She goes still. "You did what?"

"I found it."

"How on earth—And what did you do when you—"

"My friends are there, and they're in trouble."

"Tell me your friends aren't men."

"What? No. Just Dray. The rest are all historians."

She clasps her mahogany hands to her face and rubs her cheeks. "Of course it would be you. The fates are cruel to old historians. As soon as the call came in, I recognized the location and figured someone had finally found the lost facility. Of course, I immediately grabbed the assignment. I'm eager to see the place. We traveled through the night." She looks at me and frowns. "We got a message saying the dispute was settled. Do you know anything about that?"

"It's not settled. We're still under siege."

Her eyes narrow. "So, someone has lied to us."

"Yes, Luce. So she can kill us all and take the facility for herself. She said she would wait, and then she attacked us and tried to kill Onyx. You can't let her get away with it. We need to get back, right now!"

"We'll be there soon."

I sit back. "Wait a minute. If you thought it was settled, why are you—"

"I spent months out there, searching for this place. I want to see it."

She examines me and shakes her head. "But this ... I can't believe it. The two of you are the men in violation, am I right?"

"It's not like that."

"Why don't you tell me all about it? Start at the beginning."

At the beginning? I try to corral the scattered marbles of my mind and fail. My eyes are swimming with tears. "It's really you?"

She closes her eyes and exhales. "I'm sorry, Tye. I know this—"

"They don't know about me. Am I right?"

She slumps. "No. And please. Let's—not say anything about that right now."

"Why?"

"It puts me in a position of bias. I'm going to have to recuse myself, and I—"

"That's not what I'm asking."

She goes silent.

"Why did you leave us?" I suddenly realize, after a lifetime of wondering, that I already know at least part of the answer. I still need to hear it from her.

"Tye, this isn't the time—"

"*Why?*"

She sighs. "It was so long ago now ... Yes, I guess I owe you an explanation. But I'm afraid it will have to wait. Right now, we have more urgent matters to attend to, don't you think?"

The air goes out of me. Then the anger floods in. "That's all you've got?" The impulse to strike out must show in my eyes, because she pulls back. I bite out the words. "That's the most cowardly thing I ever heard. *You fucking abandoned us.*" There. I finally got to say it. The pressure eases, my head clears, and I'm startled by the realization she's here right now, when I need her. "I'm sorry. That was inappropriate."

Mouth firm, she sits back and looks straight ahead. "I disagree." Then she nods without looking at me. "I've been dreading this moment. I always knew it would come. A lot has changed since— well, since then."

I wipe my eyes. "Yes. A lot has changed."

She looks at me again. "For one thing, you're all grown up."

"And you—" I touch her robe.

"Yes. I'm on the High Council now. And all it cost me was ... Tye, please. We'll talk later."

I clutch the seat as we swerve too fast around a clump of trees and bounce through a series of ruts. Not far now. Okay, later. And she doesn't want me referring to her as my mother. Easy enough. She doesn't deserve the title.

As the High Council convoy makes its way through the lengthening shadows, I sit alone in a private chamber with a She I have cursed for my entire adult life. A She who taught me to never trust She, who ripped out my utterly dependent heart when I most needed her. A She who hated men—as I found out too late—including me and Dad ...

And yet maybe she didn't hate us ...

At her insistence, I do my best to explain how I got here but have trouble focusing on the story. She asks about Kāya even before I mention her name. She once knew Kāya and Onyx as members of the Elite Guard.

She looks down and sighs. "Life is strange, isn't it? I have to say, though, I'm genuinely concerned about what the two of you have gotten yourselves into. Having you here changes everything. Let me think this through. I need a couple of minutes with my colleagues."

She cleans up her face, checks and smooths her robe, then opens the partition behind us. "Wait right here," she says as she squeezes through.

I sit by myself, being jostled in the fading light, knowing we're close. Wondering what we'll find when we get there. Hoping Onyx is still alive. Hoping Kāya hasn't tried to fight her way out.

Hoping I'm not too late.

43

THE ARBITER

It's dusk when the High Council convoy arrives in the encampment outside the entrance to the facility. From my seat in the front compartment, I see two campfires lighting circles of She. They all jump to their feet as the trucks approach. The Council enforcers, all Alphas, leap from their vehicles and quickly surround Luce's forces.

My compartment door flies open to reveal a She in a khaki medic outfit marked with a red cross. "Onyx. Where is she?"

"This way," I say, pushing past her to dash for the entrance. Too late, Celia's voice commands me to stop, then others. I run for my life. Several pairs of feet pound down the stairs behind me, and I don't dare look back. I reach the locked door and hammer on it, bracing against grabbing hands, but none grab me. Glancing back, I see the red crosses. They could've stopped me had they chosen to.

I hammer again. "It's me, Tye! Open up. The medics are here!"

I'm underwater, on the verge of drowning. "Kāya. It's me. It's okay. You can open up."

Even muffled, the sound of her voice is music. "Tye? Is that really you?"

"Dray, tell her it's me."

The door opens a crack, then swings wide. She confronts the

medics behind me, then beckons them in. "We have wounded. Hurry! Follow me."

Within moments, the medics are examining Onyx. "We'll take it from here," one says. Dray and Kāya step back to get out of their way, and I join them.

Dray throws his arms tight around me, and we dance together in joy. "You did it! You did it. I knew you would. Thank you, thank you." We sober as we search each other's eyes. His face clouds as he looks over his shoulder toward Onyx.

Kāya is staring at me, eyes wide. "How did you—How were you out there?"

"I brought the Arbiter. She wants to hear from you."

She blinks, dumbfounded, as I drink in her face. I ask about Onyx.

"She's still with us, but it's bad," she says. "How? How did you get out?"

"Same way I got in."

"You didn't climb the vent shaft."

I shrug.

"Tye ... you did that?"

I look down at my hands and grimace as I try to move my fingers. Her face goes flat. She pulls back like she's looking at a stranger.

"What? It's just me."

She nods, seeming unconvinced. Then she looks to the stairs with a scowl. "The Arbiter's here? I thought—Wait. They let you come back down here?"

"Yeah. It's all good. She'll listen to you, Kāya."

"How can you be so sure?"

"I just know."

She is still staring when Val interrupts and points to the medical team. "Where did they come from?"

"The Arbiter's here." I lean into Dray. "And wait till you see her."

Within minutes, the medics have secured Onyx and Mara to stretchers and are carrying them up the stairs. Kāya gathers the team to follow. "We all go up together. Everyone ready?"

We follow the stretchers up, and as we approach the top, the dark doorway reveals the flicker of lanterns. Emerging into the night, we face a wall of armed Alphas. They let the stretchers through, then close ranks to enclose us, faces stern. My confidence evaporates.

Dray tries to follow the stretcher carrying Onyx, but a pair of Alphas confront him. I try to call him back. "*Dray.*" Ignoring me, he tries to push his way through. Val gasps and jumps to restrain him. His frantic cries mimic rage as he tries to fight her off until she has to put him on his ass to settle him down. I see my own heartache echoed in Val's face as she drags him back and sits him at our feet. I kneel to console him, but really, how?

"They will not tolerate disobedience from a man, Dray," Val tries to explain, gently stroking his hair. "Please. I don't want to see you get yourself broken."

I wrap my arms around him. "It's okay, freeman. She's in good hands." His eyes are desperate as we watch the stretchers being loaded into a truck.

A striking She of six-six strolls forward with a lithe and weightless gait and examines us. Her skin is pale, her scalp shadowed with a black stubble. While the Alpha collars of the others glint in the fire-light, her gold collar sparkles with a fiery ring of diamonds, accenting her domination of the scene.

"Who's that?" I whisper to Kāya.

"That's the High Alpha of the Elite Guard. Just do as she says."

Several Alphas confront the team as the High Alpha issues a directive. "As requested, your Arbiter has arrived. We will now collect your weapons and return them to you once a settlement has been reached."

Kāya and the others kneel, presenting their weapons.

The High Alpha herself joins in the collection, and as Kāya offers up her beloved Kaybo, they exchange subtle bows of respect. The High Alpha makes a quiet aside. "Miss you, Kāya. What have you gotten yourself into here?"

"You need to see this place, Tala. Don't let Luce plunder it."

"I hope you know what you're doing." They nod to each other, and the squad moves off.

The High Alpha strides toward Luce's forces and surveys their encampment. Luce's Charlies draw back as she goes by, inspecting them. She strolls among them with complete disregard for the fact that they are all armed and potentially hostile.

Then I realize. The High Alpha. Champion of champions. Those Charlies know that attacking her would be suicide. She addresses them, repeating her directive with the voice of hard authority.

"We requested no Arbiter," says Luce, defiant.

"I have the request right here," says Celia, as the Council Guard sweeps through the encampment confiscating weapons.

"I canceled that request," protests Luce.

Ignoring her, the three Councilors ceremoniously step down from the truck. Their colorful silk robes, lined with white fur and trimmed with gold, flow in the breeze. Beneath their robes I see off-white pants and jackets, the uniforms of the High Council. The Councilor in the blue robe, now wearing the red sash, steps forward. "We will speak with the two challengers now." Flaming lamps are being lit and stationed around the area as the dusk deepens.

Luce presses on. "*I said,* your presence here is no longer required."

Celia addresses her. "Are you saying the dispute has been settled?"

Luce looks around. "Uh, yeah. It soon will be."

"Which of the challengers has withdrawn?"

No reply.

"Then we shall speak with the two challengers, *now.*"

An elevated platform, surrounded by burning lanterns, has been set up backing onto the largest bonfire. The red-sashed Councilor spreads her robe as she sits in the tallest of three chairs. Celia, in royal purple, and the other Councilor, in lime green, take seats at her sides, and around them, several Alphas take position. The rest of the force rings the entire assembly.

Dray and I are herded to the side, where we sit on the ground, under guard. Still fuming, Dray strains to see the newcomers. "Is that —that looks just like—"

"Yeah, it's her. Don't ask."

"But how?"

"I said don't—"

Her voice booms out. "The challengers will approach." I hardly recognize her with her official voice and demeanor.

Luce and Kāya warily watch each other as they move into position, their mutual hatred on display.

The Arbiter speaks. "Celia has recused herself from these proceedings, and I, Renee, will preside. Henceforth, Celia will participate as an observer only."

Uh-oh. Not what I was expecting.

The Arbiter continues. "Before we proceed with arguments, we will hear an explanation of how battle injuries were sustained while a capital challenge was pending, in violation of the rules of engagement."

Kāya glares at Luce. "Here's the way it is. The challenger took it upon herself to assemble an army and conduct a siege against a rightful claim."

Luce counters, "What army? Count my enforcers for yourself."

"How many wounded did you have to cart away this afternoon?" She turns to the Arbiter. "If you check the clinics in town, I expect you will find them full."

"It was no siege. It was a righteous enforcement action. She gave men access to a historical site. These men. She doesn't even try to hide them."

"I gave them sanctuary when you threatened to rape and kill them."

"Lies! We caught her with these same two men in the Shell, a clear violation—"

"I can explain—"

"Enough." The Arbiter is on her feet, and the assembly quiets. "Let the record show that Luce does not deny taking preemptive hostile action while a capital challenge was pending."

"It was justified!"

"We shall see. We have before us competing claims. At the heart of the matter is the question of whether Kāya's claim to this historical site is forfeit due to a Rule Six violation. Such a violation would strip her of all rights to own property. On the other side is the claim of unreasonable challenge and corrupt intent. You will proceed with arguments."

The two adversaries take turns explaining their positions. Luce continues to blame the attack on us, describing it as a necessary enforcement action in defense of the rule of law and the traditions they are all sworn to uphold. I don't need to listen. I've heard it all before.

Kāya seems flustered. Her defense rings hollow, like she knows she's in the wrong. When she questions the value of the ban on men, I read skepticism on several faces and grow concerned.

Val is brought forward to give testimony, as are two of Luce's thugs. The witnesses only confirm that charges are warranted on both sides.

Kāya needs help. The impulse compels me, and I stand. A bokken clips my ear and pushes down on my shoulder. I should sit, before—

A voice, close by, demands, "Leave him be."

Who would—*Bree?* But Bree has opposed us at every turn. She steps in behind me, unarmed, and faces down an Alpha.

Bolder now with someone on my side, I step forward. "I ask to be heard."

Everyone stops and stares. I hear a tussle behind me as Bree stands her ground.

"Men do not speak here," says the Arbiter, her annoyance clear.

"As I am a party to this matter, I ask that an exception be made."

"Shut him up," snaps Luce. "We're disputing the place of men. We can't have a man interfering."

The Councilors exchange glances. A heavy hand on my shoulder presses down, down toward obscurity and loss. Kāya will lose everything.

No. I resist and cry out, "I'm an eyewitness to these matters. If you truly want justice, you will hear all evidence." There is a collective gasp. In the sudden silence, I go on. "Judge my words as you see fit."

I have their attention.

The Arbiter speaks. "In these disputed matters, witness testimony is useful information. For the sake of thoroughness, I will make an exception and call upon the male witness. You will come forward."

To the Arbiter's lower right sits Celia, and to her lower left, the other Councilor. Their flowing robes evoke a fountain of multicolored water spilling out over the podium. Three Alphas flank them, glorious in their regalia, their curves, skin and golden collars gleaming in the light of the fires. It is a humbling scene.

The Arbiter looks down at me. "Do you understand it is a criminal offense to lie to me? If it is revealed that you have spoken anything but the truth, you will face justice. Confirm your understanding."

"I understand." I thought she would be on my side. My mother would—she's avoiding my eyes. I don't even know if *she's* on my side. I know nothing about her.

The Arbiter examines me with a scowl. "Were you witness to the challenge?"

"I was."

"Tell us what you saw and heard. Be thorough. Then we will question you."

"Luce had trackers tailing Kāya, watching for an opportunity to take her claim. It's piracy. Luce demanded a capital challenge and then violated the rules of engagement by allowing secondary fighting —an attempted gang rape—with a challenge pending. And then she attempted to preempt arbitration and take the site by force. Worse, she attacked with an illegal army. I counted at least twenty fighters."

Luce yells out, "Why are you listening to a man's lies?"

Bree and Val shout her down. Kāya adds, "Her criminal behavior strips her of her right to challenge. You must declare her challenge null and void."

The Arbiter holds up a hand. "Her alleged crimes do not negate yours."

"That's right," says Luce. "She has been teaching history to men, then harboring them. She must be held accountable, or our society will crumble."

"Enough," says the Arbiter. She returns her glare to me. "Your presence here is being used as justification for a capital challenge. That presence has yet to be explained."

I find Dray's eyes and feed off the fire in them. Newly empowered, I address the Arbiter.

"I am happy to explain. Exploring in a legal area, I discovered a historical site. This one. By the scope of it, I judged it required the oversight and protection of a strong and honorable She. I found one in Kāya. I brought her here and have since refused to leave. My freeman friend and I have been staying right over there. You can see our tent. After we were sexually assaulted by members of Luce's army, Kāya gave us refuge inside. She saved our lives." I nod respectfully to Kāya. Her stare is unnerving.

The Arbiter speaks. "It is alleged that you have been taught history by Kāya. Is this true?"

Crap. I can't implicate her. I glance at Dray, and he points to me with the freeman salute. I point back. Wait. She didn't actually do the teaching. "I am a freeman. I'm quite capable of learning on my own."

"Did she or did she not allow you access to historical information?"

The truth ... the truth ... "It is I who allowed *her* access. I was in there well before her."

"And she allowed you to stay?"

"She did not. She forced us to remain outside in this tent until our lives were in jeopardy."

"And once inside, you were allowed to learn history?"

I choose my words carefully. "They failed to stop me."

The Arbiter pins me down. "So, you learned history from the site."

"Yes. From the site, not from ..."

My mother's face falls, eyes closed tight, and I falter. I've just confessed to knowing history.

44

RULE SIX

NOW THEY ALL know I'm guilty. So be it. "Kāya and the others cannot be blamed. This site has the power to teach anyone exposed to it, regardless of intentions."

The Arbiter squints at me. "Explain."

"The site before you is a window into the past. You need to witness this for yourselves. If you think you know history now, wait 'til you have experienced it happening in front of you. You're in for a surprise."

A murmur ripples through the assembly.

"And what, exactly, have you learned about the Before?"

"Enough to know that it is not the brutality of war that you seek to hide from men. It's the Inversion. The whole prohibition against men in the Shell, against men possessing artifacts or learning history—it's all to prevent us from learning of the Inversion. You ban all of history to hide one fact."

"So you admit to knowing of the Inversion."

"Yes, I was shocked by it." There are gasps around the group. "You will be too, when you learn the truth about it." I look at Celia. "Well, maybe not you."

She clasps her hands to her face, eyes riveted on me.

The Arbiter starts, "What truth—"

"What's going on here?" demands Luce. "He has confessed to his crime. Arrest him!"

A ripple of uncertainty flows through the Alphas of the Guard. I startle as one grabs my wrist and another prepares handcuffs.

Kāya's voice rings out. "The men are already in my custody. Leave them be!"

Luce counters, "You have no authority here, criminal."

Our captors stop and look to the Arbiter. My mother sits facing away with her head bowed as the other two Councilors confer. The Arbiter speaks. "I'm sorry, Kāya, but you are implicated in this. Until we can determine what's going on here, you are relieved of your responsibilities." She motions to our captors. "Proceed."

I stand bewildered. I explained everything to them, and they're taking Luce's side? Arresting us? And my mother is doing nothing to stop them?

The shock of sudden arrest paralyzes me. Handcuffs are for dangerous people. How does that now include me? I wince as a large hand clamps my wrists together in preparation. On the edge of hysteria, the absurdity tickles. I look up at the big Alpha holding the cuffs. "Why are you"—I gasp—"so scared of me?" She freezes, eyes wide.

Defying her guards, Kāya pushes forward. "Is that really necessary? They have nowhere to go and pose no threat. Surely that's obvious."

After conferring with the others, the Arbiter nods to the guards. "Just watch them."

I collapse to my knees, and they let me.

"We will now return to the proceedings—"

Nance steps forward, arms spread in submission, and stops at the point of a bokken. "I demand a voice," she says. "I have vital information."

"She has lies to spread," says Luce.

The Arbiter holds up a hand, then turns to Nance. "Present your information."

Nance addresses the assembly. "The historical records found

within this site provide evidence that refutes the very premise of the Rule Six prohibition against men learning of the Inversion. As such, this new evidence has direct bearing on these proceedings."

"What is this evidence?"

"These records show that the Inversion was not the result of a random mutation, nor natural selection. The change was a deliberate act of genetic engineering on a global scale."

The group erupts in a jumble of angry and incredulous voices. "This is nonsense," cries Luce. "Our history is well known. You can't rewrite it because of one suspicious find. Why, these men could have planted false evidence before you arrived."

Nance sneers. "When you see the evidence, you will find this accusation laughable. This is not a new idea." She nods to Celia. "We have merely lacked confirmation until now."

Luce objects. "Are you going to just sit there while she calls all She *unnatural*? The rules of the ForeMothers—"

Nance cuts her off. "The ForeMothers knew nothing of the cause of the Inversion. They assumed, and we have long accepted, that it was a result of natural selection. Only the strong survived the bio-war. It was never explained why men lagged behind. Yet we have always feared and expected that men would one day catch up, that they would evolve to again match or exceed us in size and strength."

My mouth falls open. Men would return to power. No wonder She are afraid.

Nance continues. "We have sought, through the history prohibition of Rule Six, to purge the memory of power from the male psyche. The ForeMothers hoped doing so would extinguish a simmering male resentment that might one day lead to retaliation. Our goal has been to create a male population accustomed to She leadership, so that when they returned to physical dominance, they would lack the thirst for power."

Celia speaks up. "In that regard, I'd say we have succeeded."

"Indeed," says Nance. "I've seen how the Inversion was created. You can see for yourselves how it required technology that is far beyond us. The change would be impossible to replicate, impossible to undo. Since men know nothing of the Inversion, its cause is irrelevant to them. But it matters to us. We now know that all She are safe from a return to subjugation by men. There is no need for Rule Six."

Luce objects yet again. "Even if this nonsense were true, it would not mean that She are safe. It might be difficult today, but men would never give up until they found a way. If they did it before, they can do it again."

"Before," says Nance, "they had the unlimited resources of an advanced civilization, billions strong. We're a thousand years away from being able to do what they did."

Kāya steps forward. "Yes, in the Before, they had the power to change us. That power is gone. We are what we are. Men are what they are." She looks over at me. "They're not so scary."

The sneer returns to Luce's face. "It's obvious you have a thing for this little criminal. Do you really think you can trust a man? You, of all people? After what happened?" She turns to me. "Did she tell you about snuffing out her last man?"

"Luce!" cries Kāya. "Shut up!"

"Told him she loved him as she *strangled him to death*."

I blink in shock.

"Luce, you fucking pile of puke! I'm going to—"

I turn to ice. Two guards jump between them, weapons drawn. Kāya rocks back and forth, seething.

Luce taunts her, "You're so naïve, Kāya."

Kāya slowly deflates, face flattened in defeat. "Perhaps I am. I had hoped to use this man ..." Her eyes drop. "I had no right to use him." She straightens. "... to use this man as a wedge to push for change. But clearly, when Luce forced my hand, I lost control of the process."

Celia again speaks out. "Push for what change?"

The Arbiter silences her with a hand. She's only here to observe. But the Arbiter repeats the question, and Kāya proceeds.

"Throughout our society, our whole dominance structure is merit-based. Yet our dominance over men is not earned. We have an unfair advantage. Perhaps I have become oversensitive to injustice. Training to become a historian exposed me to a different way of seeing things and reinforced my concerns. Some of our laws are unfair to men."

She continues over Luce's jeers. "The fact is, I've encountered freemen across all the region, and what I've found is that, in general, they're a harmless bunch. And yet, as an enforcer, I've been expected to treat them as if they were dangerous, simply because they're not under the control of a She. I've locked away or shipped away many of them"—she sucks in air, then sighs—"and it wasn't right. Most of them were harmless, scared, small men, and I ... I validated their fears, brought their nightmares to life. I did my duty, administering harsh punishment reserved for dangerous offenders." It is long seconds before she breathes. "I don't feel good about the role I played. Couldn't do it anymore."

I swallow, trying to absorb all this, as a murmur rolls through the assembly.

"There," shouts Luce. "That's a confession."

Kāya ignores her and addresses the Alphas. "It was my greatest honor to serve with and help train many of you. And now, my sisters, the golden treasures of our people, *you* carry the torch. Heed my words one last time. Let duty guide you, not enslave you. We are sworn to enforce the law and protect our people, our We. Don't do as I did and forget that our We includes men."

Sitting stunned, I'm blind to the reaction around me until Luce yells out, "This goes beyond a confession. She is openly inciting sedition in our own ranks. Arbiter, you must put a stop to this." Angry looks are aimed her way, betraying a loss of neutrality among the Guard.

The Arbiter asks, "Kāya, is this a confession?"

Kāya looks toward Luce and clenches her teeth. "Here's the way it is. We did not show this place to men. These men showed it to us. They found it when we could not. They got inside when we could not. They let us in. It belongs as much to them as to us. And it is forbidden to them for no good reason."

My mouth falls open.

"Ridiculous!" bellows Luce. "Do you see how unhinged she has become? She needs to be stopped!"

The three Councilors are hunched in animated debate until Nance demands their attention. "Regardless of Kāya's motivations, Luce has challenged for the corrupt purpose of taking this site from her. This site is far too important to be allowed to fall into the hands of scavenging thugs or Quo extremists who would destroy it. We invite you to enter the site and see for yourselves what is at stake here."

"Libelous!" hollers Luce. "We're not here to go on wild goose chases, we're here to protect our way of life. Do your duties and confine these criminals!"

The Arbiter again holds up an annoyed hand. Then she confers with her associates. "By consensus, we will see your evidence."

It takes a wall of Alphas to restrain Luce. Her outrage echoes off the vehicles as the delegation makes its way down the stairs, guards barring the entrance behind them.

45

A FIGHTER

To my surprise, when the others enter the facility, Celia doesn't follow. She paces back and forth out front, looking my way now and then, as everyone else settles in around the fires. What's going on? She was eager to see the place.

Luce and her enforcers withdraw to gather around their own fire, and as soon as they are gone, the Council enforcers seem to relax. Several go over and speak quietly to Kāya.

My mother heads straight for me, her bodyguard in tow. Her face is hard until she sees Dray beside me. He's staring at her with a gaping mouth. She composes herself and addresses the Alphas guarding us. "Please take this one over there and give us a moment." The pair of large enforcers nod and herd Dray over near the trucks as he cranes to look back.

Shoulders hunched in anger, she keeps her harsh voice low. "Confess to knowing history? Why would you *do* that?"

Shrinking, I struggle for words. She instructs her bodyguard to stay put, then takes my arm and gruffly steers me to a secluded spot away from the fire.

"Tye, you've put me in an impossible position." She gestures emphatically at her robes. "I have responsibilities. Do you realize now we have no choice but to send you away?" Her welling eyes glisten.

"You wanted me to lie to the Arbiter?"

"I wanted you to keep quiet and let Kāya and her team justify their actions."

"I am part of Kāya's team."

Startled, she looks around. "Don't let anyone hear you say that."

"Yes or no. Do you hate men?"

"What? No, of course I don't hate men. Why would you think …? Oh. Tye, leaving you and your father behind was the most painful thing I ever did. If there had been any other way to keep you safe …"

"You could have let me know. Could have sent word—something. All of a sudden, you were just gone. And I'm supposed to—what? Be okay with that?"

She squeezes her forehead. "No, no, of course not."

"You thought you were protecting us? Okay, I get that, but when did the danger end? A year later? Five years?"

"Tye … I'm sorry. I'm so sorry. You're right. I should have …"

"It doesn't matter anymore." I see her wince. Good.

"Tye, I'm going to do everything I can—"

"Then get on with your work," I say. "Do the right thing."

She hangs her head. "There is so much I need to tell you."

"Yes, but right now, you have urgent work to do." I look to the entrance. "Mom, I need you to know that, despite what Kāya said, she did her best to stop me from learning, to keep me safe from knowing. I made her life miserable because of it. But she came to see, as you will too, that the whole effort is pointless. In fact, I want you to see now. The evidence is waiting. You need to go see it. I know you're desperate to see what's in there. So, go. Please. Go. I'll still be here when you come out. Go."

She wipes her eyes and studies mine, then nods. We briskly walk toward the entrance, joined by her bodyguard. I break off and wave her on when we get close. I have to let go. I have to. Returning to Dray, I see we're still on a tight leash.

Under the watchful eye of our guards, he rouses and quietly asks about my mother. I tell him what I can, which turns out to be next to nothing. Not that it matters. I'll probably never see her again anyway.

Bree and Val appear out of nowhere. "How are you two doing?" They don't get much of a response.

"It's wrong, what's happening here," says Val. "We're going to do whatever we can to get you out of this."

"Thanks," I say. They're facing discipline themselves. There's nothing they can do.

As they leave, I turn back to Dray. He's worried sick about Onyx, but I want to make sure he understands his—our—situation. "They'll be sending us away."

He looks around, glowering. "It's what they do."

I see grim determination on his face, though I don't understand it. The She who changed everything for him has been ripped out of his life. And now our freedom—my chest is buried in mud again—our freedom, a freeman's very life force, is gone.

Onyx has been taken away from him, she's hanging on to life by a thread, and he can't even go to her. And if we're sent off and isolated from the world, he may never even know whether she lives or dies. She could be dead right now. My heart drops. Either way, he'll never see her again. He has lost her. And I'm about to lose him, and I've lost my mother again, after just finding her. And soon I'll lose Kāya. Just when we were starting to ...

The ground tries to drag me down into itself. I have no will to fight it.

I notice he's watching me. "Go ahead. Say it. I've cost us our freedom."

Dray shakes his head. "Tye, we're not freemen because we *have* freedom. We're freemen because we *fight* for freedom. Are you gonna keep fighting or not?"

I blink. But ... but ... "Yeah, fight." A veil lifts.

We fight. I told Kāya I was a fighter. I told her that when I get knocked down, I get back up again.

I'm still breathing. It's not too late. I'm gonna get him out of this.

Okay, how is this gonna work? I'll need help. Social power. I grab

Dray and shake him. "Keep fighting, freeman. I've got to go, but I'll be back soon." I give him a passionate kiss, then back away as he straightens in puzzlement.

My guard follows but stops at a respectful distance when I approach Kāya. She glances up as I sit beside her, then stares into the fire. It could be the flickering firelight, but her eyelids seem to pulse with tension, like they're bracing against invisible attacks. Wherever she is, it's not here. With Onyx, clinging to the edge of the abyss? Raging at Luce with suppressed fury? Mourning the loss of the facility and all her hopes and dreams along with it?

Maybe this isn't a good time to ask for help. If only I could help her. But how do—

"How's your mother?"

"Not too happy with me."

Her words turn bitter. "No wonder. Why the hell did you do that?"

"You mean, tell the truth?"

She turns on me. "I was trying to protect you, you *stupid man*."

A week ago, I'd have been scared, but now I know that when Kāya shows anger, it's to hide her fear. She knows she can't protect me. "Thank you for trying. It's a hopeless task."

She eases. "I can see that."

I wish I knew you, Kāya. Every time I think I do, I'm wrong. But I need to hear it from you. "Kāya? It's true, isn't it."

"What is?"

"What Luce said."

She hangs her head and shrinks from me, rigid, jaw tight. "Not like she said."

But ... bad. "It must have been necessary," I say.

She stares into the fire, then gives a subtle shrug.

I stiffen.

"My daughter"—she seems to fight for breath—"was already dead when I found her."

I gasp.

She continues, barely audible. "Cody was ... sick. I was so blind I couldn't see it. A mistake I'll never make again. I should have ..." She hangs her head. "You think a man couldn't hurt me? You're wrong. It was me he was punishing, when he ... killed her."

I sit stunned.

An inconceivably heinous betrayal. How could she ever trust a man after that? I see her as if for the first time, and my heart pours out. "Kāya, I'm so sorry." My eyes flow as I take her big hand in both of mine.

She gazes into the distance, taking deep breaths. Finally, she says, "That was a long, long time ago. And yes, I may have been overly hard on men since. You didn't deserve ..."

I offer my broken heart as our eyes meet, just for a second, before she turns away.

"They're going to send you away, and I can't stop them."

I look down. "I know."

She gently pulls her hand away.

I make a blind leap. "I lost a son."

She goes still.

"An infant ..." A single sob bursts out before I can catch it. I suck air to recover. "In his crib. No one could explain it. It's not the same for a father, I know. I didn't carry him in my womb. I ... I can't imagine your pain."

Her eyes stay on the ground. "I'm sorry, Tye. How long ago?"

"Not long enough."

"It will never be long enough." Her voice softens. "How do you bear it?"

"I was hoping to learn from you."

Her chin drops to her chest, then she slowly straightens. "You focus on the art. Hone it, craft it, perfect it, practice it. Use it to express the pain, use it to inflict justice on an unjust world—"

She abruptly stops and checks my eyes, uncertain.

"Thank you," I say, though we both know her advice was not for me.

Our wet eyes meet and hold firm. It is a connection as solid as a weld.

Then she blinks away and looks down. I cringe. Dangerously intimate. I've threatened her.

"Grief does funny things," I say, back-pedaling. "It pushes to be shared."

She studies the ground, then finally speaks. "Your size is deceptive. You're much bigger on the inside. It always surprises me."

I try to read her face, but she gives me nothing. Yet I know the danger has passed.

Val interrupts. "Kāya, Luce is still pressing to lay charges against you. Maybe sitting here with Tye isn't—"

Kāya doesn't look up. "He can sit where he likes."

Val dips her head. "Yes, of course."

I touch Kāya's hand, eyes full of gratitude, then catch Val as she turns to leave. "Val, can you stay for a moment?"

She stops and shrugs.

"I need help with something. What would give a freeman safe passage to stay with a comatose She in a hospital?"

The two exchange glances. Kāya speaks first. "He would need authorization. A note from an Alpha would do." She turns to me with suspicion. "What do you have in mind?"

"Dray needs a hospital pass."

"Not going to do him any good in custody."

"The pass is all I need. Apart from that, I don't want you involved. Please, Kāya." I stand. "Val, about your earlier offer: can we walk?"

Kāya sits up as we head off. "Val, what are you up to?"

Val glances over her shoulder. "Stay out of this, Kāya."

46

A SINGLE QUESTION

A CLAMOR ROUSES ME. I must've dozed off. Dray is asleep on the ground beside me, and the fire is down to embers. It must've been hours. Our guards have risen to their feet. Then, in the ample torchlight, I see what's going on. The delegation has returned from the facility. Kāya greets them as Luce and her team emerge from their tents.

I can see from her face that my mother is excited by what she's seen. The delegates continue their animated conversation even as the others assemble.

As soon as everyone settles, the Arbiter announces, "We are ready to proceed."

Luce jumps in first. "You've confirmed it is a historical site?"

"Yes, indeed. A most remarkable site. We commend Kāya and her team for their astonishing work in such a short time."

"And she taught history to men. Those men. By the laws of the ForeMothers, you *must* rule in my favor. Now, are you going to impose righteous punishment, or am I?"

Tyrant. A freeman fights. I nudge Dray and whisper, "Now."

His voice rings out. "Coward!" Beside me, Dray has risen to his knees, pumping his fists at Luce. He's screaming in rage. "You stabbed her *in the back*! You *coward*!" Hands grab him by the shoulders from behind and try to push him to the ground, but he resists.

A clamor among the assembled brings the Arbiter to her feet. She raises her hands and commands, "Hold!" Those nearby withdraw as the commotion beside me spreads.

"Silence!" says the enforcer struggling with him.

Ignoring her, Dray hollers, "All of you! You condone murder! How many have died because of this murderer, and you let her keep killing? You're a bunch of barbarians!" He is driven down hard on his face, and I cringe. "Go ahead!" he yells from the ground. "Beat me! Kill me! It's what you do best! You animals!" He's bawling now, and right on cue, Val is here, wrestling with the enforcers on Dray, shouting, "Back off! I'll deal with him. Back off."

She picks him up and carries him off into the shadows as he sobs. Our guards exchange looks of relief.

The Arbiter calls for order, and the buzz settles. "Let us resume."

Luce jumps in. "Another man driven insane from learning history. What more evidence do you need?"

Nance counters, "To question the sanity of a man in love is to question the wetness of fire. His knowledge is immaterial. The She he loves is on the verge of death due to the criminal actions of this one. Do you consider his anger unjustified? Excessive?"

As the debate rages, I make my move. Sitting on my ass, I shift bit by bit into the shadows as Bree kicks up a commotion away from me.

As soon as I'm clear of the assembly, I slink off toward the parking area, a good forty yards away. At its edge, I run right into Val coming the other way. We exchange nods, and she circles around to blend back in from the other side.

I find the jeep among the other vehicles, then take a flashlight from one of the trucks. A single flash toward the tent draws Dray with his pack. "You got Kāya's note?"

He nods, face grim.

"The closest hospital is in Cedarton. They'll be headed there. Don't race. Drive safely so you don't end up in the ditch."

"Keep them off my tail," he says, "and I won't need to race."

"I got your back. Don't turn the lights on until you get into the trees."

"Tye ... thank you." We hug and then point at each other as I walk out in front with my flashlight to show him the way. The jeep silently creeps forward in electric mode. When the headlights come on, I hurry back to the parking area, feeling a sudden void. He'll be okay. I have to think that.

Now comes the tricky part. If I'm lucky, no one will hear this. I watch the assembly as I start up the truck and inch it forward. Around the fire, several She look this way. My guard must have noticed me gone, because the Arbiter stops the proceedings, and everyone looks over.

Within moments I see several She dashing this way. I jump down from the truck and check that it is squarely blocking the other trucks in. Now to sneak back to the fire, following Val's route.

I freeze as a pair of trackers head for the jeep I forgot about. *Guns.* And there's an opening they could drive through. I can't let them follow. They'll catch him for sure. And there's no time to pull an obstacle into place.

When the headlights come on, I am standing in their beams, hands out in surrender.

"Out of the way!" shouts a tracker.

I stand there, playing dumb, trying to give myself up. The seconds tick by.

Their threats intensify, and I know what's coming, but I need to stall them. I need to. My heart jumps when one leaps from the vehicle and strides toward me. I try to evade her grasp, but my efforts are futile. She picks me up with a painful grip and throws me off to the side of the road. I cry out as I land hard on my hip. I try to scramble to my feet, knowing their next deterrent will be far more severe, but the jeep lurches forward before I can get in front of it. I cry out in despair.

The jeep slams to a stop. A swirling purple gown shines in the headlights, hands signaling to stop. *Mom?* She stands her ground as the jeep creeps forward. I back into the shadows.

"Stand down!" It's a voice of authority. "He is off to deliver an urgent message for me. Let him go."

What?

"Apologies, Councilor. We didn't know. No one informed us."

"We did not require your participation. And still don't. You are dismissed."

Several She climb down from their vehicles, then head back toward the assembly. I stare at my mother dumbfounded as she stands catching her breath. Then she follows behind them, and I run to catch up with her. There is no surprise on her face when she sees me.

Before I can find my voice, my guard arrives to escort me back. "Apologies, Councilor. I didn't—"

"No harm done," she says. "He's quite harmless."

When Celia takes her place back on the podium, the Arbiter demands an explanation. I ready myself to confess but don't get the chance.

My mother says, "I asked someone to deliver an urgent message for me. I didn't mean to disrupt the proceedings."

"An urgent message? I hope it was not in regard to these proceedings. You know that's not allowed."

"It was not."

"Then what? What was so urgent?"

Celia gazes at the ground, and I tense. How can she justify letting him get away? She has put herself in jeopardy for us. She could lose her position. Why would she do that?

Celia straightens and surveys the assembly. "He is to tell Onyx how loved she is."

My jaw drops.

The other two Councilors exchange glances, while around the ring, Alpha heads nod.

She picked the right man for the job, I want to say, knowing she did no such thing. The trouble she's in is revealed on her colleagues' faces.

The Arbiter looks down at me. "And where were you?"

"I was giving directions to my dearest friend."

"Who was under arrest."

That does it. "Yes, and for what? What happens when a man learns history?" All faces turn to me. "Do you think you know? Aren't you interested?"

Luce calls out above a sudden buzz of chatter. "Enough! Shut him up."

The Arbiter raises her hands, and the assembly goes quiet.

"You have me curious. You may speak."

"First, I have a single question."

She scowls. "Ask."

"I now know what I shouldn't; I've seen what you've seen. Given that every single one of you can easily kill me, why am I so dangerous?"

It is Luce who answers. "It's not you who's dangerous, little man. It's what you know."

"Why?"

"I do not answer to you."

My mother jumps up. "He deserves an answer."

"Celia, sit," says the Arbiter. "I will answer." She squints at me. "Ideas lead to expectations, and thwarted expectations lead to discontent. We do not want frustrated men striving for a return to power. We now know we have less to fear than we thought. Nevertheless, the reaction of men is a concern."

"A concern. I'll tell you something, as a man. Knowing of the Inversion is trivial compared to the anger men feel about being denied the dignity of making our own choices, denied full participation in our society, denied the right to know of our roots. And trivial compared to the goodwill that would be gained by educating us."

Luce is yelling disparagements, and I see annoyance on faces. I don't care. What more can they do to me? "Men once held power, and now they don't. The whole thing about men seeking revenge for that is *nonsense*. What is there to avenge?"

The Arbiter frowns. "Why, the loss of power, of course."

I shake my head. "*I have never known power*. No man alive has ever known power. How could we be angry about losing something we never had?"

There is silence until Luce speaks out. "You didn't know you'd lost something until you learned history. Now you know."

"So what? This knowledge changes nothing."

Luce addresses the assembly with a sneer. "Have you forgotten how our ForeMothers suffered? How they were forced to fight for their lives? We heed their warning. If men find out they once held all the power, they will *never rest* until they have found a way to take that power back. All She will suffer under a return to oppression."

Nance interjects. "Impossible."

"No! Not impossible. Inevitable. Men are stubborn and tenacious. They will never give up."

I shake my head. "I'm still waiting for a reasonable explanation. How could men possibly oppress She?"

"The same way they did it in the Before."

"You mean, the way you oppress men now?"

Luce glares at me, clearly furious.

I look to those assembled. "Historians mine the past to enrich the future, yes? In there"—I point to the entrance—"lies a treasure trove of information that will soon be introduced to the world. What are you gonna do? Banish every man who shows curiosity about it?"

Luce is adamant. "Men must be controlled. If you know history, as you claim, you know what happens when they are not."

"Yes, I do. And that's why any man who knows history will want to cooperate in avoiding the same mistakes."

She ignores me. "We *must* control them. Without strong guidance and firm limits, they would be building weapons, assembling armies, dumping poisons into the air and water, oppressing entire populations. Let men run wild, and who would care for our children? For our homes? No, men must be taught obedience."

"Luce, your ignorance of men is unfortunate. Allow me to educate you. Men do not learn obedience. We learn how to *fake* obedience."

A clamor arises until the Arbiter stands and settles the assembly with outstretched arms. My mother is hiding her face. *Deal with it.*

I continue. "Obedience is a choice. We can fake it to avoid punishment, or we can choose it to express gratitude or fulfill a desire to cooperate. If men were properly educated, we would be perfectly capable of controlling ourselves. And we will certainly never be in a position to control She."

Nance again. "You've seen the evidence, Arbiter. He's right about that."

"We want only fair treatment, and a say in our own lives."

Luce huffs. "You don't speak for all men."

"And you don't speak for all She."

She steps at me, eyes burning, and is blocked by crossed bokken. "They say what they think we want to hear," she sneers. "But among themselves, the talk will be different. Enough of this nonsense."

Nance counters, "Arbiter, you saw for yourself how the change was made. Without advanced computers and genetics research capabilities, it would be impossible to replicate. If you so choose, you yourself can destroy all record of how it was done. The change process will be lost forever. It will be perfectly safe to let men learn about the past."

The Arbiter leans back. "I'm here to resolve a dispute, not change the rules of the ForeMothers. We've lived by these rules for generations. They've kept the peace."

I hear the words of Onyx in my ear and give voice to them. "Those who can enforce the rules dictate the rules. You're in charge here, Arbiter. Don't hold us back. Lead us forward."

47

THE RIGHT TO CLOSURE

SOONER THAN WE EXPECT, we are called back from the recess. The Councilors take their places, and the Arbiter speaks.

"We have heard arguments and seen the evidence. It has been a long-held fear that one day the Inversion would be undone, and we would again be at a disadvantage. After a mere sampling of the stunning records found here, we are convinced, with great relief, that there is no such danger."

On the verge of jumping for joy, I restrain myself to listen.

"In light of this, there is only one justification for continued prohibition: our fear of how men will react to learning history. We are not persuaded that this fear is unwarranted. We don't know how they will react to learning of the Inversion. Perhaps more alarmingly, we don't know how they will react to having been misled for so long. However, we do agree that the matter deserves further study. Accordingly, we will recommend that Council review the prohibition against men learning history."

I tremble, uncertain, as murmurs crescendo through the assembly.

"On the matter of the dispute before us: in light of the aforementioned, and in accord with evidence presented, we rule that giving these men access to this historical site was both unavoidable, since they found it, and reasonable under the circumstances. Access was granted for humanitarian purposes."

Nance and Aida throw their arms around each other.

"The site is to remain the claim of Kāya, under her capable management. It will remain her responsibility to manage the men in question, under legal exemption, until such time as the matter is decided in law."

I cry out in joy. The team collides in a jubilant mass. Big Val beckons me over, and I run to join in.

"We further rule that Luce's challenge regarding the presence of these men was reasonable."

My breath catches.

"However, the other actions taken, including the amassing of an illegal army and the incitement of hostile action while arbitration was pending, are criminal in nature and will be prosecuted."

There is a sudden commotion, and Luce jumps forward. "No! This is an outrage! I protest! It is clear the Arbiter is biased in Kāya's favor. I challenge! I challenge you, Renee. A capital challenge. Now!"

The Arbiter is taken aback. "You appeal our ruling? You must know, Luce, that's not how this works. Not for a long time. The whole purpose of arbitration is to avoid such loss of life. According to modern rules, if you wish to challenge me, a member of the High Council, you will face my High Alpha."

"And I will defeat her! I have jurisdiction over this area, and I will not allow this farce to continue. I demand the right of capital challenge!"

My mother steps in. "The prospect of facing the High Alpha is supposed to discourage such nonsense. Don't be a fool, Luce."

"You're the fool, Celia, thinking you can conspire with criminals to take from me what is rightfully mine. I, at least, will respect our traditions and reverse this ruling by force. Prepare your champion."

"No!" yells Kāya, stepping forward. "This challenge is mine. I accept it."

Luce grins.

"*No!*" I yell. "Kāya, don't do this! *I* challenge!"

There is a bustle of confusion until Bree grabs me and slams me down on my ass. "Just sit and shut up. What's *wrong* with you?"

My mother glares down at me, the same words echoed in her eyes. *How can they not understand? I can't lose her now. I just can't.* I draw my knees up and cling to them, my stomach coiling in dread.

The High Alpha says, "Are you sure, Kāya?"

Kāya's icy eyes never leave Luce. "Please, Tala. I need to do this."

I see Onyx go down, see that agony on her face, Kāya's anguish, Dray's grief. I see Dray's eyes burning with hatred. He would have challenged too, if he could. It has to be Kāya. She's doing it for Onyx, for Dray, for all of us, just as she said she must. And I can't stop her.

She and Tala both exchange nods with the Arbiter, who shakes her head and confers with her colleagues. Finally, she announces, "The challenge is accepted. So ... Proceed."

As they prepare, I protest to Bree. "Is Luce insane? Why would she do such a stupid thing as challenge the High Alpha?"

By mutual agreement, both fighters waive battle armor in favor of the lighter regalia. The contest will be quick and lethal.

Bree grinds her teeth. "Luce would never go to prison. If she tried to run, she'd have to go up against the whole Guard. She'd have no chance. By challenging, she only has to go up against one. Slim chance, but at least a chance. But she knew Kāya would want in. Now she has a good chance. It was a clever move."

And Kāya walked right into it. I bury my face in my hands.

Torches ring the clearing beside the main fire, and the assembly spreads out around the ring to witness a fight to the death. The two Alphas, magnificent in their regalia, glare at each other, their golden collars gleaming in the firelight. The temperate breeze has stilled as the world itself holds its breath.

The Arbiter says, "I had hoped to never have to officiate one of these. And yet here we are." She stands to address the combatants. "A capital challenge offers final resolution to a dispute. The disputed matter is settled She to She. Confirm to me that the capital nature of this challenge is clear to you."

"To the death," they say, in unintended unison.

The Arbiter sighs. "We need strong She to fight for the common good, not against each other. Your strength is wasted when we lose you."

"Listen to her, Kāya," says Luce. "There is no need for you to die. Submit now, and you will get a fair trial."

"Here's the way it is. You will withdraw your challenge or die," says Kāya. The two glare at each other, eyes already locked in battle.

"I see," says the Arbiter. "Such a waste."

She stands, looks from one to the other, then raises her arms in ceremony to encompass them both. Her voice rings out over the assembly. "To the winner: the dispute is settled in your favor, as per the rules of the ForeMothers. You have removed an obstacle and gained influence, but your oath to the High Council remains in full force."

She looks from face to face, as if saying goodbye. "To the loser: at the moment of your death, you will reach out and touch the face of the Great Mother. Your needs, your fear and your pain will be gone. She will grant you eternal peace."

With that, she returns to her seat and settles. "You may engage— to the death."

In refrain, a chorus echoes through the assembly. "To the death."

The Arbiter nods, and both take their weapons. Kāya examines her bokken, Kaybo, lovingly rubs her hand along the length of its blunt blade, then faces her enemy. I grasp my head in my hands and squeeze my eyes shut. Is this what it's like to love an enforcer? To live every day with the fear of losing her? It would take astonishing strength. Despite myself, I look up. It has already started.

The two warriors circle each other, tapping hardwood blades. They exchange thrusts and parries, testing, measuring. Both switch to one-handed show-off swordplay. More lunges, thrusts, and parries, each getting bolder, more aggressive. The flickering light throws false motion into the scene, and my heart jumps into my mouth as I see disaster over and over, only to have it disappear again. They continue to circle.

Kāya says, "Is it true you took down my second from behind?"

"You took down mine."

"Yours attacked me. Did mine attack you?"

"It was battle," says Luce. "A righteous fight."

"Liar!" says Kāya. "You attacked us to avoid arbitration. You're a disgrace to the gold collar." Her voice is trembling with rage. "In the back. You *coward!*"

"You're the one who refused to face me. *You're* the coward."

The Arbiter abruptly stands and calls out, "Hold!" The fighters withdraw and turn to her. She addresses them both. "It seems we are still at the stage of talking. Perhaps if we continue the dialogue, we can arrive at a resolution that does not involve the loss of a life."

Luce snarls, "You will not deprive me of my victory."

"We fight," says Kāya.

The Arbiter sighs, then sits. "Very well. Are the challengers ready to resume?"

"Emotions, Kāya." It's Bree's voice. Kāya glances her way, hesitates, then nods. Then she sinks to her knees as Luce announces, "Ready."

What the hell? Get up, Kāya. Get up.

There is a hush around the ring as Kāya sits on her heels, erect, eyes closed, breathing deeply. I see her shoulders loosen and, in her face, see the release of the turmoil within her as she breathes away the rage, the pain. Luce sees it too.

"Get up, coward," she demands. "Let's get on with it." ... No response. "Are you going to fight or not?" ... Nothing. "Arbiter, unless she fights, she forfeits."

Kāya takes another deep breath, opens her eyes and rises smoothly to her feet. "Ready."

A swell of hope.

"Proceed." The Arbiter sits, and the opponents square off.

My heart jumps as Luce immediately leaps to the attack, hoping to catch Kāya off guard. She launches a barrage of strikes, pressing and slashing from the left, then the right, then straight on, then feigning left and slashing right, keeping Kāya purely defensive with no opportunity to strike back.

I press my clenched fists to my mouth as Luce drives her back and back, around the confines of the ring. Kāya is in trouble. My throat closes in as Luce does, my whole body twitching with each crack of blade against blade. At any moment, one of these vicious jabs will get through, and it will be the end of her. I hear a loud whine of terror and realize it's coming from me. I clench tighter. Kāya stumbles backing up and goes down on one knee, and my heart punches my ribs. Luce leaps at her with a vicious overhead slash that Kāya manages to deflect just past her ear to bang off her shoulder guard, sending another jolt through me. Then she's back on her feet.

Luce bares her teeth, breathing hard. Even I can see her frustration growing as Kāya continues to fend her off. The attacks slow. She's fatigued.

Kāya reveals her strategy. "Is that all you got?"

Instead of responding, Luce reaches behind her and pulls something out.

"Knife!" yells Bree. "She'll be looking to get in close."

"Wait!" I cry. "That can't be fair. Stop her!" A warning hand presses down on my shoulder. Everyone else ignores me. I squeeze my head between my hands to suppress a wail.

Bree sees my distress. "It's legal but not smart. It weakens your sword. She's desperate."

I chance a look. Breathing hard, Luce circles with bokken in one hand and knife in the other. She can deliver death from two directions, and I taste the bile rising in my throat. Kāya steps back, and with one hand holds her beloved Kaybo out between them as they circle, its blade straight up. I choke. What is she doing? Conceding? Eyes locked on her opponent, she ceremoniously wraps the fingers of her second hand into a solid two-handed grip. Then she drops into her fighting stance. Ice runs down my spine as I see her, my beautiful predator, poised to strike.

Luce lunges and thrusts with her long blade. In one quick motion, Kāya parries and slashes across into the knife hand. The knife flies into the dirt. Luce suppresses a howl and clutches her wrecked hand to her body. Keeping her bokken raised, Luce blocks two quick strikes, but the second overpowers her one-handed parry and glances off the side of her head. As she backs away, off balance, Kāya leaps forward, drops and spins, and snaps out a kick, catching Luce on the side of the knee. With a sickening crack, the leg buckles sideways, and Luce cries out as she goes down hard. Kāya is above her in a second, and as Luce grabs for her weapon, Kāya stomps on her sword hand. A moan rolls through the assembly as Luce writhes on the ground, one leg and both hands ruined.

I'm coiled like a spring. *Finish her. Finish her.*

Kāya stands above her shattered foe, blade poised, then looks around. Her eyes find me, and she hesitates. *Do it, Kāya! Do it!*

Her chest is heaving. What's she waiting for? She drops her arms, steps away, then re-sheathes Kaybo. Around me, there are gasps and murmurs.

The Arbiter calls out, "This is a capital challenge, Kāya. You have the right to closure."

Kāya takes a deep breath, then looks up into the stars. A hush falls over the scene, and in my heart, I know she's conferring with Onyx. Finally, she looks at the Arbiter.

"No," she says. "That's not who I want to be."

My face flushes. I wanted her to kill. It's my turn to hang my head. But my joy simply won't allow it.

48

ROBES OF SHAME

THE SUN IS ALREADY high in the sky when I step out into the open air. They've dismantled Luce's encampment, and the field now sits empty. Her entire team was carted off in the custody of the Elite Guard. All that remains are the elaborate tents of the Councilors and their guardian Alphas.

I wander out to their encampment and find my mother surrounded by her associates, eating breakfast. They're all dressed in casual sweaters and slacks. She sees me and calls me over. "Tye. Sit. Have some breakfast with me. Cheese and chicken omelets. Good food is one of the perks of office." She sees me sheepishly eyeing her colleagues. "It's okay. They know. I confessed yesterday. It's past time I came out of the closet."

I do my best to be gracious as I accept and join them.

"I don't know if you've heard," she says, "but Luce is dead."

"What? How?" We knew she'd never fight again, which would strip her of all rank and power, but I didn't think her injuries were life-threatening.

"She faced a life as a disabled prisoner. A She like that could never accept such a life. Her final command was to end her misery, though no one is admitting to injecting her."

I sit back, suddenly lighter. I didn't know I was still carrying the fear of her until it lifted from my shoulders. I wonder how Kāya will feel about it.

Her colleagues drain their cups and head off, leaving us alone.

After washing down a savory chunk of chicken with a sip of coffee, I say, "I want to thank you for yesterday. You saved my life."

"Tye, your influence on the arbitration was decisive. I ... underestimated you." She squints at me. "You are an extraordinary young man."

"I meant when you found me on the trail."

"Ah, yes. Of course."

"Then you helped Dray get away."

"I'm being censured for that little stunt, though not expelled. Had the ruling gone differently, I'd be up on charges myself. 'Observer only' my ass. I had to do something."

"You were brilliant, and I'm grateful."

We sit in silence. She looks down, like she knows what's coming.

I say, "Can we ... go for a walk?"

She fills her lungs. "Yes. It's time, isn't it."

We head out into the field, afforded space as long as we're in sight of her bodyguard, and stroll together through the tall grasses.

My mother breaks the silence. "I must say, I'm impressed with the person you've become. Perhaps it's a good thing I wasn't there to interfere." She winces.

I look down, holding back. "So, what do you think of our find?"

She seems to welcome the reprieve. "I may be on the High Council now, but I'm still a historian at heart. I'm more excited than I've been in years. This is a truly major find." She looks away and shakes her head. "Perhaps if I'd let you help me search, all those years ago, I'd have found it then."

I shrug.

We both look away as the turmoil roils up within me.

She preempts me. "Tye, I was young and foolish back then, and I made grave mistakes. One was not recognizing the hostility our work was stirring up until it was too late. A hate group, the Quo, didn't want the public exposed to my hypothesis. The idea that we were somehow created by the men of the Before threatened the whole She identity."

"Which is ...?"

"She are strong by nature, tested in the fires of competition, our dominance achieved through our own efforts. We were all taught that She fought for and earned our place of power and are entitled to it. My hypothesis about genetic manipulation—well, it suggested otherwise."

She checks my eyes. I wait for more.

"A sense of entitlement is a dangerous thing to challenge. The Quo embodies such entitlement."

"Yes, that political group that opposes progress. All freemen know of them. They actively campaign against us, though I don't know why they hate us so much."

"They believe men should be kept subservient. Freemen oppose that. The Quo justify their position by promoting fear and quoting the ForeMothers, who were, it should be said, still afraid of men."

"So, the Quo didn't like what you were saying."

"Traitors to all She, they called us. They were convinced our society would crumble if people believed us. The ruthlessness we faced shocked us. Our enemies were desperate to silence us, but we hid away. When they couldn't get at us, they threatened to kill the son of a colleague instead, to send a message. I feared what they might do to you."

Anguish creases her eyes, and I break away, off balance.

She goes on. "Fortunately, they didn't know of you. My life in Hillhaven had never been public. I had been telling people it was a retreat for me, a place to study and write."

"I told people you died in the Shell when a building collapsed."

She hangs her head. "Tye, I'm so sorry."

"Me too."

She wipes her eyes. "Everything changed when we went into hiding. I always meant to come back for you when things settled down, but then, I kept getting more enmeshed in the politics, until ... I ... kept putting it off."

I can't look at her. "So, we were just ... what to you?"

"Oh, Tye." She grips my hand. "I need you to know I've always loved you."

I pull away, my voice firm. "No. That's not what love looks like."

"You're right. You're right. But I'll tell you what can distort love into an unrecognizable form."

I wait. "What's that?"

"Shame."

I sniff. "Shame?"

"You saw my robes. They're exceptionally good at covering up shame. I had no idea when I started out how much I would come to need them." She looks off into the distance.

"Why didn't you come back when the danger had passed?"

She rubs her neck.

"Was it another man? Do you have another family somewhere?"

She gives a sad smile. "No, you are my only child, and your father is the only man I ever loved. No, my preference has been for She."

That's news to me.

"The first time I saw your father, I knew I wanted his seed. But at seventeen, there are still a lot of things you don't know. Like what you're going to do with your life. The fact is, some careers, like historian and enforcer, simply don't allow for a normal family life. It turns out I was not matria material. Not all are."

"So you live alone?"

"No, I have a longtime partner. Jula was an enforcer when we met. A Bravo. She's retired now, but back then, she was on contract in the Shell, and we happened to end up working together. I was instantly attracted to her, but I wasn't looking for a partner. I had a family."

"Us."

"Yes. Then, one day, I guess you were around the age of nine, I got cut off from my team—my own carelessness; you just can't be careless in the Shell—and ended up surrounded by a gang of bandits. I knew they were going to kill me for my valuables. I honestly expected to die. Then, out of nowhere, this avenging angel swooped in and scattered the gang like fleeing prey and carried me off to safety. And, my boy, if you think that wasn't romantic, think again."

"No, I can see how it—"

"We worked so well together, complemented each other's skills. Our success gained us influence in the city, and we became known as a power couple. Jula knew about you, of course, but no one in Provender did, and as we spent more time there, it got harder and harder to get home to see you. And then my first book was published, and everything blew up in our faces. When my colleagues and I had to go into hiding, Jula came with us. That's when I hired Elona to care for your father. I—It still breaks my heart. I should have been there for him at the end."

"And what about me?"

"Tye, I knew you'd be well taken care of. I'd never have left you there if I thought—"

"You left me with a tyrant. Elona and her daughters drove my father to an early grave."

She looks at me with a blank face. "What are you talking about?"

"With her demands. She pushed him and pushed him until he collapsed. She killed him. And you call that 'well taken care of'?"

She covers her mouth with her hand, concern in her eyes. "Did your father not tell you he had colon cancer?"

I stop in my tracks. "Cancer?"

"He got quite depressed in the final year. Elona did her best to keep him on his feet, encouraging him to keep going, keep moving as long as possible."

"My father had cancer?"

She frowns. "You thought Elona ... killed your father?" Her face collapses. "Oh, Tye. I'm so, so sorry. It must have been ..."

My head falls back. Pieces of Tye ricochet around in a shattered world until a firm hand grips my shoulder.

"Tye. Your father died of cancer. Elona was no tyrant. She was under a lot of emotional stress, I'm sure, but who wouldn't be? No, if you need to blame someone, blame me. Elona offered me an opportunity to stay in hiding and escape the agony of watching your father die, and, to my shame, I took it. Then you were in boarding school, where I knew you'd be safe, and I was thrown into a different world. A world I couldn't fit you into."

All those well-worn memories, events filtered through a child's eyes—eyes incapable of seeing life's complexities. I see it all now as if for the first time, and notice that the customary sting is missing.

She continues. "And there you have it. For years I've been telling myself that you were probably better off without me. No mother wants that to be true. But look at you now."

The rustle of the breeze through the tall grasses fills the enormous void as we stand staring out in different directions. She stoops and picks a wildflower and holds it to her nose, then lets her gaze roam the surrounding wilds. "I always loved this land. It's so ... free."

49
———

A DELICIOUS IRONY

Back in the encampment, they are packing up for the return to the city. My mother invites me to sit with her for another coffee. As she hands me a mug, she gazes at me, nodding approval. "I'm so pleased to see that you found your own strength."

I did what?

"Our female-dominated society has trained men to think that being strong means being more like a She. It leaves you playing to your weakness. You may be weak when it comes to brute force, but persuasion is power. Ingenuity is power. Coordinated effort, determination, reliability, consistency—all power. You'll find that—"

She abruptly stops, looking over my shoulder. "Kāya."

I turn, and there she is, talking with one of the Alphas. My mother beckons her over.

"Kāya, I got word this morning—I don't know if you've heard—but they got Onyx to the hospital, where she's in critical condition, but stabilizing."

"I had heard, thank you."

She was on the radio all night, getting updates. She seems a little less frantic now, but it's probably the fatigue. I wish I could reassure her.

Celia continues. "Apparently, the young She being transported with her offered her own blood, and they were able to transfuse her on the way. The new blood likely saved her life."

Mara. Even with her own injuries.

Kāya glances at me, then opens her mouth to respond but looks down instead.

I say, "Yes, we're grateful." I intend to thank Mara someday. "And they'll be transporting Onyx to Provender City Hospital as soon as she's stable. Dray plans on following."

"And you know of Luce's death?"

"I just heard," says Kāya. "Justice finds a way."

"I must say, you are still a magnificent fighter. I know you are sorely missed in the Elite Guard, and I'm supposed to invite you back into a leadership position, if you're interested. It would mean moving back to the city, of course, but you would be very well compensated."

I tense. *No more fighting. Please say no.*

Kaya sighs. "Thank you, Celia. The offer is flattering. In fact, I'll be heading into the city as soon as I get the site secured, but only to see Onyx. After that, I'll be hiring more staff, and we'll be busy here at the site for some time."

I nod my approval, trying to keep my face neutral.

Mom says, "The role of enforcement is changing, and you could play an important part in helping to reshape it. Surely, you'll have your new people do the grunt work here. And Tye, I'm sure you'll find Provender exciting."

Kāya's voice is firm. "I want to be here. I'm a historian now. I'm glad to hear things are finally changing, but I'm finished with enforcement. I'll leave that to the young."

"What are you talking about?" says Celia. "You're still in your prime."

Kāya's eyes compress, and I know her fear of losing Onyx is taking another bite out of her. I start to rise to go to her, but her flinch tells me to stay put. *Don't embarrass her.*

Mom nods. "Ah, yes. The life of an enforcer is a hard one."

Kāya sniffs and straightens. "And I've been at it far too long."

"Well, I've made the offer. Truth be told, I'm glad you turned it down. What you've got here with this find is extraordinary. It could enable you not merely to contribute to the We, but to reshape our culture to the benefit of all. A 'once in a generation' opportunity, Kāya. Do this right, and I can see you winning the Medal of Honor."

Kāya's eyes flare. The Medal of Honor? I've heard of that. A rarely awarded prize for exceptional contribution to the betterment of society. It's the greatest honor that the We can bestow.

Celia continues. "So I can certainly see why you'd want to stay here. I miss fieldwork myself."

"You are welcome to come and join in whenever you like. There is always room for experienced hands."

"I will definitely take you up on that."

Kāya turns, then hesitates. "I'm hoping Tye will stay and help out."

Her eyes question me, and I light up inside. She's asking me to stay. To help out. On a team of real historians. My heart bubbles. I can almost hear the gurgle of the river flowing by under the bridge; the unformed ache, the half-glimpsed dream, now fleshed out and fulfilled. I bring her back into focus as she towers over me. She's waiting for a response.

"I'll need some time to weigh my options," I lie.

She smiles, seeing right through me.

———

ALONE TOGETHER AGAIN, my mother examines me with concerned eyes. "You seem to be holding up quite well, considering what you've been through."

Still bubbling with joy, I shrug.

"So," she says. "You've chosen to live as a freeman. An odd choice. It's a difficult life, though it would give you instant credibility in the equal rights movement.

"The what?"

"In the city, men are clamoring for more rights and better treatment, and it's getting harder and harder for She to ignore them. The review of Rule Six is only going to empower the movement. Unfortunately, it's also given new life to the Quo, who are intent on blocking all change. Given what I heard from you last night, I think you would be a splendid spokesperson for social justice. It's time for change."

"It's long past time, I'd say."

"Hey, it took men a thousand generations to recognize the strengths of the 'weaker sex' and start including them in leadership positions. We She are reaching that point in seven."

"Enhanced intelligence. I get it. Do you She have to rub it in all the time?"

"Yes, about that: according to the records, the Eve-2 genome does enhance cognitive potential. But innate intelligence is merely a potential resource. Unless one puts hard work into developing it, it goes wasted. We're a wasteful species, I'm afraid."

"Only according to all the evidence."

She chuckles.

I have to ask, "How could the Inversion have been kept hidden for so long? Surely some men would find out and spread the news. You can't have banished all of them."

"No, of course not. I imagine it's common knowledge among men who know better than to talk about it. It's easy to suppress the spread of information."

"By using the threat of banishment."

"That's one component. But deterrents would never work on their own. To suppress history, it's far more effective to turn truth into myth. That way, even if a man hears the truth, he won't believe it. All those children's stories about giants and hulks and ogres and such. Remember those?"

"Sure." My mind does a flip. "Wait. You mean—"

"Every male child knows that big, powerful male figures are fantasy. It was easy to create a new mythology to cover up the past."

I shake my head.

She moves on. "How on earth did you manage to attract the attention of a She like Kāya?"

"I have no idea. Mom, it's the strangest thing. We are inept with each other. Our misunderstandings are epic, our misinterpretations comic—"

"Like She and men everywhere."

"—yet I trust her with my life. And she respects my independence. Can you believe that?"

"Whew. It's worse than I thought. Still, it's not what I would expect from a freeman."

"A freeman can still love."

She dips her head to look up at me. "And get his heart broken."

"Hers to break."

"It's a delicious irony, isn't it? A man demands the freedom to make his own choices and then chooses servitude."

I smile, remembering Kāya's admonition: *You do not serve me.* I straighten. "What I choose is to serve my own heart."

Her eyebrows arch. Then she shrugs. "You do what you need to do. I wasn't there for you when I should have been, but I'll be here now, if you need anything." She settles back. "It's always going to be complicated between us. I know that."

"I'm okay with complicated, as you may have noticed."

She chuckles again, nodding.

I say, "Maybe, if Kāya will take me on as an apprentice, I'll get my certification to be a historian, and then, who knows?"

A grin spreads across her face. "My son, the first male historian. Yes. I like the sound of that. And wouldn't that shake up the establishment, to have a male historian in the books."

"Now that I know where you are, I'll come visit you. And you'll come here, won't you?"

"Let's just say, even if I were a man, you couldn't keep me away."

"Ha-ha. Very funny."

We both burst out together, and I'm a child again, wrapped in the healing sound of her laughter.

50

THAT FACE

I EMERGE into the daylight and stretch. There's nothing like the end of a three-day storm to mark a new, calmer beginning. I sniff the warm, damp air and get notes of burnt wood, axle grease and burlap. In the field, the wind-flattened grasses are already springing back up.

These last few weeks have been a bewildering swirl of heartbreak and triumph, and I'm eager for a new beginning. I've known bittersweet times, but never like this. How do you live with the guilt of having your wildest dreams come true, but at too high a cost?

It's hard being here without Dray and Onyx. But spending a week in the city, visiting her in the hospital every day, seeing progress, has made a world of difference to Kāya. Dray is still there, of course, representing all of us who wish we could be.

Bree and Val will head off soon to recruit a new team of enforcers for site protection. They're determined not to get caught shorthanded again.

Aida sees me and waves, and I admire her gait as she flows across the uneven terrain toward me. She and Nance have their hands full doing tours while trying to continue the work of developing the site. They'll be hiring a small team of historians to help as well.

"Glad I found you," says Aida. "I wanted to thank you for helping us install those new pipes yesterday. Don't know what we would have done without you."

"It was pretty tight under there," I say. "Glad I could help."

A peace comes over me as I watch her sashay away. I take a deep breath, and the sunshine swirls within me. So this is what it feels like to be part of a team.

I look off into the hills, then turn back toward the entrance. I miss Dray terribly, though it occurs to me that I have female friends for the first time, along with a taste of what 'safe' feels like. I can't wait to share this new world with him when he and Onyx get back.

The facility is by far the best storm shelter I've ever been in. The storm raged for three days, but down there I hardly noticed it. A dozen guests, village leaders and respected historians who pushed for an early viewing all needed refuge when the storm hit. Though it was tense at first, I was pleasantly surprised by how quickly they all came to accept the presence of a man. I didn't expect it to be so easy to accommodate them or put them to work. Turns out, even She can do a good job with cleaning when they put their minds to it. We have years of work ahead of us, and already historians from all over are clamoring to come and see the place. And the Medal of Honor keeps coming up. They seem to think Kāya has a real chance, if she manages to fulfill the potential of this place.

What's holding her up? Waiting near the entrance, I turn as I hear Kāya approach. In a tank top and tight shorts, she stops, turns her face to the sun and closes her eyes. Her smile tells me the sunshine is working its magic.

When she gets within reach, I playfully poke her with my finger, center chest, and she lets me, then in mock reprisal pokes me back, and we laugh. She knows I feel compelled to point out the absence of regalia, and how elated I am by that. It means she's left that precarious life behind.

She holds out a set of keys. "I've been meaning to give these back to you. They might come in handy when you're on a supply run into town."

It's the keys to the twin-dome. I try to hand them back. "It wouldn't feel right. Not my home anymore."

"Tye, it is your home."

"No, you bought it. It's in your name."

"Only until you buy it back from me. You have income now, you know."

Income? I run my hand through my hair. "You'd sell it back to me? I thought you wanted ... Why'd you buy it, then?"

She shrugs. "Injustice pisses me off."

I stand in stunned silence.

"Besides, I knew they'd leave it alone if it was in my name."

Indeed they would. "Kāya, I don't know what to say."

"Then stop right there, before you say something unfiltered that will get you arrested." She wrinkles her nose in a taunt, and my heart melts.

I look away, then hand the keys back. "Don't really want them anymore. I doubt I'd go there often. I'm ... attached to my work here."

"Yes, I've noticed."

"And having a satellite office in town is gonna come in handy. You'll see."

She looks down at the keys in her hand. "We'll share it then."

I blink, then leap to accept. "Deal. Once I've paid for my share."

She smiles, shaking her head, then looks at the sky again. "Beautiful day. We won't get many more of these before the season heats up. You ready to go? Let's stretch our legs."

Those legs. I love our walks together. I can't come close to matching her stride, so I usually fall behind. At least, that's what I tell her. Fact is, I could watch her behind for hours and be completely entertained.

Forty minutes out, we're exploring fresh territory. Fewer rocks, more grassy meadows, and squat deciduous trees. We climb to the top of a hill and stand surveying the landscape. From here, there is nothing but windswept wilderness in every direction, thriving with vibrant and hardy grasslands, scattered dwarf hardwoods, squat evergreens, and colorful patches of wildflowers. I know there is wildlife around—wolves, deer, and foxes—but it keeps its distance, as if sensing the presence of an apex predator.

Indeed, her towering figure, formidable and enticing, still exudes power, and my body thrills in response to her dangerous proximity.

She senses my gaze on her and turns to me. Her eyes meet mine, and I fall in, helpless, until she smiles and says, "What?"

I can't expect expressions of love from her. I know that. And I'm okay with it. Moments like this. They're enough.

But that face.

From that first day it took me and owned me, that face has never released me from the exquisite agony of its spell. I see the sun and the moon and the stars in that face. I see my children in that—

I shake the thought away. That's not up to me.

"Come on. What are you thinking?"

"Just enjoying the day," I say.

She lets it go, freeing me. "Yes, isn't it glorious?" She spreads her long arms to the sky and stretches with abandon, arching her back and spreading her shoulders ... Okay, I've lost my train of thought.

"I love it out here on our walks," she says, "away from all the responsibilities, no regalia, no threats to worry about. Isn't it just ..." She opens to a long, full breath.

"I love it too."

"Let's run."

"You know I can't keep up with you."

"Then I'll chase you," she says with a mischievous grin.

"No, I'll chase you for a change." I lunge for her, but she leaps out of my reach and we're off. She lets me catch up, then darts off, laughing. I chase, always tantalizingly close.

Too soon, I'm winded. She slows, pretending to be winded too, and when I catch up, I leap at her and pull her down, and we roll and tumble, laughing and squealing, and somehow, she never lands hard on top of me and always catches my head before I bang it. And I wish I could give her the world. We find ourselves lying in each other's arms, and I surrender there, basking in her new, sweet scent. It's ridiculous to be missing the smell of leather.

"Look at us," she laughs. "Acting like a couple of kids."

We settle back and watch the clouds float by, until I lean up on an elbow, take her eyes in mine and drink in that luminous aquamarine.

And now my thirst rages. I can't resist. I try, but simply can't. I cautiously find her lips with mine, and she lets me. More. She kisses back. With urgency. And all at once we are joined at the mouth, pressing, melting together, clinging, nibbling. Her tongue parts my lips and thrusts into me, and I open to her. An electric current surges through me as our tongues touch, and my heart shudders, losing all restraint as I taste her. I push back with mine and enter her, and we hungrily explore, each of us with equal access to the other, each open, eager, each of us penetrating and being penetrated. And our tongues dance and grasp and caress as equals, and all I taste is ... bliss.

And when we withdraw, I search her eyes for reassurance that it wasn't a mistake, a slip on her part. And when I do, time stops.

There, in the depths of her eyes, I am awed by what I see. She is laying open to me her inner self, small and fragile.

And my heart sings to her its promise.

You are safe with me, Kāya.

<<<<>>>>

ACKNOWLEDGMENTS

I am grateful to Eve Silver, my primary editor. In addition to her razor-sharp editing, she is a prolific author and a stellar writing coach. Her enthusiasm for the craft is an inspiration.

Thanks also to Laurie Chittenden and Arran McNicol for their editorial assistance.

I thank my first readers, friends and family, who suffered through those painful early drafts and provided the feedback I needed to see beyond my own blinders. These include Ann Tassonyi, Bill Ralph, Michael MacDonald, Ron and Dianna Budreau, Jean Bridge, Verna Linney, Tom Darcie, and especially Carolyn Hafer.

For assistance in the various stages of cover concept and design, I thank Larry Rossignol, Timothy O'Donnell, Bill Ralph and Bruce Thompson.

I also want to acknowledge you, precious reader, because if you've made it this far and are still reading, it means we share an intangible bond. You are why I write.

ABOUT THE AUTHOR

Author photo © Robert Nowell

G. W. Darcie, Ph.D., is an award-winning Canadian author who studied at the universities of Waterloo and Windsor before enjoying a long career as a clinical psychologist and couples therapist. He has always been fascinated by people, science and technology, a mix that is reflected in his heartfelt speculative fiction.

In 2022, he was awarded First Place, New Voices: General and Literary Fiction (League of Utah Writers), for his first short story, *Machine* (available through his website, https://gwdarcie.com).

He has gone on to receive several awards for his speculative fiction novels, *Guardian Android* and *World of She*.

A former recreational pilot and scuba diver, he is still drawn to sky and water. He is married and lives in St. Catharines, Ontario.

THANK YOU.

I hope you found the story engaging, and I would be thrilled if it even touched your heart in some way. My goal in writing is to offer readers a unique experience, a refreshing break from normal life, maybe even a new way of looking at something. I hope I succeeded, but there is only one way I'll ever know.

If you have a minute, I would be grateful to hear your honest feedback about your experience of reading the story.

Every acknowledgment helps. Please leave a review wherever you got the book, or at

worldofshe.com

Thank you! I look forward to our next.

Speaking of ...

BONUS

To download the **Epilogue** to *World of She* for free, visit https:// gwdarcie.com and sign up for my author newsletter.

For **book club members,** along with the epilogue, you'll also find a list of discussion questions related to *World of She*. Get this free download and look forward to some lively discussion.

Ready for more? Return to the world of She in Book Two of the *Inversion* Series,

Burden of She.

Since the fall of the last patriarchy, the laws of the ForeMothers have kept men subservient and powerless. Kāya, throughout her years as an elite enforcer, felt justified in upholding these laws – until she let the gentle freeman, Tye, much too close.

Having uncovered a shocking historical revelation, Kāya holds the key to moving their society toward a new era of inclusion. But those desperate to stop change are gaining power and closing in with deadly intent, determined to silence all opposition.

With her society on the brink of falling into the clutches of a brutal dictator, Kāya unexpectedly faces a death match she can't win. Tye will give his life for her—unless she can stop him. But duty and love both demand sacrifice ...

Burden of She reveals this intriguing world through Kāya's eyes, as she gains insights into the hard lessons of life and love.

For a free preview and more, visit

https://worldofshe.com